Acclaim for Amy Yamada and her debut nov~~~~

"*Trash* is an engaging look at the travai~~~~ ~~~~
ing for love, trust and comm~~~~
broken homes and addict~~~~
vides a touching and belie~~~~
where people can still come ~~~~ ~~~~nd
memories ought not to be co~~~~

 —*The Wall Street Journal*

"It's been a long time since I was so captivated by a new voice. Yamada is a terrifically compelling writer, funny, wry, and enormously wise about the complexities of the human heart. Cool, sassy, big-hearted Koko should make legions of fans for herself and the superbly gifted Amy Yamada."

 —Jaime Manrique, author of *Latin Moon in Manhattan*

"A heartening book to experience, revolving as it does around the tremendous faith it takes to relinquish old dependencies in favor of a more fulfilling love."

 —*Los Angeles Reader*

"[Yamada] has demonstrated an uncanny skill not just for navigating difficult psychological terrain, but also for bestowing an all-encompassing dignity to her givers and receivers of pain and pleasure, sex and love."

 —*The Washington Post Book World*

"Ms. Yamada gives us a story about love, life, and the complex web of circumstance and simple need that sometimes forms the fabric, or at least the *fabrication* of an American family today. . . . Coming as she does from another culture, [her] view of our own may amuse, anger, or even embarrass us . . . but then so might *Brave New World*."

 —Jess Mowry, author of *Way Past Cool* and *Six Out Seven*

"Absorbing . . . insightful, funny and sophisticated."

 —*USA Today*

"The Big Apple will never be the same! [Yamada's] assortment of quirky-yet-lovable characters travel from the East Side to the West Side and all around the town, making their mark on Manhattan's hip, downtown East Village club scene—to uptown, Harlem, USA—and *really* far uptown, to the Bronx! Throughout, Ms. Yamada dazzles the reader with her charming and irreverent prose, her unique world view, and her great depth of feeling."

 —Janice Eidus, author of *Urban Bliss* and *Vito Loves Geraldine*

PENGUIN BOOKS

TRASH

Amy Yamada is one of Japan's most popular novelists. She once worked in an S & M club and wrote about it in her novel *Kneel Down and Lick My Feet*, the first chapter of which appeared in the anthology *Monkey Brain Sushi: New Tastes in Japanese Fiction*, edited by Alfred Birnbaum. Born in 1959, Amy Yamada has written more than twenty books in Japanese, many of them bestsellers. Her first novel, *Bedtime Eyes*, won the Bungei Prize, and in 1987 she won the Naoki Prize, Japan's equivalent of the Pulitzer, for her novel *Soul Music Lovers Only*. *Trash* is her first full novel to be published in the west. Amy Yamada lives with her American husband near Tokyo.

T R A S H

AMY YAMADA

Translated from the Japanese by
SONYA L. JOHNSON

PENGUIN BOOKS

PENGUIN BOOKS
Published by the Penguin Group
Penguin Books USA Inc., 375 Hudson Street, New York, New York 10014, U.S.A.
Penguin Books Ltd, 27 Wrights Lane, London W8 5TZ, England
Penguin Books Australia Ltd, Ringwood, Victoria, Australia
Penguin Books Canada Ltd, 10 Alcorn Avenue, Toronto, Ontario, Canada M4V 3B2
Penguin Books (N.Z.) Ltd, 182–190 Wairau Road, Auckland 10, New Zealand

Penguin Books Ltd, Registered Offices: Harmondsworth, Middlesex, England

First published in the United States of America by Kodansha America, Inc. 1994
Published in Penguin Books 1996

1 3 5 7 9 10 8 6 4 2

Originally published, in slightly different form in 1991 in Japanese, under the title
Trash, by Bungeishunju Publishing Co. Some portions were originally published
in the author's novella *Jesse's Backbone*.

THE LIBRARY OF CONGRESS HAS CATALOGUED THE HARDCOVER AS FOLLOWS:
Yamada, Eimi, 1959–
[Torasshu. English]
Trash/Amy Yamada; translated from the Japanese by Sonya L. Johnson.
p. cm.
ISBN 1-56836-018-5 (hc.)
ISBN 0 14 02.5418 8 (pbk.)
I. Johnson, Sonya, 1963–. II. Title.
PL865.A489T6713 1995
895.6'35—dc20   94–3758

Printed in the United States of America
Set in Bitstream Elegant Garamond
Designed by Janet Tingey

TRANSLATOR'S NOTE

This English-language translation of *Trash* includes several sections from the author's earlier novella, *Jesse's Backbone*, which is about the same characters. These additions were made in consultation with the author, as were slight adaptations and excisions undertaken specifically with an American reader in mind.

CONTENTS

PART I

IF SOMEONE were to ask her the one thing she longed for most in this world, she would probably say without a moment's hesitation, "*A bed!*" But not that old friend of a bed she slept in every night: the one that always had a lazy warmth all its own curling through its sheets, the one with the big reading pillow with a permanent depression in it the exact shape of her head, the one with blankets rumpled from contact with human skin. No, the sole purpose of the bed she had in mind was sleep.

She wondered if she had ever slept in such a bed. If she had, it must have been an awfully long time ago. A bed dedicated to sleeping. A real *bed* bed, the kind that made you think sometimes that sleeping is like dying. "I think I'll die now," she would say to herself and burrow under the covers. She longed to sleep in such a bed from the bottom of her heart—a bed that provided both serenity and solitude. No one's emotions would seep into that bed to wend through its surfaces and twine around its legs, not even her own. Her emotions were, for the most part, like fish snapping at baited hooks, always catching her off guard. It was as if she had no will of her own: the moment she saw that bait dangling in front of her, she'd be off.

She was thinking of things she'd longed for at one point or another and trying to pinpoint the moment that her longing for each of them had evaporated. She'd become fascinated with the project and had spent hours lost in thought. Then suddenly it occurred to her how strange it was to be sitting on the floor. Why couldn't she lie down when there was a bed right next to her? Sitting next to a bed, muttering about how much she longed for a bed—it was stupid. But what she longed for was a bed and yet not a bed. That warm, comforting thing she had loved for so long was not there anymore. It was just a big piece of furniture, nothing more. And right now she was sitting handcuffed to one of its legs.

So you can feel handcuffs on your wrists without having committed a crime. But maybe everyone goes through life with handcuffs on, she thought. There are handcuffs you can see and handcuffs you can't see.

Handcuffs you can see are for crimes you can see. And handcuffs you can't see are for crimes you can't see. So I must have committed some crime. After all, it was a fact that these steel circles were biting into her wrists. Didn't it go against the rules to have to wear real handcuffs for a crime you couldn't see? "It's unfair," she muttered. Hearing herself, she despaired at her own coy words, so ill-suited to her predicament.

Jesse'll probably be back soon, she thought. And when he sees me handcuffed to the bed he might cry out from the shock. Or maybe he'll go off to Daryl's without coming in. Jesse steered clear of the bedroom, knowing that too many things went on there he wasn't supposed to see. He wouldn't see her here now unless she called out to him. But even if she got Jesse to help her, it wouldn't change anything. He could take off the visible handcuffs, but that wouldn't make her free. She was still tied down by love. And hate. She couldn't just ball up either one and throw it away like so much trash. Both were still alive. Alive and threatening her. Sins she couldn't see lay half buried in her path, making it impossible for her to walk without tripping.

Jesse's eyes will probably be full of sympathy when he frees me. The thought made her feel it might be better to stay cuffed. No matter how mature he'd become, it was still too early for him to see all this. Love was OK, but not hate.

It was one thing for Jesse himself to hate, but there was nothing good in letting him see someone else's hatred.

She knew Jesse would say something like "Koko, you like to stir things up, don't you?"

She wished she didn't, which is why she wanted to lie in that deathly silent bed.

She had been happy yesterday. And she was happy a week before that, too. What about a year ago? Koko thought about it. She would have to say she was happy. It had been a kind of indefinable happiness that you couldn't get your hands around.

No, she'd have to say she was unhappy back then. Unsatisfied with all things in her life, she'd desperately filled in the gaps with new things until everything overflowed. She had lived with an uneasy feeling, as if her heart were an ill-fitting sweater she kept on wearing. She'd been miserable, yes. But maybe it *hadn't* been like that, after all. You could also say it was like wearing an old sweater, frayed around the edges, homey. When she looked at it that way, she thought she must've been happy. She didn't know. Why, she wondered, does trying to define happiness involve trudging through so many memories of unhappiness?

○

ON THAT SPRING DAY a year ago she'd been passion-
ately in love with Rick. Koko could say that for sure. And
she got on well with his son, Jesse. The three of them had
been living together for two years. It surprised her how fast
Jesse was turning into a grown-up. As he had learned to
avoid getting into trouble, she had learned to relax with
him. Meanwhile, a new problem was developing that Koko
was determined to overcome somehow with her love for
Rick. After all, there isn't a woman alive who can love Rick
the way I do, she'd thought. This conviction had become
Koko's entire strength. She wasn't about to be discouraged
by something like this.

That evening, Koko and Jesse were thrown into confusion by an unexpected visitor. It had drizzled the whole day.
When the doorbell rang, Koko opened the door to find a
white woman with a vague smile on her face. She was soaking wet. A tiny, kittenlike boy stood with her, just as wet.
They're selling something, Koko thought, but the outside
door to the building was locked, and no one would let a ped-
dler in.

"Uh . . . who are you?"

"Hi, you must be Koko. I'm Eileen. I have a little favor to
ask of you. Can I come in?"

Koko had never met this thin blond woman in her life.
She stood there, hesitating.

"Who is it, Koko?"

Munching on tortilla chips, Jesse came out of his room,
where he'd been playing a computer game. He stopped
short when he saw the dripping-wet pair.

"Eileen . . . and Jeffrey, too! What are you doing here?"

"Hi, Jesse. Long time no see. Can we come in?"

There was a touch of servile appeal in the woman's grin. Jesse looked at Koko as though he didn't know what to say.

"You know these people, Jesse?"

"They're Daddy's friends."

"Oh. . . ."

Even if this woman was a friend of Rick's, it didn't make sense for her to drop by without phoning first, Koko thought, as she let the two in.

"God, what a hassle it is to get here from Brooklyn!" Eileen said, brushing the raindrops from her shoulders.

"Um, I'm afraid Rick is on graveyard tonight; he won't be back until morning," Koko said apologetically. She wasn't worried, as Eileen seemed like a nice woman and Jesse said she was Rick's friend. And she was amazingly friendly toward Koko, considering they'd never met.

"I know. He works graveyard every Wednesday night. I came to ask a favor of *you*, Koko, not Rick. . . . Hey, Jeff, you're not supposed to open up other people's refrigerators. Get out of there!" She turned back to Koko. "I'm sorry. He's just learned how to do that."

Jeffrey stuck his tongue out at her and ran into Jesse's room. Koko thought he looked exactly like a doll with that blond hair bouncing lightly off his neck. A doll one didn't ever see for sale in this neighborhood.

"What a cute child you have."

"You think so?"

"There aren't any children like that around here."

"I'll give him to you, if you like."

"What?"

"Just kidding. I've always wanted to say that, just to see how it sounds. Hey, Koko, I've heard a lot about you from Rick. This room, too, is totally different from before. Are you an artist? That picture is really great." Eileen seemed genuinely impressed as she looked around the room.

"I work in a gallery in the Village. I'm not an artist."

"Oh, yeah? But you've got style. I can tell from the apartment. And Rick told me he'd found someone with much better taste than the one before."

"The one before was awful."

Every time the subject of Rick's former wife came up, Koko saw red. She told herself any number of times that the woman was, after all, Jesse's mother, but she couldn't control such deep-seated disgust. It was practically physiological. Koko had tried to behave maturely with her, but Jesse's mother refused to act in kind. She had torn Koko's thin cloak of goodwill into pieces and then disappeared. Koko had believed, still wanted to believe, in the essential goodness of people, but Jesse's mother had destroyed that faith forever. Koko hated her for it.

"You really seem to dislike Rick's ex-wife," Eileen said, with the trace of a smile.

"I don't like thinking about that woman."

"Did something happen to make you feel that way?"

There were any number of reasons she could give, but nothing anyone who did not know her could understand. Only Koko herself, Rick, and, of course, Jesse—they alone—understood a thing that can only be understood by those bound together over time by living and breathing the same air of life.

"She's not a smart woman, that's all."

Eileen looked at her and shrugged, as if to say she didn't know what Koko meant.

"You said you had a favor you wanted?"

A tense look crossed Eileen's face as she lit a cigarette. Holding it between two fingers, she rested her forehead on the other three.

"You'll probably tell me I'm not smart, either, but there's no one else I can ask. My husband would blow up if I hired a baby-sitter. What I wondered was if you'd watch Jeff for a little while."

Koko stared at Eileen in shock. This woman has got to be kidding, she thought. Koko was a congenital flop at watching kids. That's why she had suffered so these past two years living with Jesse. There are people in this world who are good with kids and people who aren't. A simple distinction, just like there are people who excel at math while others are good at language. Those who apply themselves to something they're not naturally good at have to expend a huge effort for a small result.

"Why ask me? We've only just met. Does your son mean so little to you that you can leave him with someone you barely know?"

"Don't make it into such a big deal. People who don't have children of their own are quick to make a big deal out of watching kids."

"It's a big deal to me. Just hearing the word 'child' makes me think of responsibility. If you tell me any different it means you have no sense of responsibility, even if you are a mother. No, you *do* have a sense of responsibility; you're just good at shifting it to someone else."

"You're the only one I can ask."

"You don't have any friends?"

"Yes, I do. . . . "

"Then why don't you ask a nice friend who has kids?"

"Women with kids don't understand."

"I don't understand a word you're saying myself."

Eileen had smoked her cigarette down to the butt. She ground it out in the ashtray.

"An hour, that's all I ask. You can do that, can't you? Jeffrey and Jesse used to play together a lot. I don't think he'll be any trouble. He's a bit of a brat, but basically he's a good kid. If he does something bad, go ahead and yell at him."

"This isn't a joke. I can't go around yelling at someone else's child."

Eileen looked at Koko imploringly. The color of her eyes had gone from blue to gray. And her blond hair, half dry now, was straggly. It irritated Koko. Strangers letting themselves look shabby in front of others was the most offensive thing in the world to her. The greater part of her hatred for Jesse's mother had to do with that. Koko wasn't used to seeing misery. And when she saw people in wretched circumstances, she couldn't bear the feeling of superiority that would flash across her heart, catching her unawares. Feeling superior felt good. Nevertheless, Koko didn't have it in her to feel good at someone else's expense, someone who was having a harder time than she.

Koko broke into a cold sweat at the sight of those straggly wisps of hair plastered to Eileen's cheeks. Honestly. How can a mother let herself be seen in public like that? What am I going to do? I can't handle this.

"OK. I don't know why, but I'll do it. Only for *one* hour, though, like you said."

Eileen seemed relieved; she lit a second cigarette. Looking at her, Koko wanted to take back her words. Pulling deeply on that second cigarette, Eileen didn't seem to be a mother anymore. Maybe she was going to see a man. The thought occurred to Koko, but what man could Eileen be going to see looking like that?

"Thanks a lot, Koko. I won't forget this, babe."

"I feel sorry for you, Eileen, having to ask someone you've just met for a favor like this."

Dropping her gaze, Eileen chewed on her lower lip. Koko was afraid Eileen might take her words to mean Koko felt some sort of missionary sense of duty. She was ashamed when people thought of her as a "kind" person. There were more complicated emotions than kindness at work within her.

This was definitely the case in her behavior with Jesse, with whom she'd lived for so long. Koko's ideal person wouldn't take her hard talk seriously, would understand it was discomfort, not malice, that made her act so tough. And, indeed, Jesse saw right through her. No matter what kind of tongue-lashing she gave him, he'd merely shrug, as if to say, I understand how you feel. That's how quickly he'd grown up in the last two years.

On this point, Rick was hopeless. Once a boy became a man, he could be wounded by the slightest turn of phrase and become intent upon inflicting the same measure of pain in return. Sometimes it made Koko so tired. Maybe men who had a sexual tie with a woman depended on it alone, which made them dense when it came to affairs of the heart.

"Hey, if I'm taking care of your child, you'd better tell me where you're going and when you'll be back. I can't go running around in circles if something comes up."

Eileen looked down at Koko's words.

"I'm going to a friend's place."

"Tell me the phone number."

"I don't know it."

Dumbfounded, Koko stared at her.

"Nothing'll come up. I've always kept my kid with me thinking something might happen to him, but nothing ever does."

"I can't believe your logic!"

Koko still somehow believed in the superstition that no harm, no unhappiness would come to a child so long as its mother was near. Of course, she knew from being with Jesse that children can get along without their mother. Even so, she felt there was a special power inherent in mothers, and children needed to be protected by it. She'd come to think, through taking care of Jesse, that blood ties had nothing to do with it. Even so, when things got tense, she'd find herself all but praying: if only she and Jesse were of the same blood. . . . There was nothing that could be done. She simply was not his mother. No power of God could do anything about that.

Koko knew such an emphasis on blood was terribly out-dated. Still, when she remembered how she'd grown up, enveloped in her parents' love, she thought her emphasis on blood might be outdated but it still had its place. She'd been protected from all kinds of anxieties by having her mother near.

Koko realized with a start that Eileen was putting on her coat. The straggly hair, too, was now secured with a clip and she had reapplied her caked lipstick. She was pressing her lips together to even out the color. Her lips had flaked badly since she'd arrived at the apartment. It occurred to Koko that perhaps this was why she couldn't refuse to take care of Jeffrey. After all, it was raining out. You had to pity a woman whose lips were so dry on a rainy day.

"I'll call you a few times, Koko. Jeff, Mommy will be right back, so you listen to what Koko says. Take care of him, 'kay, Jesse?"

Jeffrey had been playing on the computer with Jesse, but he reappeared now, looking worried as he watched his mother getting ready to leave.

"Where are you going, Mommy? I'll go, too."

"Don't worry. Probably Clara's."

Jeffrey looked up at Koko. "I don't like that lady. She always gets mad."

"So that's why you should stay here and play computer games with Jesse, right?"

"Yeah. I'll beat him for sure."

Jesse, silent, shrugged and looked at Koko. I've been letting him win, the gesture said.

"You really will call, right, Eileen?"

"Of course. I'm his mother," Eileen said, closing the door behind her. Her perfume hung in the air, stirred by the motion of the door. When had she put it on? Koko sighed and turned around. Jesse glared at her, put out.

"What, Jesse?"

"You're an idiot, Koko."

"Why, just because I agreed to baby-sit?"

"No, not because of that. Because you listened to Eileen."

"What can I do? I couldn't send them away. She'd made up her mind to leave him here. But you know, I don't understand how she got upstairs. The building's locked."

Koko looked at Jesse. He glared back at her, fed up.

"She must have a key to the outside door. She must've made a copy, don't you see? Daddy's so careless."

"What do you mean?"

"Man! Sometimes I just don't understand you. Eileen is Daddy's woman from before."

"You gotta be kidding! And she comes and asks *me* to baby-sit?"

Jesse was too disgusted for words. He merely looked at her.

"It's unbelievable," Koko added. "That's why she came when Rick was working graveyard. She knew he'd say no. The nerve!"

"You talk as if it had nothing to do with you. You're weird. I'm surprised she remembered this place. She and Daddy went out an awful long time ago."

As she listened to Jesse, Koko was thinking there were some strange people in this world. She could never visit some long-ago boyfriend's place and ask his present lover for a favor. And a favor to do with her child!

"Jesse, c'mon, let's go and play." Jeffrey wanted to go back to the computer.

Jesse went to get two chocolate pudding cups from the refrigerator. On his way to his room he asked Koko, "Are you mad?"

Koko shook her head vigorously. "Of course not!"

"You're *ve-ry* nice." With an ironic glare, Jesse shut the door of his room behind him.

She wasn't angry or anything, Koko told herself. She poured a glass of red wine and sat down, lighting a cigarette. She was not angry at Eileen, nor was she scandalized, not after the initial shock. Koko had felt from the moment she met Eileen that if they had been friends, they would probably have had a pretty easygoing relationship, razzing each other about this and that. Koko had girlfriends like that. They dissed each other loudly, just like men friends did. It was a game, all lively tussle and posturing. And yet, each was aware of the sort of remark that would really hurt the other, and it was tacitly understood that such words would never cross their lips.

But Koko knew she and Eileen could never be friends. She was not interested in becoming friends with a woman who had had a relationship with the man she loved.

Koko thought few women were as fastidious as she when she felt deeply about someone. If a man Koko was falling in love with said to her, "Look over there; see the third woman from the left sitting at that table? I slept with her once," the confession itself—a simple, even puerile one—wouldn't faze Koko a bit. But the fact that they were in the same place, breathing the same air—the man, Koko, and some woman she'd never laid eyes on before—would be enough to make Koko feel like throwing up. She would flee on the spot. The man wouldn't understand why Koko was so revolted. He'd come running after her with, "Hey, wait. It's just something to say. I thought you might be interested." Thought it might make me more interested in *you*, you mean. Whether she forgave him or not depended on how much she really liked the guy, but at such times she truly felt that men didn't *think* enough. A woman would never inject a foul thought into a new relationship with, "Hey, I slept with that guy over there once."

"Koko, can we go and eat at Roy Rogers? That'll be our dinner." Tired of computer games, Jesse and Jeffrey had come into the living room.

"Sure, but it'll be dark soon, and it's raining."

"We don't mind. It's only a block away. I'm not the right age to get kidnapped anyway."

"It's not *you* I'm worried about, Jesse. It's Jeff."

"Hmph! He'll be all right as long as he's with me."

Jeffrey looked excitedly at Koko and Jesse in turn.

"No. We'd better not chance it. Go by yourself, Jesse, and bring us all take-out. Ten pieces of chicken; Rick'll have some later. Make five of them wings. Fries and biscuits too."

Jesse put on his jacket, slipping Koko's twenty into his pocket.

"Make sure you give me the change."

"OK."

Jeffrey watched Jesse and Koko's exchange anxiously. Rumpling the boy's hair, Jesse told him, "I'll be back before you know it. I don't give Koko her change, she'll fry my butt."

Koko shot Jesse a look. She would have liked to respond with a sharp rap on the head. She and Jesse weren't at each other's throats anymore, but there was a certain coldness between them. They couldn't reach each other. They were a lot closer than before, but theirs was the closeness of two wary adults. They both had a knack for sidestepping around emotional situations that would allow them to enter deeply into the other's heart. They simply didn't hassle each other, and while Koko liked the smooth surface of her relationship with Jesse, it also disappointed her. In a way the two of them were overly adept at dealing with their fate: without discussing it, they'd made a tacit pact that their course together would be a calm one. Jesse understood this. He was trying to help create a harmonious atmosphere.

But it was not simple harmony that Koko or Jesse really wanted. They wanted something more, but they knew fights and hurts would surface if they tried to change their polite distance into intimacy. People can get by with just eating, sleeping, and laughing. Meals don't have to be home-cooked, and children don't need a lullaby sung at their bedside. People can get by without such niceties. Yet they also knew that small domestic gestures nourish a person's heart. Their eyes would meet and fall away. The same roadblock stood at the intersection where their eyes met, and both of them were careful to drive around it.

Only Rick had no inkling of their tacit understanding. No complexity shadowed his happiness at Koko and Jesse's getting along. That was what he had hoped for: his girlfriend and his son were not hurling insults at each other anymore. Rick always lived his life optimistically. More than anything, he hated bitching and bickering. He'd had enough of that with his ex-wife.

Koko remembered how it had been at the beginning.

"SHE'S NOT what you'd call cute—more like so-so, wouldn't you say?"

That was the first thing the brat had said when he saw her. Koko had a sinking feeling as she eyed the eleven-year-old picking at his scrambled eggs. This kid would be a great source of torment to her in the months to come.

Rick was in a great mood. It wasn't even noon yet, but he was pouring gin into a glass and booming jovially. Koko, hung way over from the previous night's excesses, could barely look at liquor without feeling nauseated. She held a large glass of icewater in front of her and was sipping steadily from that.

"Look at her! She's a *babe*! You can't help but kiss her. And she's a sex bomb—everything in all the right places; can't help but want to *do* her."

So saying, Rick had landed a big wet one on Koko's mouth. Gagging at the liquor on his breath, Koko had barely managed to keep from vomiting then and there.

The brat, Jesse, had glared at his father and slapped his fork down. He hadn't touched the vegetables Koko had put out for him to go with the eggs. He got up from the table.

"You better remember. I hate all vegetables except okra."

Koko had been speechless. Ignoring her, Jesse had put on his jacket to go.

"I'll have lunch at Daryl's, Dad, so don't worry. You have *fun*."

He'd slammed the door, leaving Koko and Rick alone in the kitchen. Koko had turned to Rick, relieved, but he was looking at the floor as if suddenly abashed. Draining his gin, he stood up and left the room. Koko felt a sweet warmth course through her lower body. She'd gone to the bedroom and, stripping down to her silky boxer shorts, slipped into bed. Rick would join her momentarily, she was sure, lie down beside her, and continue the hot, white-hot play of the night before.

This was the moment Koko loved best, when she first stayed over at a new man's place. To her it was a heady distillation to be savored, that moment when each examined the other, eyes cleared of alcohol, and decided whether or not they could go on as partners.

There was a mirror over the dresser. Koko had sat up and looked at herself. She preened, running her fingers through her hair with a satisfied little smile. Much of her makeup had worn away to leave her own skin peeking through. She knew that her bare skin had much more allure than it did carefully covered in makeup. Bare skin was her strong point. She had buried her face in the pillow with a smile and blushed at seeing last night's lipstick on the sheet.

Koko had arranged herself artfully, showing herself off to maximum advantage. Tucking the sheets strategically about her body, she waited for Rick.

Rick, however, was not forthcoming. As Koko's position was by no means natural, her back had started to ache and her leg was threatening to fall asleep. Tired of waiting, Koko had tiptoed into the next room, then the next. She was surprised to find Rick doing laundry, gin glass in hand. She sighed. Although she was confident of herself as a love professional, nothing in her mental files on the subject could explain to her the psychology of a man who would be doing his laundry the morning after making love with a new woman.

"What are you doing?"

Rick had let out a shout and dropped his glass. It'd shattered on the floor.

"I'm sorry. I scared you," Koko had said.

"Uh . . . uh-huh . . . I guess."

"You like doing laundry?" Koko'd asked, bending down to collect shards of glass.

"Uh . . . well . . . I, uh . . ." Rick took a shirt from the washing machine and started squeezing, even though he could have put it in the dryer.

Maybe he's shy, Koko thought. How old did he say he

was? With a kid that big, he must be thirty-five, at least. What was his problem? They'd already done it and all, no reason to get uptight now.

"Come."

Koko had taken Rick's hand and led him back to the bedroom. She'd slipped into the bed while Rick had closed the blinds and begun to undress.

His hands were cold and damp from the laundry water. Koko had caught a whiff of soap powder when they stroked the back of her neck. As Rick's body, cold from the air outside, had begun to take warmth from hers, he finally entered the realm of what Koko's catalog of love said the proper "morning after" should be.

Koko and Rick had met for the first time the night before. While Koko's friends partied, the two of them earnestly searched each other's eyes and talked. Rick praised Koko extravagantly, but Koko was used to that, so it didn't impress her much. What did catch her attention was the way he'd scurried to the men's room, glancing back at her over his shoulder, afraid that someone would steal her away while he was gone. He'd emerged in almost no time, ecstatic to see her waiting quietly and alone for his return.

The liquor relaxed him. It didn't do a thing for Koko—she was the same as ever. This sort of meeting was as common to her as bread and tea. While she was mildly curious about how he would proposition her after the partying, she had no illusions about his fine-sounding phrases. Or about him, for that matter. She was merely enjoying the start of the game, the tantalizing beginning of a new affair. No big deal.

Rick drank a lot. Koko sipped at her own drink to keep him company. Skillfully, she elicited the key bits of information she needed to determine whether or not he would be a fit companion for the night. This was done through jokes and tidbits of flattery designed to make him want her.

He wasn't married. Koko had no interest in getting involved with a married man. She wasn't concerned about breaking up a home as much as going to bed with some other woman's used goods. There was a particular smell to married men's bodies that had to do with bored, boring sex—sex out of inertia. Nothing made her skin crawl faster than a married man telling her he loved her and her alone. On that point, Rick had passed her test.

Sensing her interest, Rick became more and more animated. It pleased Koko to see him so happy to have monopolized the attention of an attractive woman.

Now and then, Rick would tickle Koko and she'd shriek like a child. Then he'd tell her that if she came back to his place he'd tickle her all over with his tongue. She'd imagined how he would be in bed and decided she'd probably end up going home with him that night. But when Rick lied about his age, Koko had lost some interest. Koko could tell he was far older than he admitted. She was disappointed he would do such a womanish thing and decided to hold off sleeping with him for a while. Later wouldn't be too late. More than anything, she didn't want to waste her time. Experience had taught her that delicious affairs were the only ones worth having.

Rick seemed to take it for granted that Koko would be coming home with him. When he told her they should be going and Koko said she'd like to go to another bar, Rick's face had crumpled. He looked about to cry. Shocked, Koko had cast about for a way to comfort him.

She told him that since she was a lady, she absolutely, positively could not go to bed with a man she'd only just met. Koko could barely suppress an impish smile at the white lie, but Rick seemed convinced. Resigned, he'd stopped talking about anything sexual and begun to tell her about his son, Jesse.

His son was the most handsome kid in the world. Not many parents could say they were friends with their children, but he and his kid were *tight*. Rick hung his head shyly as he talked about the boy.

It was a topic that interested Koko deeply. She didn't know any children. She knew pretty much all there was to know about men, but nothing about a man-child. She couldn't control her curiosity; she had to see that child. If, in so doing, it meant she had to spend the night with Rick—well, that wasn't so bad either.

When she'd stood up and said, "Well, then, shall we go to your place?" Rick stared at her, open-mouthed. He could not believe his good fortune. Catching Koko up in his arms, he'd kissed her and thanked her profusely. There was no way he could've known why she'd acquiesced.

The moment she'd stepped through the door, Koko had demanded to see the boy. Grinning, Rick had opened the boy's bedroom door cautiously and motioned her over.

"Handsome, huh?" he'd whispered.

Koko hadn't known what to say. The boy was half black, from his father. But his mother must have been Asian, and the mixture wasn't a fortunate one. The boy bore a striking resemblance to a monkey. Disappointed, Koko murmured something noncommittal.

Rick's hands had fluttered and faltered over the glasses as he fixed drinks for the two of them. He was very drunk. Koko watched, aghast. She was by now terribly disappointed. But contrary to her expectations, Rick's lovemaking—something she had thought of as incidental—left nothing to be desired. Koko forgot all about the child sleeping in the next room.

• • •

RICK WAS extraordinarily indulgent with Koko in those early days. He treated her like a little baby, which was a new experience for her. She'd always been on an equal footing with her men, whether loving or fighting, and hadn't realized how exhausted she was. Koko reveled in Rick's way with her. When they went out together, Rick's hand would always be on some part of her body, and when she was asleep she would periodically become aware of him kissing her cheek. With Rick, there was no need for witty conversation, nor was there the constant negotiating and jockeying for power that Koko had always accepted as part of a relationship. The sense of relief was overwhelming. It was like coming home. All the gestures and mannered poses she'd collected in her arsenal of lovemaking had no meaning with Rick. She could simply be herself, and while it went a little against her sense of aesthetics, Koko found herself relaxing around a man for the first time in her life.

Koko began going to Rick's place every Friday night and spending the weekend with him and Jesse. She was soon dreading Monday morning, when she'd have to get up, go to work, then back to her own place. Every time Monday morning came around, Koko would kick off the bedclothes, shouting, "I hate these blankets! Hate 'em! I hate having to *go*! I don't wanna leave!" Rick would rub and pat her on the back as if she were a baby. Mollified, Koko would lean back in his arms and doze again for a few sweet minutes.

While her relationship with Rick was a source of stability and comfort, it was one surprise after another with Jesse.

One morning, when Koko had gone to the kitchen to make breakfast, Jesse was already there. He said he wanted raw eggs.

"Raw eggs? You want to be Rocky or something?"

Jesse had merely glanced at her. He'd found a bowl and

cracked a couple of eggs into it. Pouring in a generous amount of soy sauce, he'd dumped in some rice and stirred the whole thing together. Koko felt sick watching him spoon the mixture into his mouth.

Koko pointed silently at Jesse when Rick had come up behind her.

"Hey, rice and raw eggs. Make some for me too, will ya, babe?"

Seeing father and son slurping the yellow-brown mass together, Koko trembled with horror.

"You're not having any?"

"Don't be ridiculous."

"Jesse's mother used to make this a lot. She's Japanese too."

Koko wasn't a Christian, but she couldn't help crossing herself and muttering, "Help me, Lord." She and Jesse's mother might both be Japanese, but they were not the same kind of Japanese.

Jesse didn't know how to use a knife and fork together. His mother had left before teaching him such things. He'd pick up his steak with both hands and gnaw on it like a dog. The first time Koko saw him do that, she flew to the kitchen to get him a knife and fork. All she could find were one plate and a single fork. This isn't a household, she thought. How do they live every day? Koko prayed she'd never have to go to a restaurant with Jesse.

Koko was used to sophisticated dinners alone with her lover. Seeing Jesse eat was enough to make her lose her appetite, and she began to dread mealtimes with him. Rick, however, wasn't perturbed at all. When Koko, beside herself, shouted that something had to be done, Rick calmed her down with, "Don't worry. He'll learn table manners soon enough, when he gets interested in girls."

Koko couldn't understand why Jesse wasn't living with his mother. She asked Rick about it.

"He was at first. But after a month he came back with all his stuff on his bicycle. He said it was no fun over there—they were fighting all the time. Said he couldn't stand living with a woman who was always screamin'. That's just how I felt after I got married. It's the worst thing for a man. I figured, Jesse's a man too, he'll be better off livin' with me."

"That's too awful."

"When he wants to see his mother, he goes by himself. She lives nearby, and all. You shouldn't worry, Koko. Kids are their parents' problem. You're here 'cause you're my girl, right?"

Rick kissed her, trying to distract her. Koko let him, but she was thinking about how Jesse came between her and Rick. She was becoming aware, for the first time, of the existence of deep, complex human relationships that you could neither run away from nor soften with sex.

Koko couldn't understand why she felt the way she did about Rick. Rick certainly wasn't the type Koko would ordinarily fall for. For one thing, if he kept up his drinking, he'd be living in a stupor within a year for sure, unable to work or do anything.

Rick cherished his liquor. He was loath to let a single drop escape him—he'd lick and suck the ice cubes. Koko loved liquor, the taste and the feel of it, but it sickened her to see the way Rick drank. He gulped it down without even tasting it, intent on getting drunk faster than anyone else. However, this rarely happened. His body was too used to alcohol. He had to have at least two bottles of Bacardi to get really drunk.

A middle-aged man with a kid. A man who liked nothing better than drinking himself into a daze. So why did she get hysterical every time Monday morning rolled around and she had to leave? Koko couldn't understand it.

Although Rick never failed to please her in bed, that in and of itself was no reason. Koko had never once been a slave to sex. She loved having sex with whomever she happened to like at the moment, but she could solemnly swear it had never clouded her good judgment. Good sex was one thing, and a relationship was something else entirely. Koko kept the two separate—or, rather, sex was an independent pleasure to be enjoyed within a relationship but never allowed to color the whole thing.

Rick had no cool attractions. Not to say that he had any hot ones, either. He was like the blankets on his bed, warm and damp with sweat, that twisted about Koko when she woke up in the morning. He wrapped himself around her every night. It annoyed her at first, but after a while she found it hard to sleep without him. Your own sweaty blanket, the one that is yours and yours alone, is the one you can't let go.

Once when they were drinking together at the apartment, Rick said his problem was women. Whenever he passed a good-looking woman, he couldn't help but turn around for another look at her. Koko was charmed. She, of course, always turned to get a second look at a handsome man. She'd even been known to find some pretext to speak to such juicy specimens. She'd even managed to get a couple into bed. Koko hugged herself, laughing. She was sure Rick could never pull off something like that. Whenever she thought of Rick's awkwardness with women, she'd smile, remembering how shy he looked that first morning doing his laundry.

Indeed, Rick was a constant source of smiles for Koko. When he got drunk, she'd glower at him, but then that telltale smile would come tugging at her lips. There was nothing she could do about it. Silly Daddy, she'd think, as if he were her own father. Can't do anything right.

It used to be so easy, she thought. She was nervous over meeting people, true. But it was a pleasant sort of nervousness, a part of the freedom of her lifestyle. The excitement of a grand game.

As she met more and more people, she selected some men for serious loves and a few women for friends to talk to about them. These carefully chosen confidantes were fine women who shared a liberal worldview with Koko. Her lovers were progressive, modern men. They'd share good times and a few tears. When love ended, Koko would confide to a woman friend, tears in her eyes, about how wonderful it had been. "I took a lot and I gave a lot," she'd say. "We're even." Her friend would listen earnestly, then say, "He's not a bad guy. You two just weren't meant to be, that's all. You didn't have that soul connection."

No matter how many loves her friends went through, they shut their eyes to the fact that love, especially passionate love, always comes to an end. They'd see the guy over and over, even when it wasn't fun anymore, always thinking there was a "soul connection" with *this* man that would keep them together forever.

Koko met Rick hoping against hope for the usual things. So I'm starting a new relationship, she thought. What'll it be like this time? Koko went to bed with Rick with lighthearted anticipation. Maybe we'll play, maybe we'll get serious. She couldn't say. It was a gamble.

Koko reveled in the thought that only *she* knew Rick's charms. His dirty face in the morning, that hangdog, apologetic look he'd get after a fight. Koko had never seen anyone who could look so sorry. When she was feeling really blue, Rick could always kid her out of it. All these things made her smile, and it excited Koko that nobody, but *nobody*, knew how wonderful Rick really was. Others saw him merely as an ordinary man, and that made him even more of a precious gem to Koko. As she gradually realized how important Rick was becoming to her, Koko had to ask herself if maybe this was the beginning of true love.

Koko burst out laughing. Her, in love with that drunk? Then Rick's drunken image appeared in her mind's eye, and her throat caught.

It dawned on Koko that love doesn't announce itself with a huge crash, nor does it set one's heart pounding. I must be in love, Koko thought. Doesn't the thought of not being with him make me cry? She touched her wet cheeks, amazed at herself. So this is love, Koko thought, smiling wryly. She almost felt like chucking the whole thing, and yet she had to admit that it was kind of nice.

KOKO LOOKED at the blond little boy in front of her. Jeffrey had gotten himself a magazine and spread it out before him. How long will he stay quiet? she wondered. She opened a book herself in order not to break the silence. We must look like a study in tranquillity, Koko thought. A boy and a woman reading. Who could know that this sort of silent stillness was excruciating for Koko? Her eyes were on the page, but her nerves were intent on not breaking the mood. Koko waited, knowing if the child moved an inch, she'd see it. If only he would stay that way, she thought, but children aren't dolls. They don't sit still forever.

It was the same when she was with Jesse. And what was even more disconcerting was that Jesse's nerves were no less on edge than Koko's, and he too was only pretending to be relaxed. Somewhere along the way he'd started to put on this act. Jesse realized Koko was always tense, on the edge of some sort of explosion. So they avoided spending time alone with each other. If they had to, one or the other would quickly get up to stir the air. Jesse would say, "There's something I want to watch on TV; I'll be in my room." Or Koko would say, "I think I'll take a bath. You're not going to need the bathroom right away, are you?"

Jeffrey couldn't be expected to understand the household rules. He started to whine.

"Hey, when's Jesse coming back?"

"Soon. This time of night Roy Rogers will be crowded."

"Koko, when's Mommy coming back?"

"I don't know, but soon, I think. Does your mommy often leave you somewhere like this and go out?"

"No. We go out together a lot. Mommy likes to go out a lot. When we go to people's houses she buys me toys and candy, so I like it, too."

"Do you remember coming here before?"

"Yeah. I played with Jesse. You weren't here. Jesse's daddy and my mommy played here and I went to the park with Jesse."

"They got rid of you, huh?"

"What?"

Koko clammed up. Why am I so bad with kids? She could never remember that children had a later start than adults. Koko looked at Jeffrey and thought, What an adorable little creature. She felt a tenderness welling up inside and regretted her immaturity.

Jesse finally arrived with the bucket of chicken. His jacket was wet from the spring rain. Koko handed him a towel.

"Rain's almost stopped. Here's your change."

"Was it crowded?"

"Not really. Hey, Koko, who do you think I saw?" Unable to wait, Jesse stuffed a french fry in his mouth.

"Who, Kay? Maureen?"

"Nope. A man."

"Who? Honestly, can't you come out with it already?"

"It was Greggory. You know, your *old* man."

"Jesse, quit saying 'man.' Can't you say 'boyfriend'? I don't like the way you've been talking recently. Girls are not 'chicks,' and I know you call them even worse things sometimes."

Jesse shrugged, not minding her a bit, as he put the chicken onto plates.

"That's how people talk, Koko, it's *in*. Daddy says it all the time."

"Your father doesn't say it because it's 'in.' He's always talked that way."

"C'mon, Jeff, let's play s'more computer games."

Jesse piled two paper plates with chicken and headed for his room.

"So what about Greg?"

Jesse looked over his shoulder at Koko. He grinned mischievously like a naughty child.

"He might be coming to see you soon."

"Did he say that?"

"Uh-uh."

"Then how do you know?"

"Because he said his wife is pregnant."

Koko looked at him, unable to speak. Pregnant? What did that have to do with her? Besides, Jesse didn't even know how a woman *gets* pregnant.

As she poured hot sauce on the chicken, the phone rang. It was Rick.

"What's up? You're at work, aren't you?" Koko said, her mouth full of chicken.

"Jesse didn't tell you?"

"Tell me what?" Koko asked.

"He needs the paper he brought home yesterday signed by a parent. I forgot, so can you do it? It's for a field trip or something."

"I'm not his parent. Are you saying anybody can sign it?"

"Yeah, sure. You signed his homework all last year, right?"

Koko was fed up. "That's because you didn't take care of it. And furthermore, do you know what's going on here?"

"Did something happen?"

"Your former *woman* showed up and pushed her kid on me."

"What woman?"

Jesse appeared behind her and said, "It's not 'your woman'; can't you say 'girlfriend'?"

Koko handed Jesse the receiver.

"Hi, Daddy. . . . Yeah, it was Eileen. She left Jeff here and went somewhere. . . . You'd better not say 'bitch.' Koko'll get mad."

Incensed, Koko grabbed the receiver from Jesse.

"Rick, I'm not kidding. Why in hell's name do I have to take care of your former woman's kid, huh? Don't you think there's something odd in that?"

"I'm Daddy's former woman's kid, too," Jesse said, grinning. Koko motioned for him to go away.

"It's all right," Rick said. "Eileen said it's only for an hour, right? She'll be back soon, baby. She won't be riding the subway back to Brooklyn in the middle of the night."

Koko was infuriated at Rick's nonchalance. He never took responsibility for what happened around him—even when it had to do with Jesse.

"It's been two hours already. I'm sick of this."

"Jeff's being good, isn't he?"

"You and Eileen both . . . honestly. You can't say he's going to be good the whole time, can you?"

"Think you can't do anything except wait for Eileen to come back."

"And another thing, she has a copy of the key—"

Rick hung up in the middle of her sentence. Furious,

Koko slammed the phone down. She always ended up doing exactly what Rick wanted her to do. He leans on me too much, Koko thought. She used to be carefree, only interested in men and clothes. Since living with Rick, she was forced to do all kinds of shit-work things she wasn't good at. It had taken her two years to realize this. Koko, despite her casually negligent manner, had discovered she had a puritanical core that pushed her to do everything that needed doing. She didn't think it was so great to find out she was, deep down, an upright, serious person. It only meant a rapid increase of things she felt she must and must not do. There was a time, long ago, when she'd been afraid of nothing. Now a lot of things frightened her. Like children crying.

The thought made her realize Jeffrey had been crying for some time now. She looked into Jesse's room, assuming there'd been a fight.

"Jesse, please don't fight with Jeffrey."

"Ah, c'mon, Koko. Jeff started crying by himself. I've been letting him win and everything."

Jeffrey was sitting on the floor, sobbing quietly like a girl. Koko leaned over and put a hand on his shoulder.

"What's wrong? Do you hurt somewhere? You're not happy with something? Jesse, get me some Kleenex."

Jesse sighed and handed Koko several tissues. Wiping Jeffrey's tears, Koko asked him again why he was crying.

"When is my mommy coming back? She's not gonna come back at all, is she?"

Ahah. So that's it! Koko glanced at Jesse. He said nothing, only pressed his lips together tighter.

"She'll be back soon. She only went to her friend's place."

"That's not true. Mommy's left me here forever."

"Of course not. Oh, what am I going to do? Jesse, what should I do? Say something. Tell him Eileen'll be back soon."

Jesse sat on the bed. "It won't do any good."

"Why not? It's not like Eileen's not coming back."

"Yeah, she'll come back. But it won't do any good to tell Jeff that. He understands. He knows his mother didn't leave him here like any old baby-sitting job. She wasn't going out like that and he knows it."

"So what should I do?"

"He'll go to sleep after he's cried himself out."

"I can't let him do that!"

"Why not? He's a crybaby anyway. He's always hanging on to his *mommy*."

"He's a child. That's natural."

Jesse turned back to his game. Jeffrey cried harder. Rubbing his back and patting his head, Koko was almost in a panic. I can't even get a child to stop crying, she thought, I'm so pathetic.

Jesse had already stopped crying for his mother when Koko first knew him. Maybe he never had cried for her. If he had, who'd been there to pat his back?

"Jesse, really, what should I do?"

Jesse glanced at Koko and went back to his game. "Why don't you call Jeff's daddy and have him come over? You won't get anywhere yourself. You're no good with kids."

"Oh, is that so? You were pretty small yourself when you first met me, and I spent a lot of time with you then."

"That's because I'm good with adults. And I didn't have many friends."

"*That's* because you had a big chip on your shoulder." Still do, Koko thought. She glared at him. Jesse ignored her, pushing the control buttons of his computer, yelping at the screen. Jeffrey had stopped crying and was looking at the TV screen. Koko suddenly felt this was all very foolish. She stood up to go.

"Don't you need the phone number? Their last name's Bedden and they live in Brooklyn, OK?" Jesse said.

"No, forget it already."

"He'll start crying again."

Koko went out and called information for the number. Area code 718. Looking at the number, Koko poured herself a glass of red wine. Whom would Eileen be coming all the way out from Brooklyn to see? How could a white married woman, trailing her kid behind her, have an affair with someone like Rick? Koko remembered Eileen's blue eyes and thin blond hair. Pitiful woman. If her husband found out what she was up to, there'd be hell to pay. Just by looking at Jeffrey, you could tell he came from a good "normal" home.

Koko didn't have a bit of prejudice in her, but when she saw a black man and a blond woman together she couldn't help wondering how they had become a couple. They must have all kinds of problems, she'd think. A Japanese like herself, coming from a different country, ran into fewer problems living with a black man. White people don't care how nonwhites pair off. People don't flaunt their prejudice as long as something doesn't disturb their own little community. Thus Koko could get along well with both blacks and whites. She knew instinctively if she didn't invade their territory, they wouldn't invade hers.

It's easy to say people shouldn't discriminate on the basis of race, but it happens all the time. If a raving liberal's cousin marries someone way outside the family, even the liberal will be unnerved by it. Facile theories may claim humankind can rise above instinct, but reality is something different. You can't go around every day worrying how to uphold theories. Nobody does, except those who've made a profession of it. If you're not a yuppie and you go to a yuppie bar and the yuppies give you the cold shoulder, you can't chop off their heads for it. Koko believed that people react to other people with their instincts more than their intelligence.

Koko didn't think women like Eileen were especially courageous. Only women whose confidence made them beautiful had courage. Women like that had beautiful, sparkling eyes, without wearing makeup. Not like Eileen's: servile, stealing looks at people. Eyes that begged others to excuse her. Koko believed those were the eyes of a person who didn't strive for freedom but was letting herself slide into darkness. Whenever she saw such eyes, Koko had to look away. She found herself having to look away a lot in this city.

Rick had slept with Eileen, Koko thought suddenly. She tried to imagine how he did it with that skinny white body. It made her feel strange. If I were a black man, would I feel like doing it with that woman? No way. I don't understand men, Koko thought. What makes them choose women to sleep with? Faced with a woman he doesn't like, a man will more often than not get it up anyway. Why is that? Even so, I can't understand why Rick would sleep with Eileen. Because she's someone else's wife? No, that couldn't be it. So was it because Eileen's white? That couldn't be it either. If it'd been a white woman with her head held high, walking into a black bar on 58th Street with a black woman friend who looked like a model, then maybe, Koko thought.

But a woman like Eileen? She didn't have any leeway, couldn't hit the town and risk it getting back to her husband. She wasn't the kind of woman who exuded the authority needed to make people around her accept what she was doing. And Rick wasn't the sort of man who'd go seeking a white woman, let alone a *married* one. Their coupling unsettled Koko.

To be sure, a little jealousy clouded Koko's thoughts. When jealousy surfaces, the most unbiased person turns into a bigot. In her calmer moments, Koko was almost ashamed of herself. She was able to see that they'd been two people who didn't love each other, didn't have fun with each other, and this saddened her.

After all, I know everything there is to know about Rick, Koko thought. He's never once decided on a course of action and followed it through. I don't know how things will turn out for us. We started living together because I loved him and I wanted to be with him. Sure, he loves me now. But his love started passively. He merely accepted me. And so long as I can keep him in a good mood, he's expansive and generous.

But Koko worried about one serious difference between her and Rick. She was a person who would decide first, then act. Rick was the opposite, acting and reacting without thought. It was only a matter of time before this difference would cause a huge rupture. One of these days, Rick would wander off someplace where Koko's determination would be of no avail.

Rick's younger sister, Grace, once said to Koko, "My brother is a very nice person. Chances are good that you'll be happy with him, Koko. But you gotta understand exactly where that 'niceness' is coming from. He can never say no. It's easy for him to accept anything. It's up to you to understand that and control him. Black women can get a hold of black men's feelings, but it might be pretty hard for a Japanese like you. Question of blood. White women are terrible at it; they'll say 'He's very nice' and leave it at that. They never have a good time of it."

Koko sighed. There's nothing I can do. Worrying about the future won't do any good. But she was troubled by the constant thought that the only time she hadn't had anxieties about Rick was in the first few months they lived together, when she and Jesse were at loggerheads every day. She'd only wanted things to go well with her lover's son then, and needed Rick as a warm blanket. But now she needed more.

Sometimes she felt something heavy weighing on her heart. In such moments, a subway token would feel so heavy she could hardly get it from her purse to the wicket, or she would be pouring sugar into her coffee and she'd pour in too much, not being able to pull back the jar of sugar in time.

Jeffrey was crying again. Koko hurried to Jesse's room.

"What happened?"

Jesse rubbed sleepy eyes. "I said I was going to bed and he started crying again. I give up already. I told Daryl I'd meet him early at school, too."

"What's wrong, Jeff?"

"I wanna go home. I don't wanna sleep here."

Koko hugged him.

"Call Jeff's father, will you, Koko?"

"I wonder if he'll come."

"It's twelve already. There's nothing else you can do."

Jeffrey continued to sob quietly.

"What do you want to do, Jeff? Do you want to wait for your mommy? Or do you want your daddy to come and get you?"

Jeff nodded at the second option. Koko put him down and went to the other room to phone his house. She was worried the call would cause an uproar there, but she thought there'd be a bigger problem if Eileen didn't come back at all. She remembered what Eileen had said about giving Jeffrey away if Koko wanted him. Eileen *had* looked peculiar when she said that. Clutching the receiver, Koko felt her hand sweat.

A man came on the line after several rings.

"Yes?"

She asked timidly, "Are you Jeffrey's father?"

"Yes."

"Well, um . . . your son is here at our place and, uh—"

"Could you give me your address? And your telephone number. I'll drive over and pick him up."

The voice was calm. Koko gave him the address; he didn't ask about the circumstances. He merely said he was leaving immediately and hung up. Koko was stunned.

"Is Daddy coming?"

"Uh . . . uh-huh. Why don't you go and sleep in Jesse's room? I'll wake you up when your daddy gets here."

Jeffrey had completely recovered his humor. He jumped into Jesse's bed and burrowed under the covers.

What a strange man. He didn't ask anything. "I'll drive over and pick him up"; that's it? His son is all the way uptown in the middle of the night and he doesn't want to know why, he just jumps in his car and goes? What's that supposed to mean?

Koko sat down, perplexed. That quiet voice. Husbands and wives were beyond her. So many different kinds of couples: Rick and Jesse's mother used to come to blows when one of them was going out. When Grace went out at night, her husband always accompanied her. When Sue, Koko's co-worker, went out, her husband would say with a smile, "Have a good time!" And when Rick went out alone to drink, Koko would say, "I'll miss you." Saying that didn't make him stay home, though.

THE NEXT MORNING, Koko was awakened by the smell of liquor on Rick's breath. Jesse had already gone over to Daryl's, having finished his usual breakfast of raisin bran and milk. Rick, still fully dressed, was snoring away next to Koko. Oh, no! How did it get to be so late? She jumped up. It was all Eileen's fault. Koko's head felt like a balloon from the Courvoisier she'd drunk on top of the wine.

After Jeffrey's father had collected him the night before,

Koko couldn't sleep. She'd had three cognacs in a row and was finally starting to nod off when the phone had rung. It was Eileen.

"Hi, Koko, how's my baby?"

The woman was clearly drunk and spoke above the pounding of nightclub music. Koko felt like screaming, You fob your kid off on me and then go off to play at a club, huh, you bitch? Instead, she'd hissed, "Your baby isn't here anymore."

"What's that supposed to mean?"

"He cried so much I called your husband and had him come get him."

"You're kidding!"

"No, I'm not. He came about two hours ago."

"Oh, my God! I'm in deep shit!"

"Well, you got yourself into it."

"Why did you do this to me? Was it so hard for you to baby-sit for one night? You couldn't do that much? Couldn't you have thought there was a reason and left him where he was? What'm I gonna do now?"

Eileen had suddenly sobered up. Her voice carried real fear.

"Well, he was crying and asking for *you*."

"So what? You don't understand one bit how a mother feels, do you?"

"That's right, I don't."

"I thought we could be friends—"

"Why? We have nothing in common except we both slept with the same man. I am not your friend, I have never been your friend, and I never want to be your friend!"

"I wanted to be friends with you. . . . I liked Rick, and you like him now, right?"

Fed up, Koko'd been about to slam down the receiver

when she heard a man calling, "Yo, Eileen!" A young voice, the kind of voice that belonged to someone who cruised the streets.

"Eileen, I think you're crazy."

"What'm I gonna do? I wrote a note saying I'd be at Clara's—"

"Seems your husband called Clara."

Eileen was silent. She hung up without another word. Koko was past the end of her rope. She staggered back to the bedroom and collapsed on the bed.

"Hey, Rick, get up, will you? I have to talk to you about that woman last night."

There was no way Rick was going to get up. When he was dead drunk like this, it took a lot more than someone talking to him to wake him up.

Koko suddenly thought of Eileen's husband. The poor man had been so apologetic, had gathered his son in his arms and left. Jeffrey, exhausted from crying, barely woke up. The husband was a good-looking man, but an air of fatigue hung about him. When Koko had asked, "Are you sure you're going to be all right?" he merely smiled, as if he didn't know how to reply.

He seemed nice enough. Koko wondered if he knew what was going on. He probably could not imagine any mother past thirty hanging out with street punks, let alone his own wife. Or maybe he knew all about it. Whichever, Eileen's house must be wrapped in a cold darkness about now.

Irritated at Rick for not waking up, Koko slapped his cheek a couple of times. He turned over.

"Lemme sleep, will ya?"

"*Rick*. We have to *talk*. Why do *I* have to take care of Eileen's kid?"

"Huh? I dunno. Jeffrey still here?"

"I called his father and had him take Jeffrey home."

Rick whistled. "You are one tough woman."

"I got mad."

"Oh, yeah?"

"What's this 'Oh, yeah?' That woman is taking you cheap. She thought it'd be OK as long as it was at your place. Any woman living with that *Rick* won't be able to say no; that's what she thought."

"So what?"

Rick covered his head with a blanket. Koko pulled it off him.

"She went to a club. Somewhere where they play rap and loud music. You know what *that* means, don't you?"

"That woman likes black guys. She'll sleep with anyone. Everyone on Seventh Avenue knows her. She used to hang at the Seventh Avenue Baby Grand."

"So you thought you'd sleep with her, too? Because she sleeps with anyone? Or was it because you both had kids, so it was convenient? I saw her husband. I saw the man you two made a fool of."

Koko was getting more and more agitated. Her voice was shaking. Rick was now completely awake and looking at Koko with amazement.

"Hey."

He pulled Koko into his arms. Koko buried her face in his chest as the warm liquor-breath she was so used to descended upon her.

"What's wrong with you? All that was a long time ago."

"She thought . . . as long as it was your place she wouldn't be turned down. I could never do that. That woman took *me* cheap."

Rick lay down on his side, pulling Koko down with him. This really is the best place to be, Koko thought. As long as I'm here, everything else just disappears.

"You know?" Grasping Rick's chest hair in her fingers, Koko spoke. "What I really want is for no one to look pitiful in front of me."

"Who's pitiful?" Rick asked lazily, reaching for his cigarettes.

"You wouldn't understand. Absolutely, positively wouldn't understand," Koko replied.

"You think too much," Rick said, as he began to love her with his free hand.

KAY CALLED Koko at work a little before lunch. "You want to have lunch? I'll treat." Kay lived with her boyfriend near the gallery where Koko worked. She was a friend Koko could be herself with.

Kay was already drinking wine when Koko arrived to meet her.

"What's up? Are you off today? You're the one who never likes to drink in the daytime."

Kay laughed.

"I'm celebrating."

"What's the occasion?"

Koko asked the waiter for the same wine Kay was drinking.

"The sautéed portobellos are good here. Their angel hair pasta's really good, too."

"So what're you celebrating?"

Kay looked up from the menu at Koko and laughed. "We broke up."

"What? You broke up with Brian?"

Kay nodded emphatically.

"Wasn't it going well?"

"Only because I was *making* it go well. Ah, I feel so *light*! I can smoke anytime I want to, I don't have to drink that shitty Perrier with meals anymore, I'm free from aerobic sex.

Finally, I can start living like a human being again. You know, I'm the type who likes to start the evening with a couple of martinis. I'm going to eat and drink my fill today, you betcha. And after lunch I'm going to have a *sinful* dessert."

"Isn't all that kind of old-fashioned?" Koko said, surprised at the change in her friend.

"I finally realized that what was old-fashioned was changing my lifestyle so goddamn much for *him*."

"When did you break up?"

"Last night. He left. He said he'd send a friend later to pick up his stuff. If I knew where he was, I'd get a moving company."

"I thought all this time that everything was fine. You didn't tell me anything."

"That's because I didn't want you to think I couldn't handle a man or two. Truth is, I'm exhausted."

The Italian chef came to their table to greet them. An expensive restaurant, it catered to a dinner crowd and had few customers at lunch. Bordering the Village, it got busy at night with people going to jazz clubs or the theater after dinner.

"Hello, ladies. If it's all right with you, why don't you leave the menu up to me today? I'll make you something very nice."

Koko and Kay nodded their assent.

"Put in some mushrooms."

"I love fried zucchini."

"And may I have another glass of wine?"

After the chef left, the two looked at each other and laughed.

"I'll bet the food must not have come in yet."

"Surprising such a small restaurant can get by without doing lunch specials."

"Well, from now on I can't come here very often. No

more access to Brian's money." Kay sounded regretful as she lit a cigarette. "Ah, those NO SMOKING pricks can eat shit. I can't believe that I, who couldn't live without my Newports, actually went *two years* without smoking."

"You two didn't break up over cigarettes and alcohol, did you?"

"No, but *everything* was like that. Cigarettes and alcohol were merely the tip of the iceberg. Like, we'd have to go all the way to One Hudson Café in Tribeca for what he'd call 'brunch.' He said the food there was good and didn't fill you up. So we'd eat that anorexic shit with Perrier and lime. I would've been happy with Ray's Pizza. I like drinking and having a good old time at rip-roaring bars in the East Village. *He* says those places stink. We couldn't agree on anything in the end."

Koko thought of the handsome young man who worked at a law firm. Brian was delicately featured and obviously well-bred.

"He sure was nice-looking."

"Well, yeah. But he wasn't my type."

"He was your type at first, wasn't he? You're the one who would pull nasty faces when I had a gin and tonic in the middle of the day."

Kay didn't reply. She merely transferred some of the appetizer to her own plate.

Inserting her knife into a large portobello mushroom, Kay said hesitantly, "I don't think it was because we weren't compatible that things didn't go right. It's because things didn't go right that after a while we couldn't get along anymore. Believe me, I know."

"You think so?"

"Yes, I do," Kay said simply. "When we first started going out, he'd take me wherever I wanted to go. He'd look kind of out of place. And I tried to live the way he liked. Would you believe Brian actually went with me to the T. Connection?"

"He went with you there? He must have had an awful time. Brian at that club? Wow."

"He heard some coke dealers talking, didn't even think they were speaking *English*."

The two laughed heartily. Koko's laughter died when she saw large tears rolling down Kay's cheeks.

"Don't cry, Kay. It's not like you. Cheer up. You'll find another man. It'll take all of two minutes."

"But I'm miserable."

"C'mon, eat up. If you eat good food, you'll feel better."

Kay wiped her tears with a napkin. "I'm sorry. I know how you hate scenes. But you know, everyone has times when they don't look good. Everyone, that is, except you. You've got style, Koko, in times like this."

"That's not so. I bawl and scream just like everybody else."

"Come to think of it, I remember you having a big crying jag over a fight with Jesse. How is he doing? It's about time for him to start having a girlfriend of his own, isn't it?"

"You gotta be kidding!"

"You're probably the only one who thinks so. Koko, can I tell you your weak point?"

"What?"

"You tolerate too many things. After a while, you don't know what's what anymore. Sometimes you have to throw things away. If you don't, they pile up and you can't see what's real."

"What're you talking about? Tolerate what? You're being too abstract, Kay."

"Never mind. It's just something I wanted to say. Well, you can say that's your good point, too. Christ, I'm sounding like you now."

"You're drunk, aren't you?"

"I'm clear. My head is so clear it's like I'm on coke. After all, I don't have to be thinking about men."

"For how long? One week? Two weeks?"

"How do I know? Until I can enjoy being by myself. Then I'll look for a new man."

Koko raised her glass. "I'll drink to that."

Laughing, Kay touched her glass to Koko's.

"About Jesse, though."

"What?"

"Kids mature a lot faster in this country than in yours, Koko."

"Thanks for the warning."

"I slept with my first man when I was eleven," Kay said, heaping a mound of pasta onto her plate.

THE HANDCUFFS were biting into her wrists. Koko thought of that warm creature, that mischievous black boy, always jumping around like the California raisins on the TV commercial. Whenever she saw him, she felt like squeeze, squeeze, squeezing him.

There are people who can't get along without me, and I can't get along without Randy. Randy, Randy, Randy. She said his name over and over, pulling out his gestures from the file of her memory, and tears welled up behind her eyes.

She couldn't predict how things would go, nor did she care. She knew there was nothing she could do, so she contented herself with the sweet fluorescent candy of fantasy. You can't live without something sweet, she told herself. Her fantasy was stronger and sweeter than any drug.

But unlike a cat, you can't lick your own body. So her thoughts went. She wondered how she'd get out of these handcuffs. Her despair began to melt away. Jesse said it was cool to hang cuffs from your belt. He'd clip them on and take them off, over and over. He'd use one of Koko's hairpins to unlock them.

Randy told her he liked her hair. He'd run his fingers through it, gather it up. He never listened when she protested that she wasn't a Barbie doll. He'd play with her hands and feet, use her whole body as a plaything. And she liked it.

The hairpin was worth a try, but what then? She felt weak. "If I don't see him, my heart will be in pain." Could she actually say something like that? And would he feel sorry for her?

Premonitions terrified her. She'd had one for some time

now; its vagueness frustrated her. She knew she wouldn't understand it until too late. Premonitions all lead to death in the end, she thought. People go through so many hardships to get to their end. So much futile scrambling around. Oh, God, we are all lost sheep.

She remembered that Sunday in church. She wasn't even Christian, but there she was with Rick's sister, Grace. She watched Grace listen to the sermon, saying, "Thank you, Jesus," again and again. Koko moved her lips to the words, mimicking Grace, who, dressed to the nines, sang "Halle-fuckin'-lujah!" But you're not supposed to use such language in front of God, she had thought. Suddenly, she understood that swearwords should only be used sparingly. She'd been far too free with them—as if they were toys. Just like Randy. He'd say, "You know goddamn motherfuckin' what I mean?" Everyone talks like that, he'd tell her.

Intense feelings about how she and others behaved twisted through her. She would have to untangle them one by one. She started to search for a hairpin.

ONE FRIDAY, near the start of their relationship, Koko had arrived at Rick's to find him packing a suitcase. He told her, when she asked, that his family had called to tell him his father was about to die. He was packing to go home to North Carolina for ten days. Listening to Rick hum as he chose what clothes to take, Koko thought he was being all too cavalier and told him so.

"He ditched Ma 'n' the rest of us. Haven't seen the dude since I was a kid. 'Spect me to be sad? He was a drunk anyway."

"Like father, like son."

"Well, booze does run in the family. Oh, poor Daddy. Better have a drink to the old man," Rick said, pausing to drain his glass. Jesse was at his side, silently putting some toys into a small backpack.

"Is he going too?" Koko asked.

"Yup."

"What about school?"

"He'll have to miss it. There's no one to watch him here. When I asked his mother to, she got hysterical. Said she wouldn't consider it unless I forked over two hundred dollars. Pissed me off. It's not a whole lot of money, but I don't feel like leaving him with a woman who won't watch her own kid unless she's paid. Figured he'd be better off taking a trip with me."

Jesse listened impassively as the two adults discussed him. Koko wanted to say that if his mother was going to be like that, she'd watch the boy, but she held her tongue. She couldn't get along with Jesse no matter how hard she tried.

He was a little less aggressive with her, but still sullen and stubbornly independent. He was constantly reminding her that she was an interloper in his house. Koko knew she'd been naive to think a child would be like a puppy, instantly eager to get and give affection. Jesse refused to be close to anyone but his father.

Still, to demand two hundred dollars to watch your own kid for ten days was too much. Koko had a vague dread of children and was not inclined to have any of her own. She had a great body, made for loving, and she wasn't about to ruin it by getting pregnant, she told herself. Even so, it infuriated her to think of a woman who would have a kid and then be incapable of raising him.

"I'll watch him," she said.

Rick and Jesse gaped at her.

"Are you sure?" Rick could not believe his ears. Koko could feel Jesse's eyes boring into her and was careful not to look his way.

"Yes, I'm sure."

No turning back now. Koko was already regretting her words when Rick spun her around in his arms.

"What a fine woman!" he cried. "I know how to pick 'em, huh, Jess? You're my girl all right. Jesse, you be good now. Tell me if she brings other men here." Suddenly, Rick shook his head and heaved a big sigh. "Ah, poor Daddy! Can't believe he's dyin'. He may've been a drunk, but he was a good father." Rick was suddenly desolate.

Koko fully expected Jesse to reject her offer.

"So you're gonna be here?" he asked. Koko nodded. "OK, but it might be pretty rough on you," he said. It was that mouth of his that set Koko's teeth on edge.

Though his flight was leaving first thing in the morning, Rick quit his packing and began to drink in earnest. Koko was anxious about getting everything done in time, but she went ahead and joined him anyway. It pained her to think they'd be apart for ten whole days.

"I wonder if I'll be able to sleep," she said.

"Jesse'll be quiet once he goes to bed; you'll be fine."

"That's not what I mean. Am I gonna be able to sleep without you with me?"

Rick held her tight. Then he asked if she'd be OK staying there with her commute to work.

"I'll be fine. That's only in the daytime. Oh, why did I have to go and fall for a man like you? There're four or five guys who'd be in seventh heaven if I showed up on their doorstep right now!"

"My poor daddy," Rick moaned, getting her away from the subject of other men and gaining her sympathy at the same time. When a woman is soft on a man, there's no end to what she'll let him get away with, Koko thought. She gave up. She was too crazy about Rick to argue.

And so Koko's life alone with Jesse had begun. Koko's friends were all enormously interested in her new situation, and not a day passed without at least one of them showing up at the apartment. Like Koko, none of them had ever been around children before. They came to get a look at Jesse as if he were a friend's new puppy. Jesse, not yet used to Koko, was like an animal in a cage before this stream of strangers. He stayed huddled in one corner of the room listening to his music, refusing to speak unless necessary.

Koko felt responsible to at least feed the kid, so after work she'd drag her tired body to the grocery store, then back to the apartment to make dinner.

One night Koko put a roast in the oven. After a while, its good smell filled the apartment, making Koko sad to think it would be gone without Rick having eaten any.

"Koko." Jesse had joined her in the kitchen, his voice breaking into her thoughts. "What're you making?"

"Roast beef," she replied.

"Oh, yeah?"

Roast beef was one of Jesse's favorites. Koko had never worried about cooking for anyone before, but now that she cooked for Jesse, she always took his tastes into consideration.

"I'm gonna get a cheeseburger."

Koko, washing the vegetables, paused.

"So give me money."

Koko's vision seemed to darken for an instant.

"Why would you want to do that?" she was finally able to ask.

"'Cause I want a cheeseburger."

Koko stifled her rage and went to get her bag. Her hands shook as she pulled a five-dollar bill out.

"My mom's a really good cook," Jesse said, snapping his gum and blowing a bubble. Koko threw the five at him. Grinning widely, Jesse picked it up off the floor and walked out the door.

Koko finally got a call from Rick two weeks later, the day she moved all her stuff into the apartment. He was absurdly cheerful, given the emotional stress Koko thought he'd be under, losing a parent and all. When she asked him about it, he said, "Well, we all thought he was a goner, but he started getting better soon as I got down here. Now he's fine, even askin' for his whiskey. So I went over to my mom's place and I've been goin' around the old hangouts and stuff with my bro's. You know, clubs 'n', shit. Figured since I'm out here, might as well have myself a little vacation. So how's Jesse?"

"He's fine."

All that worry for nothing. Koko felt like an idiot. Rick said he'd be home in a few days and hung up. That's it? Koko thought. That's all? When they first met, he seemed to notice every little thing she did. Now he was down in North Carolina having himself a good old time without a thought for her, struggling alone in New York with his son. Well, you could say it was all part of his easygoing nature. And it was that very easygoing nature that Koko loved most about him.

"Your daddy's coming back in another two or three days."

"Oh, yeah?" Jesse didn't seem much interested. He was busy looking at Koko's things. Koko knew he only offered to help her unpack to see what she had in all those boxes.

Still, Jesse had become surprisingly talkative in recent days. He'd taken to sprawling on a chair, watching her cook dinner after work. Now and then something like, say, a steak she was preparing to cook would disappear and when, bewildered, she'd look for it, he'd urge her into the bathroom, barely able to suppress his laughter. There hung the missing steak, splayed out on the bathroom wall like an amoeba. He'd have vanished by the time she turned to yell at him. Keeping up with such silly pranks tired Koko out, but she was getting used to it. Jesse was as rude as ever and refused to get close to any of her friends, but he seemed finally to be letting down his guard around Koko herself. The tricks he played on her were different. They used to be malicious, whereas now they just called out for attention.

One night Jesse told her he wanted to make dinner. Koko had no problem imagining what would happen if she said no. He would go ahead anyway and make a big mess in the kitchen to boot. So she waited anxiously in the living room for the longest time until Jesse called, "Dinner's ready!" Going into the kitchen, she was surprised to find the table set with a lone baked potato on each of two large plates. Koko and Jesse faced each other across the table and began to eat. The long wait had made Koko famished, but after her initial disappointment, she found that lots of sour cream helped make the simple baked potato more satisfying than most meals. Koko and Jesse wielded their forks and knives with the formality properly accorded a Cordon Bleu chef, and Koko felt she was eating something really precious indeed.

The day Koko finished putting away all her things, they decided to celebrate by watching TV. Jesse said he'd make popcorn on the stove, and they hurried to get everything ready before his show started. Koko loved nothing more than hot buttered popcorn. She was searching the shelves for a mug for Jesse's Ovaltine and the things she needed to make herself a martini when the telephone rang.

Greggory's low voice came over the line. Koko was in such a good mood, from having finished her move, and now hearing from this dear friend, that she forgot all about making the drinks. She wanted to tell Greggory about how well things were going with Jesse. Greg joked around with her, pleased to hear her so happy. Koko had always loved his deep, melodious voice. She was so caught up in the conversation that she didn't hear Jesse ask her how much butter to put in. Something caught her attention out of the corner of her eye, and when she looked up, there was the frying pan, full of burning butter, coming closer and closer. Before she could let out a shout, Jesse had flung the butter in her face.

Koko crouched over, squatting on the floor, her hands over her face. Her shrieks filled the kitchen, and she could hear Greggory shouting through the receiver she had dropped.

Jesse stood there stock-still, frying pan in hand. Koko got up and, shoving him aside, flew to the bathroom. There in the mirror she saw the burn welts already rising on her face.

"Oh, God! Oh, my God!"

There was nothing else to say. Her face was rent like a

dress torn on a nail. The burn stretched from her temple all the way down her cheek.

"I'm sorry, Koko. . . ."

Jesse appeared behind her. Koko turned on him in fury.

"Get away from me! I hate you! I don't want to see you, *ever*! You could *die* for all I care, you brat!"

Her rage poured out. Koko had no idea what she was saying, nor did she care. After a while, a modicum of reason returned. She remembered she'd left the phone off the hook. Pressing a towel to her face, she went to the kitchen and replaced the receiver. The popcorn sat in its bowl on the table, untouched. A huge lump, impossible to swallow, rose in Koko's throat. By the time she had opened the refrigerator to get some ice out, she was bawling. Jesse was nowhere to be seen, and Koko couldn't bear to even say his name aloud.

ONE DAY AFTER Rick's return an unexpected visitor came to call. Koko opened the door to find a woman she'd never seen before.

"Hi." The woman smiled at her.

Koko didn't know what to say.

"Mom!" Jesse had come up behind her. Koko looked hard at the woman: thin lips and small slanted eyes. She looked a lot like the Chinese women from Koko's childhood picture books. Koko hesitated, but the woman, who introduced herself as June, walked in before Koko'd had a chance to invite her.

June hugged Jesse with an exaggerated "My baby!" Koko, remembering the two hundred dollars, wasn't taken in. What a hypocrite! she thought.

The woman continued to make a big deal over her "baby," loudly lamenting how lonely she was without him. Koko went in the kitchen to make some drinks. Soon she was hearing the woman say angrily, "Why have they fallen so much? Answer me that. I'm not here and they get this bad?" Koko went back into the living room.

Rick had walked in, and he answered. "Why've his grades dropped? 'Cause he don't study, that's why."

June glared at Rick, whose lips were set in a tight line. Koko had never seen him so angry and upset.

"Why haven't you been studying, Jesse?" The woman turned to her son.

Confused and shaken, Jesse began to sob. Koko stared at him in disbelief. The brat was trying to get on his mother's good side! He was making a bid for her sympathy. Koko had never hated him so much as in that moment. She'd expected, even hoped he would respond with his usual smirk and wisecrack, but no, there he was, blubbering away and saying, "I'll do better next time, Mom, you'll see, OK?"

Rick seemed repulsed by the scene. Koko wished he would say something.

Jesse continued to cry. He produced no tears, just screwed up his face and made noises. Suddenly, his mother seemed to remember Koko's presence. June turned to Koko and said, "Don't mind me. I *despise* this man. I shudder to think I actually lived with him for more than ten years. There must be something wrong with you to move in with him. Well, not that it's any of my business."

Koko let her talk. She was more interested in what she looked like than in what she had to say. June's face wasn't so bad, but hatred had given a hardness to it that made her look twenty years older than Koko. There was no joy at all in that face. Koko felt wretched to think that years of living with Rick had molded it. The woman's clothes, too, were from a different time, gaudier than the simple, sophisticated things people Koko's age preferred. The effect was pathetic, and

Koko couldn't help but feel sorry for her. Koko was aghast at the ravaging effects a long-held hatred had on a person.

". . . such a stingy nigger."

It took Koko a few moments to realize June was still talking about Rick. Shocked, she looked at him, but he merely pulled on his cigarette. Koko could see he was furious. The woman continued to pour out all manner of abuse. Koko could hardly believe a woman could treat a man she'd once loved like this.

"This isn't your place anymore. Leave, why don't you." Rick's voice was steely.

June paled, and her lower lip trembled. She'd worked herself up into a fury with her own words. "That's not so. Jesse is my son."

Jesse was looking at the floor, his hands jammed in his jeans pockets. Koko wanted to run over and put her hands over his ears.

"Jesse, is she good to you?" Not getting anywhere with Rick, June changed her tactics.

"No!"

Now it was Koko's turn to stifle her rage.

"Does she cook for you?"

"No!"

"Does she wash your clothes?"

"No!"

"Does she clean your room?"

"No!"

Koko felt herself grow faint. Jesse had tried in various ways to use his father against her, and now he was striking out at her through his mother. Koko's eyes locked onto the rear end of the boy standing in front of her. Myth had it that demons have a special mark on their rumps. Koko wondered if there might be one under those jeans.

"A girl like her can't possibly take care of Jesse. He's coming home with me."

"Koko does take good care of him." Rick sounded tired.

"You heard what Jesse said! Jesse, you're coming with me, OK?" Jesse was silent. "Sweetheart, your mom has a boyfriend too. He'll be your new daddy."

Jesse didn't say a word. Rick held his breath as he looked at his son. This one was up to Jesse.

Koko's heart was hammering. If Jesse said yes, she'd be released from the burden she had been shouldering for so long.

The three adults waited intently for what this small boy would say next. The thought flashed through Koko's mind—he's going to start crying again to get out of answering—but answer he did.

"I'll stay here for now."

The tension was broken. "I'll stay here for now": five little words that made Rick happy and his mother relieved. Koko grasped for the first time just how intelligent Jesse was.

"My poor child! My poor, pitiful baby!" his mother wailed. What a show, Koko thought, revolted. This woman is so blind. Blind to how her son must feel, hearing his mother heap abuse on his father. Blind to how wise that son of hers is. And blind to what fires forged his wisdom. Stupid woman, Koko thought, it's nothing to have a kid; the real test is in raising one.

Jesse's mother was getting ready to go. She seemed a totally different person from the one who'd talked her way into the apartment. She snatched up her purse with such force that the clasp flew open, scattering the contents: a cheap tube of lipstick, a wallet about to fall apart, a garish handkerchief. The sight of the woman crawling after these shabby things reminded Koko of a scene in a French movie of a peasant on her knees gathering up fallen leaves. Koko's heart contracted with pity. This woman will go on gathering up dead leaves, she thought.

"I'll be coming to get you, you hear? So you take care now," Jesse's mother said to him as she left. All lies, Koko said to herself, walking June to the door; if she really cared, she would be asking me to be good to her son. Koko loathed going back into the living room to face all the hatred June had left behind.

RICK LEFT the apartment and didn't come back that whole evening. When he got his jacket out of the closet, Koko wanted to say, Don't go, but the words stuck in her throat. The woman had dirtied the air, and Koko knew Rick couldn't bear it. She knew only too well that Rick had to run away from what he couldn't bear.

Koko didn't want to be alone with Jesse. She was burning to ask him why he'd lied to his mother about her, but she didn't have the courage to do so without Rick there as a buffer. Koko sat alone in the dining room, cradling a bottle of gin.

A man and a woman living together. Why did one extra person in the picture throw everything out of whack? Koko hadn't borne ill will toward Jesse when she'd started going out with Rick. She'd been willing to accept him as something that came with the man she wanted.

I put myself out for Jesse, she told herself, more than I ever thought myself capable of doing. Koko remembered how it used to be with her and men. One smile from her would be returned with heaps of loving words. She'd thrown all that away to sit here alone on this couch, and still she didn't have regrets. She'd been happy simply to have Rick's warm body warm hers, to feel his love for her. She'd been able to shut her eyes and ears to everything else. But it was different now. Those moments Rick held her and whispered loving things into her ear were like eating candy: the pleasure gone with the moment. Blackness loomed in Koko's heart as soon as such pleasures ended. Images of Jesse's lips, his fingers, his fingernails, even, would go around and around in her head, tormenting her to no end.

Jesse had grown up bathed in his parents' hatred. He'd never had the right to refuse it. All those layers of hatred piled up on him—was there any way to peel them off, one by one? Could all that hardened hatred be cracked open to expose the tenderness inside?

I want a man, Koko thought, a nice hot body. Even if it can't heal the hurt, I want to be transported, if only for a moment. Now Rick isn't here to give me even that.

The alcohol was coursing through her but not warming her heart. Koko was ready to explode when Jesse came in and sat down in front of her as if it were the most natural thing in the world.

Jesse calmly opened a magazine. There were so many things she wanted to say to him, she didn't know where to begin.

"Daddy's awfully late," Jesse said, without looking up.

Now that he mentioned it, Rick *was* late.

"Would you be mad if he was with someone else?"

Someone else? Koko moved restlessly.

"Would you start to hate him?"

Koko looked at Jesse. He didn't have the usual know-it-all look on his face. Instead, his eyes were full of silent entreaty.

"If he were . . . I've never thought about it." Her voice trembled.

"There's nothing to worry about. It happened all the time when he was with Mom."

Koko's heart started to pound. How could Jesse be so sure

that his father was with another woman? she wondered. The way Rick held her with such love, as if willing her to understand how much she meant to him—how could that same Rick leave her in the apartment to go off and do something like that? Impossible. It was impossible, but . . .

"What am I going to do? If this is true . . ."

"Liquor and women are good escapes, aren't they?"

One tear, two, welled up and spilled over. Then all the feelings Koko had kept tamped down so tightly came rushing out. She felt her body caving in to a flood of emotion.

Jesse stared at her unblinkingly. Koko had her face covered with both hands, but she could see his beat-up basketball shoes in the cracks between her fingers. She'd never noticed before, but his feet were bigger than hers. Those basketball shoes came toward her, and the next thing she knew a hand was quietly patting her back.

It felt so good, Koko didn't want to stop crying. She wasn't crying anymore from anxiety about where Rick might be or with whom; she was crying about all her hurts, past and present. It felt so good.

After a while, Jesse heard the key turn in the lock and pulled his hand away from her back, but not before Koko felt him stiffen. She looked up to see Rick standing in the door. He was a little surprised to see the two sitting there like that, but he quietly pulled up a chair.

"Can I have some of that gin?" he asked.

He was drunk, but not so much that he couldn't talk straight. Koko, ashamed of her swollen, reddened face, escaped to the kitchen to pour gin and lime juice into a glass for him.

Jesse headed silently for his room, but Rick stopped him and motioned for him to sit.

"You and me, we're going to have a talk," he said.

Jesse shrugged.

"You got somethin' against Koko?"

Jesse was silent.

"Answer me, boy."

Koko had never seen Rick act the stern father.

"I don't dislike her," Jesse said.

"So how come you don't let her in? I know you love your mother. I know you want the two of us to get back together. But you know there's no way that woman 'n' me can get along, don't you?"

Jesse nodded, and Rick continued.

"Koko loves me. That's how come she's trying so hard cookin' and cleanin'. That's for *you*, Jess. If I'm hungry, I can eat out. I don't have anything to wear, I can buy somethin'. I won't die if the apartment needs cleaning. You think she does all this stuff out of the goodness of her heart? She's only doing it because she loves me. You oughta thank her. It's your mom who should be lookin' after you, but you don't see her doin' it, do you?"

Jesse shook his head.

"I know you don't want me having any other woman around 'sides your mother. But that only works for normal families. This ain't no normal family—you can see that for yourself, can't you? Jesse, your parents hate each other. You know what it means when a man and a woman hate each other? It means there's no end to it."

Rick rubbed his face.

"I want to be happy, Jess. I was too young when I married your mother, and I couldn't make her happy. Seein' her unhappy made me unhappy. But now I want to be happy. Listen, Jesse, I'm the only real father you're gonna get. You're gonna need me until you grow up. Can you stand by and see your father lonely without a woman of his own to love? I need Koko. What'm I gonna do if she goes away, 'specially if she goes away on account of you? Are you tellin' me to get by without a woman? Your dad wants a woman, Jess, and the woman I want is Koko. If you need your father, you're gonna have to accept her. You know what it means to love a woman? It's a good thing."

Jesse looked thoughtful. Koko felt she couldn't be happy, even though Rick had come out and said he needed her. If Jesse were forced into accepting her for his father's sake, the most she could hope for was a distant albeit cordial truce. That's what she'd wanted at the beginning, but now it wasn't enough.

"Did you love Mom as much as you love Koko?"

"I loved her. But I loved her in a different way. So how 'bout it, Jess? It's a good thing to love a woman. How about you tryin' to love Koko?"

Jesse looked down at the magazine on his lap. He slowly turned its pages, thoroughly rubbing each one.

"You *don't* like Koko, do you?"

"No, that's not it."

"The truth is, you're starting to like her, aren't you? When you start likin' a woman, you gotta tell her. Otherwise she'll run off on you."

"I . . ." Jesse started to sob. "*I hate her!*" He began to bawl, emitting a series of howls, over and over, like a wolf. "I love Mom! I . . . love . . . *Mom!*"

Koko sighed. It's over, she thought. That's it. Underneath all that hatred, the boy's backbone was made of love: a love toward his mother that wasn't returned. There's nothing I can do but leave, Koko told herself.

Her eyes were dry. She felt she had come all this way with Jesse only to hear those words. There were the early weeks when she was getting used to him, then the short period when she was actually feeling close to the boy. . . . Rick could say he loved her, and she loved Rick, but it was Jesse who needed Rick most.

Jesse couldn't help his misbehavior with her. He knew what it was to love, but there was a thick membrane around his heart that prevented him from showing it no matter how hard he tried.

Jesse was crying hard while Rick looked on, shocked to see his son like this.

Koko had made up her mind.

"Jesse, I'll move out. So you be a good boy and listen to your father. One thing, though: I was ready to like you."

Jesse, head down, didn't stop crying, but his wails had abated. Koko was as desolate as if she'd been dumped. She turned to go.

"Koko, you don't have to do that," came Rick's low voice.

Koko hesitated; she could hear the despair in Rick's voice. He didn't want to lose her.

"Jesse, if you don't say something right now, you and me are gonna end up alone again."

Koko wasn't expecting anything from Jesse. Even if he did say something, it would only be because his father had pushed him into doing so; it wouldn't be from the heart.

Jesse stood there, open-mouthed. Koko glanced at him, then composed herself for his next words.

"I . . . I . . ." Jesse gasped and threw up, an amazing amount, on and on, all over the carpet. Koko stared at him, aghast. Jesse writhed and continued to vomit, and the next thing Koko knew his nose was bleeding.

Koko was rushing to grab some tissues to wipe up the blood when Jesse began to howl again. Blood and vomit and that awful beastlike wail. Koko was scared witless. Not knowing what to do first, she stood there in a dither when Jesse shouted, "I do like Koko! If Koko'll like me, I'll like *her*!"

Koko stood rooted to the floor. Jesse ran off to the bathroom, cleaned himself up, and bundled himself into bed.

"Koko."

She came back to herself and saw Rick grinning at her widely.

"Well, then." Rick got up and stretched. "I'll beg off on that, if you don't mind. It's not my thing." He motioned with his chin at the mess on the floor.

Koko blanched. It was impossible to leave now, tonight, she thought. Koko felt she'd been completely taken in by this father-son pair. All right, she decided, I'll take care of this mess. But not before she asked Rick where he'd been all night.

Rick snorted and said he'd been bumming around by himself. Koko told him what Jesse had said.

"Look, Koko." Rick struggled to keep down his anger. "I'm not young anymore," was all he'd say as he left the room.

And that was how, early on, Koko lost her chance to move out of that apartment.

KOKO AND her friends liked to drop by a Village bar in the evenings. Happy hour, crowded with people who came for the discounted drinks and pizza, lasted until eight. It was a good way to separate day from night. They'd talk about trivial things like stingy gallery owners, how Macy's would soon bite the dust and they should turn it into a club, the worst is the Palladium, and so on.

That evening four of them showed up: Maurique, an up-and-coming artist who turned out inscrutable art objects; his black boyfriend, Buckey; Sue; and Koko.

Their get-together turned into a farewell party for a piece of Maurique's that had just been sold.

Koko ordered her second gin and tonic, after having called Jesse to tell him to eat dinner without her.

"So, how's your kid these days, Koko?" Sue asked. She'd

recently grown out her butch cut into a frizzy bleached ball of hair. She ran her fingers through it pretentiously.

"If you're referring to Jesse, he's pretty much the same. Does everything by himself now. He's so busy with his friends he doesn't have time to complain to me much."

"No! You have a kid, Koko? I don't *believe* it!" Buckey said with exaggerated surprise. He greeted everything with more excitement than necessary. When Maurique admonished him for it, Buckey would defend himself, insisting that for a member of the proletariat he had a rare sensitivity.

"Idiot. It's not Koko's kid. She lives with her boyfriend and his kid."

"So you're raising the child?"

"That's right. But I can't say I'm raising him, really—he was already eleven when I moved in."

"How old is he now?" Sue asked.

"Thirteen," said Koko.

"Is he cute? Does he do some sport?" Buckey asked, his eyes shining.

"Cute?" Koko replied. "I don't know. He's mixed, Asian and black. He really shot up recently. Maybe from your point of view he'd be cute."

"*Our* point of view? What's that supposed to mean? We have a very strong aesthetic sense, I'll have you know. Just look at us."

Buckey rolled up his jacket sleeve and put his arm in Maurique's, who smiled.

"His pale skin and my dark one make a *marvelous* harmony."

"I *see*," Sue said, revolted. Koko grinned. She was inured to such talk, so common in New York.

"I have been *so* influenced by Maurique, it's like I can understand art now, too. I haven't even been to M.43 in ages because *he* hates it."

"What's that?"

"A gay disco. You gotta see it to believe it," Sue explained.

"I wonder if everyone changes for the person they're in love with," Koko said, staring as Buckey flirted with Maurique. She could see he had it bad.

"We all change. You too, Koko," Sue said. "It doesn't hurt at all at first. You throw away your old life as if it's been a lie. But throw away too much and the parts you tried to toss come back to haunt you. Your old life wasn't a lie. Everything you do is real and remains with you. When you throw away too much of yourself, you start forgetting who you are. It's been that way every time I've been in love."

"You aren't in a very good mood, are you, Sue? Something bad happen?"

"I'm a little depressed, that's all."

"Hey, ladies. Do you ever talk about whether or not to throw things away?" Buckey asked, waving his hand up and down to disperse Sue's cigarette smoke.

"Why? Are you referring to that piece of trash we just sold?" asked Sue.

"That's awful! Did you hear that, Maurique? How can you take it? These people don't understand art at all."

Maurique smiled amiably and drank his Corona. "I thought it was rubbish myself," he said.

"To tell you the truth, I'll miss it. It always gave me such a sense of reassurance at work to see it," Koko said with a wink at Maurique. She liked him. When she felt troubled, Maurique's tranquil air always calmed her down. She was sure his lover spent each day luxuriating like a child in the peaceful atmosphere he created.

"Koko, don't stare at Maurique," Buckey said.

"I can't help it. I'm mad about you, Maurique." She turned to Buckey. "If he had any interest in women, I wouldn't let you have him. What a shame. The thing that surprised me most when I first came to New York is that riffraff like you get all the good men."

"Isn't your man a good one, Koko?" Buckey's eyes glistened with superiority.

A good man? Rick? Could you call a man who traipsed around unshaven on his days off, interested in nothing but sleep and alcohol, a good man? All Koko knew was that everything in her heart—every sadness, every happiness—was something Rick made. He held her emotions hostage. Was that what you called love? If she asked him to let them go, he probably would. It was Koko who wouldn't let him let go.

"He's a good man to me, I guess," Koko said haltingly.

"Koko's boyfriend drinks like a fish," Sue said.

"The type who gets a release from liquor?"

"Guess so."

"How old-fashioned." Buckey spooned up his frozen margarita and licked it as though it were ice cream.

"Better than drugs," said Maurique.

"Not necessarily."

"Well, moderation in everything. That's the ticket," said Buckey.

Sue laughed scornfully. "Come now, Buckey. You? Moderation?"

Buckey looked away, pouting.

"If it gets too awful, you can always run away. Come to our place," Maurique told Koko.

"Thanks. But I wouldn't want to intrude on you two love birds."

"Everyone has problems; no one can say he or she is truly happy. Asian or black or gay has nothing to do with it. And the smallest problem feels like a big deal to the person who has it," Sue said.

Buckey nodded at Sue's words and held out a hand for her to shake.

"That's right!" he said.

They bantered on, and at last Koko left them to go home. She found the door chained and heard laughter coming from Jesse's room. He must have friends over. Just as the thought crossed her mind, Jesse's door opened and a tall young man came out.

"Hi, Koko."

She had to look up, he was so tall. "Do I know you?"

"You don't remember me? Come on, Koko, it's me, Daryl."

"Daryl? *That* Daryl? I don't see you for three months and you turn into a giant?"

Koko remembered the white boy from downstairs who used to come over to play games with Jesse. He had suddenly gained several inches in height and lost them in girth. He didn't look at all Jesse's age, he looked like a young man.

"I don't believe it. How'd you lose all that weight?"

"I didn't go on a diet or anything. It just came off."

"How?"

Daryl grinned. "A broken heart."

Koko snorted.

"Hey, can I have a soda?" he asked.

"Sure. There's some in the fridge."

Daryl took out four cans of Coke. Koko was amazed. Clumsy, pudgy Daryl had turned into a good-looking kid. Teenagers were full of surprises.

"How are Kevin and Lisa?"

Daryl shrugged and said with a smile, "Yeah, well, it looks like Mom and Dad are splitting up; they're separated now, but they're fine. Mom's living in the Bronx with her parents."

Koko was fond of this boy who was always baby-sitting his younger brother and sister. The three were constantly hungry and loved to eat anything Koko made. Daryl would say to Jesse, who barely touched his food before he was ready to chuck it down the garbage disposal, "You're gonna throw away that good food? You don't understand a thing." Daryl could accept love from others and be thankful for it. He'd help Koko clear the table and carry groceries upstairs, which once prompted Koko to tell him, "Your mama raised a fine son." Daryl had replied with a big grin, "My mom is the best woman in the world."

"Daryl, it's your turn!" Jesse called.

Daryl shouted back, "OK!" and gave Koko a kiss on the cheek. "I missed you," he said.

Koko was floored. Daryl went back to Jesse's room, as Koko pressed her hand to her cheek, muttering.

"Unbelievable. That kid is a full-fledged adult."

At what moment does a boy-man become a real man? In three months everything about Daryl had fallen into the right places. He's been with a woman for sure, thought Koko.

"Have you eaten?" Koko opened Jesse's door and looked in. Shiny blond hair caught her eye. Another girl, black, waved. The blond girl giggled shyly and shrank behind Daryl. Jesse's boisterous laugh contrasted with Daryl's dark muttering as they counted up domino scores.

"Isn't it a little late for you girls to be over?" Koko asked to cover her surprise.

"It's OK. We live in the next building," the black girl said.

She wore large fake gold earrings. Her tight T-shirt emphasized her chest area and her jeans had been assiduously ripped to shreds. *Hey, boyz, do you like what you see?* this girl's body would be saying as she prowled the streets.

"I'm Roxanne. The same Roxanne as in Roxanne Chianti. Everyone calls me 'Real, Real Roxanne.' The shy one over there is Tracy. Pleased ta meetcha."

"I'm pleased to meet you too," Koko said curtly. She was no good with kids like this: brash, swaggering girls who, for all their adult exteriors, were still children. When these girls saw a woman Koko's age—not old enough to be their mother but older than they—they would pounce on her and try to compete.

"I heard 'bout you from Jesse, but you're real different from what I thought. He said you're Japanese, so I thought you'd be like the Korean women at the corner deli, but you look just like a Puerto Rican."

Tracy giggled incessantly through Roxanne's speech. What a pretty girl, Koko thought. Tracy's makeup had been applied with a careful hand. She looked a little familiar, Koko thought. Without the red lipstick, she might be able to recognize her as a girl she had passed somewhere.

"Hey, Koko, the girls'll be leaving in about an hour, but is it OK if Daryl stays over? He hasn't been around for ages."

"What would Daryl's dad say?"

Lining up his dominoes, Daryl answered. "It doesn't matter. My policy is to never listen to what my dad says. Plus, he has work tonight."

Koko remembered Daryl's father, who lived downstairs. He seemed like a nice man. He worked as a bartender at a nearby bar.

"Please, Koko."

"Please, Koko."

Roxanne parroted Jesse's words, and Koko started to feel harassed.

"OK. Keep it down, though, will you? Did you have dinner yet?"

"We had pizza delivered. We used the money from the shelf," Jesse said.

"Oh. Did Rick call?"

"Not once. Does he ever?" The other three burst out laughing at Jesse's reply. Koko pulled the door shut without saying another word.

Jesse sure is confident when he has his friends around to pump him up, Koko thought. Usually he'd be the one to say, "I wonder where Daddy is."

Jesse knew Koko all too well. When her heart had a lump in it, Jesse would pick it out with sharp fingernails and place it where she had to look at it. The truth was, and Jesse knew it, she wanted to go out now and search the streets for Rick. She imagined entering bars where young men paid respect to this older, seemingly wiser man, where he played the part of the once-dashing now-tired man of the world; and the women who stared at him thinking, This guy's safe—not the type who'd rape a girl—don't look like he's got AIDS, either. Or maybe Rick'd gotten so drunk he couldn't make it home and was sitting on some fire hydrant a few streets away. Koko wanted to go searching, as if finding him would assure her things were still all right with the world; that is, still all right with them.

Still all right. What did that mean? she wondered. It meant that anything was better than breaking up altogether. That no matter what abuses she took, their relationship still had meaning and would see them through. How had things gotten this bad?

Koko realized she'd long ago forgotten how it was to live like that. Everything felt so leaden and difficult. Growing up, she'd been surrounded by kind people who didn't know how to hurt others.

It wasn't that she'd come home now to find strange women in her bed who'd provoke knock-down fights with Rick, after which he'd go out and get so drunk someone'd pick a fight with him in the street, and he'd come home covered in blood. No, no such drama. Things were bad with Rick simply because nothing was particularly good with him. Not one thing.

Koko used to like spending time alone when she was a girl in Japan. She had felt smothered by those around her. Now she hated to be alone. And when she managed to get Rick to spend time with her, she felt alone then too.

Please, everyone, please do what you're supposed to do, Koko would plead silently. Don't fall apart. If the people around her would be happy, her unhappiness could slowly transform into pleasure. Jesse's loneliness terrified Koko because it reminded her of her own. Two independent, lonely people, existing side by side in the same apartment; the idea of it made her hands and feet turn cold.

Koko enjoyed seeing Jesse having fun with his friends. His pleasure pushed away her negative thoughts and premonitions.

After the girls left, Jesse and Daryl stayed up talking late into the night. Koko called out when she saw Daryl walking to the bathroom.

"Hey, are you going with one of those girls?"

"That what it looked like?"

"Is Tracy your girlfriend?"

"Are you kidding? My girlfriend is way older. There's no way I'd go out with anyone my own age. I prefer adults."

"Is that so."

"Tracy is Jesse's girlfriend. I don't think they've been on a date or anything yet, though."

"No! I don't believe it! Jesse on a date with a girl?"

"Why not? That's how you start, right? You go out a few times. How else are you supposed to get to know a person?"

Koko was speechless. He was right. But she had never

once found a boyfriend by going out on a series of dates. That wasn't her style. She never went out with a man unless she'd already chosen him for a lover.

"Put it that way, I guess you're right. But I just can't see Jesse doing anything with a girl."

Daryl laughed. "We're growing up. Once we grow up, we'll be equal."

"With who?"

"Whom. With you and Kay and all the other many and beautiful women of the world. Once people cross the line into adulthood, everyone is the same. Age doesn't matter then."

"That's not true. There are adults and there are adults, you know."

"Yeah," Daryl said, as if admonishing the older Koko, "I'm referring to age in and of itself. The most pitiful ones of all are the overgrown children."

"Yeah? And to *whom* might you be referring?"

"My dad, Jesse's dad, lots of others. It seems many men who go by the alias 'Dad' are that way."

"Is that so? And what makes you so smart?"

"I'm going to be a young adult pretty soon. When that time comes, Koko, will you go out with me?"

Koko laughed.

"It's nothing to laugh about. Sooner or later you're going to have a bunch of young men coming around you. I intend to get a jump on them."

"Do you, now?"

"Yes, I do. Koko, I'm serious. I really like you. Jesse doesn't understand at all."

"What don't I understand?" Tired of waiting, Jesse had emerged from his room.

"I've never seen an idiot like you," Daryl said. "You're so ungrateful to Koko."

"What's that s'posed to mean? You want me to get down on my knees and kiss her feet? That'd make you happy?"

"No, 'course not. But Koko's terrific, and you know it."

Jesse looked at Koko furiously. Koko didn't want them to start fighting.

"When people live together they don't go around saying things like 'Thank you' or 'I love you' all the time. But things go well even without that."

"Maybe when everyone feels those things, they do. But I think such things need to be said in this house," said Daryl, looking at Jesse and Koko in turn.

That night Koko could not get to sleep. Every time she started to doze off, Daryl's words would come back to her and she'd wake up again.

Rick doesn't say anything like that. Neither does Jesse. And neither do I. I don't say them because they won't let me. I always want to say "Thank you" or "I love you," but I never get a chance. Maybe Jesse's the same way, Koko thought. He can't tell when's a good time to come out and say things from the heart. Jesse will say "thanks" at the dinner table, but it doesn't mean more than good manners.

Koko needed to hear "thanks" when it wasn't expected; she needed to hear the sincere thanks that would express his gratitude for her presence in his life.

Koko wrapped herself in the blankets that smelled so much of Rick and wished she could cry. She used to be so damn confident. Not now, not anymore. She couldn't even keep in her bed this man who looked so easy to handle.

"Koko's terrific." That's what Daryl had said. "I'm terrific." Koko willed herself to believe it. Lots of men have called me terrific. I look pretty good. I work a lot harder than most Americans. I don't think I'm too bad in bed, either. And I have a good heart. Most important, I worry about others. My problem is I worry because I have to, not because I want to.

Why won't Rick let our love flourish? Why won't he set me at ease? All he'd have to do is let me come near him, touch him. Why won't he let me? So many people can't let themselves be touched, and yet they expect to be loved.

Koko tossed in bed until she heard the key in the lock, then put on a robe and went to the door. Rick was fumbling, trying to get the key out of the lock.

"Hey, Koko."

Rick looked at her. Koko had just enough time to think how pathetic his eyes looked before Rick slumped against her. They sank together to the floor.

"Are you all right? Where'd you get this drunk, Rick?"

"The usual place."

Koko had no idea where that was. Rick never took her to his "usual place." Manhattan could sink into the Atlantic before he'd do that.

Koko shook him to wake him up. If he fell asleep here, she'd never get him to the bedroom. She called his name over and over. Koko could see it was hopeless. Rick's eyes changed once he passed a certain stage of drunkenness. They looked like they belonged to someone else. No one could tell Rick to stop drinking; they could all see he needed it. "You don't care that people see you use alcohol as a crutch?" she'd once screamed at him, but he didn't care. Once Rick was sober, he had no recollection of how he'd been when drunk.

Everyone must think he drinks because he can't get what he needs from me. There was a time when, out of love for Koko, Rick would sip shamefacedly at his liquor. Passion is a necessary element in love. Rick had said that, making Koko laugh. There was no laughter anymore. She couldn't imagine Rick having passion for anything now. She felt like telling him, Happiness is right in front of your face, idiot. Why couldn't he see that?

Rick started snoring. His mouth was open and saliva was dribbling out. What was it Daryl had said? "Once people cross the line into adulthood, everyone is the same." Can you look at this man and still say that, Daryl? He's not an overgrown child. He and I got to know each other as two adults. Consenting adults.

Koko continued to shake him.

"Koko."

She turned around to see Jesse standing in the doorway.

"Daddy drunk again?"

"You can see that for yourself. Hey, come and help me get him to bed, will you?"

"Shit, no. He stinks."

"He's your father."

Jesse squatted down halfheartedly to help move Rick to the bedroom.

"Sorry, Jesse," Koko said ruefully.

"What're you apologizing for?"

"I don't know."

"I thought Daddy had straightened up quite a lot. It's started again."

"He was like this before?"

"He was much worse. But my mom was strong too. Once when they were goin' at it, Dad picked up a Bacardi bottle and broke her arm. It was awful."

"He broke her arm with a Bacardi bottle? Is that true?"

"Yeah. Sometimes I stopped their fights. They really hated each other."

"Hey, Jesse." Koko paused. "Why do you think your daddy has started to get like this?"

"I dunno. Because of you, I guess."

"Me! You're saying it's *my* fault?"

"Maybe it is. And his straightening up for a while was because of you, too. Not because of me. I don't have that kind of influence on him."

"I feel so tired."

"Daddy's heavy."

The sweat stood out on their faces as they pulled at a snoring Rick.

"What happened?" Daryl had woken up and joined them. "Geez. This is a lot worse than our dad. Lemme help you, Koko."

Koko looked up at Daryl. She felt like crying. Rick was her and Jesse's problem alone. They could take care of Rick's shameful state themselves, however clumsily. Daryl was an outsider. Koko dropped her eyes in shame.

Daryl went and lifted Rick's torso. Just then, the three looked at each other in shock, mouths open. Rick was comfortably peeing, right in the middle of the living room.

"Oh, my God! I don't believe this!" Jesse jumped back, disgusted, and bolted out of the room. Koko could hear him in the bathroom washing his hands. She sighed deeply and started undoing Rick's belt to take off his pants.

"Koko, you're getting your robe wet."

"It doesn't matter," she muttered.

Daryl helped Koko pull at Rick's jeans.

"Thanks," Koko said, glancing up. The sympathy in Daryl's eyes made her look away. The two silently worked Rick's soaked jeans down, then his underwear.

Jesse came back with a wet towel and a couple of dry ones. Koko wiped Rick's groin and thighs with it. She couldn't stop herself from sobbing. Jesse stood watching, despondent, and Daryl, flustered, rubbed Koko's shoulders.

Don't look, she kept thinking, please, just don't look. Gripping the wet towel, Koko still wept. Can you believe there was a time when the thing that made this rag wet with piss brought me to ecstasy?

"Koko, are you OK? Don't cry."

"I'm OK." Koko nodded over and over. "Don't worry, I'm all right."

This person is part of me. I couldn't do this for anyone but Rick.

○

THE HAIRPINS were in a silver box on top of the dresser. She moved around, handcuffed as she was to the headboard, and positioned herself to just reach it with her toes. If she missed and the box fell over, scattering the pins away from her, she'd be stuck for good.

She'd stretched out her leg to measure the distance between her and the box when her eyes fell on her brightly enameled toenails. She had to laugh. Compared to her fingernails—which were chipped and broken from resisting—her toes were positively cheerful.

No matter how bad it gets, people always keep a part of themselves proud and hopeful, even amused. Laughter gave her just enough distance from her distress and her fury. For an instant, she wanted to forgive everybody everything.

"Draw a line." Daryl had said something like that. If she was going to separate the past from the future, the time was now. The present is no more than a line drawn with chalk between the past and the future. If you rub it with your fingertips you'll erase it, but unless you draw it you can't go forward. Tossed between past and future, she only had to draw a line to separate them forever, this she knew. She hesitated. So long as she held back, she couldn't go on. But the thought of that slender line paralyzed her.

She wondered when Rick would be back. Soon, now, she guessed. He'd reaffirm the present for her with hands shaking from liquor. How many times had he cleared the drunkenness from his mind and tried in his own way to draw a line, to make a new beginning. This time she'd tell him. She'd draw a line for him. Instead of crying out "I love you," she'd say "I loved you." Probably I was the one who made the mistakes, she thought. Rick never lied to me. He's merely been silent. He doesn't have the words to lie. With Rick, what you see is what you get. It was his smell, emanating from his damp genitals, that he gave her, and the vomit after he drank; this is how he revealed himself to her with all too much clarity.

What the hell is love, anyway? Attachment, fondness, passion—it seemed to her that any of these terms were interchangeable with the word "love." And yet she couldn't change her focus. She could care deeply for innumerable people, but Rick was the only one she could say she loved.

She wondered if she could bury a love she had no more use for. Time could cover it, like earth covers the dead. Then, for the first time, she'd have a grave in her heart. Yes, she had to bury her love, she thought, as she lay there gazing at her toenails.

WHEN GREGGORY came by after so many months, Koko was annoyed that Jesse's prediction had come true. It didn't please her to think that children were surprisingly perceptive about what adults might do. In contrast to her discomfort, Greggory sat before her, grinning away.

"Jesse told me he saw you a while back."

Greggory laughed, drinking the Crown Royal she had offered him. "Yeah, at the chicken place. They make a good couple, those two."

"Those two? Jesse wasn't alone?"

"He and some girl were standing outside Roy Rogers, talking. They were getting wet in the rain and laughing. I thought, 'teen love'; then I saw it was Jesse."

"Hmmm. So that's why there wasn't much change that night."

"I guess Jesse's reached that age."

"Teenagers surprise you. It's like they hit the accelerator and turn into adults overnight. So, Greg, I hear your wife's expecting. Is that true?"

Greggory scratched his head.

"Yeah, second time. I'm gonna be the father of two kids at my age, can you believe it?"

"How is she? Is everything going OK?" A little jealous, Koko fixed her eyes on her former boyfriend.

"Yeah, I guess so. But why do pregnant women have to be so bitchy? Every time I go out, it's 'Where're you goin'? Who're you gonna see? What time're you gonna be back?' Bitch, bitch, bitch."

"She's worried. She's afraid something or someone is going to take you away. It's proof that she loves you."

"Well, it's a tremendous pain in the butt. All those questions. And she knows I'm coming back."

"When she stops asking, that's when you know it's over. There isn't any love that doesn't have its problems."

"I guess there isn't, huh. But sometimes I remember how much fun you and I had, and I miss it."

"But you didn't love me, did you?"

"I loved you. You weren't the kind of woman, though, who'd wait around for me. I never knew you could be the kind of woman who would be able to live with Rick like this and make things go so well."

"Every woman can become that kind of woman, once in a while."

Koko remembered her time with Greggory. She'd really liked him, but she hadn't loved him. She realized she loved him more now, as a friend. If Greggory had treated her the way Rick was treating her now, she wouldn't have put up with it. Koko told herself that putting up with someone's abuse was a form of love.

"You know, Greg, now I can listen to any problems you might have and happily give you advice. You're very, very important to me."

"Thanks, Koko. You are to me, too. It's great to have women friends. Tell me, though: things still going well with you and Rick? I've seen him at Cerise's a lot. Gets blasted out of his skull. But he seems like a good guy. The regulars there like him a lot."

"Yes, he's a good guy, a really good guy," Koko said, with an ironic laugh. Greggory hated to see her like this. Koko never used to laugh at herself or at anyone else with such scorn. Her laughter used to be a sign of strength, so much so it made him feel she didn't need him.

"You're not very happy, are you, Koko?"

"Why do you say that?" Koko's eyes widened in surprise.

"Just a feeling I get, that's all. I don't want you to be sad. You never looked sad the whole time you were with me."

"How awful. You mean I look sad?"

"You're beautiful. Much more than before."

"What do you mean? Explain."

Greggory laughed aloud. "There you go. That's my Koko."

My Koko. Koko thought about those sweetly sentimental words. They weren't lovers anymore. And they weren't husband and wife. But they did have a relationship where they could call each other "my Koko" and "my Greg." A warm feeling washed over her. Maybe this is what friendship means, she thought.

"You had a wild sort of beauty about you back then. Now it's like, I don't know . . . it's like you have a focus now."

"I'll have you know I didn't suffer from astigmatism back then."

"Shit, I know that. But it's like I said. And on top of that, your eyes are always shining now, like you want to cry, or maybe laugh. An unreadable sort of expression."

"I want to cry."

"You do."

"But I also want to laugh."

Greggory tilted his head and laughed as though he didn't know what to make of her. Long ago, so long ago, Koko had loved that expression. Greggory was one of those open men who would look at an ex-girlfriend with such a loving expression. No wonder his wife is worried, Koko thought, looking at him.

"To tell you the truth, sometimes I don't know what Rick's thinking. No, actually he's not thinking anything. But if that's so, why doesn't he *try* to think? Greg, are there people in this world who don't *want* to be happy? That's how I feel when I look at him. He's running away from happiness on purpose. He's so lucky and he doesn't even know it. He has a nice apartment, a job, he's raising a kid, and he has a girlfriend living with him. But he feels like it's all a big burden. Greg, is it a big burden? And if so, is there any burden as wonderful as this?"

Greggory listened to Koko in silence.

"So what do you think? Greg, I want to know. If he really doesn't like everything around him, he's free to reject it. But he doesn't. For one thing, he could kick me out of the apartment, right?"

"He doesn't do that because he needs you. He knows he can't do anything without you. He knows, but he can't believe in his own happiness, so he's always striking out at it and breaking it down. That's just the way he is. Everyone carries that sort of destructive tendency in themselves. It's just that in Rick that tendency is very strong."

"I don't believe it." Koko looked ready to laugh. "It's not like he's an artist or anything. Why would he be so tormented?"

"You can't say I'm wrong."

"Well, if it's true, then he's really fucked. Nothing good ever comes from people who can only destroy."

"But you do love him, don't you?"

"I love him."

"Rick can still take pleasure in a lot of things, I'll bet."

"He sure can."

"You're certainly clear on that, aren't you? You really know how to hurt a guy." Greggory shrugged and grinned.

"There's lots of stuff I don't like about being with Rick. But when I go off to sleep with the crook of his arm as my pillow, I think there's no place in this world I'd rather be. I have friends who tell me I should break up with him. But when I think about losing that pillow I wonder if I'd be able to sleep at night at all."

Greggory whistled. "You got it bad, girl."

"Yes. I hate it, but I do have it bad. It's a sickness. I know that myself. Why, *why* do I feel that it has to be *this* man, huh? Other men ask me to go out with them. But it's this broken-down, messed-up man I want. Why does just imagining breaking up with him make me start to cry?"

"Well, I wouldn't say it's a chemical reaction exactly, but when you get hooked up with someone, you can't see where one of you ends and the other starts; you're one person."

"So why didn't I feel that way with you?"

"Shit."

"Don't take it the wrong way. I feel really close to you, like I would with a good woman friend."

"OK, you're not interested in me. I can take it like a man."

They looked at each other and grinned. A warm feeling enveloped them that made speaking, even looking at each other, unnecessary. Merely being in the same room was enough. They both knew as they sat there that this was something precious.

THE NEXT MORNING Koko made Ovaltine for Jesse as he sat eating his toast.

"So why're you making breakfast for me all of a sudden?" he asked mischievously.

Koko put his cup in front of him and poured some coffee for herself.

"No reason. I'd like to do this for you every day. But you wouldn't eat it. I'm not going to get up just to pour milk on your raisin bran."

"The truth is, you're feeling guilty."

"What for?"

"For last night, after I went to bed. It's a good thing that guy left before Daddy came home. Not that Daddy would be suspicious. Even if he came in as Greg was going out, he'd be so drunk he'd just think, Geez, I didn't know plumbers came this late at night."

"Jesse! Greg's an old boyfriend of mine, and now he's a very dear friend. I don't have anything to feel guilty about."

"Oh, is that so. That drippy voice. 'Koko, you're *so* bee-yoo-tiful.' I felt like puking."

"You were listening?"

"I have ears. I heard some."

"Eavesdropper! That's a bad habit. Very rude."

"You're the one who's being rude. You're Daddy's woman. You shouldn't be letting other men in."

Koko sat down, pouting, acting as though she'd been injured. But she wasn't really upset at all. Letting another man in, huh? Sounds kind of nice, she thought.

Jesse finished his breakfast and ran around the apartment, brushing his teeth and putting his books in his backpack.

"How come you're leaving so early in the morning these days?"

Picking at his hair, Jesse glanced at Koko. "None of your business."

Annoyed at Jesse's impertinence, Koko held her coffee cup in both hands and breathed in the steam. That first cup of coffee in the morning was something she always looked forward to.

Taking the chain off the door, Jesse said, "Hey, later I want to talk to you about something."

"What?"

"I want to ask you about how to do something."

"Ask *me* how to do something?"

"Yeah. How to say something."

"How to say what?"

"You know—that kind of thing. 'You are *so* beautiful, baby.'" Jesse imitated Greggory.

"Is that something you need to know?"

"Maybe."

"What for? And quit making fun of my friend, you brat."

Jesse rubbed at his nose, embarrassed. "Well, uh, it's gonna be her birthday soon. Tracy's."

By the time Koko could reply, Jesse was gone.

Why am I like this? I immediately imagine something bad, but I can never imagine anything good. Jesse, who'd always resisted her, was now asking for her help and she had to go and scold him.

"Hey, baby, what's with you? Why so low?"

She turned around to see Rick taking Evian out of the refrigerator. He drank straight from the large bottle.

"What are you doing up? You hardly ever get up by yourself."

"I was thirsty."

Rick drank deeply. He looked completely exhausted. Not many people look so tired first thing in the morning, Koko thought.

"I'm not low," she said.

"Oh, yeah? Looked that way to me."

Koko pouted. Her look reminded Rick that she was a lot younger than he.

"Are you getting up now?"

"You kidding? I'm goin' back to sleep for a couple of hours. Come with me."

"I don't have that kind of time."

"I'm not asking you to spend the whole two hours with me. You know what I mean."

"You wanna have sex?"

"Kiddies shouldn't say such things." Laughing, Rick took

Koko by the hand. She let herself be led to the bedroom. Right now I really do feel like a child, hand in hand with her father. Only at these times do all confusion and anxieties lift and let me be completely innocent. Having a person around to lead you by the hand makes time go backward, she thought. She found herself toddling along like a child, puffing out one cheek, her eyes cleared of all worries. Holding in the laughter bubbling up in her, Koko raised her arms to encircle Rick's shoulders.

Rick made love to Koko as if washing a small child in a warm bath, and Koko was seized the entire time by the hope that there could be some miracle that would let it be like this all the time. . . . She felt like weeping. She, who had so hated children, now wanted nothing more than to go back to being a child. She wanted to borrow a pair of masculine arms and take a long, long rest in them.

This feels so very good, something should be born from it. From two bodies joined in love, sometimes it's a child that's born, sometimes an overwhelming sadness; sometimes a suicide with no regrets, only complete contentment. When one threw away oneself, threw oneself into a despair full of love, anything became possible.

So this bed remained impossible for her to leave. Even if Rick weren't here, she could smell him. She didn't care what happened. As long as she had this bed, it was enough. So long as she had this, it meant she hadn't yet lost everything.

You have within yourself the key to release yourself from the ties that bind you to a man. Kay had told Koko that. But Koko felt there could not be anything harder.

"I wish we could be like this all the time, forever," Koko murmured, grasping Rick's sweaty chest hair in her fingers. She knew exactly how each hair on his chest grew. No other woman knows him so well, she thought again.

Rick pulled silently on his cigarette. Putting Koko's head

on his shoulder and holding her next to him, he thought how precisely this girl fit against his body. It had happened somehow all of a sudden, while he was not paying attention. This girl was always here, never away from him, and he, too, had gotten used to her weight on his arm. The thought filled him with a vague fear. He knew how empty a man felt when he lost a lover he'd gotten used to.

"Did you hear me? Rick. I said I want to be like this forever. Next to you, always drowsing like this."

Rick's laugh was low. "Then it'd be like you had sleeping sickness."

"You don't like that idea? I'd think you would. You're the one who likes to be lying in bed all the time."

Maybe so, Rick thought. Maybe he really would like to be sleeping all the time. And Koko simply liked to imagine it; she didn't really want anything of the sort. She just liked to think so.

"Your friends'll laugh at you, you go and say stuff like that."

"Why?"

"Well, you have a lot of weird friends. Space cadets. Cruising around West Houston."

"That's not so. No matter how different people are, they all want pretty much the same things."

"You think so, huh. Well, I don't get along with most of those people you hang around with."

Chewing her lip, Koko fought down her irritation.

"Can I ask you something?" she said.

"What?"

"Rick, do you love me?"

Rick could not say anything. When Koko had wanted to move in, he didn't have any reason to refuse. It was only after they'd started living together that the problems started, when Koko's intuition had turned into determination. Rick couldn't keep up with her. She needed him so much. The terrible knowledge was always before him, day in and day out. He'd laugh and keep up the banter, but underneath, the cold sweat was running. Who would have thought that the woman who was always so fun-loving at the club every night would turn out to be so intense? Rick could not begin to understand. Young people were attracted to intensity like bees to honey. Intensity only made him want to flee.

"Answer me. If you answer me this once, I won't ask you again." Koko did not ordinarily ask these questions. She understood how disgusting men found them. And she knew such questions had charm not when a woman asked them but when a big-bodied, lumbering man did the asking.

"What do you want to go and ask that for?"

"The women you play around with are a whole lot worse than me—trashy and stupid."

"What's that supposed to mean? Are you trying to say I've been sleeping with other women?"

"No. But I can't say you haven't. Your shoulder always fits under my head perfectly. That's still true. But I don't understand you at all. I can't sleep at night, but I want to be here. You're hateful. I can't understand what it is you want."

"Not a thing."

"Is that so. You go on like that and you'll die for sure. You won't be happy with anything. Even if a thousand wonderful things are around you, you won't be able to see them. If you keep on drinking the way you do, you're gonna die, no doubt about that."

"What wonderful things? You're talking about yourself, aren't you?"

"I'm one of them."

Rick's tight smile was more of a grimace.

"Rick. The woman here with you now wants you so

much. She's crying, *shouting* that she loves you and you are making her so unhappy!"

"Shut up already!" Rick roared. Shocked, Koko was silent. After a few moments, tears welled up in her eyes and spilled over.

"I'm just so worried," she whispered.

Rick gathered her close. His face was twisted with pain.

"Koko, let me tell you something." He sighed deeply, try-ing to get hold of himself. "If I'm not here, there is only one person in this world who would be in trouble. That person is Jesse. He is blood of my blood and he's just a kid. Neither you nor the boy's mother would be troubled at all. I want you to remember that."

"That's so selfish. You think the world is set up that sim-ply? It's easy to die, but when I think of the people I'll leave behind, I can't do it. It hurts too much, right here." She laid a clenched fist on her chest.

"You're a spoiled little princess. You can't even imagine how it feels to hurt so bad that you don't have the margin to think about other people's hurts."

"No, I can't."

Rick put on a robe and went out to the kitchen. Dully, Koko watched him go. She heard the refrigerator door open and the sound of a beer tab being popped. Her tears would not stop. "Such a degenerate," Koko muttered. She tried to laugh. The corner of her mouth tugged up. Anyway, I'll make the bed, Koko thought, and stood up. Shaking out the bunched-up sheets, she found they were soaking wet. She would have to wash them. Koko sighed. This bed is a wreck. Like a bed at some roadside motel.

"You don't have to make the bed. I don't have to get up yet, so I'm goin' back to sleep."

"The sheets are all wet from sweat."

"I don't care." Rick piled up the pillows and lay down, drinking his beer. Now he'll press wrinkles into the sheets, Koko thought. I give up. She went to the bathroom.

LARRY'S TUMMY on West Broadway was always crammed with people like Koko and her friends, the ones Rick called "space cadets." Stopping by after work, Koko would usually see someone she knew. She had a date to meet Kay there that night. She was hurrying along Sullivan Street when she ran into Buckey on a bicycle.

"Buckey! Long time no see!"

"You done with work?"

"Yeah. I'm on my way to Larry's Tummy to have a drink before going home."

"Oh, yeah?"

Buckey was dressed in cycling pants and a jacket. Their colors were subtly matched and offset perfectly by the earring in his right ear. How come gay boys are such good dressers? Koko wondered, eyeing his outfit.

"You always dress so well," she said.

"I know. They tell me that at my new job all the time. I just *love* working at that boutique," said Buckey.

"How's Maurique?"

"He's fine. But recently he's come out with the most shocking thing."

"What?"

"He says he can sleep with *women*, too."

"Is that shocking?"

"Of course! Maybe a girl like you wouldn't understand, but every night I'm *so* worried."

"Why?"

"Well, I have twice the love enemies you do. Double the competition, you know?"

Koko snorted. Buckey looked at her with disbelief. "I'm

sorry. But, hey, it's not like any woman has come sniffing around, huh?"

"Well, Maurique is straight. Forward, I mean. I think he'd tell me if anything like that happened. But I'm so—so worried I can hardly *bear* it. Please, Koko, promise me you won't make a play for him, will you?"

"Now, I can't make any promises, Buckey."

Shocked, Buckey pulled up short.

"Sorry! I was just kidding. I have my own man. I won't go horning in on yours."

"That's a *relief*. Hey, are you meeting someone at Larry's Tummy?"

"A good friend of mine. Her name's Kay. You want to come along?"

"Can I?"

"Sure."

"Thanks! I *love* talking with girls. You don't have to worry with them."

"Is that so?"

"Oh . . . but is it the kind of bar I can go into?"

"Of course. Why?"

"Well, you know, recently this area has been *crawling* with *those* people."

"What people?"

"The yup-yups."

"Relax. We kicked out all the yuppies ages ago. No one will say anything because you're black and nobody cares if you're gay. More than half the people there are black, gay, artists, eccentrics, or any combination of the above."

"Really? Then I'll go. When I was little I got beat up on for being black; now I get beat up on for being gay. I just don't want to be anywhere but downtown, and preferably Christopher Street!"

"Come on. Not everyone's a bigot, Buckey."

"You know, now the prejudice wolves dress themselves in sheep's clothing so you don't know who to trust. I was born in New York, but I've never once been to a bar on the Upper East Side or anything."

"Neither have I, but that's because they're so outrageously expensive. I've had problems too, being Asian, especially with the owner of the gallery where I work. He's gay himself, but—oh, I'm sorry—anyway, he's always nasty to me. A real dickhead."

They soon reached Larry's Tummy. Pushing the door open, Koko spotted Kay at the corner table farthest in the back.

"Wow, Kay! What's going on? You're so dressed up."

"Well, a little. So who's this stylish boy? A friend of yours?"

"This is Buckey. Buckey, Kay."

"Hi, Kay. Pleased to meet you. But I'm not a boy; I'm a *man*."

"I'm sorry, it's just that you're so cute."

Buckey cheered up immediately and plunked himself down.

"So how's it going, Kay? Have you forgotten about Brian yet?" Koko asked.

"But of course. I have a date tonight after this. We're going out for dinner."

Koko whistled. "Go get 'im, girl. What a relief. Hey, Buckey, would you believe that only one month ago this pretty girl here was crying over a guy she'd just broken up with?"

"Oh, yeah? She looks fine now. You're pretty tough to get over a guy in just one month." Scooping at his frozen margarita and licking his spoon, Buckey looked Kay up and down. It seemed he didn't have any affection for the type of strong woman this city seemed so often to produce. They may look tough, Koko thought, but in reality they're brittle and easily broken.

"I don't know, Kay. Somehow I feel a little envious."

"Why, Koko? Something going on with you and Rick?"

"No, same as ever. But somehow we're not really *connecting*, you know? I always feel like we're two totally different people."

"What makes you think you could be the same person? Doesn't do a bit of good to wish for that. It's an old wives' tale that love makes you one. You always stay different people, going along on parallel tracks. It's the same with marriage. Whether you break up or not, love doesn't make those two tracks cross. You're always two different people: a man and a woman."

"How dull it must be to have to think like that." Buckey sounded fed up. His big hoop earring glittered in the bar's light.

"You know, I understand what Kay is saying." Koko was thoughtful. "But I feel the same way you do, Buckey, that it's awfully empty. I want to love a man like a part of myself, something I would absolutely never let go. And I want to be loved in the same way." Koko was thinking of Rick as she spoke.

Kay looked at her. "So does Rick feel the same way?"

"I don't think so. But I want to believe he will come to feel that way."

"Women like you are a big burden to men."

Buckey's eyebrows shot up at Kay's words. "What a perfectly awful thing to say!" he exclaimed.

"I'm sorry. But listen to me, Koko. I'm not saying your way of loving is wrong. Everyone has their own idea of what an ideal love should be. And everyone tries their best to get closer to it, even if they get hurt from the trying. And even if they get hurt, the love they create may be a good one. Maybe getting hurt is inevitable, but I don't like it. When I was living with Brian I really used to think sometimes that a person's life is predetermined. The best thing to do is relax and take it easy. Easy come, easy go, just like money."

"I don't think that way at all," said Buckey.

"I don't think you can understand what I'm saying, Buckey. No gay can."

Koko was aghast. She looked at Buckey, but contrary to her expectations, he didn't seem offended at all.

"Yes, I am gay. And I want to love intensely. I can't help it, and neither can Koko. We're simply made that way. You should be able to understand that, Kay. You were in love with that—Brian guy, wasn't it? You broke up with him, but you'll fall in love again. When that happens, you can push it down and push it down, but the desire will come. I'm not talking about a desire of the body, either. Mark my words, Kay, you'll want a love that is unique in all the world, a love for you and you alone."

Kay was silent for a while.

"You're right, Buckey. I'm sorry I said you wouldn't understand because you're gay. I apologize. But I want to avoid all that. It's so scary. I think you have guts, Koko," Kay said, sipping her drink.

"I don't have guts or anything. I've been thinking that maybe I'm just stubborn. After all, I'm lonely all the time. I don't know how to get away from this feeling. I feel lonely even when I'm with him."

"And yet before he loved you, you felt fine," Buckey murmured.

Koko looked at him, surprised. "Are you saying he loves me, Buckey?" she asked.

"That's what I think. You don't feel lonely when you're caught up in the chase. You might feel hungry, but not lonely. That's something you feel after you get love, don't you think? It's impossible for people to be easygoing when they love and are loved."

"You know, Buckey, talking to you makes me feel a lot better." Koko's eyes blurred with tears.

"If all men were as smart as you, Buckey, we'd be able to have such fabulous romances," Kay put in. She was looking at Buckey with admiration. She seemed to have completely changed her opinion of him. Koko could tell she was starting to like him.

"I'm not particularly smart. But I do go after good things. I never settle for anything less."

"Oh, yeah? What if one of those good things gives you AIDS, huh? What then?"

"Well, that goes with the territory, like mustard on a—"

The two women burst out laughing.

"You know, I hope the man I'm meeting tonight might turn out to be a good thing for me too. He's a terrific guy."

"Really? He'll be here soon, won't he? I think I'll order another drink. I'm not budging until I get a look at him," Koko said.

"I'll have another frozen margarita myself," Buckey said. "A double."

"You guys are embarrassing me. And after all my crying over Brian, too."

"That's right. Can you believe, Buckey, that this woman was sitting in front of me a month ago, angel-hair pasta hanging out of her mouth and tears running down her face?"

"Koko! That's awful! I did not have pasta hanging out of my mouth!"

"Indeed, that must have been a performance to see," Buckey observed. Kay pushed him in the head and he squealed. "Hey! Women are so *violent*."

"Is that so. It's men like *you* that makes us that way."

Koko was gently wrapped in an alcoholic haze as she watched her friends razzing each other. Kay looked at Koko dazing out and laughed.

"What's with you, Koko? You've only had two martinis on the rocks. Don't tell me you're drunk already."

"Don't be silly. I was just thinking how nice this is. Wouldn't it be great if it could be this nice and easy with a man? Why can't it be like this?"

"Because it wouldn't work, that's why. That's what makes things between men and women so interesting. You're either way up or way down, one or the other."

"You always state everything so definitively, huh, Kay," Buckey said.

"You know," Koko said thoughtfully. "Something halfway in between would be nice."

"That's impossible. Then it wouldn't be a love affair."

"So what would it be?"

"Well, I don't know. But it wouldn't be a love affair, that's for sure. And anyway, I couldn't bear anything so wishy-washy. It'd be like death."

"I wouldn't want it to be dead or anything. But no matter how unhappy I get over Rick, I always feel we should be living together peacefully and all this trouble is something temporary."

"So what are you going to do if that temporary trouble goes on forever? Koko, if he makes you go through sad times, he has a duty to make you really happy at others. That warm and fuzzy stuff you were talking about is only for people who haven't had any experience with either extreme, or for those who have been through the whole gamut hundreds of times. We here are far too young to be included in that latter group."

Buckey listened to the women's exchange with great interest. Women certainly liked to analyze things to death, he thought. He himself always went straight for what he wanted, and as a result had gotten himself into any number of unbelievable situations, all for the sake of love. He went for what his hands wanted. What his heart wanted. And what his mind wanted. He never went against his desires: that's how he picked men and that's how he ended up living with them. To Buckey, it was a dreadful thing to be the one who was *wanted* instead of being the one who wanted. And yet, to listen to these two women talk, it seemed that what they really desired was for someone to want *them*, even though they spoke in terms of their wanting this or that. It was weird, he thought.

"So, Kay, does the guy you're meeting tonight want to be a couple with you?"

Kay reddened at Buckey's question.

"I don't know yet. I can tell he likes me, but he hasn't really said anything yet, you know? I can't exactly *ask* him. . . . Oh, geez, there he is."

Kay half stood and waved. Koko reached out to steady the daiquiri that her happy friend was about to tip over and glanced around. The next moment, she was looking at Buckey. His eyes were wide with disbelief. Kay was waving at *Maurique*.

Maurique stood stock-still for a few moments. His hands were in his pockets and his head was slightly tilted in a bemused What-the-hell's-going-on-here? Then, resignedly, he began making his way to Koko's table.

"Hey."

Maurique looked ill at ease as he greeted them. Surprised, Kay looked first at Maurique and Koko, then at Buckey, who was chewing on his lip.

"You all know each other?" she asked.

"Uh-huh."

Koko ordered herself another martini. "Who would have

thought you'd arrange to meet a date here. Didn't it occur to you that you'd run into me sooner or later, Maurique? Or if I were alone, you thought you'd simply slime your way through, not explaining anything? Sorry, but I'm not that close-mouthed." The waiter came with the martini. Koko drained it in one gulp.

"What's wrong? Koko, what's going on here?" Kay asked nervously.

"Well?" Koko smiled tightly and stuck a cigarette between her lips. Maurique lit a match for her, but Koko put the cigarette down and blew the match out.

"It's nothing for *you* to be so upset over," Maurique said quietly. "It's no big deal."

"No big deal? Is that what you think? I hate this! I hate this whole thing! You're supposed to be a friend, and you put me through this?"

Buckey had been fiddling with his napkin ever since Maurique arrived at the table, crushing it, smoothing it out, and crushing it again. He finally looked up. His eyebrows were pulled together, but he smiled and said gently, "Koko, it's no big deal."

"You too, Buckey? How can you say that? So what'm I supposed to do?" Koko took out a handkerchief and wiped her eyes. She didn't know why she was crying. It was simply that she was so angry, her eyes kept getting wet. She couldn't stand the moment when love died.

"I'm sorry, Koko," Maurique said.

"Why are you apologizing to me? You've nothing to apologize to *me* for. You don't have anything to say to Buckey?"

"No. We don't have the sort of relationship where we have to apologize to each other."

"I don't understand you at all. People should talk more in relationships, but nobody does. They try and show things with attitudes or by making things happen. Everyone's so talkative when love *starts*, but once it's going, it's like everyone forgets *how*. Everyone's *human* at the beginning, but in the end, people turn into *animals*."

"This is our affair, Koko. It has to do with Buckey and me, and with Kay and me. You can say this and that, but it will be settled among the three of us."

"Is that so? You think you're the only ones that get hurt when you get together and break up like this?"

Kay, white-faced, had gradually grasped what was going on. She seemed to want to say something, but she was so shaken it was impossible.

"Hey, Koko, if you're mad on account of me, let it go, OK?" There was no strength in Buckey's words. "I'm used to stuff like this."

"On account of you." Koko thought about it. Her angry tears weren't only for Buckey. Well, then, who were they for? For all the poor wretches. And for the one poor wretch that was herself.

"You know, Koko, actually I'm having a very difficult time right now. The reason I'm not saying anything to Buckey is that I can't find the right words to say. And if I say something to Kay, she'd probably pass out. Why do I have to explain myself to a third person like you at a time like this?"

Koko looked away at Maurique's words and shook her head. "I can't feel sorry for you, Maurique."

"Of course, I'm not asking for your pity. Koko, I don't understand very well why you're so angry. This is something that happens a lot between people like us, as I'm sure you know. Perhaps you and that alcoholic—what was his name? I forget. Maybe you and he have about reached the end, huh? Are you so angry because you're confronting that through Buckey and me? If that's it, I wish you'd stop."

No sooner had Maurique finished than Koko's hand was

flying through the air to land on his cheek. Maurique's gold-rimmed glasses went skittering under the next table.

"You bitch!" The next moment, Buckey's margarita was flying into his face.

"Shit!"

Maurique reached for a napkin, but Buckey was already hurrying Koko out of the bar.

THE TWO walked along Canal Street through Chinatown without saying a word. The pre-dinner clamor soothed them. Someone with his arms full of dinner groceries bumped into the bicycle Buckey was pushing. Without cursing it for being in the way, the man continued hurrying down the street.

Koko finally spoke. "You want to leave your bike somewhere?"

"No. I don't want the saddle to get stolen."

"Is that bicycle important to you?"

"Uh-huh. It even has a name."

"Yeah? What's its name?"

"Whoopi."

Koko snorted. "Like in Whoopi Goldberg? You're weird."

"Yeah. If you don't take care of her, she rattles on just like Whoopi."

"You really do care about your bike, huh?"

"Yeah."

Buckey laughed, embarrassed, and chewed on his lip. His artless expression made Koko's chest hurt. He looks like a child somehow, she thought.

"Hey, Buckey, let's go eat some Chinese food. It'll make you feel better."

Buckey looked at Koko and hesitated. They weren't so close as to have dinner alone together.

"OK, but I don't have any money."

"I have some. C'mon, let's do it. Or maybe you don't eat with girls?"

"Of course I do."

"OK, let me make a call. I'll tell Jesse to stay over at Daryl's. Do you have a quarter?"

Buckey watched in a daze as Koko ran off to make her call. She doesn't want to go home, that's why she's doing this, he thought. Well, the same goes for me.

The two picked up a bottle of red wine at a liquor store and went into a Chinese restaurant. The owner didn't mind their bringing Whoopi inside with them, so Buckey was happy. They toasted each other with the wine and began to eat.

"You know, this duck sauce you put on the spring rolls? It's something you only find in New York," Koko said.

"Oh, yeah? I can't imagine spring rolls without it."

"I didn't see it anywhere in California."

"Gee, you were on the West Coast? Wow, Koko. I've never been outside of New York. I envy you."

"I was on vacation. It was a long time ago. I didn't have a boyfriend or anything. So it was boring."

"Are you having fun now?"

Koko looked at Buckey.

"No, what I mean to say is, do you think New York is so great?"

Koko looked down and dipped her spring roll into the duck sauce. "You know, Buckey."

"What?"

"You don't have to be so careful. It's not like you and I have to do that anymore."

Buckey was silent.

"I happened to be there when you saw Maurique and Kay, and you know how awfully unhappy I am. I like you, Buckey."

"Is that because you feel sorry for me?"

"No. I'll tell you what it is. It's that no matter how close I am to a woman friend, no matter how much I tell her about myself, I always protect myself somehow. And with male friends, I want to show them my good side. But with you I don't feel I have to do either. It's different with you. I'm not trying to hit on you or anything; it's nothing like that."

"I know. It's the same for me too. I feel like I can relax with you. I'm not sure why. But I think it's because with you I don't have to act gay and I don't have to act 'like a man.' You don't care a bit that I'm a black fag."

"Yeah. You're right, I don't think about any of that at all. So I might say something that'll hurt you or be harsh. If I do, I apologize for it in advance, OK?"

"OK. Actually, the only people who can truly hurt you are the ones you really like. I'll grit my teeth and bear whatever abuse you heap on me."

"Am I abusive?"

"I didn't say that. Wow! What a humongous crab!" Buckey yelled as the waiter brought over their food.

"The stuff under this shell here is really good."

"We call that poison."

"Americans are so close-minded. Shut your eyes and try these eggs. They're fantastic. It's not the season for it, though, so they've been frozen."

Buckey reluctantly put some in his mouth.

"They're great, aren't they?"

"I can handle it." He chewed at the crab shell for a while. "If you only give it a try, there're lots of good things to eat," he said.

"That's right. If you don't ever taste it, you never know."

Buckey gave a big sniffle. Koko looked up and saw he was crying. Buckey quickly wiped his tears and blew his nose on the handkerchief Koko held out.

"Why did Maurique have to choose that woman?"

"Don't call her 'that woman.' She's a friend of mine."

"Sorry. But it's awful. I can't even bad-mouth her because she's a friend of yours."

"I can sympathize with you on that point. But didn't Maurique give you any indication?"

"What kind of indication?"

"That he wanted to break up with you."

"Not at all. He always used to say he was honest. But even that was a lie."

"I wonder why he did it? He knew you'd be hurt. I can't believe he'd end the relationship with such a scene."

"Well, he probably thought he'd break the news to me after everything was going well with Kay. He wouldn't want to do it before he was sure this new thing would work out. That's the way he does things. As long as he's happy, the injured can take a hike. People who have happiness in their hand can afford to leave without extending courtesies."

"That son of a bitch! Lying, underhanded jerk."

"I can kind of understand," Buckey said quietly. "People break up after they've found a new lover."

Koko suddenly thought of Rick. If he wants to break up with me, why won't he do it? Is he waiting for a new lover?

"Are you thinking about your boyfriend?" Buckey looked at Koko and sipped his wine. He wasn't crying anymore. Far from it, he seemed completely matter-of-fact as he dug into the broccoli. Here was a man who didn't mind at all that the woman sitting in front of him was thinking of a man other than himself. It set Koko so much at ease that she was able to taste her wine.

"Why is it that everyone goes with men they can't get along with?" she asked.

"Everyone needs to pass the time."

"I guess you're right."

"Falling in love in this town is like eating pecan pie when you're on a diet," Buckey said.

"Oh, yeah? I like apple pie. With a slice of cheddar melted on top."

"Yuck! That's what you get at a hick diner."

They broke open their fortune cookies and read them.

"'Don't be a bigot; love women too,'" Buckey said.

"Liar."

"Yeah. It says, 'If you continue along your chosen path, fate will smile upon you.'"

"Really? That's what mine says."

"They probably all say the same thing. Must be cheaper that way."

"Maybe. Anyway, I'm not going home tonight. I'm going to drink all night; that's my chosen path."

"Well, if you do, I guess I have to, too."

The pair left the restaurant and went bar-hopping. It was about 2 A.M. when they were thrown out of a club on Avenue A for being too rowdy.

"I haven't been so drunk in ages. I feel like I'm not afraid of anything."

"Koko, you're awful when you're drunk! All messed up! Really awful!" Buckey himself had trouble keeping his balance. He kept dropping Whoopi. Here and there they met up with a few bums who were still awake, who scurried off, frightened by the pair's raucousness.

"Hey, you! If you get scared on Avenue A, you'll never be able to show your face in the South Bronx!" Koko shouted.

"You can't even go to Brooklyn!"

"Hey, Buckey, what should we do if we get mugged?"

"We've got Whoopi."

"Yeah? Well, what if they pushed us off the bike and raped me?"

"I'd say I was a fag with AIDS, and I'd get my own butt out of there fast."

"You're cold. I'm so sick of it all! Fags're cold; men're cold!" Koko squatted in the middle of the street and began to cry. A couple of Puerto Rican men walked by, whistling. Buckey squatted down next to Koko and held her.

"Koko, if we stay here we really will get jumped. My place is across Tompkins Square Park; let's go there."

Koko did not even wipe her face. Messy with tears, she gaped at Buckey.

"But Maurique will be back, won't he?"

"Probably not. 'Specially not tonight."

"Do you have any liquor?"

"Yeah. There's whiskey and gin. And if you need it, there's Maurique's coke."

"No, that's all right. I don't do anything like that. But I do want a drink."

Maurique hadn't come back to the apartment, just as Buckey had predicted. Koko sat on the couch and smoked a cigarette. Her mind was strangely clear. Buckey had bolted for the bathroom the moment they got there. He didn't come out for a long time.

Koko looked around the room. Sure is sophisticated, she thought. It didn't look like anyone lived there. After a while, she heard the toilet flush and Buckey came out.

"You threw up?"

"Yeah. I feel a lot better. You want to do it too, Koko?"

"No way. I've never thrown up in my life."

"You're strong."

"No, I'm scared to. I keep thinking, what'll I do if my whole stomach comes up, and my intestines start coming—"

"Ugh. Stop it. How come women can say stuff like that?"

"It's our nature."

Buckey made a gin and tonic for Koko. She watched him the whole time.

"You really are a nice-looking boy, aren't you?"

"You only noticed now?" Buckey said, holding out Koko's drink. He opened a wine cooler for himself.

"Hey, Buckey, do you get a lot of grief because you go out with men?"

"Yeah. I get shit about it from everyone: men, women, family, and friends. I used to hate lots of people. But my weak point is I never could hate myself."

"Oh, yeah? I don't think that's a weak point at all. It's a good thing to like yourself."

"Koko, don't tell me you dislike yourself?"

"I don't know. Maybe I'm starting to."

"Well, *don't*."

Koko's eyes rounded at Buckey's forceful tone.

"Let me tell you something," Buckey said, sitting down next to her. "Death is not the end for a person. The end is when a person hates himself or herself. Once you dislike yourself, it's hard to start liking yourself again. Everyone has two sides. One is negative and one is positive. You understand? Once the negative side starts to take over, a lot of things in you are on their way to being destroyed."

"Wow, Buckey, you sound really wise. Have you ever thought about becoming a priest? Oh, but I guess you can't. Priests aren't supposed to be gay."

"I'm serious."

"I know." Koko stroked Buckey's cheek. It was so smooth. She stroked his whole face. Dear God, she thought, what were you thinking when you made such a beautiful creature?

Buckey sat quietly and let her touch him. Koko wanted to touch . . . what? Someone who is really and truly concerned about her, he thought. She'd probably be doing the same thing even if I were a woman. It seems she hasn't touched the skin of someone who cares about her in a long time. My brown skin, it probably feels warm. Koko's hands are warm, too. She likes me. Even though I'm black, even though I'm gay, she really cares about me. She wants to touch me and I want her to touch me. And the reason why is that we really and truly like each other.

"You're such a beautiful man. The other kids used to pick on you, huh? How can people be prejudiced against you when you're such a good person? If I were God, I'd never let you suffer."

Koko was crying. Buckey held her in his arms. She was the first woman he'd ever held who was not a member of his family, but he didn't feel grossed out. It was like holding a kitten. And he thought he might start mewling like a kitten himself any minute now. The two held on to each other and felt they'd become two fluffy balls of fur.

"Shall we go to bed?" Buckey asked.

"No, we don't have to. I don't want to push you."

"You aren't. I can't have sex with you, but I'd feel a lot better if we slept in the same bed. To be honest, I hate sleeping alone. I can't bear not having someone in the same bed with me."

Koko laughed. "I'm the same way," she said.

Koko borrowed a sweatshirt and pants from Buckey and changed in the bathroom. There were notes fixed to the mirror that read *I love you* and *You're mine*. Buckey probably wrote them, she thought. It's those who say the words of love who get hurt. The more they say, the more they hurt, she thought absently, sitting on the toilet.

When she came out of the bathroom, the light was already out. Koko made her way to the bed with the help of the streetlight coming through the window. The bed sat behind an Asian-style screen. Buckey had already rolled himself up into a sheet. He looked like a jelly roll. Seeing his feet sticking out at the bottom, Koko sighed. It'd been a long time since she'd seen bare feet in bed in a darkened room, lying there waiting for her to get in. They made her realize how much solitude she'd been enduring.

"Come on in. Plenty of room." Buckey moved over for Koko. She slid in and then found the tears welling up all over again. She struggled to get hold of herself.

The two lay quietly side by side in the dark. The buzz from the liquor had long since worn away. They heard some drunks making noise somewhere outside.

"Koko, are you asleep?"

"No. I don't know why, but I can't sleep."

"Are you thinking about that guy?"

"Rick? No. I'm thinking how long it's been since I've been in bed and felt so peaceful."

"It's quiet here, isn't it?"

"Yeah. You can hear drunks sometimes, though."

"That makes it seem even quieter."

"Yeah."

"It makes me remember being a kid."

"What kind of kid were you, Buckey?"

"A weird one."

"Really? I was a weird kid, too."

"Everyone kept saying I was weird."

"Me too. That's probably why I left Japan."

"I didn't know you were Japanese, Koko."

"Of course I am. What did you think I was?"

"I don't know."

"Not that it matters." Koko sighed. "The first time I came to America it was just as a tourist, to California. I wasn't planning on living here or anything. But then later I came to New York—supposedly to study English, but really just to get away. And after I got here, I felt I'd found a place where maybe I could make a life for myself. More than anything I wanted to be left alone. I wanted to lose myself in the crowds, you know? I thought it would be easier to be alone in a place like this, packed with strangers. But the irony is, now that I've got what I wanted, and I'm on my own, I find myself wanting to be with people."

"Uhmm . . . did you play with dolls when you were little?" Buckey asked.

"No. I hated dolls."

"Why?"

"Because I thought they were hateful. They *are* kind of hateful, don't you think?"

"Probably you were the one who was hateful," Buckey said, propping himself up on one elbow and looking at her. His eyelashes were so long that Koko reached up and pulled them. His lips were so broad that she pinched them together, too. Buckey laughed and pinched her nose, saying it would be nice if it were longer. Koko pulled his ears. He grinned and said his ears were on the small side. Even so, he had three holes in them for earrings.

"If only Jesse were this cute."

"Is that your boyfriend's son?"

"Yeah. He's not cute at all. Compared to him, you're . . ." —Buckey looked at her expectantly, his large moist eyes like Bambi's—"a total child."

"Oh, shit!" Laughing, Buckey plopped back down onto his back. Koko remembered how she used to sleep with her younger sister, nestled together, front to back. They used to call it making spoons.

"Buckey, let's spoon."

"OK."

He seemed to understand what she meant. He twined his body around hers, and they drifted off to sleep.

• • •

THE NEXT MORNING, Buckey made coffee while Koko called Sue.

"What? You're at Buckey's? Something happen with you guys?"

"Of course not." Koko and Buckey's eyes met, and they burst out laughing. Koko told Sue she was going home to change and then to work from there, so could Sue tell the boss that she had a dentist's appointment and she'd be late. Their boss was exceptionally finicky about hygiene, and that sort of excuse worked best with him.

"He'll chew you out again. He's so prejudiced against Asians."

"Well, that Jewish prick is not at the top of my list of favorites himself."

"Tell me about it. So, there isn't anything *going on* between you and Buckey, is there?"

"Well, something did happen. We didn't have sex, though."

Buckey grabbed the phone and said into it, "I don't do that sort of thing with women!" and hung up.

Koko finished getting ready and then thanked Buckey.

"Call me. And if you have trouble with Maurique, I'd like to help *you* out this time," she said.

"Thanks. But I don't think anything like that will happen. I'm sure he'll move in with Kay."

The two exchanged kisses on the cheek and parted. Looking for a subway station, Koko walked quickly down the street, which was still sleeping off its drunk. She was lucky Buckey had been with her the night before, she thought. She'd been in such a bad way, she could've easily gotten herself killed. Koko felt truly grateful to Buckey.

A strange stench assailed her when she opened the door to the apartment. Little patches of vomit lay here and there in the living room. Koko cursed. It seemed that Jesse had fled to school, jumping over the wet spots. She could see evidence of his footprints.

"Rick! What have you done here?" Koko shouted. Rick was in the bedroom, snoring on the bed, his shoes still on. He had urinated next to the bed. The side table and everything on it was soaking.

Koko stood in a daze for a long moment. I'm supposed to like myself in this house? she thought. She sat down next to Rick. She didn't even have the strength to cry.

○

THE SUMMER was hot. Summer's always hot. But there are various kinds of hot. Like the hot when you're on the verge of a totally hot love. Or when it feels like your skin is struggling to breathe. So hot you want to go out and kill someone. But you feel something's going to happen to relieve you at any moment, which stops you from falling over the edge. Summer's hot. So people kill people. And people fall in love. Before you know it, a whole saga's been born, to be laid on top of other sagas. You don't watch out, you become part of them.

I could've stood back and simply marveled at life and marveled at love's complexity, she thought. I could've chosen to freeze up and avoid letting my feelings get mixed up with those of others. But she hadn't taken that route, she hadn't become an emotional zombie. Proof was in how much her heart hurt. Her body, too.

Sunlight streamed through the blinds. She saw shadows of people walking by on the street. There was no coolness from the shadows her eyelashes made. Because they're constantly wet with tears, she thought. She stretched her leg as far as it would go. Her foot barely grazed the box of hairpins. She'd used them before to keep her hair from moving. Now she'd use them to free herself. She spread her toes and tried to grab the box. I've thought so much about Jesse and Rick that I've become incapable of thinking about them anymore. I want to leave. My heart, the one that exists in this place, is dead. I have another heart that's alive. If I go now, she thought, I can make it.

She'd try to unlock those handcuffs.

KOKO'S HEART nearly stopped when she heard Jesse's voice on the line. He had never called her at work before. She thought for a moment that Rick had been in an accident. Jesse wasn't forthcoming at first. He kept saying, "Um . . . um. . . ."

"It's all right, Jesse, I'm listening," Koko said, trying to keep her voice from trembling.

"Well, actually, I didn't want to ask this of you, but—"

"What are you saying? We live together, don't we?"

"Yeah, well. Thanks. . . . I think maybe I won't have enough money, and . . . uh—"

"What? Money?"

"I was thinking about earrings."

"Earrings? What about earrings?"

"You don't have to shout. I can hear you. I thought maybe for Tracy's birthday present. Daryl said if I got you to come, I could get a really nice pair."

"So nothing's happened to Rick?"

"Huh? Something happened to Daddy?"

Koko sighed. She remembered what Eileen had said. You always think something will happen to your kid so you stay with him all the time, but nothing ever does. Koko realized that her tired sigh had been just like Eileen's about her son. She smiled wryly.

"So you want me to buy a present for Tracy."

"I'm not saying that. But I only have five dollars. That's barely enough for lunch."

"Now look, Jesse. You're supposed to buy a present for the girl you like with your own money even if you have to go *without* lunch. And what's more, you'll soon be old enough to get a job pushing carts at a supermarket, won't you?"

"No, not for ages. You have to be a senior before you can do that."

"Oh, yeah?"

"C'mon, Koko. Daryl and I will come downtown tonight and meet you."

"OK. You two coming together?"

"We were thinking about going to SoHo or somewhere like that."

"That's expensive."

"You're coming, aren't you?"

Koko arranged to meet them at Ray's Pizza after work and hung up. How did Jesse learn that women like earrings? She wondered if he was falling in love. He was just a kid. Even so, the farther a person stuck his neck out for love, the more of an adult he was.

"What's up? Earth to Koko. Who was that on the phone?"

Koko came back to herself. Sue was standing beside her, holding a huge painting.

"Oh, is that the piece everyone's been talking about?"

"Yup. Nice, huh? This kid's gonna be bigger than Basquiat. So who was the call from?"

"Jesse. He's coming downtown tonight after work with his friend Daryl. He wants to buy a gift for his girlfriend."

"That's great!"

"What is?"

"Has he ever asked you for your advice before this? If he asks you for advice, it means he's opening up to you. He thinks it's OK to talk to you more."

"I wonder."

"I guess it's the girlfriend. . . . When a man gets a woman, he becomes happier and friendlier to everybody."

Maybe that's so, Koko thought. The old Jesse would've rejected any advice from Koko about his private affairs. He's exposing himself, Koko thought.

"Is he on vacation now?"

"Uh-huh. Just started. He's busy having fun. I don't see him except late at night."

"He must be out dating. Hey, Koko, I have some time tonight. Can I go shopping with you guys?"

"Sure, but I don't know how much fun it'll be for you with the kids along. What about your husband?"

"Oh, he'll be fine. And anyway, recently he's been so *boring* to be around, I can't stand it. So can I go with you guys?"

When Koko and Sue walked into Ray's Pizza, Jesse and Daryl were already waiting for them. They wore camouflage pants and high-tops and waved when they saw Koko.

"Oh, geez, they're wearing that awful stuff."

"It's cute. They look like that rap group, Hammer and the Pistons, or whatever they're called."

"People will think we picked up two punk teenagers."

"Koko. Japanese people think too much about what other people think."

Koko introduced Sue to the boys, then went to place an order.

"Two coffees and a slice."

"We have decaf and regular," the black youth at the register said, glancing at Koko. A small diamond stud glinted in his left earlobe.

"Make it decaf."

The boy called the order out.

"Do you live around here?" he asked.

"No, but I work around the corner. Why?"

The youth grinned and chewed on his lip. Koko waited for him to reply, but when she realized he wouldn't, she took the tray back to their seat.

"Did he say something to you, Koko?" Daryl looked at her suggestively.

"Why? Nothing to do with you."

"Because, look—he's still looking at you. Maybe he's mistaking that counter of his for a bar."

Looking around, she saw the young man leaning on the countertop, chin in hand.

"He probably commutes from Jersey," Jesse said, laughing.

"Well, I think he's pretty cute, Koko."

"Don't you start too, Sue."

The boy really was looking at Koko. Feeling awkward, she lowered her eyes and poured cream into her coffee.

"Koko's being shy!"

"Shut up."

Daryl and Sue burst out laughing. Only Jesse didn't smile.

"What's his problem?" he asked.

"What do you mean?" Sue held her cup in both hands and tilted her head to one side.

"He must be weird, staring at Koko like that. He doesn't even know her. It's rude."

"Goodness, Jesse. When men and women meet, one way to make an impression is to be a bit impolite. Koko still has more than enough appeal to make young men like that want her to notice them. You see her every day, so maybe you don't notice. I don't know what it's like in your house, but that's how people outside see her."

"Sue!" Koko was worried about Jesse, who was silent. Sue always had to be so blunt. It was one of her attractive qualities, but Koko didn't expect a child to understand it. Jesse didn't seem upset as much as perplexed.

"Koko has sex appeal, is that it?" Jesse asked Sue.

"That's right. So if you and that father of yours don't treat her like a lady, some guy is liable to come along and snatch her away. I don't think you understand yet, Jesse, but Koko is one type of woman men like."

"I knew that," Daryl put in. "Women like Koko turn me on."

Koko reddened. "Daryl! Would you please not say things like that?"

"Wow, Koko, you're getting red," Sue said.

Jesse was looking seriously at Koko. He didn't seem to know what to say.

"Koko's terrific, but you're pretty terrific yourself, Sue."

"Gee, Daryl, what nice things you say. You're going to be a very attractive man yourself. You'll have to lose those camouflage Rambo pants, though."

"What, these? Everybody wears them."

"Hey, how come Daddy doesn't treat Koko like a lady? He doesn't see her like that guy at the counter does?"

Everyone fell silent at Jesse's abrupt question and looked at one another. It was easier for Koko if Jesse didn't wonder about such things. The one thing she couldn't bear was someone close to her feeling sorry for her. Rick and Koko were not husband and wife, nor were Koko and Jesse mother and son. So it was natural the three should live together without becoming very involved. At least, that was what Koko wanted Jesse to believe. Not that it was, of course, how she really wanted to live.

"You don't have to say anything. I just wanted to bug you. I wouldn't ask that kind of question for real." Jesse laughed slyly. He looked pretty pleased with himself.

Koko sighed.

"Grown-ups can't handle unvarnished questions," Daryl observed.

Koko and Sue snorted.

"If we don't say anything, grown-ups think we're not thinking anything." Jesse was triumphant.

Sue poked him in the head. "Grown-ups are too polite to psychoanalyze people."

"Yeah, they're too cowardly to face the truth; they'd rather keep their heads in the sand," Koko shot back.

"Koko, you always get so serious about everything. Hey, don't look now! That guy at the counter is still staring at you."

Koko looked up at Daryl's words. "He's a beautiful boy. But he's awfully young."

"Like you're ready for the embalming fluid yourself."

"Jesse, don't you go mouthing off like that. Show respect to women older than yourself. Koko takes care of you. You ask me, she does a heck of a job. You're not even her child."

"Is that right."

"Yes, that's right."

Koko could see Jesse was starting to lose it. He didn't show it as much as he used to, but it was clear to Koko, who lived with him. The corner of his mouth was crooked as if it had been cracked. Whenever Koko saw that childish expression of wanting to say something sarcastic but not having the words, something would twist inside her heart, imitating Jesse's mouth.

"As long as I'm in the house, Daddy always comes back once a day. Koko should be thankful I'm there. I know sometimes they think I'm a pain, but if I weren't there, they would've broken up a long time ago."

"Why don't you just shut up? You don't know a thing about it. You're still wet behind the ears. You couldn't last four days without adults around to take care of you. I don't have to listen to your guff." There, she'd said it. Koko instantly regretted her words. She bit her lip. She could suppress her rage up to a point, but the moment always came when her reason would fly out the window.

"I don't remember ever asking you to take care of me. I accepted you because you're Daddy's girlfriend, but that's as far as it goes. If you think I'm included in Daddy's and your relationship, you're wrong. You're the one who came into Daddy's and *my* space—*our* space."

"I'm sorry, Sue, but can you take these two kids shopping?"

Before Sue or Daryl could answer her, Koko had stood up and run out. "I hate you!" she thought she heard Jesse shout behind her.

Koko ran along Christopher Street. She felt if she stopped running she'd start crying, and if she started crying it would be the end. Her breath came in ragged gasps. They helped blunt the sadness. She stopped, then began walking very slowly. There were a lot of gay couples along this street, walking with their arms around each other. All at once, Koko felt like seeing Buckey. If she could sit with Buckey and cry and bawl and wail, she'd surely feel better. She didn't, however, have the courage to go walking around Alphabet City by herself at dusk, so she doubled back to the Village, simply looking for a place to cry in peace. She knew, too, that if she went to Buckey's now she'd just be using him.

Guess I'm not much of an adult, Koko thought, as she trudged along. But who can be an adult when someone hits your sore spot? Jesse seemed better at handling things, but nothing had really changed. He had simply learned how to voice his discontent. He learned fast; Koko admired him for it. His words could sometimes claw at her and rip apart her carefully constructed reasoning. But if Koko felt pain, Jesse felt assailed by the fear that he'd done something so bad he couldn't take it back. To protect himself, he'd attack her even more. Koko, in turn, would lash out at him.

"This is what people call a vicious circle," Koko mut-

tered. Why did she feel what Jesse said was so unreasonable? The fact was that Jesse was not her younger brother, or
her child. He was the kid of the man she was in love with.

Even though Jesse didn't talk much about his mother
anymore, Koko knew he thought about her. She also knew
that sometimes when he said he was visiting a friend he
really went to see his mother. That in itself didn't bother her.
But if he had a mother to go and see, why did she, Koko,
have to be worrying about him all the time? A person who is
not your lover but always around you, always around . . . it
grated on Koko's nerves and made her jumpy.

Koko had heard from Grace that Jesse's mother lived
with a younger man. Must be nice, Koko thought peevishly.
The woman had a lover, and a son she saw every now and
then. Though it looked like she'd thrown everything away,
she had everything in her firm little grasp. Whereas Koko
looked like she had everything, but in reality she had nothing for sure.

I hate you. Jesse's words went round and round in her
head. I'd like to say the same thing, she thought. I'd like to
turn to everything I find less than pleasurable and shout *I
hate you!* But I can't do that. If I did, I'd be surrounded by
things I hate, and I myself would be among them.

I wonder if Buckey'll pass by. That'd be nice. She bought
a bottle of beer at a deli and sat on a bench in Washington
Square. She drank it straight out of the bag. Homeless people and drug pushers passed by, but no one spoke to her. On
summer evenings, the sun took its time going down.

Maybe Jesse, too, got through each day feeling everything
was absurdly unreasonable, Koko thought. It couldn't feel
good to have a woman who's not your mother watching you
all the time. But at his age, he couldn't live by himself. He
had to have someone around. And there was no one to be
that someone except Koko. Probably Jesse was grateful for

Koko's being there but felt inadequate taking help from an outsider. The only thing he could do to feel manly was to rage at her sometimes.

Logic is not enough to understand what's going on inside a person's head, Koko thought. If Rick had kept his drinking down, would she and Jesse get along? There was no telling.

"KOKO! What's going on? What're you doing here all by yourself?"

Kay and Maurique were standing in front of her.

"I was just thinking. Hey, long time no see, you two. How've you been?"

"We're fine. Is something wrong? What're you doing in the park at night drinking beer?"

"'The park at night'—it's still light."

"Well, yeah."

Maurique was standing next to Kay, looking distinctly embarrassed. This guy never changes, Koko thought, glancing at him. I'm sitting here on a park bench, miserable. Buckey is tossing and turning at night from loneliness. And here he is, the same as ever.

But Koko could not be angry at Maurique. Indeed, she felt strangely comforted at seeing him: looking nonchalant, yet gathering happiness about himself faster than anyone else. He always had a pleasant warmth about him.

"How've you been, Maurique?"

"OK, I guess." His hands stuck in his Levi's, Maurique shifted uncomfortably. "Are you still mad?" he asked.

"Are you kidding? It doesn't have anything to do with me, really. I'm not that immature. More important, I have to apologize for hitting you."

"That's OK."

"That must have been the first time you've ever been hit by a woman, huh?" Koko said.

Maurique laughed. "So we're still friends?" he asked.

"Sure. Why not? But I do have one condition. I'm all by myself and not a thing to do. Buy me dinner?"

"That's all? Sure. But Kay handles all the money; you'll have to ask her."

"There's nothing to ask. She won't say no. Right, Kay?"

"'Course not. Sometimes it's more fun to be with Koko than with you."

Maurique shrugged and grinned. The three decided to go listen to some jazz. Koko stood up, feeling calm enough at last to walk. She might have sat on that bench for hours if no one had come along.

Koko and Kay walked along, talking, hanging back a little behind Maurique. It was the time of evening when the smell of fresh liquor permeated the Village, stimulating one's senses.

"You're living together, aren't you?" Koko asked Kay.

"You can tell?"

"Of course. Soon as you get into a man, Kay, you start changing. I can tell just by how you're dressed. What's with the Fiorucci-esque hand-me-downs?"

"When you're together a lot, things change naturally."

"*You* change, you mean. Sometime you should get the guy to change."

"Oh, that's no big deal to me. I'm not going to fuss about some guy's clothes."

"So no more Perrier lawyer?"

"Brian? He came for the rest of his things, you know. Maurique helped him pack."

"I give up."

"Brian has a girlfriend already, too. She lives in Chelsea; she's a singer. Just starting out."

"He never learns, does he? He should get himself a nice rich girl."

"It's what he likes. I think I was perfect for him, but I couldn't handle it. I'm never going to go out with a guy like him again. I could drop dead tomorrow, so what's the use of busting my butt at the gym all the time?"

"You may end up living to ninety. Think you can handle being with a man who makes rubbish every day?"

"It's called *art*, Koko."

Maurique had reached the club first. He was waiting for the two women, who were taking their time, strolling along and talking.

"You two seem to have a lot to talk about."

"Oh, nothing important. Right, Kay?"

"That's right."

Koko had never heard of the band that was playing. Because of the early hour, the tables were fairly empty, but people stopping by for drinks at the bar on their way home from work made the place feel lively. Koko and her friends took a table near the entrance, not wanting to disrupt the performance.

"I love coming to a place like this early in the evening. Makes you think something fun might happen that night. Of course, nothing does, usually," Koko said, sipping her drink. The moment even a little strong liquor passed her lips, her vague feelings of unease would retire to a hidden place within her and she'd feel better.

"You seem worried about something, Koko."

"Not really. It's not like I have any special problems today. It's just that today my problems won't listen to me."

"You mean Rick?"

"I feel like all my problems began when I started living with him."

"And all your happiness too, right?"

"Yeah. Why should happiness and unhappiness be bound up together like this? Pisses me off."

"It's because you don't hunger for happiness unless you have unhappiness," Maurique said. Koko looked at him, amused.

"My. And how is it *you* should know such a thing?"

"Maybe you think I never have any problems, Koko, but you're wrong."

"Am I? I thought you were a lighthearted bimbo who only accepted happiness, or else a cold-blooded S.O.B. who turns away from anything sad."

Maurique looked a little injured at Koko's referring to him as a bimbo, but he quickly recovered his amiable smile. Koko could tell there was nothing artificial about that smile. Its genuineness was a relief to her. He must really love Kay, she thought.

Koko was silent for a while, her eyes on the pianist doing his solo. Maurique was wary of her sharp mouth, her barbs always directed at him. But Koko wasn't plotting her next zinger, she was merely listening to the music. She seemed to be thoroughly enjoying their company. She must be alone a lot, Maurique thought.

Koko wondered suddenly if Jesse had found his earrings. It's all right, she thought, Sue's with him. Koko regretted she couldn't be along for this rite of passage. If she'd kept her cool and cheerfully changed the subject, none of this would have happened. But when she was hurt, the only thing she could manage was a quick escape. Koko thought of Rick. What was that man trying to escape? she wondered.

"What're you thinking, Koko?" Kay asked. She'd been playing with Maurique's fingers and watching Koko. People who had someone at their side, a warm body they could touch at will, looked upon the world with magnanimity. Kay, whether alone or in love, worried when one of her good friends was at the end of her rope. She was worried now. Koko could see Kay was wishing fervently she could be of help.

Sitting across from these two happy lovers, Koko felt sad. It wasn't that she was envious. Seeing them made her nostalgic for the honeymoon period she and Rick went through when they first fell in love. She could sense Kay and Maurique's concern for her, and it hurt. At the same time, their concern enabled Koko to begin approaching, however tentatively, her own pain.

"I'm not thinking about anything, really, except . . . well, that I'm not alone."

"That's right. We're always thinking about you, so don't you go getting depressed, Koko."

"I guess one's man makes the difference."

"What do you mean?"

"There are so many people who care about me, who like me, who help me. Everything should be going my way, but if things with my man aren't right, I'm miserable. Guess I'm at his mercy. I don't know what to do. It'd be better if he'd disappear. Maybe if he'd die. . . . Then I could take all the misery all at once and get it over with. Maybe total misery is the start of happiness. Huh? Whaddaya think?"

"Koko, what are you saying?"

Koko looked up. Kay was pale. Koko realized she was frightening her friend.

"Koko." Maurique lit a cigarette. Did he used to smoke? Koko wondered suddenly. "You should break up with that man. No question about it."

"I don't have any place to live."

"You can move in with us," Maurique said.

"You said the same thing before." Koko's laugh was low. "I don't have any place to live."

"So—"

"I don't have any place to live except that one."

"Yes, you do, Koko," Maurique said. "There are any number of places for you to live. Look, I can tell you still have some misgivings about me. But I want to give you some advice. You should try to become shrewd, like me. Find yourself a place to live before you break up. You understand what I'm saying? A place to live is not an apartment. Find yourself some happiness before you get unhappy. Before you lose love, get your hands on another love. If you do that, you can change the present into the past without crying about it."

Maurique's voice had risen. A man at the next table motioned him to keep it down. At that moment, the piano solo ended and the drums and sax competed with the applause. People stopped looking at their table. The waiter who'd been trying to listen in on their conversation went back to the bar. Maurique put his elbows on the table and looked at Koko.

"I'm not sorry about what I did, Koko," he said. "You know, there's a certain amount of volition at work when people get together and break up. If you don't see someone you love anymore because he died in an accident, you're not going to be able to accept it. But if you don't see that same person anymore because one of you wants it that way, it's actually much easier to get over."

"Yeah, you can talk 'cause you've always been able to pull it off. Some of us can't do that, you know."

"I think it would be best for you to try to become one of the ones who can. You should be more centered on yourself."

"Koko loves Rick. He's not a bad man. I don't dislike him. He's no one to depend on, but he's a good person." Kay turned to Koko. "So what do you think? Maurique told you to make a shrewd move like he did, but he's not saying you should be underhanded. He's completely honest with me. When it comes time to break up, he'll probably do the same thing to leave me that he did with Buckey. But I can't say that's a bad thing. He's simply taking care of himself. He's finding ways to get on with his life without hurting himself any more than necessary. That doesn't change the fact that he loves me. And Koko, unhappy people can't love anyone. People who don't love themselves can't console others. I don't think you can make Rick happy the way things are now. The best you can hope for is that things don't get any worse than they already are."

"Thanks, Kay. You understand a lot of things. I thought you'd be blissfully basking in a certain someone's love, not a thought in your head."

"Oh, I am, believe me," Kay said, laughing. Koko excused herself and headed for the ladies' room. The club had filled up and she had to thread her way through the crowd. As she did, she caught the eye of a number of men. Jazz was a good backdrop for that favorite masculine pastime: ogling women.

"Hey, baby, you were having a fight with that couple a while back, weren't you?" One man spoke to Koko.

"No, I wasn't."

"If you need someone to take your side, tell me. Any time."

"Thanks." Koko threw the reply over her shoulder and opened the door to the rest room. Shutting it behind her, she sighed. I do need someone to take my side, she thought. The pain became keen. She looked up at the mirror. I can't start crying now. Maurique and Kay will be worried, she told herself firmly. She looked intently at her eyes in the mirror, swimming with tears that threatened to spill over, and willed them to obey her. I sure have a lot of friends who are on my side, she thought. But I can't let myself cry in front of them.

The door trembled from the bass, and the piano riff was clear and sweet. It was a good band. They were jamming. Koko finished her business and went back to the mirror to fix her lipstick. This band's gonna be famous for sure, she thought. She put her fingers on her temples and tried to make herself smile. The tears came all at once, and she had to grab both sides of the sink to steady herself. She wasn't crying about Jesse, or about Maurique's stern advice. She was crying because she felt so small and helpless.

WHEN KOKO got home that night she could hear the TV in Jesse's room. Koko was on her way to bed when his door opened. Jesse looked at her anxiously.

"Did you buy your earrings?"

"Uh-huh. Sue bought us dinner, too."

"That's nice. I hope you thanked her."

"Uh-huh."

Koko said good night and was about to go on into her room.

"Koko." She turned to look at him. "I didn't mean what I said."

"Let's forget it already."

"It's not because Sue said all that stuff, but . . . I don't want you to go on a date with any other man. You won't do that, will you, Koko? Even if some other guy asks you, you won't go out with him, will you?"

"What's it to you?"

"Because if you go out with some other guy . . ." Jesse struggled to find the words. "I can't live with you and some other guy!"

Koko looked at Jesse earnestly, trying to understand what he was saying. Jesse bit down on his lip. He was trying to think of what explanation he could add in case Koko took what he'd just said the wrong way. The right way for him meant he wouldn't have to speak plainly. Koko was the same. The two understood each other without the use of kind words. That was how they'd built their relationship. They depended on one other now, but neither wanted to admit it.

"I'm not saying I want to live with you forever, Koko. And it's not like I'm jealous if you go out with anyone besides Daddy."

"I know. You don't like me enough to be jealous."

"What I mean is . . . Daryl would be able to explain this better than me, but . . ." Jesse smacked his forehead two or three times with the palm of his hand, trying to put what he wanted to say into words.

Koko looked at him absently. He's gotten so big, she thought. The cloud of depression that had weighed on her earlier in the evening had disappeared, dissolved into precipitation that settled, along with everything else, at the bottom of her heart.

"It'll be awfully tough."

"What will be tough?"

"If you're not here it'll be tough for me. I don't like it, but I'm not old enough to live alone yet. I can't get along without you here. I don't want to live anymore like how it was when just Daddy and I were here. I don't want to go back to that. Back then I was smaller, so I couldn't do anything except accept it, but now I know exactly what I need. I need a woman like you."

"Like me?"

"I can't explain it."

"That's all well and good for you, but it's awfully selfish. I'm not your mother."

"I know that."

"Sometimes I think you don't. You and I are not related. But we live together. And now you say I'm necessary for your day-to-day life. If so, why can't you work to make our life together go better? Maybe you're too young to know that it takes effort to make things go well when you live with someone, but it's your duty to learn it."

"Duty?"

"As in 'to respect.'" Jesse was silent. "If you don't know what that means, why don't you look it up in your father's Webster's? Jesse, let's make our life easier on ourselves, huh? I don't want to feel like this anymore."

"Yeah."

"You don't like it either, do you? It's a pain always thinking how much you hate me, right?"

"Uh-huh."

"I feel the same way. I guess I'm not grown up yet myself."

Koko sighed. Taking off her earrings, she thought how tired she must look. It made her even more disgusted. Jesse looked at her earnestly.

"What is it?" she asked.

"Nothing. I was thinking how young you are, Koko."

"Not tonight, sorry to say."

"My mom is young, too. Maybe you think she's old, but she's young."

"What's that got to do with anything? You sure are a weird kid."

"It's good to be young, isn't it?"

"Where'd you get that idea? Jesse, the answer's yes, but it's also no. Depends on who and where you are."

Jesse laughed, embarrassed. "Mom says she wants to take me out to dinner tomorrow night. Do you mind?"

"No, why should I mind? It sounds nice. And I won't have to cook; that's a big help. What I do mind, Jesse, is when you sneak out to have dinner with your mom without telling me. Not that I'm jealous or anything. Same as you not being jealous if I go out with some guy. But it's hateful."

"I think I understand. I'll ask you before I go out. That's part of showing respect, isn't it? And you won't be going on a date with another man without telling me about it, right?"

"I can't promise that."

"Why not?"

"A mother and son getting together is totally different from a man and a woman getting together. It's not something between you and me; it's between me and your father."

"Shithead."

"What was that?"

"Nothing. Isn't there respect between men and women?"

"Jesse. In situations where men and women are involved, respect doesn't do any good at all. Unfortunately."

"Are you going to dump Daddy?"

Koko looked at Jesse, surprised. Dump Rick? she thought. Dump Rick? Maybe he'll dump me.

"I feel sorry for him," Jesse said flatly. He didn't look particularly anxious. He seemed to simply be stating a fact. "Daddy's the one who really doesn't know how to make life easier on himself. He does respect you, Koko, I know he does. But he doesn't know how to be respected himself. Don't dump him, Koko. He'll get more white in his beard."

Koko thought of the stubble on Rick's chin. The hair on his head was completely black, but he had a lot more white hair on his chin than a man his age should. It was one more thing that made trouble for Koko. No matter how mad she got at him, when she saw that stubble she felt like taking him in her arms and cradling him.

"Hey, Jesse."

"Yeah?"

"What should we do about Rick?"

Jesse shrugged and grinned uneasily. "I don't know. I'm just a little kid."

"That's not fair. If you're a little kid, why aren't you in bed?"

"I've been with him a lot longer than you have. Man, what a problem." Jesse stretched. Koko giggled. Jesse looked at her questioningly. Koko shook her head and told him good night. She went back to her room thinking how at times like this she could almost like the boy.

Koko removed her makeup and lay down on the bed thinking about what Jesse had said. What did he mean by his mother being young? she wondered. It was almost as though he were apologizing for her about something. People did tend to forgive things on the basis of youth. And criticize when the transgressors were not so young: "You're not a kid anymore." Maybe he was trying to find a way to accept his mother even though she did nothing to take care of him.

KOKO WAS drifting to sleep when she heard the sound of the key in the door. She jumped up and hurried out. Rick had flung his keys and a newspaper onto the chair and was lighting a cigarette.

"You're early tonight."

"Uh-huh. Did I wake you up?"

"Oh, I'm always up when you come home. You may not have noticed, though."

Rick laughed and took his shirt off. He wasn't drunk.

"You want something to drink?"

"Yeah. There's some Michelob in the fridge."

Koko took out two bottles, setting one on the table and opening the other for herself. She always felt optimistic when she saw Rick sober. Times like these, she'd completely forget her depression. Times like these, though, came few and far between.

Rick sat on the easy chair, smoking and looking at the paper.

"Anything interesting happen?"

"Not really. 'Policewoman dies from overdose.' Awful shit."

"Oh, yeah? That reminds me, Jesse's going to see his mother for dinner tomorrow."

"I know."

"Jesse told you?"

"No. His mother did."

"You saw her?" She could feel the rage boil inside her. Rick felt it too. He looked up from his paper.

"Don't look at me like that. She's Jesse's mother. It's natural we see each other sometimes and talk."

"But I didn't know you were seeing each other. I hate that woman. She doesn't do a thing and then asserts her rights as a mother whenever it suits her. She doesn't do any of the work. It'd be OK if she always worried about Jesse. But she doesn't. She only wants to pick up the fun stuff and leave me with all the shit work. Do you know what she says about me to people? I heard from Grace. She says she feels sorry for Jesse for having to live with a girl like me who don't know nothing about nothing."

Rick laughed. Koko looked at him, aghast.

"It's nothing to laugh about."

"I just thought how like her it is."

"It really pisses me off. She's the one who doesn't know anything."

"She does know. That's why she goes on, sayin' shit like that. She's protecting herself so people don't tell her what you're saying—you know, about her not taking care of her own son. She knows everyone around her has their shit more or less together and she's the only one who's always fucking up. Must be hard for her. She can't feel right unless she thinks someone besides herself is fucking up too."

Koko chewed on her lip. She thought maybe she could understand. She herself was the same way, wasn't she? Jesse's mother wasn't such a bad person. If it hadn't been for Jesse, maybe Koko would've even liked her.

"Oh, I hate this feeling," Koko said, plopping down next to Rick.

He grinned and patted her on the head.

"It's horrid to hate another person, isn't it?" she said. "It makes you hurt inside. Sucks the fun out of everything."

"Everyone hates at least one person. Sorry to say."

"You're different, you don't hate anyone. You don't even feel bitter toward that ex-wife of yours, do you?"

"She was a good woman. At least until we got married, that is. And I think I was a good man for her. But everything changed. Probably my fault. But maybe she was the one who made me that way. There's no point in trying to figure it all out now. I talked to her the other day, and she was real worried about her future. She knows she's not young any-more. But she doesn't want me to know she knows. So she acts like she's real proud about living with a younger man . . . but I know that guy's gonna leave her."

"Do you think she loves him?"

"She doesn't seem happy with him, so I don't think so. Oh, she acts happy up front."

"Why doesn't she want to look after Jesse?"

"Maybe because she thinks happiness comes from men, not boys. She has to have everything going just right before she can take care of a child. Jesse understands that. But hap-piness, man, the more desperate you get about it, the more you can't get your hands on it."

"It seems if she'd just look at things differently, everything would work out."

"She doesn't look at everything psychologically like you do, Koko."

"I do not look at everything psychologically. I just think that everybody should work hard and get their act together and then they'd feel pretty good about themselves—and about everything."

"Not being able to get one's act together is part of being human. What you're saying is an ideal. You probably can't understand a guy who chips the rim of a coffee cup by mistake and then feels he has to go on using that broken cup forever."

Koko drank her beer silently. She was beginning to think the world she and her friends occupied was very different from that of Rick and the people around him. She wondered why. It didn't seem to be the difference between young and not so young.

"I don't know, but this friend of mine said there are two sides to every person: a negative one and a positive one. When the negative side gets too strong, the direction of the person shifts. It seems to me that the people around you are going in the negative direction, Rick."

"Probably. Not that they want to," Rick said, kissing her. What a happy night this is, Koko thought. When she tucked her head into the crook of Rick's arm like this, she felt like babbling something meaningless, like babies do before they learn speech. Koko wished she could be reborn into something that made soft mewling noises, rubbed its furry face against the furry face of another creature, and ran around in a field.

Rick stroked Koko's hair and thought how happy this made her. He'd known it for a long time. He himself liked this quiet time with her. It was relaxing. A wonderful woman next to him. But the next moment, he'd want to jump up and rush out the door. Oh, Jesus, I'm still holding on to that chipped coffee cup I should let fall. Rick put his hand to his forehead. Breaking into a cold sweat, he tried to figure out if he was living in the midst of a dream or a reality, but he didn't get anywhere. Despair froze his hands and feet. Maybe I'm sick, he thought, Why else would my chest start hurting so suddenly? I've got my woman and my son, what more do I want?

Koko felt Rick's chest tense. She looked up at him. She was relieved to see the same old gentle, slightly care-worn expression. She put her full weight onto the easy chair and snuggled up to him. I wonder if Maurique and Kay are still out drinking. The thought made her smile.

Koko gripped Rick's hand in both of hers. I'm not going to let this hand go, she thought. I can't do anything without it. Maybe this hand isn't really holding me. But I'm held by it.

"Hey, Rick."

Rick came back to himself. He looked at her. Her tiny face was resting on his knee and her ear was peeking through the drape of her hair.

"Wouldn't it be nice if things were always like this?" Koko said. Her eyes were half closed.

Rick could not bring himself to drop the words she wanted to hear into that waiting ear. He knew exactly what they were.

"I'm the only one who can love you like this," Koko continued.

"You're something else."

"Am I?"

"Uh-huh. By the way, what're you doing this weekend?"

"Nothing. Why? I don't have any plans. I never make any plans. Why?"

"Let's go out."

Koko jumped up.

"Really?" Before Rick could nod, she'd thrown her arms around his neck.

"Don't be so surprised."

"But I'm so happy! What'll I wear?"

Rick looked at Koko's bright face. One word from him and she was so happy. He shut his eyes. He couldn't bear to think that he controlled this woman's feelings. Slowly, he untangled himself from Koko's arms and stood up.

"What's wrong?"

"I'm going over to Cerise's for a little bit."

"Why?"

"Have a drink."

"Did you mean what you said about this weekend?"

"Sure." Rick put his keys and wallet in his pocket and kissed Koko's cheek.

"You don't have to go out now."

"I told you. I'm going to have a drink."

Koko put her hand to her cheek in blank amazement. The sweetness from the kiss had completely disappeared. And before she could think of anything to say, she heard the sound of the door closing.

Koko poured herself some red wine and went back to the easy chair. She felt worthless. They'd lived together for so long and she couldn't even get him to stay with her for one evening. I irritate him, she thought. But how? Everything seemed to be going so well. Every time I start feeling relieved, Rick runs away from me. The same thing, over and over. I love it when he's cheerful. I'd do anything to make him feel that way. But he always rejects my efforts. Maybe people don't like it when you try to do too much for them.

The warmth of the wine spread through her, but it only made her feel more disconsolate. Why do people drink? she thought. It doesn't make you forget anything at all.

When Rick came home at dawn, Koko was lying, passed out, on the easy chair. It was awfully quiet, he thought. Koko looked cute lying there like that, her mouth half open. Rick's legs were shaky, but his head was surprisingly clear. I can cry if I see, say, a sad movie, he thought. But seeing a woman passed out drunk on account of me doesn't make me feel sorry for her. He felt, rather, relieved. She still wasn't hurt so bad she was going to dump him. He picked Koko up and carried her to the bedroom. Even fast asleep, she was light. She must have unconsciously very much wanted to be picked up. She was so used to the feeling of longing. At that, tears did rise in his throat, but they were gone the next moment. It made him happy to pick her up like this without a second thought. He didn't feel any sympathy for her, and to him that was a good thing. Liquor helped him avoid sympathy, precisely the emotion Koko was always trying to pry from him.

○

A CAR ALARM was blaring nearby. "Fucking noisy," she muttered. But that was the least of her worries. Damn thing's just like me, she thought. My alarm had been howling for quite some time, until somebody turned it off. Or maybe it shut itself off. If someone were to try to take Randy away from me, it'd go on again. Her right hand hurt from being cuffed. I pity you, Rick, for having to do something like this.

For so long now he had been cutting off the hands she'd been stretching out to him. She had no more hands to hold out to him. Why couldn't he understand that was what was making him want her now? He should've realized all this before those terrible words "I don't love you anymore" had formed on her lips.

She sat now, rattling the headboard, turning over in her mind the good and bad things she'd done. What was it Maurique had said? You can't deny the things you've done. You even start to feel that fate decided your actions long ago.

Hello.

You don't know me, but I see you all the time. You always order two slices with extra cheese and onions, a small fries, and two decafs. So, what do you think? I have a good memory, don't I? I'd like to talk to you. Please forgive me for writing to you like this out of the blue. But don't you think we really should get together and talk more than we do now? (Smiles.) Your friend is beautiful too, but I'm always thinking about you. I work part time, so I never know when I can see you. Won't you please give me a chance?

From your
Randy
(Smiles)

Sue was collapsed in laughter while Koko was reading the letter. Koko picked it up gingerly between thumb and forefinger and waved it at her friend.

"What is this?" she asked.

"What do you think it is? It's a letter. It's cute. He's got style."

"It looks like something by a child."

"He wrote it that way on purpose. He thought it'd amuse you."

"He seems to have done a pretty good job with you. And how did you get this?"

Sue finally got her laughter under control and began to explain.

"Last night I went to Ray's Pizza. You remember that kid

who was there before, right? The one who was looking at you when we went there to meet Daryl and Jesse. He came to my table to talk to me, asking me when my friend was coming. I acted stuck-up and wouldn't tell him, you know? So he goes into the back and comes out a couple minutes later with this. He asked me to give it to you."

Sue continued to laugh, and Koko took another look at the letter, a pained expression on her face. After a few moments, her discomfiture dissolved into sweetness and a smile crept onto her lips.

"You're happy, aren't you?" Sue said, glancing at her.

"Well. I guess. But how odd that that boy at the counter should feel this way about me."

"There's lots of that kind of oddity where this came from. You're the only one who doesn't notice. It's fine to worry yourself sick over a heavy relationship, but if a woman doesn't have these little things in her life, she dries up. This boy would be really fun. He writes this letter to an older woman, trying his best to make a good impression—it's cute."

"You're a real fan of his, aren't you?"

"To tell you the truth, I've fallen in love myself recently."

Koko looked at Sue, puzzled.

Sue simply laughed. Then she took up Randy's letter and kissed it loudly.

"You haven't fallen in love again with your husband, have you?"

"What, are you kidding? Come on, Koko. I wouldn't be getting hot over that seen-all, done-all man. It's excruciatingly boring when nothing excites your husband anymore. No, it's a different guy."

"And you intend to keep it a secret."

"Well, for now at least. I'll tell you about it when the time's right. Not now. I'm too excited—it'll just make you feel bad. Besides, you're such a prude sometimes."

This wasn't the first time Sue had told Koko about having an affair. How those affairs ended was something Sue never mentioned.

"Don't do anything stupid, Sue."

"I wouldn't dream of doing any such thing. Only stupid women do stupid things."

"What am I going to do with you? And what am *I* going to do? Now I can't go to Ray's anymore."

"Why not?"

"If I go now, he'll think I want something."

"What's wrong with wanting something? That's when a woman shows that lovely animal side of herself. The catching of the scent, the padding along the trail—it's great. Letting a man see a crack in the fortress is a form of consideration, you know. Look, Koko, you can get a slice of pizza anywhere, but Ray's is the only place you'll find that kid."

"He's not something to eat, Sue."

"Of course not. He's a lot cheaper than food. And you don't have to worry about your weight."

"Yeah? Well, I could get a disease."

"So? My husband works at a hospital."

Sue and Koko gave each other a high five and went back to work.

That whole day, Koko was in high spirits. A man out there had his eye on her. She couldn't have imagined that such a trivial thing would make her feet light and soften her lips so that a smile constantly threatened to tug at the corners. How delightful to think that a man's gaze had fallen here and there upon her body. It wasn't the hot gaze of a lover. It was a playful interest, a love affair there for the taking if only she felt like it. And that letter sent to make her understand this wasn't an interest thrown at any number of women; among crowds of women, it was for her alone. Koko thought of the diamond stud in his ear. She had to hand it to him. He'd managed to convince an older woman who didn't know him from a hole in the wall of his interest. And, like Sue said, he'd done it with style.

But that's as far as it goes, Koko thought, sighing. She was far too involved with Rick to respond to another man's interest. She knew her ties to Rick would prevent any fun she might have with another man. A relationship she couldn't concentrate on would be pointless. With that thought, she folded Randy's letter into a tiny square and put it away. She forgot about it for a while, but later took it out again. She couldn't believe what she was doing. What she wanted, she thought, was some tiny kindness to find its way to her. She needed warm little fragments of love and friendship to comfort and sustain her. A lifetime could be a long, long time, and the only thing you could do to last its whole length was gather up such tiny fragments and keep them here and there around you.

"Randy," Koko murmured. Maybe he's thinking of me right now with the same light heart. She wished she could tell him thank you. Just that. Just because such a small thing had made her step so lightly. It's exhilarating when you have pleasure and no responsibility. How old was that kid? Not as tall as Daryl, but probably a lot older. Still, a lot younger than herself.

Koko suddenly thought of Jesse. That night after he'd come back from dinner with his mother, he'd asked Koko, "How come it's OK for me to live here with you and Daddy, but not with Mom and her boyfriend? I even ate asparagus, and I *hate* asparagus. I can't go on like this. What should I do?"

Koko had shrugged and said, "Why don't you try liking asparagus?"

"You don't understand. I hate asparagus. You know that, don't you?"

"What would your mom say if you left it?"

"Nothing."

"So what's the problem?"

Jesse started to get mad at Koko for not involving herself in the conversation.

"I'm not saying that asparagus is the problem. I'm not saying that at all."

"I know." There was no strength in her words. She looked at Jesse.

He gave a small sigh and then squared his shoulders. "Hey, Koko. Can we talk?"

"Anytime. You want to sit down?"

Jesse pulled out a chair and faced her shyly. His hair had been carefully picked, very unusual for him, and even his shirt had been ironed. His usual clothes—that is, the cool stuff—had been replaced with what a child wears when he's trying his best to be accepted into the world of adults. He really is trying, Koko thought, feeling a stab of jealousy.

"So how was dinner? Did your mom bring along her boyfriend?"

Jesse nodded.

"What sort of person is he? Handsome?"

"Kind of. He seems like a nice guy."

"That's good, isn't it?"

"Koko." Jesse folded his hands and looked at her. Koko was startled; it wasn't the gesture of a child.

"There have been many times when I've been mad at you since we started living together. You and Daddy fight all the time. Every day I wonder why I was born into this environment. That goes for the way I'm being raised, too."

"Don't get mouthy, Jesse."

"Well, you guys do buy me what I want to a certain extent, and I can play all I want with my friends. I appreciate your not being strict with me. In those things, I do get my own way. But that's not what I want to talk about. It's like this. When Mom introduced me to that guy, she said that as long as it was all right with me, I could move in with them anytime. But even though I'm fed up with living with you, I told her I couldn't do that. I have this feeling that even though I'm always mad at Daddy and you, I can't escape. If I moved in with Mom and that guy, I wouldn't know what I could get mad at. Her boyfriend is a nice guy, but I couldn't live with them. What I want to know is, why is that so?"

"I can't answer that, Jesse. You make me mad all the time too, ever since we started living together. But even so, I'd get mad if you moved out. Hey, don't you ever hate your mom for not taking care of you at all? Don't you think that's awful of her? I know it's kind of a harsh question."

"She's my mother. Mothers make their kids suffer. But I still love her. Maybe I should love you too, but I do love Mom and Daddy. Why can't they get back together again? I guess my being here doesn't have much meaning to them, huh? I can't believe Mom likes that guy more than my dad."

Koko felt keenly that she had to give Jesse some sort of answer. But she didn't know what to say. It was irresponsible even to attempt to explain the love between a man and a woman.

"I think they both tried to make it work in the beginning. These things can't be helped."

"Does trying to make it work mean fighting right in front of me? They'd yell at each other every day, ever since I can remember. And after all that, then what? She finds another man and runs off. My sorry butt was left out there in the cold. And you know what she says? That boyfriend of hers is different from Daddy because he's a college graduate. But why do I have to eat my asparagus when I'm with him just because the guy graduated from college? I don't get it. So that made me think there's lots of stuff I get mad at, living with you and Daddy, but it's better for me to be somewhere where I *can* get mad. . . . I want to know, Koko, aren't there any relationships that absolutely never break up? Isn't there anything solid?"

That was Koko's question too. She was starting to feel worn out by the search for an answer. Maybe there was only one true happiness to be had. But if you had to lose so much trying to pin it down, maybe it was best to give up. Maybe it was better to settle for the little things close at hand. Thinking this didn't make it any easier to do, though.

Jesse was looking at her. He was waiting for an answer he could understand and accept. Koko broke into a cold sweat. She was horrified to realize that though she had lived so much longer than Jesse, she hadn't yet developed any ability to explain life's vicissitudes.

"So you're saying you'd rather live with me and your dad than with your mom and her boyfriend?"

Jesse nodded ambiguously. Koko could see his confusion. A clear "yes" here would mean choosing his father over his mother.

"I wonder if that has to do with me versus your mom's boyfriend. Or maybe it's the difference between your dad and your mom."

"I don't know. Probably it has to do with you versus Mom's boyfriend. But I don't think I can live alone any more with just Daddy or with just Mom. Neither of them can take care of me alone. There are lots of people who could, but those two can't. I think just having me around would be enough to keep them from being happy."

"That's not true, Jesse. I don't think it's so hard for a parent to raise a child."

"That's what I'm saying, Koko. But that's exactly what those two can't do. It doesn't have anything to do with money, either. I've pretty much known they can't deal with raising me ever since I was little. It's too bad. When I was little I used to be scared, wondering what'd happen to me if they split up. I'm not scared anymore. I just wonder why it has to be this way."

"You sound really troubled."

Jesse looked at Koko over his laced fingers, his elbows on the table. There was no trace of his usual animosity toward her in his eyes. He looks almost like a gentleman, she thought. Maybe a child becomes a little more of an adult each time he turns to someone in all seriousness. If that's so, then maybe I've never grown up. When it comes down to it, Rick is the first man I've been really serious about.

Koko sighed, and Jesse shot her a reproving look.

"Nobody will give me an answer. That's why I'm asking you, and all you do is sigh. I guess it's something I have to figure out by myself."

"I'm sorry. But maybe you do. The only thing I can say is this: I don't have a right to influence your choice between living with your daddy or your mom."

"Even if it means choosing between you and Mom's boyfriend?"

"Yes. As long as I want to live with your daddy, that is."

"Don't you have a self?"

Koko looked up, surprised.

"Daddy, Daddy, Daddy! Everything's about Daddy. If he doesn't come home, you mope around the apartment; if he comes home drunk, you get mad. I deal with *my* problems, why can't you deal with yours?"

"Wait a minute. Don't you go talking to me like that."

"I'll say what I have to. You love Daddy. It's simple, isn't it? I love Daddy and Mom myself. I need them both, but they don't need me. Can you understand how that makes me feel?"

Koko felt the blood rushing in her ears. She struggled to get hold of herself. Jesse continued.

"I totally know already. I know even if I kick you out they're not going to get back together and take care of me. They're so full of themselves they don't give a shit about how I might feel. I don't have to be told that. When things are like this, the only people who'll help are outsiders like you. You do think about me, don't you, Koko? I'm part of your life, aren't I? When you cook, you always automatically make food for three. That means you're thinking about me, right?"

When he put it that way, Koko was forced to admit that she did think about him. But her cooking three portions was as much from habit as anything else. Even though Koko was always hoping Jesse would open up to her, one part of her kept pushing him away. She lived in constant fear that her cooking for three had some deeper meaning. And yet she longed for Rick to see their life together as having a significance beyond a string of petty details.

"Do you like me?" Jesse lowered his eyes as though ashamed of his own question.

"I don't think it's a question of liking or not liking. I don't know what it is."

"Same goes for me. That's how I feel about you. I hate it, though."

"I'm sorry, Jesse."

Jesse shook his head. A quiet resignation descended upon the pair. It was a new feeling for both of them. Jesse put an elbow on the table and rested his forehead on his hand.

"You and I, we're kind of similar, huh?" Jesse said.

"I never thought so before, but I guess you're right."

Their eyes met and they shrugged simultaneously. At that, they both started laughing. They could look each other full in the face without embarrassment. They weren't particularly happy, and they weren't having fun, but they were getting somewhere.

"Mom looked OK. And she looked like she was having fun. But that's only because she had a guy with her. When I see her alone, she always looks unhappy. Daddy's different. He's always the same."

That's because Rick knows that being with a woman doesn't make him a complete person, Koko thought. He knows that trying to give something means taking something away.

"I don't mind living with you, Jesse," she said. Maybe sometimes I get mad, but it's no big deal."

"Thanks. But when I think that you're here basically because of Daddy, I get nervous. It's OK now, but after a while there won't be anyone around to look after me."

"Don't say that. Your parents are both in good health."

"It's not a question of my parents being healthy. Maybe you don't understand."

"There's that mouth again."

"Maybe so. But I really think you don't understand. And I don't understand how you feel."

"Let's wait on it. I'm sure something will change."

"So you're saying that while we wait we'll be in the same place, huh?"

Jesse stood up. Koko half rose. She was just about to sit down again when he kissed her on the cheek.

"Good night, Koko."

They had said good night to each other many times, but it had never been accompanied by a kiss before. Koko was speechless.

As if in contrast to her consternation, Jesse was perfectly calm. "Wake me up at seven," he said, and went back to his room. He was so natural that Koko had to wonder why she herself was so flustered. People who lived together kissed each other good night all the time. She wished she could kiss Jesse back easily, and with joy.

There's something similar about Jesse's good-night kiss and Randy's letter, Koko thought, opening the letter up again. They're both so natural. And they both gave her such pleasure.

She'd go to Ray's soon and see what happened. Koko didn't think of it as anything more than a little treat to look forward to. It didn't occur to her that what kept prompting her to open Randy's letter was the will to save herself.

THAT WEEKEND, Koko put on bright lipstick to seal in her high spirits. She was embarrassed to be so excited about going out. There was no reason to hide her happiness, but she felt that showing this much joy at something so simple was proof of how dreary her everyday life was.

Rick shaved while Koko chose a dress. Jesse was watching her with great interest.

"What time're you guys coming back?"

"I don't know. But it doesn't matter, does it? You don't need a baby-sitter anymore."

Jesse shrugged. Koko peered into the mirror and carefully put on her earrings.

"Hmm," she said. "Do you think these should be bigger, Jesse?"

"I think they're fine."

"You'd probably say that about anything." Koko looked at him in the mirror and laughed.

"It doesn't matter what I think, does it?"

"Of course it does. You're sulking because you have to stay home. That's it, isn't it?"

"You gotta be kidding. Daryl'll probably come over. You two go and have a good time."

Koko looked at Jesse over her shoulder. She had put on a deep rose-colored lipstick. Her lips looked moist. Jesse couldn't help thinking she looked totally different from when she was home alone with him. Seeing her like this, he understood she wasn't a "mother" type.

"You're going to be with Daddy, aren't you? What are you getting so dressed up for? Seems like a waste of effort."

"Why?"

"Well, you and Daddy live together. You see each other looking pretty awful. Frizzy hair, trashed sweats—the whole bit."

"I want to show everybody how happy I am with your daddy. And of course I'd like to get some compliments from him. He hasn't seen me dressed up in a long time. But—"

Koko halted. But what? Rick would surely say something nice about her appearance before they left the apartment, or perhaps over dinner. But there was no telling what would happen once Rick started drinking. So often liquor would cloud his eyes until he didn't see her. She couldn't be sure she'd still be registering in Rick's eyes by the end of the evening.

"Don't worry, Koko. I don't think Daddy will get as drunk as usual tonight, not with you with him."

"Could it be you're a little worried about me, Jesse? If you are, then thanks. I appreciate it."

Jesse reddened. Koko laughed and dabbed perfume behind her ears and onto the backs of her knees.

"Why do you put perfume there?"

"Perfume is something you put in hidden places. Where the eyes don't reach."

"Oh."

"The nose takes over where the eyes leave off."

"Do men do that, too?"

"No! Men can go ahead and splash their cologne any old

place. Women's eyes are so penetrating, there's no use trying to hide anything from them."

While the two were talking, Rick came back to the bedroom. His chin and cheeks were neatly shaven. He seemed to be in a good mood.

"Ready to go? Hey, Jesse, get your shoes off the bed. Mmm, baby, you smell good. Let's have a drink and get this show on the road."

"You'd better not drink so much tonight, Daddy. You're driving to midtown, aren't you?"

"Man, you two act like a couple of old 'fraidy cats at me having a drink."

Jesse and Koko exchanged glances. Here was one thing that held them together. They had a common anxiety and, because of it, they'd long ceased their childish squabbling.

"I'll make us both one," Koko said. "Will gin and tonic be all right?"

She went to the kitchen. Jesse could see her legs through the slit of her dress. He wondered if his father would really notice the perfume down there. He thought it highly unlikely. Koko's wasting her time, he thought. If Daddy could notice perfume behind the knees, he wouldn't be going out to bars like he did.

"Hey, Daddy. You and Mom aren't gonna to be getting back together, are you?"

"I don't think so."

"Are you gonna marry Koko?"

"I don't know yet."

"Her friend says Koko's pretty hot. She says Koko's the type men like."

"Don't talk shit, boy. Go to your room. You're not done with your homework yet, are you?"

Jesse wrinkled his nose and jumped off the bed. He went to his room, grumbling about how his father only brought up homework when he wanted to get rid of him. Turning on the radio in his room, he sat thinking. He remembered how abandoned he'd felt when his parents left him with a baby-sitter and went out by themselves. He'd bawl helplessly. That was when his parents used to go off arm in arm. They got along then. After a while they started going out separately. Jesse stopped crying then. There were nights when there wasn't even a baby-sitter. Jesse didn't care. He'd lie, not stirring, in his bed in the middle of the night and stare at the ceiling. He never thought that he was unhappy. He just wished they'd hurry up and put an end to their misery. He never thought that end would be a divorce.

Jesse thought he handled himself pretty well compared to other children. He couldn't touch Daryl, of course, but at least he didn't bawl, grumble all the time, or cling to anyone like children from normal families did. Children who had everything.

Jesse couldn't settle down. It'd been so long since his dad and Koko had gone out together for a night on the town. He wasn't sad or lonely. After all, he was all grown up now. And he really felt sorry for Koko. Those two weren't doing very well. The thought made him restless. Seeing Koko and his dad together didn't make him feel abandoned anymore. He felt the need to plug up the emptiness that an absence of feeling had left.

Jesse went out into the kitchen. Koko and Rick were laughing at the table, drinking gin and tonics. They sat with their backs straight, different from usual. They looked like they were getting along well. But that was only a danger signal to Jesse. Koko's eyes were already shining. They became more transparent as he looked, brittle and fragile as glass.

She's happy, Jesse thought. She doesn't regret anything. His feelings toward Koko had undergone a change recently. Of course, she still made him mad sometimes, but what made him mad was different from before. Sometimes, when he looked at her, Jesse couldn't help but think of Koko as a little kid easily taken advantage of by others. You do that and you're gonna end up the loser, he'd say to her silently, over and over. His father could look like a nice guy, but he was downright selfish. On the surface, Koko looked like the self-ish one. But she really wasn't. Jesse understood now that being unselfish was not necessarily a good thing.

"What time you guys coming back?"

Koko laughed at the question. "I don't know. But you never ask that. Why tonight?"

"No reason. It's just that you two haven't been out together in a long time."

"Daryl can come over, but don't stay up too late," Rick said. Koko took that as a signal and stood up. Her glass was empty. The one gin and tonic had loosened her hair a little and removed the excess lipstick. She looked very beautiful, Jesse thought.

Rick seemed flustered at Koko's action. He had barely started on his second gin and tonic. He hesitated a moment, glass in hand, then drained the contents all at once. He tipped the empty glass to his mouth again and again, as if to taste the gin smell left on the ice.

Listening to the sound of the ice, Jesse looked at Koko and Rick in turn. His father was pathetic. Before all the fun began he was trying to lick the alcohol off some ice cubes. He seemed to think that if he let any trace of it get away, he wouldn't have any more that whole night.

Looking at Rick, Koko's face clouded for an instant. But she put on a smile and ignored what he was doing. They put on their freshly polished shoes at the front door and compli-mented each other on how they looked. Jesse thought they went well together. They both smelled faintly of gin and they both had the same smile on their faces.

"I'll call later to see how you're doing," Koko said, looking over her shoulder to check the seam of her stocking. The femininity of the gesture startled Jesse, but Rick didn't seem to notice anything. He was absorbed in the mirror on the wall, comb in hand. Jesse felt strangely anxious.

"Don't forget to do your homework," Rick said.

"Say hi to Daryl," Koko said.

The two went out. Jesse could hear their voices going down the hall. He shot the bolt and put the chain on, muttering "Good luck" after them.

JESSE SEEMED different to Koko after that weekend. She didn't say anything. Nor did she ask him anything. But just as Jesse could tell from Koko's manner that something had happened between her and his father that night, Koko could sense that something in Jesse had changed.

Koko wasn't about to ask him what had happened. Jesse wanted to talk to her, and wished he could do so as casually as Daryl talked to older women. He couldn't talk to his mother or father about such things. They'd forget about their own mistakes and focus on his: the ones he made or was about to make. Jesse knew that with something like this, far from being angry, Koko would be an ally. If, that is, he could find a way to let her in on it.

Maybe he could bring it up like this:

"Hey, Koko, you probably noticed my girl stayed over the other night. Let's keep it quiet from Dad, OK? You know what a hassle 'rents can be."

Or maybe he could say:

"My girlfriend came over the other night and we went to bed early; didn't hear you guys come in at all. So what time *did* you two get in?"

Jesse sighed. He couldn't say it. What prevented him was the certainty that something was weighing on Koko's mind.

His father and Koko hadn't come home together that night. Koko had come back by herself, crying. She'd glanced into his room and then shut herself into her own. She was so done in, she couldn't have said anything even if she'd noticed Tracy's blond hair hanging over my bed, Jesse thought.

The next morning, after he'd snuck Tracy out, Jesse went to the kitchen for some water and spotted Koko's high heels in the trash under the sink. They were in terrible shape. One heel had come off and the leather of both was cruelly scraped. Lifting them up, Jesse saw the stockings that Koko, the image of an adult woman, had inspected the previous night before going out. They were now in shreds.

Ever so carefully, Jesse opened Koko's bedroom door. She's not dead, is she? he thought. He was afraid he would find her in a pool of blood. But far from being murdered, Koko was lying face down, fast asleep. Relieved, Jesse shut the door, but his heart was hammering. Something had happened.

Whenever Koko thought of that night, goose bumps of rage would rise on her arms. In essence, that was the night she learned beyond a shadow of a doubt that once Rick had liquor in him he didn't need her. It was as if she'd put on her favorite dress and gone out with him just to learn that lesson.

Dinner had gone well. They'd ordered champagne cocktails to start, talked and laughed as they carefully went over the menu. The man at the next table kept looking at Koko admiringly, to Rick's vexation. Koko felt it was just like the dinners out they used to have when they first met. Their food came, and they shared a bottle of wine. Rick was in a good mood, laughing a lot. He's such a sweet man. He does love me, Koko said to herself over and over, as though it were some new discovery.

Koko finally had what she'd wanted for so long. It was incredible, she thought. She knew she was looking good; happiness poured elegance all over her. The attentiveness of the man she loved enfolded her gently and straightened her back like a hand. This is what I needed, Koko thought.

"I wonder why I feel so wonderful when I'm with you. I can't imagine feeling this way with anyone else."

Helping himself to the seafood appetizer, Rick looked up at Koko and smiled. He too felt that this free and easy space could only be created with Koko. Rick couldn't imagine not having her around. The best thing about her was that she didn't bitch all the time like some women. He couldn't bring himself to think that this good-hearted woman might someday leave him. And yet he couldn't imagine her staying with him forever.

Koko used the L-word easily. She'd jump right in there and say it: "I love you." Rick would look at her, amazed. She'd be beaming rapturously, as if she had a mouthful of chocolate, and out it would come: "I love you." Rick and his ex-wife weren't used to loving. They could count the number of times they used the word "love" on their fingers. And, of course, when they really needed to use it, they forgot all about it.

"What should I do? What should I do? I wonder if it's all right to be so happy tonight."

"You make it sound like every other night is awful."

"No, but when you're not with me I get lonely."

Rick stretched out a hand and touched Koko's cheek. She needed him so much. It was a relief. At the very least, he wouldn't be lonely any time soon. She was very dear to him. And he felt so sorry for everything he'd done to her. He knew well that the things he did hurt her. Sometimes he thought it'd be best to simply put an end to everything. Something in him made him crazy, made him choose stupid fleeting pleasures over this woman who clearly loved him. He didn't think about it, it just sort of happened. Love to him was always one step away from raw fear.

Rick couldn't begin to explain his feelings. He didn't understand that if, for him, fear came before love, it was because he himself had put it there. His sisters didn't have that fear. His older brother didn't seem to either. Only Rick. His childhood had been one sad incident after another, but he couldn't explain the whys and wherefores of what had made him into the man he was now.

Watching Koko talking, her cheeks flushed, Rick had to admit he felt restored. He wished he could make her happy, but at the same time he felt like saying "what the fuck" and chucking the whole thing. Was making her happy going to make him happy? Fuck that shit.

Rick thought that happiness was something you won all at once, like a slot machine jackpot. He didn't know it was something you had to work at, day in and day out, building it up a little at a time. Rick had no way of knowing these things because he'd never had enough happiness around him to get used to it.

"Hey, Rick, what do you think I want more than anything?"

"I don't know."

"What I want is a normal life."

"What do you mean by normal?"

"A life where people worry about each other."

Rick laughed. "How about saying something bigger, like money or a good career? You're a funny woman."

"You don't understand at all. I'm talking about the hardest thing there is to get. Things like money, a career, a big house—"

"'Scuse me." Rick called a waiter over to ask for the check. "I'm no good at that kind of talk. Save it for your screwball friends. They probably like that kind of stuff. Talkin' about dreams and ideals and all. I'm not like that. All I'm thinkin' on is the food and drink that's right in front of my face. And let me tell you something you might not know: most people in this world are like me."

"Maybe so. But dreams and ideals are born even out of the cheeseburger and beer sitting in front of you."

"I see. That's an interesting way to look at it. But you know, Koko, I'd appreciate it if you'd lay off that kind of thing around me. I can't work up any concern for anything other than things that will actually happen and their results."

Koko chewed on her lip. She could feel the anger start to rise, but she killed it. She knew her tendency to be emotional irritated Rick and often led to terrible fights.

Tonight of all nights she had to love him lightly, Koko thought, sipping her drink at the club they went to after dinner. Her effort was paying off. Rick was in an expansive mood. Downing one drink after another of hard liquor, he kissed her again and again, laughing all the while. Koko returned his kisses with heartfelt words and gestures of affection. And then the moment came when Rick's kisses suddenly felt mechanical. Koko looked up at him. Rick seemed stiff as he straightened his tie. He finished off his drink in a single gulp. A line appeared between his eyebrows as he lit a cigarette and raised his hand. He's going to order another drink, Koko thought, as he motioned the waiter. Rick's eyes had turned leaden, and he was no longer paying any attention to Koko.

"Rick, did I say something wrong?"

"Uh-uh. Why?"

He emptied yet another drink as he spoke and ordered the next. Koko simply stared at him, flabbergasted. What the hell is going on? Their evening had hardly begun. She hadn't done anything to set him off, and here he was, trying to forget she was with him. Rick gave her another kiss. He kissed her again and again, as if it was his duty to do so.

Koko's eyes filled with tears. Rick was beyond seeing them. He'd forgotten all about the "special evening" that Koko had so looked forward to. He was drinking like it was any other night. Only his lips remembered, swooping down onto hers time and time again like a woodpecker on a tree. There was no love in the gesture. Her lipstick was getting stamped all around her lips. I'll have to go to the bathroom and fix it, Koko thought, but she didn't get up from her chair. If I leave him, even for a few minutes, there's no telling what'll happen. The thought astonished her. She'd lost all faith in him.

Koko had often worried where Rick might go when he was drunk, but it'd never occurred to her what he might do with what sort of woman those nights he was out by himself. These were kisses a man might give to any nameless, faceless companion.

She'd made a mistake to come. Nothing about this Rick made her feel she should be here. Koko looked down at her dress in a daze. They hadn't been sitting there long. Her perfume was emanating from her warm body, and she was thinking how the scent's best time was being wasted. Rick's friendly expression had disappeared. He looked like an absolute stranger. Koko lit a cigarette, then froze. I've seen that look on his face once before, she thought. When it came to her, she was aghast. He looked the way he had the first time they'd met at the club. Someone who didn't know him would think Rick's expression and gestures were signs of being merely relaxed, not drunk. When she'd met him then, she'd been a party girl who took passion for passion.

Rick had gone back to being what he was before. Koko couldn't go back. Surely they'd been building something little by little, every day they were together. How could he be hunting around in the cracks and crevices of the night as if what they had together was nothing? And while she was still by his side, no less.

A couple who knew Rick came up and said hello. Rick clapped the man on the shoulder and gave the woman a kiss on the cheek. Koko stood up, feeling she had to say something. The couple merely glanced at her and moved on.

"Are they friends of yours?" Koko asked.

"Uh-huh."

"Why didn't you introduce me?"

Rick raised his eyebrows as if surprised and looked at Koko. It was as though she'd said something absurdly inappropriate. Koko sat down again. Rick said he was going to get a drink at the bar and left. Koko watched his retreating figure. He was a stranger. A number of people called out to him, and he returned their greetings affably. There was even a woman who whispered something into his ear. Koko understood that Rick had stepped into his own world the moment they'd entered this club.

"Are you here alone?"

Standing in front of her was a young man, grinning widely. Koko was sitting at a table with two glasses on it. Any fool could see she was not alone. And yet this guy was trying to pick her up. He guessed Rick was not her lover.

"I'm sorry, but I'm with my boyfriend."

"You're kidding. That guy? The one who was sitting here? He's at the bar talking to a woman, and it doesn't look platonic to me."

"I don't see how that's any of your business."

The man left, annoyed at Koko's chilliness. She didn't despise herself for the situation she found herself in, she just felt very, very lonely. She began to see that while she'd been erecting a wall around the two of them to guard their love, Rick had been busy on the other side tearing it down.

Rick came back, glass in hand, and was disgusted to find Koko sitting straight up, staring ahead, tears trailing down her cheeks. Her face was devoid of expression, and the dim light picked out the luster of her tears.

"What's with you?"

"You don't know?" Koko's lips crooked into a derisive smile.

"No, I don't. What is it now?"

"It's everything."

"If you're gonna cry, do it in the bathroom. People will see you here."

Koko looked at Rick. She struggled to put everything into her eyes. If she could look at him with all those feelings, surely he'd understand how lonely she felt. Rick averted his eyes. She could see he felt like screaming, *This is not what I want!*

The two had sat facing each other for a while when Rick brought his glass to his lips almost savagely. Koko watched him quietly. *He looks afraid,* she thought. She felt strangely triumphant. But it was a lonely triumph. She was the one looking, and he the one looking away. He couldn't look her in the eye, she thought. She had to be practically writhing in pain to get him to look at her, only to have him look away again. Maybe the relationship she thought they had was no more than a phantom. Whatever love existed between them, their feelings for each other only met in fleeting instants. Rick would try to kill those moments with silence, while Koko would grab at them so eagerly she'd crush them. Koko understood at last.

She raised her hand and motioned a waiter to order a drink. Seeing her gesture, Rick felt he had to say something.

He opened his mouth, but then stopped. The taste of alcohol was so much better than this strained atmosphere. He emptied the remainder of his drink and armed himself with a fresh one.

It was 2 A.M. when the two emerged unsteadily from the club. The air outside was warm. The music from the club followed them as they walked along. The two had the illusion that their dim shadows stretched forever before them into the distance.

Koko lowered herself heavily onto the passenger seat of the car. Her temples were throbbing from the liquor, and her eyes kept filling up. If only it'd rain, she thought, I could cry all I want and the rain would hide it.

Rick started the car without a word. No matter how drunk he got, he never lost control of the car. Rick knew that alcohol was exacting a toll on his life expectancy, but there was nothing he could do about it. There were too many things out there he couldn't face sober.

Koko gazed out the window, looking at the streetwalkers they passed. Those women are selling their bodies, and maybe I'm trying to sell Rick my love. If that's so, where's the justice? she wondered. I'm giving my love, he won't pay up with his. But she felt instantly ashamed. Love was not a business transaction; she despised herself for sinking so low.

Rick looked perfectly normal beside her. You couldn't see his hatefulness. But Koko knew that if she stretched a hand out to touch him, he'd thrust it away. As they reached uptown, Rick lit a cigarette and spoke.

"You sure drank a lot tonight."

"Uh-huh. I'm drunk. Sorry, huh?"

"That's OK. I'll make sure you get all the way home."

Koko looked at him disbelievingly.

"Make sure I get home! What do you mean by that? Are you going to drop me off and go somewhere?"

Rick didn't reply.

"Rick!" she shouted. "We're going back to *your* house. The one *we* live in, right? Isn't that right? What do you mean, you're going to make sure I get home?"

"It means I will take you all the way to the door of the apartment."

Koko grabbed the emergency brake. The car screeched to a stop. Rick was thrown forward, bumping his forehead on the windshield. Koko was thrown against the dashboard, but still she held on to the brake. Thoroughly disgusted, Rick peeled her hand off and shoved it over to the passenger side as if he were throwing it away.

"You wanna get us killed?"

"No. I just wanted to stop the car."

"If it weren't the middle of the night, we would've been dead for sure."

"Rick. I want to be with you. I want to spend tonight *with* you. If you want to drink, you can drink at home. If you get totally smashed, I'll take care of you. Tonight is a special night for me."

Rick clucked his tongue in disgust and started the engine again. This time Koko grabbed at the keys.

"What do you think you're doing?" Rick grabbed Koko's wrist and twisted it. Scowling, Koko threw off his hand.

"What's going on? You go out with me and it's such a hardship you have to go out again and get yourself a drink to recover from the trauma? I'm your woman. Are you saying you can't even enjoy your own woman's company to the end of the evening and then take her to bed? All I want right now is to fall asleep with *you*, with your arms around me. And you're going to go off to meet someone else, is that it? I'm not enough for you? So you're going to get the difference from another woman? You can't. There's no way. There isn't a woman alive who can love you the way I do."

"I can't talk to you."

Koko sagged against the seat. Her mind was blank with shock. She couldn't understand what made him like this. Koko looked at the side of Rick's face. He'd started the car again and they were moving. His beard was neatly shaven. Something close to hatred rose up in Koko at the sight of that clean, smooth jawline. Her reason snapped, and this time she grabbed the steering wheel. Rick shouted and pushed her away.

The next thing Koko knew, they were in front of the apartment building and Rick was dragging her from the car. The drunkenness had evaporated; her mind was perfectly clear. She didn't, however, feel like getting up.

"If you're awake, stand up and walk on your own."

Rick was getting mad. He'd pulled Koko from the passenger seat, but she merely lay on the sidewalk with her eyes open. She wasn't crying. She didn't feel like fighting anymore. She lay in a daze, her cheek resting on the ground.

"Do you love me?" she asked in a tiny voice.

"Yes, I love you. As long as you don't ask that. Why don't you give it a rest and get up already? You want me to drag you in?"

"Whatever. I don't care. It's not like there's a bed or anyone waiting for me. It doesn't matter where I sleep; it's all the same."

Rick grunted with annoyance. He grabbed Koko's wrists and began to pull her into the building.

"Shit. If a cop sees me now, he'll think I'm moving a stiff."

Koko's dress was being ruined, dragged along the sidewalk, but she was beyond caring. The dress had failed to do what it was supposed to do back at the club.

Rick dragged her into the elevator and all the way to the front door of the apartment.

"You have the key, right?" he said. "If you don't, get Jesse to let you in."

"I'm asking you again: are you going to go somewhere and leave me here no matter what? Is there some reason why you have to do that?"

Rick looked down at Koko. There was something close to hatred in his eyes.

"Yes, there is."

"Is there someone you want to see?"

"There's a woman I *don't* want to see. That's you, Koko."

"Oh." Koko closed her eyes. The tears came finally, and began coursing down her cheeks.

"There's only one woman I *want* to see: that's you. And you're also the one woman I *don't* want to see. I don't care anymore, Koko. You hear me, woman? I don't give a fuck."

Koko heard the elevator doors open, and the sound of his footsteps disappeared. And that's how the weekend she'd so looked forward to ended. She lay there for a while, shaking with sobs. Eventually, she got up unsteadily and opened the door. She was tired. She'd sleep. I feel the same way you do, Rick, she told him silently. I don't give a fuck.

Rick did not come back that night.

AFTER THE NEW WEEK had started and she'd calmed down, Koko could think about Jesse. She hadn't been able to imagine Jesse on a date with a girl, but now the knowledge that he'd spent the night with one didn't faze her a bit. That kid had taken on a whole new shitload of problems. Looked at that way, it was almost laughable. Daryl was one thing. If it were Daryl, it would seem a perfectly normal sequence of events, but the thought of Jesse having sex with a girl was very strange. Koko even wondered if the kid could pull it off. If she were her usual self, Koko would've liked to sit down and listen to his story. She would have patiently given him any advice he might need. But she was so tired.

Rick didn't say a word about that night. To anyone but Jesse it looked like everything was the same as usual. But Koko and Rick couldn't hide anything from Jesse. He sensed something had happened. All three knew something was going on, but no one said anything. So long as no one spoke, there would be no peace in the house.

Koko sensed Jesse hanging around her, wanting to say something. She'd been waiting a long time for this to happen, but now she couldn't take him up on his overtures. Jesse was considerate of Koko. He knew something was eating at her, so he left her to her thoughts. It was almost like a lover's triangle. While one side seemed ready to break up, the other seemed about to draw closer.

Jesse was the first to hazard an approach. He went to Koko's room and managed with difficulty to get out these words: "Koko, uh . . . if you're . . . uh . . . feeling lonely . . . you want . . . maybe I should call Greggory or somethin'?"

Koko looked up. She searched Jesse's face.

"Why would you say that?"

"Why? Well . . . I can understand how women feel."

"My goodness." Koko shrugged, feigning ignorance.

"You know what I mean." Rubbing his face, Jesse sat down and crossed his legs. His feet have gotten so big, Koko thought.

"What size are your feet?"

"Ten."

"Wow! That's incredible! That's an adult size."

"Uh-huh."

The two looked at each other and laughed. Koko's usual smile finally made an appearance.

Koko looked at Jesse, and—it was strange—she could feel her eyes soften as she looked at him. This was someone she could be herself with. The realization made her happy. The tension she felt toward Jesse ever since she met him had at some point melted away, leaving no residue. Maybe she'd finally gotten used to him. Or perhaps Jesse was able to accept her now because he'd had some experience of his own with women. Whatever it was, he wasn't rubbing Koko the wrong way anymore. He sat before her now, looking concerned, just like a good friend would—one she didn't have to put on company manners for, one who'd leave her alone except for when she really needed him.

The closer two friends are, the more frank they are with each other about their wants and needs. Needs remains hidden in good times but surface when things get bad. Then one friend whispers to the other, who's going through the rough spot, "If you're going to use me, now's the time."

Koko and her friends helped each other get through hard times. They would tell each other, "You can enjoy the good times by yourself, but I don't want to hear of you trying to get through the bad ones on your own, you hear?" Koko believed this sort of friendship could only be found among adults, so it was a surprise to find it in Jesse. He looked at her not the way a kid would look at his father's girlfriend but the way a full-fledged adult would look at a friend in need.

"Hey, can I ask you something?" Jesse leaned forward. Like anyone asking a personal question, his voice took on a conspiratorial tone.

Koko shrugged and nodded.

"It seems Daddy isn't coming back until morning a lot. Something going on?"

"He's always stayed out a lot, Jesse."

Jesse made a face. "Come on, Koko. That's not what I'm talking about. It's not about him staying out all night to drink. You know what I'm getting at, don't you?"

"Ha, ha, ha, so you noticed, huh? You're right. Before, Rick used to not come home until morning because he was out drinking all night, but now it looks different. He's going out to stay over at someone else's."

"It's not something to laugh about, Koko. What's going on? Aren't you going to try and stop him? Before, you used to cry and tell him not to go, didn't you? And when he went anyway, you'd rag on his butt when he got back."

"There's nothing to do except laugh. I don't like it, but there's nothing I can do except laugh."

"Why?"

"We've crossed a line. After this, the relationship is just going to get worse and worse."

"You don't love him anymore?"

"Don't be stupid. Of course I love him. That's why I can't reach any kind of decision even though things are like they are. I don't want to live in a situation where I have no connection to him at all. The thing I'm most regretful about is that we won't be able to be friends if we break up. We're both in too deep to come out with anything like a friendship between us."

"What are you and I going to be if you break up?"

Koko looked at Jesse, surprised. "Hold on, now. Nothing to get so worked up over. You're jumping to conclusions, aren't you?"

There was sweat on Jesse's forehead. Koko reached out and wiped it away with a thumb.

"I forgot to turn on the air conditioner."

"Koko! Who cares about the air conditioner? Are you guys going to break up? That's what I want to know!"

"Is it so important?"

Jesse searched Koko's face. Her faint smile made his blood run cold. Up until recently, Rick would come home smashed, Koko would carry on, Jesse'd sigh, and that was that. Those were the facts of life. Jesse might get disgusted, but he'd never been frightened. He'd never seriously thought that Koko and Rick might really break up.

"What happened that night?"

"Nothing." Koko's voice was dry. "I simply confirmed what I'd been suspecting all along. The two of us can't have fun with each other anymore. We both know now that we should stop forcing the issue and trying to make like we're a couple. No need to go on getting in each other's face."

"But you're still living together."

"That's only because we're stuck. I don't have the energy to move out right now. And when I'm really ready to go, Rick's not going to have the energy to stop me."

"I don't get it."

"Oh, really? I thought you said you can understand how women feel."

Jesse didn't know what to say. His face twisted like a child struggling to say something but unable to form the words.

"Was Tracy good?"

"That's not what we're talking about here, is it?"

"It's nice to make love, isn't it?"

"Uh-huh. I mean, *no*! Look, I—"

"Just make sure you're careful with your contraceptives."

"Koko! I want to talk about you and my father!"

"We don't do anything. I'm not even on the pill. But we still can't make a kid."

"I'm not asking about that!"

"We still have sex. But it's no use. I can't get into it. Something changed that night. I know we'd been waiting for something like that to happen for an awful long time. Now that it's happened, we both feel it's a great weight off our shoulders."

"Is Daddy sleeping with another woman?"

"I don't know. Probably. I haven't asked him."

"Are you sleeping with another man?"

Koko laughed dryly. "No. Maybe I should try it," she said.

Jesse was angry at Koko for not answering him seriously. As he thought about what he'd asked her, a strange realization came to him. He'd come to think of Koko as belonging to his father. To Jesse, the idea of Koko going to bed with another man made him feel like a small, defenseless child. He felt very clearly that he was losing something.

"So what were we?"

"You mean, you and me?"

"You and Daddy and me."

Koko thought about it for a while and then said apologetically, "Well . . ."

"I thought we were solid. But we weren't, were we?"

Solid. Koko turned the word over in her mind. That's what she'd wanted them to be, too. She'd hoped to make this child a part of her life from the moment she'd first seen his sleeping face.

"Jesse, right now I really don't know what I should do. So I can't answer your question. No matter how I explain Rick and me, there's no way you could understand. You haven't had any experience."

"Is it something you have to have experience to understand?"

"Yes. It's not something I would wish on anybody, but most people go through it."

"You mean the bitterness of love?"

"Where'd you get that line? No, it's more like being fed up. It's how you feel when you're giving everything you can and getting nothing in return."

Koko fell silent. Looking at the forlorn expression on her face, Jesse felt sorry for her. Something about Koko at that moment made him forget his own problems and think about the pitiable situation she was in.

"Hey, Koko."

She looked up.

"I guess I'm a nice guy after all."

"Why do you say that?"

"Because just now I was worrying about you."

"That's because you're in love. Not so long ago, you were a mean little brat," Koko said flatly, much to Jesse's chagrin. But her next words made him feel warm inside. "Thanks, though, Jesse. I'd say that what you're trying to do for me now is—well, what a good friend would do."

THE NEXT TIME Koko saw Randy, it was sheer coincidence. At first, she had no idea who he was when he walked past her, turning around to face her with a huge grin. She'd completely forgotten about Randy's letter. She looked at this smiling boy suspiciously. He spread his hands wide, perplexed.

"You didn't like my letter?"

"Huh?"

"Aw, man. You don't even remember it."

"You were kidding, right?"

"No way. Truth is, I hate writing letters. I wouldn't write one as a joke."

Randy leaned against a wire fence enclosing a basketball court. Koko twined her fingers around the wire mesh. Some kids were playing two on two to the shouts of a number of onlookers. The evening sun shone down on Koko and Randy, and their shadows stretched far into the court.

"You're done with work?" Randy asked.

"Uh-huh. I'm on my way to the subway."

"Am I bothering you?"

The sun glanced off Randy's wire-rimmed glasses, and Koko looked down, dazzled. In his long baggy shorts, he looked like a little boy. His feet were stuck in a pair of moccasins and his ankles looked strangely large above them.

"That backpack of yours looks pretty flat. Are you really a student?"

Randy laughed aloud. "If I really am a student, will you talk to me?"

"Maybe. I don't talk to punks."

"OK, then. I'll make sure I don't cut any classes. Or go to too many parties. And I'll work hard at my job. By the way, I've got my eye on you."

"I know."

"That's pretty cool of you. Your friend said she doesn't think it'll work either. But I intend to make it work."

"You're a weird kid."

"I'm sorry."

"But you look good."

"Really?"

"You're cute."

Randy grinned.

"But I'm not interested."

"Why?"

"Why are we standing here talking in this fucking heat? Why did you stop me? You wanna play 'Boy Meets Girl'? Let me tell you: I have no interest in basketball. If you want to get a woman, use your head. I'm a lot older than you."

Randy hung his head at Koko's tongue-lashing, but he didn't look particularly unhappy. The people watching the basketball game seemed amused by their exchange and kept looking at them. Koko, suddenly embarrassed, buttoned up.

"I want to know you," Randy said.

Koko was silent.

"That's all I want!" Randy said loudly.

A man who'd been listening to them called out, "Don't be so cold, babe!"

Koko looked at Randy, more embarrassed than ever. He looked down, struggling mightily to keep from laughing. Koko had no idea why she was doing this. This boy had come running after her and now they stood here, talking. He was happily telling her he wanted to get to know her. Flustered, she was thinking she mustn't let him do anything of the kind. But why was she in such a hurry to go home? Rick wasn't there, waiting. Jesse was sure to be out with Tracy. What was stopping her from talking to this kid? She'd just go back to the apartment to sit there alone.

"Randy."

"You remembered my name."

"So, Randy, let's go somewhere. It's too hot to stand out here. And would you mind dropping the performance?"

They walked to the East Village. The whole time, Randy chattered on about how he was a student, how he lived nearby with a friend of his, how his family lived in Queens Village, how he'd had his eye on Koko for quite some time.

They arrived at a café, where a waiter gave Randy a meaningful look.

"That's my roommate. He goes to the same school," Randy said.

They sat down at a table outside. Koko ordered a gin and tonic, Randy, a beer. The sun was going down and a cool breeze played with the tablecloth. The long twilight had begun. It was the time of day when Koko would usually lapse into loneliness. She hadn't had any fun at twilight for ages. Ordinarily, she would have invited a friend out for a drink, but she hadn't done that for a while. She couldn't face her good friends. She knew they sensed her trouble and would push her to talk.

"I feel like I'm dreaming, sitting here like this with you," Randy said.

"I didn't feel like standing. And all of sudden I didn't feel like going home."

"Why? Because you decided I'm cute?"

Koko laughed. The smell of gin tickled her nose. I love liquor, she thought.

"Do you mind if I smoke?" she asked.

"It's bad for the health."

"But it's good for the spirit."

Randy found matches and tried to light Koko's cigarette for her. The breeze kept blowing out the flame, so Koko put both her hands around his to shelter it as she reached over with her cigarette.

"You're not married, are you," Randy said.

"What makes you say that?"

"You're not wearing a ring."

"Well, I do have a boyfriend."

"It's not going well, is it?"

"Oh, yeah? And why do you say that?"

"Your nail polish has grown out a bit."

Koko looked down at her fingernails. There was indeed a little space at the bottom of them. She looked at Randy. He shrugged apologetically. Koko was impressed.

"Usually, when a woman's nails look like that, it means she knows how to use nail polish, but she hasn't been complimented on it for a long time."

"Are you feeling sorry for me? Or do you intend to worm your way into the crack?"

"I can't say I feel sorry for you. And I do mean to pick up where your boyfriend left off. If it was me and you changed your nail polish, I'd compliment you on it right away."

"Why me?"

"I told you, I've had my eye on you."

"Why?"

"I don't know. I thought I'd like to know you. You're different from other women."

"How am I different?"

"I don't know. Someone I like comes in and orders coffee. Do you need a reason? It's just how I feel. Tell me something."

"What?"

"Your name."

"Koko."

"Koko." Randy said it over and over. And then, as if to stop himself, he hurriedly drank his beer.

Koko stared hard at her fingernails. Suddenly Randy reached out and, to Koko's surprise, bunched her fingertips up and kissed them. Koko did not resist.

"Do you like that man?" Randy asked, looking at her sideways. Koko hesitated for a moment before answering.

"I hate him."

"So why are you with him?"

"I love him."

Randy looked a bit put out. This guy is completely straightforward, Koko thought. And he has a good heart.

"Why're you working at Ray's? If you're a college kid, surely you can find a better job than that."

"I like it, and the manager's a friend of mine, so there're advantages to working there."

"What do you study at school?"

"English lit."

Remembering his letter, Koko snorted. "I never would've guessed from that letter of yours."

"I wrote it like that on purpose. It was a literary device intended to charm you."

Long ago, Koko had so enjoyed summer evenings. It had been too long since she'd sat with a man at twilight, enjoying a drink, talking about nothing in particular. I feel good, Koko thought. But this goodness I feel only makes my life with Rick more palpably miserable.

"Are you thinking about something sad?"

"Why do you say that?"

"Because there were tears in your eyes."

"It's the alcohol." Koko laughed, not knowing what else to do.

Randy looked her up and down, putting his elbows on the table and cupping his chin in the heels of his hands. There wasn't a hint of reserve in his manner, which didn't bother Koko at all. Randy had nothing to do with the part of her heart that held passion and love; moreover, she could find nothing in his eyes other than the desire to get to know her. Randy was one of those rare people whose honesty was so artlessly frank it was a form of sophistication.

"You look like you're a good person," Koko said.

"People become good people when they're with someone they like."

"There are people who can't do that."

They each ordered another drink, deciding to go home when they finished it. Randy made Koko laugh by sipping his beer little by little through a straw to make it last longer. They exchanged phone numbers and parted.

When she got back, the apartment was empty. Jesse had left a note saying he'd gone to a movie with Tracy. That was the only thing waiting for her. She balled his note up and threw it away. She turned off the little lamp she'd read the note by and sat vacantly in the dark apartment for a while. Then, as if she'd remembered something, she got up and opened the refrigerator. The light inside went on, illuminating her face. She stood in front of the open refrigerator awhile, the cold air pressing against her legs. Bending down to get the open bottle of wine, she felt a wave of dizziness. She wondered fearfully if she was sick. I am sick, she thought. I can't stand up. I need somebody's help. I'm cold. I need somebody to stand me up and make me warm.

○

THERE WERE two things she found impossible to accept: the fact that she hated Rick and the fact that she couldn't forget him.

"I'm sorry, I'm sorry, I'm sorry." She spoke the words aloud over and over. "As soon as I get these handcuffs off, I'm going to leave you. I'm in love with Randy." The words alone made her feel capable of accomplishing anything.

But the same blood ran through her and Rick's veins; she felt it. She knew she could break it off, and that it was now or never. But then what? Would Rick's blood continue to flow forever in some corner of her heart? Somehow, she imagined, what he felt would always be what she felt, and she would never be able to begin a new life of her own, not in a true sense.

She would have liked to take a pair of pliers and move her heart to a different place. She didn't want her heart forever dragging its heels, teardrops squeezing out one by one—that sort of love did no one any good. That's why he did this. He put handcuffs on her because he couldn't stand the way she looked at him. And yet maybe this was the last kind thing he'd done for her. She'd made him do it. They'd both made her into the prisoner she was now.

She stretched her leg out toward the box of hairpins. They were on the corner of the dresser. If she could just . . . her leg trembled. She bumped the box, and it fell down the side of the dresser, scattering the pins on its way. She'd never get to them now.

Evening approached. Randy's probably waiting for me, a worried look on his face, she thought. I can't throw away what I want to reject, and I can't get my hands around what I want to keep.

You can bury love, and your memories become fossils. But she knew that despair would always be shared. She and Rick had been born and raised in different places; they were two completely different people. So why in hell's name was this strange feeling of connection tucked away in her heart, she asked herself, there to erupt whenever she remembered it? It was as if they were of the same flesh. And yet they couldn't even be friends.

IT WAS EVENING, and Koko had finished her work for the day. She was getting ready to go when Sue came up, hung an arm over Koko's shoulder, and laughed knowingly.

"I saw you guys."

"Saw who?"

"You're going with that pizza boy, aren't you?"

"Don't call him that. You know his name."

"Randy, yeah. I thought you were making yourself scarce lately—so that's the reason! You should've told me. When did all this happen?"

"I'm not *going* with him. We just hang out at a café in the evenings and talk. He's a student. He works at night sometimes, too."

"Oh, yeah? Workin' for drink money at that café?"

"Yeah, *right*. I pay once every three times . . . they're not 'dates.' He's a lot younger than me. Which reminds me, what happened to *your* young lover, huh? You two break up already?"

Sue laughed, examining her lipstick in a mirror.

"No way. We're swimming right along. He's *adorable*, simply out of this world."

"Oh, yeah?"

"Don't you think younger men are better?"

"Well . . ." Running a brush though her hair, Koko thought about Randy. That first night, after they'd sat together for a drink, Randy had called Koko at the apartment. Sorry, she'd told him, I'm not interested in going out with you. After another minute or two of conversation he'd blurted out, "Try seeing me ten times. I'll change your life—

you'll see." She'd laughed uproariously, saying, "You're one weird kid." He merely replied, "I want to make you laugh."

Koko had been taken aback by the gravity in his voice. She knew for certain she'd sleep well that night; his words had gone straight into her heart, like hot cocoa on a cold morning. And so she'd seen him the next day. And the next. They'd meet at the same café and pass some time talking about nothing in particular. Randy didn't try to hit on her. He was a well-behaved conversational partner, a perfect gentleman.

Nights had become hard for Koko. She couldn't stand being alone after nightfall. She made a ritual of returning to the apartment, making dinner for Jesse, then sitting in the empty kitchen or bedroom, not moving a muscle, contemplating the fact that she was, in reality, all alone. She'd engage in the usual banter with Jesse. When Rick put in an infrequent appearance, she'd calmly exchange some words with him too. Then the recognition of just how alone she was would overwhelm her, and she'd break into a cold, greasy sweat.

SOMETIMES RICK would wonder why she was so strangely quiet and push her down onto the bed. Koko would circle her arms around his back and let him do whatever he wanted. And she would return his kisses, as if by reflex. What's with her? Rick thought a couple of times. But he never attempted to make her explain herself. Her life had slipped into an uneventful routine. Rick believed that something had snapped inside her, just as in himself.

To rouse himself out of his black funks, he'd been drinking hard again. He couldn't get through the day anymore, either physically or mentally, without liquor. Putting the cooking wine to his lips, Rick was seized by a cheerless feeling, but once he'd drunk it the feeling was gone. He'd beaten it. He had no idea what he was beating, but he had to beat it.

Sometimes Rick would remember his father, who'd left his mother years ago to live in North Carolina. Since he was small, Rick had lived in dread of becoming like him: always drunk, hitting his mother. Even now, Rick still despised him.

Rick got his first car when he was seventeen. None of the guys at school had their own car yet. It was a birthday present and he was crazy with happiness over it. It was in that car that he first got to touch a girl's body.

And all at once he loved the same father he'd despised. What a stupid, simple thing, he thought. You could love a person just because he bought you a car. Is this what it means to be human? he wondered. The thought drained all the strength from him. What a goddamn easy thing it is, he thought, to love someone.

It looked to him like Jesse and Koko were getting along fine. Rick was relieved. And she'd stopped bawling and yelling, at least in front of him. But Rick couldn't shake a feeling of foreboding. He knew intuitively that something was wrong, and to erase the knowledge he took another pull on his whiskey. He felt sorry for his mom. But he'd been able to love that daddy of his after one car. That was all it took. Things were like that.

"DID YOU hear that thunder? I'm soaked."

Robin came flying into the gallery from the street, as Koko looked at the weather anxiously. It was raining hard. She wondered what Randy would do; he couldn't be sitting at their usual outdoor table in this weather.

"Hey, Robin, can I give you a piece of advice?" said Sue, an impish look on her face.

"What?"

"Don't you think you oughta drop some weight? How 'bout taking up smoking, huh? It'll be good for your diet—I highly recommend it."

Robin's face reddened. She was always preaching about the harmful effects of cigarettes to Sue and Koko, who both smoked. They didn't exactly appreciate hearing about it.

"And you'll get a much better workout taking a nice young boy to bed than going to the gym. Don't you think so, Koko?"

Koko glanced at the two and grinned. It was their habit to tease chubby Robin about her weight. But tonight she didn't feel like joining in. Randy was waiting at the café. That was all she could think about: shooting the breeze with Randy. That brief span of time with him was the one part of her day she couldn't do without. She had to see him.

"Sue, I'm leaving now."

"It's still raining."

"It's down to a drizzle," Koko replied, spraying the backs of her knees with perfume. The sweet scent enveloped her, smelling better even than the rain. The thought of how good she smelled made Koko blush.

"You're gonna go meet Junior?"

Sue winked and Koko smiled.

"What's that supposed to mean?" asked Robin.

"Why don't you smoke a cigarette or somethin' and think on it, kiddo."

Koko dashed into the rain, Sue's laughter ringing behind her.

As she walked down Broadway, the rain slowed nearly to a stop. Koko headed for the café, running her fingers through her wet hair. She was walking faster than usual. He's not getting wet, so why am I walking so fast? she wondered. You'd think I was hurrying to deliver an umbrella to him, when I'm the one getting wet. He wasn't a lover, she thought, he wasn't really a friend. Their lives didn't intersect at all. He was this strange person who, all by himself, had jumped straight into her heart. Randy was . . . well, Randy was Randy. She had no words to describe the odd place he occupied in her life. All I know, she thought, is he's waiting for me right now; I am the sole reason he's at that café.

The tables outside were drenched from the rain, their tablecloths had been removed. Koko was about to push open the door and go in when she noticed Randy. Standing under the eaves of the café to stay dry, he was smiling away at her. He had both hands stuck in his pants pockets and he was looking at her, his head tilted. The rain had made big dark blotches on his brown loafers.

Koko stood there for a long moment, gazing at him. Oh, how I've missed you! The words came to her lips on their own, startling her. She had to fight against saying them aloud. How could she say such a thing to someone she saw only yesterday?

"Come over here," said Randy.

Koko nodded. The rain had started up again. Squeals rose from people crossing the street who started to run.

"Come over here," Randy said again. "You won't get wet if you come here."

She didn't have time to think. She bounded over a large puddle to where he was, and he immediately caught her in his arms. She didn't know what she was doing, but she wasn't confused either: this was the most natural thing in the world. She put her arms around him as far as they would go. He was too big for her to hold, so he held her instead. The rain became louder and the light over the bar inside the café went on. Randy pushed her wet hair away from her neck and put his hand there. It was wet and cold. But his lips, when he kissed her, were warm. For a while, they stood there wordlessly and kissed.

Koko took off Randy's glasses. She had never seen his eyes from so close before. She could see herself reflected in them. He blinked, but her image remained. He couldn't see anything but her. She lowered her eyes and laid her head on his shoulder. He was kissing her hair. I am dear to him, she thought, near tears.

"You smell nice," Randy whispered into her ear.

"I put on perfume. I wonder why. It's daytime, but I put on a night scent."

"It's not night yet," Randy said.

"Yeah, you're right."

"But it will be soon."

The rain let up again, and a few feeble rays of the evening sun spilled out from between the clouds. Randy took some paper napkins out of his backpack and wiped two of the chairs in front of them.

"Wipe them all while you're at it," said his roommate, sticking his head out the door.

"Yeah, right. Why don't you make yourself useful and get us a Michelob and a gin and tonic?"

The roommate grunted and disappeared again. Randy followed him inside to get Koko an ashtray. She took a tiny mirror out of her bag and repaired her lipstick. Touching the red stick to her lips, she thought, I'm in love with that kid. Her lips were soft and full, and the bite marks that habitually marred them had disappeared.

"Hey! You're putting on lipstick? You don't need to."

"Why not?"

"I wanted to kiss you some more."

"You don't like the taste of lipstick?"

Randy shook his head and sat down. Koko looked at him

earnestly. A ray of sun glanced off his dangling gold earring and she squinched her eyebrows together, shutting one eye. At that, a droplet of rain still on her eyelash separated the ray into all the colors of the spectrum. And beyond the rainbow, Randy was laughing. Koko felt very warm. Sipping her gin and tonic, she thought how she loved the lifting of the rain, the setting sun, the smell of the gin—she loved it all. At that moment, everything around her was infused with a soft haze.

"I like the way you look when you smile."

Koko realized she'd been grinning since they sat down. Her hand flew to her mouth, a little embarrassed, and Randy looked at her with a satisfied air.

"Hey, we've started something, don't you think?" he said, removing the cigarette she'd put between her lips and kissing her there. Then he replaced the cigarette and lit it for her while she wondered absently, and with vague trepidation, what it meant to be starting something.

WHEN KOKO got back to the apartment that night, Jesse was in his room on the phone. Koko couldn't help hearing his raised voice as he argued with Tracy, who was jealous; another girl, it seemed, liked Jesse. He kept repeating, "What'm I supposed to do?"

Koko chuckled at the thought of Jesse at the center of a love triangle. She started to prepare dinner with the memory of Randy keeping her heart warm. His kiss, the strength of his arms around her, made Koko sigh. This is no time to be washing vegetables, she chided herself.

She sat down with a glass of wine. Its mellow warmth spread quickly through her body, and she felt so good her vision seemed to darken for a moment. What am I going to do? She didn't know how to calm herself. She couldn't go around bouncing up and down like some idiot who'd never been in love before.

Koko heard Jesse slam the phone down. The next instant, it was ringing again.

"Koko, telephone!" he shouted.

Koko jumped up and grabbed the kitchen phone. It was Randy. As Koko spoke to him, Jesse came in and watched her closely. Koko pulled the cord into the dining area and motioned him to go away. Jesse started to boil. Something was going on. Daddy's woman shouldn't be whispering and giggling into the phone like that with another man, he thought, enraged. Powerless to stop her, he could only shake.

After a while, Koko hung up the phone and, her cheeks still flushed, went back to fixing dinner. Jesse blocked her way.

"Was that your man?"

"What? Were you listening? That's a bad habit. It has nothing to do with you anyway."

Suddenly the doorbell rang. Koko pushed the intercom button and Greggory's voice came through the speaker.

"Oh, so that's it." Glaring at Koko, Jesse pressed the intercom and told Greggory to come up. Realizing Jesse's misunderstanding, Koko was about to explain when the door opened and a smiling Greggory walked in. Jesse flew at him, arms swinging.

Surprised, Greggory jumped aside. Jesse lost his balance and fell to the floor. He glared up at Greggory.

"What's going on here? What did I do to deserve this?" Bewildered, Greggory spread his hands wide and looked at Koko.

"I'm sorry. It's not your fault. The kid is mixed up. Jesse, that call just now wasn't from Greggory."

Shocked, Jesse looked at Koko and Greggory in turn. His anger left him. There was nothing between these two except ordinary, comfortable friendship, nothing for him to be anxious about.

"C'mon, get up. I don't know what's going on, but you shouldn't go around hitting people out of the blue." Before Greggory could help Jesse up, he'd already stood shakily on his own. He looked down at the ground, shamefaced.

"I'm sorry. I was sure you were coming here to see Koko while my dad's not here," he said.

Greggory's laugh was embarrassed as he mussed Jesse's hair.

"Well, that is the truth. I saw the car wasn't around outside, so I knew Rick wasn't home. I wasn't exactly waiting for the opportunity, but I did take advantage of it. I wanted to talk to Koko; it's true. But that doesn't mean I want to start up anything with her. I wanted to talk to her as a friend, that's all."

"Even though you guys are man and woman?"

"It doesn't always go that way when men and women get together. There are things that a good woman friend understands that no guy friend can."

"But you used to be Koko's man."

Greggory glanced at Koko. How did Jesse find that out anyway? Koko was irked, but at the same time she wanted to know what had made Jesse so upset.

"Yes, that's true. But now I like her for other reasons than when we were together. She's very, very important to me. But it's totally different from what your father and Koko have with each other. You see what I'm saying?"

Jesse thought he could understand. He remembered Koko saying that if she broke up with his father, they wouldn't even be able to be friends. It was strange, he thought, but maybe that's how it was when men and women loved one another too much. Love that became friendship when it ended was not so serious an illness; it could still turn into something else when it died.

"Koko and Daddy probably won't be like you two. Once they break up, that's it. I don't have any say in it."

Greggory rubbed Jesse's head again, gently this time.

"Why are you thinking about that? Koko's here, with you. She hasn't said anything about breaking up; she's right here. When you're talking about things between a man and a woman, only the two people directly involved know what's going on. Other people can try to figure it out, but they can't really know."

"But Koko has a boyfriend."

Koko and Greggory looked at each other. Koko's face was beet red, and though she searched for words, she could not think of a thing to say. It wasn't exactly true that she had a boyfriend, but it was true that she was in love.

"It's all over. Daddy and Koko are going to break up. I thought Koko was always going to be with Daddy even though he's the way he is, but now, all of a sudden, she's gone and dragged a man into it."

Koko's hand flew through the air and struck Jesse on the cheek. Greggory didn't have time to stop her. Koko didn't realize what she had done until she felt the stinging heat in her palm.

Jesse pressed his hand to his cheek wordlessly. Before, he would have flown at Koko and tried to return her blow in kind, but now he knew instinctively that a man is not supposed to hit a woman.

"You hit me because what I'm saying is the truth, didn't you?"

"And what's wrong with me going out with another man, huh? Is it wrong for me to do what your father's doing? Are you saying I should stay at home by myself? That I should be satisfied just cooking and cleaning? Who's going to make *me* happy? Can't *I* choose? There is nothing in this house to make me happy, not one thing."

"Then get out."

Jesse's eyes widened as if in shock at his own words. He looked at Greggory fearfully.

"You don't mean that, Jesse," Greggory said. Jesse looked at the ground, chewing his lip. "If you don't mean it, you should apologize. If you don't, you'll regret it later."

"Daddy doesn't mean it either. He doesn't mean what he's doing. If Koko gets another man, he'll regret it for sure."

"I hear you, Jesse," Greggory said.

"I don't exactly know what's going on, but I don't like it. Koko getting another man is just plain wrong. Living here, in this house, and making out with another man . . . it's *wrong*."

"Do you like Koko that much?"

"Liking her or disliking her has nothing to do with it; I can't think of her being with any other man, is all. I can't imagine her sleeping with any other man than Daddy. I don't think anything of it when she and Daddy have sex in the next room, but if it were another man I couldn't stand it."

Greggory burst out laughing. Koko was red to her ears.

"Don't use that word!" she shouted.

"But that's what it is: sex, right?"

"I am not going to have sex in this house with any other man!"

Greggory was all but rolling on the floor with laughter. Koko and Jesse glared at him.

"I'm sorry," he said, "but you guys are something else. You two have the oddest relationship. You're not mother and son; you're not really friends. Jesse, what is Koko to you?"

Jesse, looking disgruntled, refused to answer Greggory's question. He went to his room, slamming the door behind him.

Koko sighed and told Greggory to have a seat. She went to the kitchen to make him a drink.

"Sorry you had to go through all that," she said. "It doesn't have anything to do with you. The kid's got himself a girlfriend now, and he's trying his best to keep up with it. He wants to be grown up about everything."

"He *is* almost grown up. It's a hard time for him. Too bad he can't be immunized against growing up. This is the time he can catch all kinds of problems, just like that. He looks pretty upset about you and Rick."

"He doesn't have any right to talk about me and Rick. I'm not his mother."

"But he seems to like you."

"Maybe. I think sometimes he worries about my well-being. But that's only because he's afraid for himself. He'd have a hard time if I moved out. I don't have the courage to leave now." Koko sighed. "It's weird. I feel like I can't live unless I know Rick is all right. I have to always make sure he's OK before I can do anything myself. I can't let him go."

"Even if you knew he'd be all right without you?"

Koko looked at him in shock. The thought had never occurred to her.

"He can't be alone! He wouldn't survive."

"How about if he had a woman who was better able to take care of him than you?"

"Impossible."

"Koko, don't you think you're a bit overconfident?"

"Overconfident? What do you mean by that? I know exactly what I can and cannot do."

"You're making a big mistake if you think you're the only

one who can take care of Rick. The truth is, you're scared stiff that some other woman is going to come along and take him away, aren't you? That's why you've convinced yourself that no other woman can understand Rick like you do. That's the only way you can explain why you can't leave Rick. But the truth is, you still don't want any other woman to have him. So, girl, what's it gonna be?"

Koko tried to put into words what it was her heart really wanted. Her throat grew dry, and still she couldn't think of how to say it. It pained Greggory to see her like this. That wonderful insouciance she'd had was gone. He waited patiently while she struggled to find the words.

"I just want to see that look on his face one more time . . . see him look happy that I'm with him. If we break up now, I'll never get to see that. I could push myself to leave Rick, but then all I'll remember of him is that pathetic shell of a man drinking his liquor. That's all I'll have! I can't bear to go on with that image torturing me."

"Why would you be tortured by it? How come you're not thinking of trying to forget it? You think he'll be lost without you, and you're using that as an excuse to not even give yourself a chance to forget."

Koko was silent.

"I'll be frank with you, Koko. *You are not doing anyone any good*."

The emphatic way he said it hurt Koko's feelings. For an instant she thought he was hateful, but it was absurd to hate Greggory.

"Was I wrong in how I loved him?" she asked in a small voice.

It wasn't the sort of question a grown-up woman would ask. Greggory thought Koko looked like a lost little girl.

"Probably," he said. "I'm sure Rick was wrong, too. It's

rare for two people to love each other exactly the way each needs to be loved, but with you guys it's pretty bad. Is Rick still drinking a lot?"

"It's gotten even worse. His body is, unfortunately, a lot stronger than his spirit. Even when he throws up, he goes and drinks some more. He can't seem to stop until he's completely smashed. So we only talk in the morning when he gets up, or right when he's started his drinking. All I want is to have a normal life together. Is that such an unbearable burden to lay on him?"

"It would be one thing if he recognized it as a burden, but I don't think he's aware of what he's feeling or doing."

"Well, then, it looks like all conditions are go for me to fall in love with another man." Koko smiled weakly.

"What kind of man is he?"

"A young boy. A sunny boy with not a care in the world. He seems to have been raised in a good home with a lot of love. There's no hatred in him. And when he feels love, he's able to express it."

"Do you like him?"

"I like him."

"You're not simply trying to get away from Rick?"

"No, I don't think so. I've been holding myself back to make sure it's not only that."

"I'm jealous."

"Why would you be jealous? That's silly. I only felt this way about Randy—that's his name—tonight. I'd forgotten what it's like to have this sort of warm feeling for a man. With Rick, the feeling of 'Why can't he understand me?' is always struggling with the feeling of 'No wonder he's sick of me.'" Koko smiled wryly. "There's proof for you of how far gone things are with us. I'm always trying my damnedest to avoid facing that fact, but meeting Randy forced me to see it. I've found that love can be a much simpler emotion than I'd thought, one that makes you like yourself. It's a primitive feeling. Something that comes from wanting to protect another person and be protected."

"Do you want to be with that other guy?"

"Yeah, I want to be with him."

"Are you going to break up with Rick?"

"If things keep going this way with Randy, I will. But it's not so easy to break up. It takes an incredible amount of energy to throw something away that's been going on for years."

"Does he know about Rick?"

"Yeah."

Greggory was relieved, but at the same time he felt frustration that a young man had come along to suck away the heavy loneliness that had been weighing on Koko's heart. Maybe adults think too much. Maybe, Greggory thought, love was what Koko said: a simple happiness.

"He's a good guy?"

Koko laughed. "Greg, this isn't like you. Why the third degree? You never used to be so cautious."

Greggory opened his mouth to reply, then froze, his gaze fixed on something behind her. Koko turned around. Jesse was standing behind her. Tears ran soundlessly down his cheeks.

Shocked, Koko stood up and put both hands on his shoulders to try and comfort him, but Jesse shook them off.

"You're gonna dump Daddy, aren't you? He's always loved you and me. He drinks all the time, but he's a good person. He messed up, is all. You can't put all the blame on him. What about *you*? If you'd be nice and smile once in a while, he wouldn't be like that."

"Jesse, that's what I want to do. But I'm not some kind of doll. I can't be smiling all the time."

Koko struggled to maintain her composure and speak

calmly. Jesse, on the other hand, was getting agitated by his own words. He started to cry openly. Greggory stood up and put his arm around the boy's shoulders. Jesse resisted at first, but then he leaned against Greggory and cried like a child.

"If only things could have stayed the way they were when you first came," Jesse said between sobs. "You guys used to stay up late every night, laughing like you were at a party. Don't you remember? You and Daddy used to sit here, smoking and drinking and having so much fun. It was like I wasn't even around. Don't you remember? You used to sit on Daddy's lap, looking so happy."

"Koko could be like that back then because she didn't really love you and your daddy," Greggory said, rubbing Jesse's back. "As soon as she started truly loving your daddy, he couldn't handle the *way* she loved him. It was just no good for him. But you know, the very thing that didn't work for him is Koko's way of loving. She wants to cook dinner for her man, sit down and eat it with him, look into his eyes, and talk about love. Maybe she was in too much of a rush, but that's all she wanted: simple things like that."

Jesse took a deep breath, but when he spoke again, there was still a tremble in his voice.

"Actually, that's what *I* wanted more than anything else."

Koko gave a strangled cry. Her hand flew to her mouth.

"But I knew," Jesse continued. "Koko's so stupid, she didn't see it. If Daddy could do what Koko wanted, Mom never would've left in the first place. Koko, you don't understand men at all. That young guy is goin' to use you up and throw you away like a tube of toothpaste."

"You're a smart kid, Jesse. Don't you think that maybe there might be other smart young men like yourself?" Greggory asked.

Jesse didn't have the words to express what was really on

his mind. He was utterly and completely confused, shocked to learn that somewhere along the way Koko had become an important part of his day-to-day life.

"Koko, are you really gonna leave?" he asked, his eyes still wet with tears. Ah, those eyes, Koko thought. She instinctively shook her head no. At that, Greggory felt like punching the wall. Koko had no idea, Greggory thought, what cruelty she wreaked with her kindness. To him, Koko was a completely different woman from the one he'd loved long ago. The untroubled innocence that used to be in her eyes was gone, and in its place lived a vague fear.

Greggory had to fight the urge to take her in his arms and hold her tight. Koko's appeal used to come from the confidence and control she exuded. Now her appeal lay in her vulnerability; she engendered in men a desire to protect her. Anxiety dwelt constantly in some part of her body, emphasizing her femininity. Now, even when she laughed, there was a sadness about her. This was Rick's creation, Greggory thought, one that had been several years in the making.

Jesse had stopped crying. He looked embarrassed for having bawled in front of Koko and Greggory like a little kid. Well, at least it didn't look as if Koko would be leaving this place very soon, he thought. But the realization that she wouldn't be there forever weighed heavily on him. He felt stupid for having thought she was different. He should've known by now that the start of something between a man and a woman is already the beginning of its end.

Koko took Jesse back to his room now that he felt better. She tucked him into bed, covering him up to his chin with the blankets.

"Hey, Koko," he said.

"What?"

"You're nice."

"Oh, my," Koko said with an embarrassed laugh.

"If you're not nice, you'll cut off all your ties with me."

Koko was silent.

"Ties are something you have to make by yourself, huh," he said.

She turned out the light without replying. Jesse asked her to tell Greggory he was sorry and closed his eyes.

Koko left the room and went back to where Greggory was sitting. He smiled at her.

"I don't know what I should do," Koko said.

"In that case, it's best not to do anything."

"I guess so. Hey, Greg, it's not like I'm doing anything I don't want to do."

"I know," said Greggory. He put both hands on Koko's cheeks and kissed her. Her face looked very pale in the light. Only her eyes were bright as she looked at him.

"Don't do that," she said.

"I'm sorry. But old boyfriends have a right to kiss without asking first."

Koko's laugh was low. Greggory felt as though he was realizing for the first time that he would never, ever sleep with this woman again.

THE FIRST TIME Koko visited Randy's apartment was an afternoon so hot steam seemed to be rising from the sidewalk. She dropped a quarter into a public phone on a crowded corner on 14th Street. She didn't think Randy would answer. She simply wanted to try calling him. She wanted to show herself that there was someone she could call in the middle of a weekend day for no reason at all. Hearing the voice of this person who was not a friend, who wasn't yet a lover, would seem like a gift from heaven.

Randy sounded sleepy when he picked up the phone. When he realized it was Koko on the line, he excitedly gave her the apartment's address. Koko wrote it down on the back of a deli receipt. The hand holding the pen was sweaty. She hung up and headed for 3rd Avenue.

Maybe she was depressed because it was so hot. Her lashes were a dark shadow that crossed her eyes each time she blinked. She trudged along, feeling unpleasantly sticky. She wanted to drop her tired body in some nice cool place and take a rest. That was all she could think of. Every now and then, the thought of Rick this morning at breakfast crossed her mind and made her unbearably agitated. Maybe this really was the end, she thought. She'd wanted to see Randy so much, but now her depression over Rick clung fast to her spirit and made it hard for her to keep putting one foot in front of the other. A feeling of desolation came over her when she thought of how Rick looked after having been with another woman. The tiny sprigs of her affection for Randy were no match for the huge weight of her attachment to Rick. She feared her feelings for Randy would be crushed under the heaviness of all those months and years of living with Rick.

When she got to the apartment, she was shaking with exhaustion. Randy had her lie down on the couch and made her drink cold Evian.

"Looks like you have heatstroke," he said.

"I think I walked too far."

"But you called from Fourteenth, right? That's less than ten blocks from here."

"Actually, I've been walking since early this morning," Koko said, closing her eyes. Randy simply gazed at her, not saying a word. She was the most pitiful thing he'd ever seen. With her legs thrown any which way, she looked utterly defenseless. He was supposed to work that night, but he called his friend and traded shifts. He passed the early afternoon beside Koko, flipping through magazines and listening to music, as she lay fast asleep. He could see just by looking at her how tired she was, and he was happy he could take care of her.

It took a moment for Koko to remember where she was when she woke up, but the sight of Randy's bare feet near her put her at ease. His eyes were on his magazine, and a radio played softly over the hum of the air conditioner. It was very much a young man's place. The room was small, and with a bicycle, stacks of magazines, barbells, and a jumble of sneakers it seemed tiny. Koko felt peaceful there, not lonely at all.

"Where's your roommate?"

Randy looked up from his magazine.

"James is at work. Are you feeling better?"

"Yes, thanks. I didn't think you'd be home. Don't you have school?"

"It's summer vacation."

"Oh."

Koko hadn't heard the words "summer vacation" for ages. She said them over and over to herself. They brought back so many sweet memories.

"That's nice. Summer vacation. I wish I could be a student again. Summers in New York are so hot."

"So what were you doing, walking around in the heat? You looked about to drop dead when you got here. . . . You don't have to tell me if you don't want to."

"OK, I won't."

Laughing, Randy got up and took a bottle of wine out of the refrigerator.

"I was surprised. I never thought you'd come over," he said.

"Am I in your way?"

"Are you kidding? I've been trying to think of how to advance our relationship to something a bit more than evening conversation partners. I don't know what happened, but whatever it was, I'm thankful."

"What an optimist you are."

Randy held out a large glass of wine. Koko took it in both hands, her fingers encircling his.

"Can I stay here for a while? Just for today," she said.

"Of course. You don't have to ask, Koko. You know how I feel about you."

"I'm lonely. Friends are no good at a time like this. They don't hold your hand, they don't kiss you; you can't ask them to hold you. Sometimes you need more than someone to talk to."

Randy came and sat beside her. He put an arm around her shoulder.

"Is this what you mean?"

Nodding, Koko let him kiss her. The moment she felt Randy's lips on her cheek, the tamped-down lid that covered her pain lifted, and she began to sob.

Randy had never had a woman cry in his arms before. He quietly rubbed her back and thought that when sadness floods a woman's heart, older ones look the same as younger ones. She was so dear to him. Fighting the urge to squeeze her tight, he made his arms into a protective shelter for her.

Koko cried for a while, but then started to feel self-conscious.

"Um . . . I'm done crying now."

Randy was at a loss. "Well, what'm I—" he stammered.

"I think I'll have a cigarette. Do you have an ashtray?"

Randy went to James's room and got the ashtray from the bedside table. Koko's tears were now completely dry, and she was smoking a cigarette as though nothing had happened. Randy was nonplussed.

"You're not going to cry anymore?"

"Nope. I feel kind of embarrassed, to've gone blubbering away in front of you. I didn't mean to put you through that. I'm sorry."

"It's nothing to apologize for! Shee-it. You're a weird one. You know I'm crazy about you."

"I've got so many things on my mind. I don't want to fall in love with you. Let's forget about what just happened, OK?"

"Yeah, but—"

"Sit down."

Troubled as he was, Randy sat down meekly next to Koko. She drank the wine and smiled at him.

"Thank you," she said. "I realize now that I needed to lean on you. I feel better. To tell you the truth, I've been wanting someone to lean on for a long time. And that someone turned out to be you. How about if I give you a brand-new kiss? Do you mind? This is one I'm giving you because I want to."

With that, Koko kissed him. With the sweetness of the wine tickling his nose, Randy felt for the first time Koko's desire for him. He had waited for so long; he was immediately giddy with the joy of it. It was the same for Koko. All at once, she was the one being kissed, and she couldn't catch her breath.

"This is awful," she said. "My heart is pounding."

"That must be because you're feeling something new," Randy said.

The radio played on and on, music from an FM station. As they kissed, Koko and Randy lost track of time. The only sign of its passage was the growing puddle of water around the glass of wine on the floor. Drops of condensation formed and dribbled coolly down its sides.

"Will you be my girl?" Randy whispered. "I'll never make

you cry. I may be younger than you, but I know love is something that should only make people happy."

Clutching Randy's shirt, Koko nodded once. It was like being a teenager again, she thought. Hadn't she done something like this back then? The love she had for Rick, so close to hatred, could go to hell as far as she was concerned.

Randy stood up and led Koko to his room. Stumbling over magazines and sneakers, Koko made her way to his bed. The western sun streamed in through the blinds, making a striped pattern on the sheets. The sun was setting, the time of day both of them loved most. Koko told Randy she was a little chilly, but instead of turning down the air conditioner, he enfolded her with his body.

"You're my baby now," he told her.

Koko heard the words as if she were in a dream. She could see Randy; she was touching him, but she was already thinking about what she would do if she lost him. Sorrow is so intricately bound to the birth of love, she thought. She opened her eyes wide and looked at Randy so that the newly born love within her would not have a chance to slip away. She kissed away the sweat on his brow; she bit his earlobe and traced the length of his backbone with her hand. His face and body would be etched so deeply into her that nothing would be able to take them away.

"I want your being here like this with me to make you happier than anything else in the world," Randy said, his voice husky. Koko was already wondering how she'd managed to live until now without being with him like this. She tried to smile, she was so happy, but all she could do was cry.

"Promise me one thing?" she said in a tiny voice.

"What?"

"That you'll never leave me. Promise me you'll always be with me."

"OK, I promise."

Koko knew there was no such thing as a promise between men and women. For her, there was no such thing as a past or a future in a relationship, only a series of nows piled up one upon another, and to ask for a promise only meant she loved this moment more than any other she could recall.

Koko treasured most the things that settled onto her, drifting down to her like leaves from a tree. It's started again at last, she thought. The joy of a simple love in which the pleasure of one becomes the pleasure of the other.

"I've never known a woman I've felt so in tune with. My intuition was right. I knew all about you from the first time I laid eyes on you."

"What did you know?"

Randy didn't answer. Koko didn't expect him to. Both of them already knew they would no longer be alone; each would always be thinking of the other.

Koko admired Randy's body, lit by the last rays of the sun. And Randy thought Koko was beautiful against the white sheets. She looked so vulnerable to him, a small figure all but buried in the waves of sheets. Brushing her hair from her eyes, he let his lips wander as he loved her with infinite care. Had he ever loved a girl so thoroughly? Randy didn't think so. He himself was surprised at the depth of his feelings for Koko. He gazed down at her peacefully sleeping and knew it was his duty to make sure she had a quiet place to rest.

When Koko woke up, she was alone. The sun had gone down and she could see light from the next room seeping through the crack under the door. Randy had gotten up not long before and was talking to James in the kitchen. Koko felt shy at hearing James's cheerful voice and Randy's triumphant one. She burrowed under the sheets.

They were talking about Koko. Randy was praising her to

the skies and James was teasing him. The conversation grew livelier, punctuated by the opening of beer cans. Her ears tickled with the sound of Randy's voice, and she reached for a cigarette.

Suddenly Koko remembered Rick and how lonely his departing figure always looked. For a long time now, Koko had only seen him leaving. Home wasn't a place for him to come back to anymore.

Koko pitied him. Rick had come to the end of their relationship without getting anything from it, and without knowing the joy of giving. "The end of our relationship." Koko muttered the words aloud. Maybe that's what Rick had been waiting for all this time. Koko was bewildered. She had no idea what she'd been doing in this affair that she was now, finally, trying to bring to a full stop. She was starting a new love with Randy, but thoughts of Rick made Koko want to scream. There were too many wounds in her heart to chalk up her whole relationship with Rick as one big mistake.

"Koko, are you awake?"

The door opened suddenly and Randy stuck his head in. Koko could see James's head bobbing up and down behind Randy, trying to see around him. She grabbed the sheets and covered herself up to her neck. James laughed and grinned at his roommate's new girlfriend. Koko told Randy she'd get dressed and be right out.

Pulling her clothes on, Koko peered into a large mirror over the dresser. Standing in the mirror, in that dim room, a radiant young woman looked tranquilly back at her. Her hair was a mess, but she felt pulled to the laughter of the two boys in the kitchen, so she simply ran her fingers through it and put on a little lipstick. Looking earnestly at that woman in the mirror, she made herself a promise: "I am never going back." At that, Randy's smell, which hung about the room like the radio's incessant FM music, seemed to intensify. It was as though he himself had walked up beside her. Koko leaned her forehead against the mirror. Randy's smell made her think of Rick's, which was still in her nose. That was the last thing she wanted to think about. But as painful as it was to remember it, it was already over. Koko said good-bye to that smell. It would never wrap itself around her again.

"Like I've been telling you, man"—Randy's incessant chatter continued—"I'm head over heels."

James laughed and looked at Koko. Grinning wryly, she drank her wine. There was no separate kitchen; it was simply part of the tiny living room. And there was no table. Instead, they opened up an ironing board to its lowest position and set their drinks and food on it. Randy was excitedly chewing on sunflower seeds. He looks like a squirrel, Koko thought. James seemed to always take up the role of listener with Randy, laughing at everything his friend said. He turned to Koko.

"What do you intend to do about your boyfriend?" he asked pointedly.

His roommate's abrupt question exasperated Randy, but there was no sarcasm in James's gray eyes. Koko felt her brow wrinkle with distress, but she answered honestly.

"We haven't broken up yet. But it's no use. I can't make it without Randy. I like him, and I want to be with him."

"What about the guy's son?" was James's next question.

"I want to start fresh with Randy. Up to now I've been thinking I have so many problems. But now I know the only problem I had was my heart. Rick's son already knows that. I want to help him, but there's nothing I can do. I always thought there were lots of things I could do, but that's not true. I didn't think I would fall in love with Randy, but now I need him. You can't control a person's heart. I'll tell Jesse

I'm in love. And I'll tell his father the same thing. I'm so happy I'm dizzy—that's what I'll say."

"Things might get complicated." Randy looked at Koko, his eyes serious. "I've been pretty selfish up until now. I don't want you to be thinking of what I want when you decide what to do."

"Thanks, Randy. I'm not. You don't have to worry. But your bed this afternoon—and everything else—was wonderful."

James let out a long, low whistle. Randy was terribly embarrassed. Koko looked at him, amused, as she helped herself to blueberries on the ironing board. Stretching out a hand, Koko popped a blueberry into Randy's mouth. He accepted it docilely and thanked her with his eyes. Those eyes waited expectantly for every move she made toward him. They were full of trust and confidence.

THE NEXT DAY Koko borrowed one of Randy's shirts and went straight to work in it. Sue came over to talk to her.

"I heard you didn't come home last night. So what's with the shirt? I didn't know you liked Ralph Lauren. I hear he's hot nowadays with young black guys."

"How do you know that?"

"I know all there is to know about what's going on with young men."

"No, not that. How do you know I didn't go home last night?"

"There's a missing person's report out on you."

Koko glared at Sue, annoyed. She laughed and put an arm around Koko's shoulder as if about to tell her a secret.

"Jesse was worried. It seems he went around with Daryl, looking for you. You know, Daryl looks pretty old, so he can get into places. They checked out the bars you might be at."

"How would Daryl know what bars I might be at?"

Sue merely grinned. "I can't stand it any longer," she said, groaning. "I gotta tell you, Koko." Sue confessed she was having an affair with Daryl.

"You gotta be kidding!" Koko tried to imagine that tall boy next to this friend of hers. "Oh, my God," she said, putting a hand to her forehead.

"It's nothing to be *that* surprised about. And it's not what you'd call on God for, either. Not for something like this, anyway."

"I give up."

"Why?"

"Do you know how old Daryl is? He's the same age as Jesse. It's unthinkable."

"Daryl's totally different from Jesse. He's far more adult, both in body and mind."

Koko didn't like what Sue's laugh suggested. "It seems you have no intention of feeling guilty about this. It's a sin, you know," she said.

"Why? Are you saying it's a sin for two people to fall in love? Sin, my ass."

"So what if Daryl's mother said some witch raped her son? What would you do then, huh?"

"I'd say that before I raped him, he put a hand up my skirt," Sue said calmly. Koko stared at her, aghast. Then the two began to laugh.

"So you think it's his fault because he asked for it. You're incorrigible," Koko said.

"Give me a break."

"I *really* give up. OK. So tell me. How did a married woman manage to seduce a high school boy?"

"That's what I've been dying to tell you. Ah, secret love is such agony."

"Secret love, my left foot. Come on, out with it."

Sue began her story.

"Do you remember that evening when you had the fight with Jesse at Ray's?"

Sue said she'd fallen for the grown-up youth who had been there with Jesse.

"So that's when it all started," Koko murmured.

"That's right."

Sue told Koko that Daryl gave her his phone number, and they began seeing each other. Sue didn't think a boy handing her a slip of paper and saying "Call me" would turn out to be so conservative, but they'd started *dating*. She hadn't done anything so orthodox in years, but it was nice. Sue's eyes were sparkling as she talked.

Koko felt let down. To her, marriage was something sacred, yet here was her friend, chattering away with absolutely no guilt about her extramarital affair. Still, Koko envied Sue's self-assurance, so different from her own self-doubt. Sue wasn't inviting heartache upon herself, and Koko had to hand it to her for that. But Koko felt Sue wasn't inviting any dizzying, all-consuming happiness either.

"So what're you going to do?" Koko asked. "You know this thing with Daryl isn't going to last forever. You're not the type to leave your husband, are you?"

"Love that you know won't last forever is the best kind! That's what makes it so exciting."

"Well, it's not for me."

Sue looked at Koko as though she were a little girl. Koko could see the sympathy in her eyes, and it hurt. She hated to think Sue might be worried about her.

"You should let up a little, Koko. That's your weak point, you know. I guess it's also your strong point, but it means you get all worked up over people."

"You mean I'm too serious?"

"Uh-huh. You expect too much from people. Love should only be one small part of your life, but you try to make it everything. It's very hard for a man to make a woman like you happy."

"I want to love a man with my whole being."

"But that means you have to have *his* whole being. No man can bear that. How about it? You think that pizza boy stands a chance?"

"I think he might. He knows how to give. He says love is a tool to make people happy. I think he loves me a lot. And I want to love him, too. But I can't."

"You'd better drop Rick like a hot potato, girlfriend."

"Don't say that. Oh, Sue, what'm I going to do? I was planning to tell him tonight about Randy, but I get shaky just thinking about it."

"Jesus, girl, I was all set to tell you about how much fun I've been having with Daryl, but now you've gone and got even me serious. Look here, a man who can't keep even one woman happy is no man."

"So what about a woman who can't keep herself to one man?"

Sue just winked and laughed. Koko passed up her invitation at the end of the day to have a couple of drinks—"Just the two of us, c'mon, it's been so long"—and turned her reluctant feet home. They felt so heavy.

When she opened the door to the apartment, a small black cat jumped out at her. Koko scooped it up. Jesse came out, laughing.

"Where did this come from?" she asked.

"Somebody gave it to me."

"Who?"

"Tracy's aunt."

The cat, hardly more than a kitten, lay comfortably in Koko's arms.

"Do you like him?"

Koko handed the cat to Jesse, nodding. It wouldn't do

any good to get attached to this cat now, she thought. She would have liked to bury her face in its soft black fur, but she held herself back. Jesse seemed to be in a good mood. Koko looked at him, trying to figure out what he was really thinking.

"His name is Ninja. From now on you and I will take turns feeding him every day. And taking care of the kitty litter. I'm going to have to go out and buy more kitty litter soon."

"Jesse, you know, I——"

"Tracy says the grocery store on the corner is no good. She says you have to go to the place across from the theater."

"Hey, I have to talk to you."

"She says there's all kinds of cat food there."

"Jesse!"

"And I got some leftover fish from a waitress at Sylvia's."

Koko decided to hold back what she had to say for a while. Jesse watched her fearfully as she headed for her room to change.

Koko had the strangest feeling upon entering the bedroom, after only one night away; this room had ceased to be the place for her to sleep. Koko stood in the doorway, looking at the unmade bed and the clothes flung on the floor any which way.

"Koko, you should play with Ninja," Jesse said, appearing behind her.

"I'm sorry, Jesse. I can't do that right now," Koko said quietly.

"OK." Jesse went back to his own room. He's anxious, she thought. He can guess what I'm going to do. But Koko couldn't help him now. The old familiar smells of this room couldn't hold her any longer. She thought about the many times she and Rick had created happiness in this room. "I can't say I was unhappy," Koko muttered, covering her face with both hands. "It's simply that this air is stale." Koko thought nothing was harder than building up the warmth that was necessary to keep two people together. Thoughts of Rick fell about her softly. She'd wanted to stay locked away forever in this room with him, just the two of them. In this sacred place, money, jewelry, anything material would have had no meaning, Koko thought. They would have known that most primitive state of being: two naked human beings possessing nothing but intangible love to save them. It was not to be.

Opening the closet, Koko took out enough clothing and shoes for work so that she wouldn't have to return for a while, and packed them into a suitcase. She'd intended to talk to Rick, but there was no telling when he'd be back. She feared she'd change her mind if she waited for him there, so she decided to go. Anyway, Rick would be drunk when he arrived, she told herself, and she didn't want him to be in an alcoholic haze the last time they talked.

Koko whirled through the room as if possessed, hurling underwear, accessories, perfume, and the like into the suitcase. There were three bottles of perfume. After hesitating for a few moments, she returned the one Rick liked to the dresser top. She knew such fine points of politesse only suffocated Rick, but she couldn't change herself now.

Suddenly, Koko heard the cat wail from Jesse's room. It was actually more a tortured shriek than a wail.

"Jesse, I'm coming in." She opened the door to Jesse's room. "What are you doing?"

"Nothing."

Jesse had the cat in an empty bucket and was trying to put a lid on it. Koko took the lid away from Jesse and picked up the terrified cat.

"What an awful thing to do, trying to stuff a cat into such a small space! He's not a fish."

"But he was trying to run away."

"That doesn't mean you go and put him into a bucket! Poor thing. He's so scared he's shaking. Jesse, cats and fish are two different things."

"Of course they are."

"So then, why—"

Jesse glowered at Koko. "It's none of your business, is it? This is my cat. I told you, he was trying to run away, so I was showing him he wasn't supposed to do that."

Jesse tried to grab the cat from Koko's arms. The cat shrieked, jumped to the floor, and disappeared into Koko and Rick's room. Two scratches had appeared on Jesse's cheek, blood oozing from them.

"Are you OK?"

Koko reached out to touch Jesse's cheek, but he evaded her hand and wiped the blood away with his own hand.

"That cat is mine. It's up to me where I put it. He's the only thing I've got," Jesse said, his eyes on the floor.

Koko put her hands on his shoulders and turned him around to look at her. There was more fear in Jesse's eyes than in the cat's.

"That's my cat," he repeated. "I was the one who named him Ninja."

Unable to bear it any longer, Koko held the boy tight.

"But it's no use now. Ninja hates me. Hey, Koko, how come I don't have anything, huh? I don't have anything, do I?"

"You do," said Koko softly. "You have all sorts of things."

"I want something that moves. I want something that'll answer when I talk to it, something that'll laugh, that'll go wherever I go."

Koko didn't know what to say.

"Koko, are you going to leave?"

Koko tipped her head down once in a vague affirmation.

"Can I go with you?"

Koko was hard pressed for a reply. Jesse put an arm around her.

"I didn't mean it. I just wanted to see what it was like to say it."

"I'm sorry, Jesse."

"That's OK. I want to leave too," Jesse said quietly. "But I can't leave Daddy here alone. Koko, I finally understand. You feel the same way I do now. It's hard to leave, isn't it? There's nothing harder than to leave Daddy."

Koko could not keep from sobbing. Jesse rubbed her back quietly. Koko put her arms around Jesse, intending to hold him, but as he was several inches taller, it was more like he was holding her.

"You gonna come back?"

Koko looked up at Jesse and nodded.

"I want to be alone for a little while," she said. I'm planning on staying at a friend's place. I'll be back, of course. I can't break up with Rick without talking to him first."

Koko let herself be held by Jesse for a while. Somewhere along the way, he had become the person closest to her. And that was the way it should be.

"You can get hold of me through Sue," she said. "You know about her and Daryl, don't you?"

"He's crazy about her," said Jesse.

"What's wrong with that? The time to be crazy in love is when you're young. That's when it's fun."

"You're still young yourself, Koko."

"Thanks. But when you grow up, the hurt of loss kills the fun."

"Daddy's that way, too. That's why he's always trying to kill the fun right from the start."

Koko looked up at Jesse.

"You look kind of like a little kid, Koko," Jesse said.

"Shut up."

Koko blew her nose on the tissue Jesse handed her.

"Hey, Koko."

"Mm?"

"Do you know what I want more than anything?"

"I dunno. What?"

"A kid."

"Why?"

"If I had a kid, I'd take good care of it. I'd raise a terrific kid."

Wiping her tears, Koko giggled. Jesse shooed her back to her own room with an embarrassed grin. He was a bit flustered by the underwear strewn over her bed, but he helped pack the other things: a suit, some shirts and pants.

"You're making yourself into an accomplice."

Jesse chewed his lip at Koko's words.

"You know, Koko, I hate to be a pest, but I don't think anyone can look after Daddy except you."

Koko did not answer. She went to the kitchen and came back with two glasses of wine.

"Is this for me?" Jesse took the glass Koko handed him.

"I know you drink anyway."

Jesse laughed and Koko joined in.

"You'd better not go making a kid just yet."

"Don't worry. Daryl knows how to use contraceptives."

"Sue does too, of course."

They both snorted at that, then drank deeply of their wine. Ninja, who'd crept timidly out from under the bed, looked at them as though they were very strange indeed.

LUGGING HER SUITCASE, Koko took a bus downtown. When she got off, she headed for Larry's Tummy. The waiter recognized her. Koko ordered a vodka martini and asked if she could park her suitcase behind the bar. Then she went downstairs to the phone booth. After flipping through her address book for a few seconds, she dropped a quarter in and dialed the number to Buckey's place.

Buckey answered almost immediately, shrieking happily when he recognized Koko's voice on the line. Koko asked if it would be all right if she stayed the night.

"Of course! But why me? What about your new boyfriend?"

"I can't impose on him. He has a roommate."

"So you can impose on me?"

"Do you have a roommate?"

"Well, I do have a lover."

Koko stopped short. That possibility hadn't occurred to her. Buckey laughed softly as if to console her.

"You don't have to worry. I haven't seen you in ages, girl. I miss you. And I want to introduce you to my new boyfriend. Come right over."

"I'm at Larry's Tummy. Can you come pick me up?"

"Huh? That's pretty far. Don't you remember where I live?"

"I don't want to walk around here dragging a suitcase. Please, Buckey? Jump on Whoopi and come to my rescue. It won't take ten minutes."

Buckey complained a bit, but he wasn't serious. In fact, he was delighted to be the one Koko called when she was really in trouble. Before morning came and she had to face her usual day she needed not the man she was in love with, not her girlfriends, but him. Buckey told his lover he'd be back with a very important friend and went out, carrying Whoopi.

Back at her table, Koko downed her vodka martini in a single gulp and lit a cigarette. The back of her throat grew hot. She had at last crossed the line. She imagined Rick drunk, opening the door to their bedroom, seeing she was gone. Would he feel he had committed a grave error? Or, relieved, would he knock back another drink? And who in the world would wash his dirty underwear now? Maybe he'd do it himself, like the morning after she'd met him. She remembered two expressions on his face that day: joy at having met her and regret at having again started the inane drama of love when he knew from the start nothing would come of it. Rick was torn as to which way to go, so Koko had chosen for him. She must have been smiling then, full of confidence. Choose happiness, she'd thought, you can start fresh; everything will be different with me.

Koko put her forehead in her hand. "Idiot," she muttered, "to think I could've done that." She'd never known a man like Rick, who killed happiness before it began. And she didn't know that different people fall in love at different rates.

"Young girls are no good at playing the moody, tortured hero having a drink by himself."

Koko didn't have time to turn around. Buckey swept by her and seated himself across the table.

"One more of what this girl is having and a frozen margarita for me." The waiter left and Buckey reached out suddenly, putting both hands on Koko's cheeks. "Why so down, sweetie?"

"A man bubbling over a new lover is not going to understand what's going on with me."

Buckey laughed uproariously. Seeing that mirthful face, Koko immediately felt better. She understood why she'd picked him to call. He was good at letting people lean on him without acting too worried about them. What Koko needed now more than anything was a warm, uncritical heart like Buckey's.

"So, Buckey, you have a lover? That was pretty fast, wasn't it?"

"He's just started living with me; it's only been—um, three weeks. He's fantastic. And he's an artist."

"He wouldn't be Italian by any chance, would he?"

Buckey shrugged, grinning. Koko snorted.

"I give up. You'll never change."

"You could give me credit for being consistent. I have the utmost confidence in my highly developed aesthetic sensibility."

Their drinks came and Buckey raised his glass.

"To what shall we drink?" he asked.

"To the new guy I like," Koko said.

"OK, to him."

"And to your artist."

The two sipped quietly at their drinks for a few moments. Buckey could tell Koko's mind was somewhere else, but he didn't try to bring her back.

"I feel like such a shit," Koko said abruptly. Her voice was flat.

"Are you worrying about Rick?"

"Not exactly worrying. I don't know what to call it. I just feel I'm giving him a low blow by leaving so suddenly. It'll be a shock for him."

"There's nothing you can do about it. He's partly responsible for making you do this. But more important, what about your new lover? When he hears you've moved out, he'll go crazy, won't he? With happiness, I mean."

"I guess so," Koko said.

"It's wonderful to see someone happy. Especially when you yourself have caused the happiness. That's all you should be thinking about, Koko. You have in your hand one of the parts you need for building a new love. Are you saying you want more stimulation by worrying yourself about someone else on top of that? That's selfish, girl, and unfair to your new guy."

He's right, Koko thought. Why am I always thinking I can be of help to people? There's a limit to how much people can do for each other. It was arrogant of her to think she could do something for Rick.

"Rick's an alcoholic. I've always been the one who cleans up his vomit. I hated doing it, of course. And he sleeps around. I felt so hopeless. . . . I was always alone in the apartment on weekends. Pisses me off. It's the pits. But . . ."

Buckey's eyes urged her to go on.

"No other man has ever made me feel so much love."

Koko was flabbergasted at her own words. But she knew that being able to love Rick had given her a sense of superiority that couldn't come with being loved back.

"I was using him up. I thought he was the one using me, but the truth is, it was the other way around."

"What are you going to say to him when you see him next?" Buckey asked.

"I'll tell him thank you," Koko murmured.

Putting both hands on her shoulders, he leaned across the table.

"Good girl!" he exclaimed.

They each ordered another drink and left after they emptied their glasses. Koko felt calm again. Walking along with his bike, Buckey talked incessantly about his new lover. When the man in question greeted them back at the apartment, he looked so much like Maurique that Koko was jolted. Elbowing Buckey, she cried, "Boy, I'll say! You really *are* consistent."

Buckey laughed and changed the subject. He tried his best to make this first meeting go well between his new lover and his friend, the first woman he'd ever felt really comfortable with.

• • •

IT WAS STILL very early when Koko opened her eyes the next morning. The first rays of sun were just lighting the sky. She slipped off the couch, careful not to awaken Buckey and his boyfriend sleeping in the next room, and went to the phone. The shock of the cool floor under her feet wiped away the last traces of sleepiness, as James answered at Randy's place.

"Did I wake you up?" Koko asked.

"Uh-uh. I'm on my way to the gym. Randy's still asleep. You want me to get him up?"

"No, let him sleep. I'd like you to leave him a message, though. I've moved out of the apartment and I'm staying at a friend's place on Avenue D. Tell him I'll be waiting for him tonight at the café where you work."

"Such a businesslike message? You don't want me to add 'I love you' or anything?"

"Thanks, James, you're a dear."

Koko imagined Randy's face asleep: angelic, sweetly oblivious to the foulness of the world. She wished she could gaze upon that sleeping face whenever she felt like it.

Koko hesitated for a few moments and then called Jesse. After three rings, however, it was Rick who picked up. Koko was so sure he'd be sleeping, passed out drunk, that she nearly dropped the phone.

"Koko? Is that you?"

She didn't answer.

"Where are you?"

"At a friend's."

"When are you coming back?"

"I'm not. I do have to see you once more, though . . . to talk."

"This is a joke, right?"

"No, it's not."

"It's a joke, I know it. Just a stupid joke. There's no way you can move out, I know it."

"I'm in love with someone else, Rick."

There was dead silence for a moment; then Rick laughed. In the background Koko could hear the sound of ice being dropped into a glass.

"Don't lie to me, woman. No way you can be into some other man. You can't leave me. You don't have anyplace to go. There're men all over, but the only one you want is me. So hurry up and get back here. In love with someone else? Don't kid me. When did you meet this man, huh? Last night? You're saying you're in love with someone you had a one-night stand with? Is he asking you to move in with him? After one goddamn night of screwing?"

"I met him quite a while ago."

Rick laughed loudly.

"Rick. I'm serious. I want to break up with you. I've met someone else. I can't help it. I love him."

"You really throw around that fucking love word a lot, don't you? I'm sick of hearing it, and you know it. So now you're gonna go and say it to someone else, huh? What *is* love, huh? Tell me that. Show it to me."

"It's something *you* certainly can't express."

Rick cursed.

"You're drunk again. I can't talk to you when you're drunk. Let me talk to Jesse."

"You're gonna throw me away?"

There was despair in Rick's voice for the first time. Koko was brought up short.

"You're saying you're gonna dump me, aren't you? Koko, are you really gonna dump me? Answer me. You saying you're gonna dump me and make some other man happy? You're gonna be saying 'I love you,' 'I love you,' like an alarm clock every morning to some other man, huh? And is that man going to wake up, like I didn't? Is he gonna hold you, whispering 'I love you,' 'I love you' back, like a woman? Is that the kind of stupid thing that's gonna satisfy you?"

Unable to bear it any longer, Koko hung up the telephone with a sigh.

"Are you all right?" Buckey had come out from his bedroom, a towel wrapped around his waist.

"Did I wake you up?"

"Your old boyfriend sure has a loud voice. Even so, it takes an unfortunate sort of courage to be drunk at this time of the morning."

Koko twisted her lips at Buckey's words, trying to smile. Realizing, however, that it was useless, she crumpled to the floor and lay there. Buckey knelt beside her, a resigned look on his face.

"There's nothing to talk about," Koko muttered, narrowing her eyes against the bright morning sun.

"He's in a bad way. It's a pity, but there's nothing you can do about it. Why's he so prickly, anyhow? It's so much nicer to grab the one you love and hold on tight than try to escape with alcohol. And it's so easy. Cuddling up with someone, you feel so safe and peaceful. What's wrong with him?"

"You're right."

The air was growing warmer as the sun strengthened. It seemed about to become hot. Koko closed her eyes. It was bright even under her lids.

"Lying here like this in the warm sun makes me think it's not so bad to be alive. But when I get up, those good feelings evaporate. It'd be so nice if everything went along nice and easy, you know? People are stupid. They make everything complicated."

Buckey glanced down at Koko. She looked as if she'd given

up. But he knew she was merely resting. She was preparing herself for all the things that were about to happen.

"You know what, Koko?" he said.

"What?"

"It *is* easy."

Koko opened her eyes and looked at Buckey. She smiled. "I know. People are simple creatures. Animals, really. Their true state of being is snuggling up to the person dear to them. That makes them complete. I'm going to see Randy today. And when I see him, I'm going to tell him that. I don't need anything more than to be held tight."

All at once, the aroma of coffee filled the room. Buckey got up and padded off to the kitchen to give his own dear one a hug.

AS SHE entered the café that evening, Koko flew at Randy, nearly knocking him over. Love for him exuded from every fiber of her body. Her ardor surprised him a little; he thought if he weren't there to hold her up, she'd surely fall over. He was happy to hold her. She was so incredibly sweet. He'd never met a woman before who made him feel so much like a man. He didn't think of her as weak without him. Alone, she stood straight and walked with a firm, independent step—he'd noticed her strength the first time he saw her. But when she stood before him, she melted. She was a woman any man would look at twice, but she only showed the womanly side of herself to him, which made him feel privileged. His grip on Koko's shoulders tightened. I'm never going to let anything hurt her, he told himself fiercely. So this is what guys meant when they said "This is *my* woman." He felt that way about Koko, and it made him ashamed of all the other relationships he'd had before this one.

"Come stay at our apartment. It's small, but we wouldn't mind you there. Koko, I want to see you, touch you, every day. You don't have to feel like you're imposing. I'm thinking of what's best for you too, of course, but really I want to have you there for myself. I think it would be terrific if I could always have you around."

"Thanks. It would be nice if we could do that sometime. But not now. I have to get various things straight for myself in my own way."

"You mean logistically? You have to talk to your old boyfriend? Or are you talking about something within yourself?"

"All those things."

Koko touched Randy's cheek. She was older than he was, but could still feel her smallness when she was with him. She could be weak with him. The realization made her dizzy with happiness. She didn't have to always be strong now.

"Hey, Randy."

"Mm?"

"How do you want me to love you?"

"Why do you ask that? That's a stupid question. I don't want to choose some way to be loved. I just want to be loved. I guess I just want to love and be loved the way my parents love each other."

"That's beautiful."

"You know, Koko, I don't know what this Rick guy is like, but I'm going to make you happy. That's because I want to be happy myself. I don't know what he thought about you, but I'm gonna use my eyes. If a crack opens up in your heart, no matter how small, I'll see it. I don't want you to have any foolish worries. That's only wasting time. Don't you think this moment is the best? I do. Drinking my favorite beer at a café, my baby next to me, knowing we're going to be alone together soon in bed. This beats everything. It's more than enough."

Koko laid her head on Randy's shoulder. She watched the people walking by. The air and the voices hanging between them seemed to be almost visible; lovely shining particles that danced in space and seemed to come floating toward her. She took a sip of her drink. She could feel warm blood coursing through her body. Even if these splendid, elusive illusions flickered away, she'd still have that broad chest behind her.

KOKO MANAGED to see Jesse a few days later, using Sue as an intermediary. When she got to the appointed Denny's, Daryl and Jesse were standing at the entrance looking for her. Feeling like a parent, she shepherded them to a table and ordered them drinks. It felt like ages, not days, since she'd last seen Jesse. He seemed taller and thinner.

"I guess I can't say it's good news after everything that's happened, but Daddy hasn't been drinking much at all since you left," Jesse said, sipping his soda through a straw.

"Oh? I would say that's probably good. My leaving was good for his health. Maybe I should have left earlier."

"It's good for his body, but I think he'd be better off drinking."

"Why? Is he in a bad mood all the time?"

Jesse shook his head.

"It's weird, but he's up. Kind of wired, you know? I think maybe he might be losing his mind."

"Are you serious?"

"He doesn't want me to know what's happened, and he doesn't know that I know you already have a new boyfriend, so he's trying to cover up. He still comes home totally smashed sometimes, though. It takes him forever to get to the bedroom. I think he gets most of the way on his hands and knees. I'm always awake, but I don't help him. I stay in bed, thinking I have to let him get there on his own. I lie there listening, and all of a sudden it's dead silent. You know when that is, Koko? It's when he gets to the bedroom and opens the door. Then I can't stand it anymore, so I come out. And he's just standing there like he's in shock or something, looking at the empty bed. I tap him on the shoulder, and he turns around with this scared look on his face like he thinks he's gonna see a ghost. Then he realizes it's me and sighs. 'Oh, it's you, Jesse,' he says. Even though I think he has to do it himself, I give him a push. He needs somebody to do that for him. He's in trouble, Koko."

Pain seared through Koko's chest. She could imagine Rick standing there, see the expression on his face.

"He's so pitiful. That's why I told him, 'Daddy, you gotta get yourself a woman, like me.'"

"And what did he say to that?"

"'Shut the fuck up.'"

Daryl snorted.

"Don't laugh," Koko snapped.

Daryl shrugged. "I'm sorry. But he's an adult, isn't he? An adult man needs a woman. So why couldn't he keep his woman at home with him?"

"Yeah, right, Daryl. And you're having such an *incredibly* grown-up love affair yourself, aren't you?" Koko said, glaring at him. Daryl grinned, not minding at all.

"Sue's the best," he said. "I can see why she's your friend, Koko. It gets to me, though, that she has a husband. He's nothing like Rick, so I don't have a chance in hell of getting her away from him."

"Don't talk about my father that way," Jesse said.

"Yeah, that's right," Koko added.

Daryl grinned at Koko and Jesse in turn. This kid think's he's tough, Koko thought. At the same time, she felt like telling Sue a thing or two.

"Koko, isn't there a chance?" Jesse asked. "I feel sorry for him, you leaving like that. I feel more sorry for myself, though, since I'm the one he uses as a scapegoat. Don't you feel like talking to him at all? Are you so into your new boyfriend?"

Koko reddened. "Well, putting that aside," she said, "do you really think I can talk to him? If I go, do you think he'll be sober and will actually talk to me?"

Jesse spread his hands wide to show that he didn't know. He honestly didn't have any idea. If things went on the way they were going, his father would become a shabby, run-down man like so many others, he thought. Better to have a father who drank and came home smelling of women.

"He needs a woman, Koko. Things are no good in that apartment unless there's a woman between him and me."

"Come to think of it, Ninja is a male too," Daryl teased.

Jesse continued, ignoring him. "It's true, Koko. I don't know why. Having a woman there makes all the difference. Hey, can't you take a break from that other man? We need you."

"It could be any woman. It doesn't have to be me."

"Stingy."

"What kind of lip is that? You have no right to talk to me like that."

"Yes, I do."

"Why?"

"Because you're family."

Koko stared at Jesse, unable to believe her ears. Jesse hung his head. He seemed to be embarrassed suddenly.

"What I mean is—well, you were *like* family."

Daryl had to struggle to keep from laughing at the two of them. If only Jesse had said that from the start, he thought. Things would have gone fine if only they had been able to

give each other a hug. Love changes everything. Like
Randy, Daryl already had an understanding of this most
simple of truths.

"Well, I do have to go back to the apartment one more
time." Koko was careful to keep her voice flat. She didn't
want Jesse to read anything into her words. Jesse shot her a
look but immediately dropped his eyes and chewed on his
straw. Koko was sorry for him, seeing him like that, but she
refused to acknowledge his feelings. Everyone has to spend
their days secretly regretting things they did too late.

Even while Koko was pitying him, she was furious at
hearing these things from Jesse now, when it was too late.
There'd been a time when she'd so wanted to hear him say
this and was sure she never would.

"Jesse, I'm not going to lie to you. I'm not going to try
anymore to put a good face on things. The day I go back to
that apartment to talk to your daddy is going to be the last."

"And what about me and you?"

Jesse was slumped in his chair, his head hanging forward.
Only his eyes moved to look up at Koko. She hesitated,
wanting to choose the right words.

Daryl looked at the two in turn as he noisily ate the soup
crackers. "That will be the start of a brand-new day, of
course. For you guys as friends," he said.

Koko and Jesse shrugged and looked at each other.

"THIS IS the last day," Koko told an anxious Randy as she
boarded the subway. She stood absently at the doors after
they closed behind her and looked at her own face reflected
in the window. Her hair had grown to the middle of her
back while she'd been busy with other things. Koko ran her
fingers through it, thinking that as soon as all this was over
she'd cut it. "This is it," she'd told Randy as he embraced
her. She'd tried not to show him how anxious she was.

She looked at a businessman reading *The New York Times* folded up into a neat little oblong. Next to him was a boy in high-tops, rocking to his Walkman. All these people who had nothing to do with her were going about their business, the same as usual. Nothing had changed in the world; Koko tried to calm herself by remembering that fact. Everything was up to her. She couldn't imagine that Rick would try to stick to her. He'd stopped that long ago. Wave after wave of regret swept through Koko's heart, but that in itself was evidence things were over. Rocked by the subway, Koko felt sorry for them both.

Rick was supposed to be at the apartment, sober, waiting for her. Koko had called him at work the previous day and said she wanted to talk to him one last time. Rick had sighed and said, "OK." Koko had felt lonely, but also somehow comforted at that muttered assent: OK. When she heard Rick's familiar, much-loved voice, Koko had the feeling that her whole past had been capsulized into the sound of those two syllables. In that moment the future, something that should be in front of her, rose up behind her in bold relief—to lean against so she wouldn't fall. Koko gave herself up to it but then looked ahead and shuddered. She could see nothing directly in front of her. The roads she should take, the signposts along the way—everything had disappeared. It was up to her, now, to build them all over again. What have I done? she thought. Once more, she felt the weight of the years she'd spent with Rick.

No sooner did she put her key into the doorknob than it swung open from the inside. Koko hadn't expected to feel so flustered to see Rick again after not having seen him for almost a week.

"Hey," Rick said, letting Koko in. His smile was strained. It seemed to her the old familiar smells of the apartment had changed. "Do you want something to drink?"

Koko shook her head no. A regretful look crossed Rick's face as he lowered himself on the chair in front of her. Koko felt bad for him. He looked like he really needed a drink, now more than any other time. For that matter, so did she. Everything they really needed between them, though, existed in the past. Nothing could help them now. Alcohol was not going to bring them together. The only time that alcohol had ever helped them was when they'd just met, when they still looked at each other.

Rick seemed disgruntled, as if he felt the need to say something. His mouth worked, but of course the words didn't come. Rick had never once been the one to start a discussion between them in all the time they'd been together.

Koko was seized with sentimental memories. Rick's cheeks were covered with a scrubby stubble, as they'd been when they first met. As always, the sight of that stubble with all the white in it made Koko infinitely sad. But his sandpaper cheeks would never again scrape her own.

"So you're planning on leaving me?" Rick asked.

"Yes."

"Why?"

"I don't see any reason to go into that now."

"I want to know why you want to leave. You don't love me anymore?"

"I met somebody else; that's when I stopped having feelings for you."

"I don't believe it."

"Rick." Koko looked at him, troubled. "What's going on here? You're acting like you want to keep me. You've been unhappy with me for an awfully long time, haven't you? I've been an eyesore to you. You were always drinking when you were with me. You couldn't keep yourself sober. There are lots of things I want to say too, but I won't. Saying them now won't do any good. There's a mountain of things we should have discussed. I always wanted to talk with you. But I don't think it's necessary anymore. I'm in love with someone else. That wipes out anything we might have to say to each other. It's unfortunate, but we can't even be friends after we break up."

"Why are you always like this?"

"Huh?"

Koko's eyes widened as though what he said didn't register. Rick gave her a withering look. This woman, he thought, always acts so innocent. It's as if she retracts the antennae that feel people out and refuses to see what's going on. And she does it so casually, he thought, without flinching, like she doesn't harbor a shadow of a bad intention.

"What do you mean, Rick?"

Rick almost hated her then. There was no way, though, that he could put into words why Koko set off a whirlpool of emotion in him. "In other words, you got yourself a man. So you want out of our relationship. Simply put, that's it, isn't it?"

"Even if I hadn't gotten a boyfriend, you and I were beyond helping."

"And that was my fault?"

"No. There was nothing either of us could do. We just weren't right for each other, that's all."

"What kind of man is he? Does he fuck you right? Is he that *good*?"

"Rick!" Koko half shouted. "It's nothing like that. You know that sex alone doesn't tie a man and a woman together."

"Koko, there are lots of things you can lump together and call sex. That's the way it is between men and women. Sad feelings and happy feelings spill over from sex. You can't be with a man you don't feel like having sex with, can you? You love another man more than me. To me, that means you don't want to have sex with me anymore; you want to have sex with the other guy. That's the way it is, isn't it?"

"You're right about that. I can agree. When you take into consideration all the things sex brings with it, yes, I do want him."

"Not me; him. Right?"

"That's right. Not you. Him."

"Fuck!"

Rick pulled out a Newport from a crumpled pack and stuck it between his lips. Koko could tell it wasn't only anger that was making his hands shake.

"It's so easy for you to leave me? To leave this place?"

"Easy?"

Koko stared at Rick in disbelief. Then she laughed hysterically.

"Easy? Something's wrong with you. How long do you think it took me to come to this decision? Are you pretending to be ignorant, or do you really not know? Rick, we took a long, long time to kill our happiness."

Rick looked down at his intertwined fingers on the tabletop. The cigarette he'd lit went untouched in the ashtray, its lengthening ash marking time. Koko waited for him to say something. She felt faint in this cursed silence.

"Can I have a drink?" Rick asked.

"No."

Rick's laced fingers tightened.

"Why does liquor always help me more than you do?" he asked.

"Probably because you don't love me."

"It never occurred to you that it's because I love you too much?"

Koko looked at Rick and chewed her lip. She wasn't so strong she could walk away from that one. Nor was she weak enough to fall for it.

I'm not the one who made you do what you did, she shouted silently. And I'm not the one who made you what you are—that's the work of long months and years before we met. I'm not so vain anymore, Rick. I know I didn't have any influence on you.

"Have you ever heard me use the word 'love' before?" Rick asked.

"Never."

"Well, what do you think? Isn't the word 'love' a fucking joke, coming from me?"

"No. I liked that word. I liked to say it to you, and I wanted to hear you say it. I could have been happy with that one word from you."

"I couldn't love you the way you wanted. That's why you went and got yourself another man."

"Rick." Koko's voice was full of sympathy. "Everyone needs someone. I was lonely, but that's not why I went to him, why I need him. I need him because he needs me."

"What if I said *I* still need you?"

"What for?"

"For me. So I can survive."

"Rick! I don't want to just survive! I want to *live*! Living for me is a lot easier than you think. All I need is to be able to laugh with the one I love."

The corners of Rick's lips twisted into a sort of a smile. He was trying to just get through this ordeal. This, too, would pass, he thought. And once it did, he would soak himself in liquor. Then it would all seem like something out of a dream.

He now understood his father. His father had side-stepped everything, but even the things he rejected he never wanted to let go of—he was a selfish, greedy man. Rick smiled bitterly to think he'd become like his father.

Koko was exasperated. She hadn't come back for this.

Please, don't trip me up now by laying these words of love at my feet, she begged Rick silently.

"How did you get your hooks into that guy?"

"Don't say it like that."

"It's the same thing no matter how you say it."

"Are you talking about how I got him into bed?"

"What else is there?"

"So you're saying if a man and a woman don't go to bed together, there's nothing between them?"

"Is that wrong? That's how it starts, isn't it? You and I started that way. You jumped into my bed the first night we met. Why was that? Probably because you thought if you didn't, you wouldn't be able to get to know me. You wanted to see what I was really like beyond any shit smokescreen I might put up on the outside."

"You're right. That *is* how I started with you. But it's been different with Randy. I looked at his eyes, I listened to his voice, and I found myself drawn to him naturally, little by little. Going out with him means conversation, smiles, *and* sex: together, in the same place."

"Hmph." Rick sneered at her. "His name is Randy, huh? That bastard kid."

"He's an adult. He's one of those rare young adults who doesn't make things easy on himself. At least, he's not an aging child like you."

"You think you would have fallen in love with him if it hadn't been for things with us?"

"No. To be perfectly frank, I do think our problems made it possible for me to get close to him. Rick, I've never before tried to talk this way with a man when I broke with him, especially about things like this. All this is new to me, and it hurts. I love him, Rick. There's nothing I can do anymore. What do *you* want to do? I came here to tell you what *I* want to do. I'm not coming back. It's hard to break up with you.

Out of all my relationships, the one with you has been my biggest failure. It's hard, damn hard, to think nothing good came of it. But that doesn't mean I want to make up and try again. What do *you* want to do, Rick? I am not your woman anymore."

"You think I'm just gonna let some other guy come along and steal my woman?"

"Rick! What are you saying? You're not going to try to stop me, are you?"

"Of course I am."

"Why? We can't even laugh together anymore."

"Do we have to laugh together?"

Even as Koko began to get angry, she thought Rick must know how foolish it was to debate this sort of thing. There was nothing he hated more than abstractions, and he'd long ago closed himself off from her. He couldn't, she thought, want to prolong the pointlessness of the two of them being in the same room together. He must know it was too late to change anything.

"Do you want to be with me, Rick?"

Rick made no effort to answer.

"You don't want me to be with any other man, is that it?"

Rick lit another cigarette.

"Answer me!" Koko cried.

"That's right."

"Well, that sucks. I am not your doll. Why do you think I couldn't leave you, huh? Maybe you thought no other man'd find me desirable?"

"I thought you'd love me forever. I know it's selfish, but I'd never known another woman who tried so hard to stick with me. Jesse's mother didn't. She treated me like I treated her. It was easy to understand." Rick's voice was gravelly, as if it had been a long time since he'd said so much at once. "But you were different. I had no idea what to do with a woman like you. I'd never met a person like you who loved me body and soul, whose happiness was bound up in loving me. I had no idea how to love you back. No one ever cared for me so much that they tried to analyze me—not my mom, my brother, my sisters. I don't know how to describe it. It's like you had so much love; yeah, that's it. I'd never met a person who had so much love before. I don't know what kind of home you grew up in, but I'd never seen a person with so much love stored up that needed a place to go. I know you were always thinking about me. And I know you were always hurting yourself trying to show me how to be happy. But I didn't know how to answer to that kind of love. It was choking me. I wasn't really raised to love. And I couldn't accept it the way I should have. It's hard for me to let it make me feel good."

"So I release you. That's what I came here to do. I release you! I don't hate you or anything. I should thank you for teaching me important lessons. But I can't change the way I am. My love is primitive, and it doesn't take orders from anyone, not even me. It takes off by itself and gets more and more basic."

"Are we really through?" Rick asked her.

Koko nodded slowly, once. In that moment, she was thrown from her chair. She didn't know what was happening. Her eyes flew open—Rick was on top of her. She felt something warm at the corner of her lip, and when she realized it was her own blood she shook uncontrollably. Rick was crying.

"Why? Why is it always like this? Why is my life always so fucked up?" he gasped. Koko looked up at him vacantly. She was seeing his face twisted with pain, crying, for the first time.

"You don't want to sleep with me anymore?" he asked.

"No. Not anymore."

"You used to like it, didn't you? You used to really like doing it with me."

"Yes. I liked it."

"How does that other guy do it with you? Is he better than me?"

"Hey, Rick?" Koko said, looking up at him. A number of his teardrops had fallen on her face. "Have you ever put love into sex?" she asked.

Rick was silent.

"That's how he does it with me. You have never once done it with me like that."

"You weren't happy, doing it with me?" Rick asked.

"I was happy. That's how we used to make sure of each other. That's how we could tell we were still together. I'd feel reassured because I could still lie peacefully by your side, and you'd be reassured that I wasn't running away from that peace. Rick, the only time we could be at rest with each other was when we were in bed together." All at once, Koko was crying too.

"What's so wrong with that? Is it so wrong to use a bed only to take a rest on? You're trying to take away my one place of rest, Koko. What am I supposed to do? I don't have anything left anymore. Not one thing. I've lost everything. I don't even have anything left to worry about."

"You have Jesse. You told me once that if you died, the only one who'd be sad would be Jesse, right? And I don't think you have any lack of women around you. You've stumbled home often enough at dawn smelling of other women. You think I was going to stand for that? I don't want to be used as a rest stop."

"Are you really going to leave?"

"I'm sorry."

"Are you going to go and live with that guy?"

"Well. He's still a student. I'll be staying with a friend of mine for a while."

"Is he black?"

Koko looked at him silently in disbelief. Then she spoke. "What the hell kind of question is that, huh? What race he is has nothing to do with anything."

"Maybe that's what you think, but it does matter. It's hard to live with a black man. Living with me didn't go well, did it? We have our own ways of doing things."

"I can't believe you're serious, Rick. You can't differentiate people on the basis of their skin color; it's not that simple."

"Don't act so high and mighty. I know what I'm talking about, Koko. It's you who don't understand. It's never gonna work with that guy."

Koko raised her hand to strike him, but, instead, Rick grabbed her wrist and twisted it until it hurt.

"Don't bring skin color into it!" she said. "You'll make me despise you, I swear you will! I don't know what sort of environment *you* were raised in, but don't, *don't* bring race into it as one last weapon. Please, don't make me hate you."

"If you're going to leave anyway, go ahead and hate me. Despise me, I don't care!" Rick groaned like an animal. He began to cry great heaving sobs.

I can't hate him, Koko thought helplessly. If I could, I wouldn't be here now. "Your younger sister told me it's hard for any woman who's not black to take care of a black man. Sometimes I'd think maybe she was right. Maybe that's how it is in your family. But there are all kinds of people. Randy's black, but so what? He's my man. That's all there is to it. A man's a man. Nothing more, nothing less. Could you accept it if he were white, Rick? You couldn't, could you? You'd use that, too, as an excuse to hate him and me. How convenient."

"What do you want me to do? What can I do to make you stay? There's nothing I can do to make you stay. How'm I gonna live? Do you know what it's like to always come home drunk and be scared to look in the bedroom? Can you understand the relief I felt each time when I saw you were still there? Do you know what it's like to take all the love you have to give me and then be terrified, imagining the day when it'll be gone?"

"Rick, we're alive *now*. The past and the future are moments that have no meaning *now*."

"Shut up!" Rick got both hands around Koko's throat and began choking her. Unable to breathe, Koko struggled, kicking and slapping at him. She was too frightened even to shout.

"Kill . . . you're gonna kill me?" she gasped.

Rick seemed to come back to himself with a start. He released his grip.

"I don't want to die," Koko sobbed. "Don't kill me, please, Rick."

Rick's face twisted with pain. "How can you think I would kill you? I'd never do such a thing. I need you! I need you, and you go and sleep with another man. You act like you're always thinking about me, and then you go and do this behind my back. You bitch! What'm I supposed to do? How do you think I feel, huh? I thought at least there was one woman in this world who cared about me and worried about me. When I came home in the morning I'd be relieved to find *my* woman still warming *my* bed—now what'm I supposed to do? I didn't know one damn thing. I was a fool. I thought my woman had her hands full with me, and then you go and do this. Making me an idiot. What about Jesse, huh? Does Jesse know about this? Does he know you went and got yourself a young man and you're leaving me?"

Koko looked afraid. She hesitated for a moment before replying. "Yes, he knows."

Rick's vision went dark with rage. He grabbed Koko around the collar with both hands and wrenched her toward him. "You two were in this together?"

"No . . . Jesse is in no position to do anything like that. He's trying his damnedest to make a place for himself. I can't be his mother, and he knows it. He's always trying to think of where in his heart he can put me. He and I, we're like friends—"

Not waiting to hear her out, Rick struck Koko in the face several times. Feeling the blood running from her nose, Koko reached up to wipe it away with the back of her hand, but she was trembling so badly she only smeared it. Rick stared at her wild-eyed. Remembering he was sober made Koko all the more frightened. She'd left him. The structure to his life had caved in, she thought. And this was the result.

"You don't have any right to treat me like this!" she cried.

"Yes, I do. You're my woman. I can treat you any way I want. You say you're gonna leave me? You gotta be kidding. This is what I do to things of *mine* that try to run away. You're *mine*."

Koko could only stare at him.

"What're you looking at me like that for?" Rick demanded. "You feelin' sorry for me? Huh? That's it, isn't it? You're always like that. What is love anyway, huh? What the hell is love? Is it saving some poor miserable wreck? Is it teaching someone how to be saved? Fuck. God can eat shit. God, he never saved my ass once. All I ever got was pity from my woman. You'd look at me and think, 'You poor miserable fuck: here, I'll give you some sex.' Is that love? Fuck that shit. You and Jesse probably used to get together and say, 'Oh, poor Daddy, we gotta do something to help him.'"

"I don't feel sorry for you! At least, not the way you are now. Jesse's a wonderful boy. He's trying his best so he won't end up like *you*!"

Rick grabbed Koko by the back of her neck and her arm and shoved her toward the bedroom. Koko struggled and screamed at the top of her lungs, but she was no match for Rick's strength. On the way, she managed to grab hold of a leg of the dining room table, but the whole table began to move. The ashtray on top of it fell to the floor, scattering ashes in Koko's hair. Even so, Koko kept screaming, shouting Randy's name over and over.

"Shut up already! If you say that man's name one more time, I really will kill you!"

Koko struggled to stop crying, but it was no use. Her ankle was swelling up—she'd probably sprained it resisting. She didn't think she could walk.

Rick threw Koko on the bed, pulled the sash from his bathrobe, and bound her hands and feet. "Don't you dare move," he told her, and went into Jesse's room across the hall. Koko could hear him rummaging through Jesse's desk drawers.

When he came back, Rick had Jesse's handcuffs, the ones he hung from the belt of his Rambo camouflage pants. Koko remembered Jesse showing them off to her when he first bought them. Koko had laughed and told him not to do anything nasty with them. She never imagined those handcuffs would one day be used on her.

"What're you going to do with those?" There was no strength in the question. Rick silently untied her hands and feet and handcuffed her right wrist to the brass headboard. His eyes were hollow. He lay down on the bed next to her and began to unbutton her shirt. Why in hell's name am I doing this? he asked himself. Her heart has already left to be with another man. I've already hurt her so much, why add this to it now? I want to hate her, that's why; I want to spit on her, and I'll lose my last shred of dignity doing it.

Rick took off his T-shirt and shorts and lay on top of Koko. She uttered a tiny cry, but she'd given up resisting. Once she'd wrapped around him like a cute, mischievous little animal. Now she lay there like an animal sacrifice.

Even though he felt like spitting on himself, Rick kept at it. Koko lay beneath him, her eyes empty. It was strange, but she didn't hate him. In her heart was an overwhelming sadness for the pathetic helplessness of people. She thought it was strange that she wasn't angry anymore. Rick's body continued to move up and down on her, but to Koko it had no more to do with her than with a machine.

"Scratch my back with your fingernails," Rick ordered. Koko did as she was told with her free hand.

"Harder. Make me bleed," Rick said. Koko did so. Rick cried out in pain. Koko jerked her hand away, shocked to see Rick's blood and skin under her fingernails.

"More. Scar me! Put something there that will never disappear!"

Koko shook her head wordlessly and stroked his cheek.

"Rick, you really—"

"Don't talk. Please, don't say anything; just let me hold you. I love you, Koko. I don't want to let you go. I need you so much. I don't want to lose you. You're mine. I can live as long as you're by my side. What do you want me to do? What should I do to show you how much I love you?"

Koko closed her eyes and stroked his neck. Beneath her eyelids, fresh tears began to flow. Rick had never taken her before like this. If her body could help him, she would give it to him gladly, she thought, circling his neck with her free arm.

"Why didn't you ever make love to me like this before?" she asked.

Rick didn't answer. He was surprised himself that he could make love to her with such intense feeling. Though she lay beneath him now, she was gone, and Rick had no way of showing her, proving to her, how important she was to him, how much he loved her. This was how she must have felt, he thought suddenly. This cup of bitter pain that I'm tasting now, she must have been drinking from every day these last two years. Rick heaved a deep sigh of regret and then came. Coming had never carried so much meaning for him as it did at this instant. And, for the first time in his life, he whispered the words "I love you" to the woman underneath him.

They lay there for a long while. They each felt days had gone by, they were so tired. But the bright summer sun through the window told them only an hour or so had passed.

Rick slowly lifted himself off Koko and looked down at her. He traced a finger along the purple and reddish bruises on her face and frowned.

"Oh, Koko," he said. "What have I done to you?" He turned his face away from Koko's eyes and began to cry.

"Don't cry, Rick. I'm OK."

"You wouldn't take this from any other man, would you? You wouldn't lie there, not fighting, if somebody else did that to you, would you? Doesn't it hurt, Koko? How can you take it and still not hate me?"

Rick's back faced Koko. Blood was oozing from the deep scratches on it. They were the first stamps of love Koko had ever put on a man. And with those bloody lines, Rick's back ceased to be the expanse of skin she was so familiar with.

"You started everything, Koko. You started it, and now you're finishing it. It's like a joke or something. Are you going to do the same thing with that other guy? Are you going to happily take everything he has to dish out too?" Rick scrubbed at his tears with an arm. "I hate you," he said.

"Hate me?"

"Yes. Who else am I gonna hate? I'll hate you and hate you, and that's how I'll stop loving you. I'm not gonna let you go back to that other guy. I'm gonna keep you here like this."

"What good would that accomplish?"

Rick grabbed Koko by her jaw. "I don't know," he said. "But I don't care. I can't let you leave like this. I just can't; not now."

"Rick, please. Let me go. I don't care if you hate me. I'll bear the burden of any kind of hatred from you. But please, take these handcuffs off. Let me go!"

Koko was almost shouting. The handcuffs rattled against the metal of the headboard.

"Koko." Rick's whisper was tortured. "I don't know why, but I can only love what is right in front of my face. And I can only hate what is right in front of me."

Koko closed her eyes in despair. Rick stood up and went to the kitchen. He took a bottle of vodka from the refrigerator and drank deeply from it, then sputtered and coughed. The bottle was cold against his teeth, but he finished it off in one long pull. He had to start by forgetting everything; that was the only way.

As Koko lay on the bed in shock, she heard the sound of Rick's keys as he left the apartment to go buy more liquor.

PART II

SUMMER

SHE AWOKE from a deep sleep, a smile tugging at her lips.
The room was dark. She groped about in search of something she could pull toward her: some sheets, perhaps, or a
teddy bear; somebody's arm—anything she could hang on
to to help her wake up. The air was nice and cool. Why am I
smiling? she wondered. She tried to think of the reason, but
it was like grasping at soap bubbles. She gave up and turned
over. I'm smiling, grinning away like a Cheshire cat. Like
the cat who got the canary. So what did I get? she wondered,
her eyes wide open. As her eyes became used to the dark, she
saw the outlines of the pillows and sheets. She finally realized what it was. The thing I got was sleep. Simply able to
sleep without thinking about anything.

"Are you awake, Koko?"

Koko turned toward the sound of the voice. Buckey was
leaning against the windowsill, looking at her quietly. He
was a black shadow against the little bit of light coming in
through the window.

"Oh, Buckey. I hurt all over," Koko said. She was lying on
her stomach. Buckey chuckled softly and drank his seltzer.
The fizzing sound from the water blended with his laugh-

ter. A soft cloud of tiny sounds always seemed to hang about him.

"You're fine, Koko. You'll be able to go to work tomorrow. The bruises won't fade for a while, though. Boy, you scared me! You collapsed the moment you walked in."

"I wanted to sleep."

"At my place?"

Koko got up slowly. She winced at the pain in her right wrist. It was swollen.

"I'd like to say I wanted to die, but that's not what I'm into. I just wanted to sleep. I wanted to enter a realm where I didn't have to think a single thought. I finally found a bed I can do that in."

"You mean my bed?"

"I'm sorry. I'm hogging your bed. Where's your better half?"

"If you mean Spike, he's out shopping. He says he's going to make you something good to eat."

"What time is it?"

"Nine. The sun only set a little while ago."

Koko thought she'd slept for days.

"Buckey," she said, full of gratitude.

Buckey looked at her, his head tilted into a question.

"Thank you," Koko said. "I think I really am OK." She pulled at the sheets and looked down at herself.

"Of course you are," Buckey said.

Koko sighed. "I feel like I've murdered someone."

The memory of Rick's face as he took off the handcuffs came back to her, sending a sharp pain through her chest and making her moan aloud. So this is heartache, she thought. Real pain is when you know you've hurt someone. You feel like killing yourself not when *you've* been hurt but when you've torn someone else apart.

Those eyes of Rick's. I guess I'm fated to remember those

eyes every day from now on, Koko thought. I'll never be able to be carefree in love again, she told herself. No deep, death-like rest for me. I'll be crying out in my sleep for a long time to come.

"Can you give me a hug, Buckey? I really need one."

Buckey went over and hugged her.

"What am I gonna do? What am I gonna do, Buckey?"

Buckey rubbed her back. "Koko," he said. "Everyone has something he or she would like to forget and can't. You want to talk about it? I can't give you any advice, but I'll always be here to listen and give you a hug."

Koko leaned against Buckey and began her story.

"He did love me, Buckey. Basically, that's all there is to it. He really did love me."

RICK HAD come back with a paper bag and found Koko trying to shield the scattered hairpins from his sight with her body. She didn't want anything to set him off. There was no telling what Rick would do now that he had liquor in him. Exhaustion made her mind strangely clear. She could predict every move he might make. Even as she felt dread, she thought of how he'd held her a little while ago and wanted to cry for this pathetic man, trying to do some-thing *now* about their relationship. It was already dead but he refused to leave the corpse alone, pushing and pulling at it. The only thing that kept back her tears was her terror.

Rick knelt down next to the hairpins. Koko shut her eyes, waiting for his reaction, but contrary to her expectations he merely picked them up one by one. Then he began to laugh.

"What's so funny?" she asked.

Still laughing, he sat down on the edge of the bed and took out a can of beer from his bag. He drank it down in big gulps. Then he heaved a deep sigh and sat looking at the ground, his shoulders stooped.

"You were going to try to use the pins to get the handcuffs off?" he asked abruptly. "You thought I wouldn't take them off for you?"

Rick pressed his temples with a thumb and forefinger. Koko was surprised at his subdued manner. But she was shocked to find her old responses still intact: she'd nearly asked him, "What's wrong? Does your head hurt?" Unnerved, she realized that because their bodies had intertwined once more—however unwillingly on her part—she'd reverted to her subservient way of thinking about him.

"Koko." Rick looked up at her like a little boy. "Can I lie down next to you? Do you mind?"

The question was so unlike him, Koko didn't know what to say.

"I want to lie down next to you," Rick said. "I won't do anything. I won't hit you or anything. I didn't go to the liquor store. I just got some beer at the deli and came back. Can I, please? Lie down next to you?"

Koko was swept with the impulse to stop up her ears. You're asking me for something, Rick? she shouted inside her head. I don't remember you ever, *ever* asking anything of me. Koko felt something cut through her, ripping her apart. It hurt far more than when he'd rammed himself into her by force.

"Koko, please. I won't ask you for anything else. You can go right back to that other man. But please, just for now, give me a little time. Let me lie down beside you. Can I?"

Koko opened her mouth to say something, but no words would come out. A great deal of time seemed to pass. Then, finally, she spoke: one word. "Yes."

Rick stood up and took a key out of his pocket. He unlocked the handcuffs, then kissed the red marks on her wrist. He was crying silently.

"Why am I crying?" he asked. His voice was husky and

contained an infinite sadness. He lay down next to Koko, fully dressed. "I've cried a whole lifetime's worth of tears today," he said, then laughed softly.

"Don't cry, Rick," Koko had told him, "don't cry." She wiped his wet cheeks.

"There's nobody to help me. I can't help myself. So what if I cry? I'm feeling sorry for myself." He pressed a pain in the middle of his forehead with his fingertips and said, "I'm sorry I hit you. Must've hurt."

"Yeah, it did."

"But you have someone to take care of you. I won't fix up your bruises because you're the one who always fixes me up. You should go now and get that other guy to fix you up. I was always, always, the one who leaned on you. I really liked leaning on you, Koko. But I was so dumb. I didn't have to drink. I could've just laid down beside you and leaned on you like this. I was so stupid. That's what you wanted, wasn't it, Koko? For me to have leaned on you like this?"

"Yes."

Time had passed quietly as they lay together. Koko wasn't afraid anymore. She felt as if she and Rick were attending a funeral together. They only half believed that what they were burying was really dead, so they tossed in the soil—in the form of their words—ever so slowly.

"I guess it's stupid to say something like this at my age, but . . ."

"What, Rick?"

"Things we can't forget are like beads on a necklace."

"I guess you're right," Koko said. "I guess pretty soon I'll be a bead for you, huh?"

"I'll be one for you, too. I already am. It makes me sad. Families aren't any help at all when you come down to it. The only thing that holds me together are memories of the past. No one, not even people who are related to me by blood, can do anything. I am my only support."

Koko rested her hand on Rick's heart to feel it beating.

"Come here," Rick said, turning to Koko and offering his shoulder. Koko put her head on it without resisting. One more time, that pillow fit perfectly beneath her head. She'd never rest her head there again, she thought.

Koko lay there, her mind a blank. No love, no hate. The loneliness was almost peaceful.

"It'll take you more than one trip to get all your stuff."

"Uh-huh."

"What're you going to do?"

Koko didn't reply. A strange silence fell over them. The rhythm of Rick's heart was strong and regular. Koko felt her own heart's rhythm must be matching his. They felt sad but very much alive.

All at once, there was a loud pounding on the door. Rick shouted and the door burst open. It was a wild-eyed Jesse.

"Koko! You're back?"

Koko smiled weakly at him. Jesse was shaking. He looked at Koko and Rick, lying quietly side by side on the bed.

"Don't you be bothering adults, boy. Go to your room and finish your homework."

"I'll do it later. Koko, you back to stay? You're not going to go anywhere, are you?"

Koko looked at Jesse, unable to speak. Stability, that's what it meant to him to see her in bed with his father. Bed. There was no way Jesse, who'd only just begun to know love, could have any idea of the mixture of emotions that happened in bed. A lover could leave a bed, but his or her form would be stamped into the sheets, making it impossible for the person left behind to sleep. Koko herself didn't yet fully understand the meaning of bed, and she'd been wrestling with it for a long time.

"I'm sorry, Jesse. Let's talk later, huh?"

"OK. Daddy, I'm going to go to a movie with Daryl, so I'll be taking the money on the shelf, all right?"

"Don't be out to all hours of the night like last time."

Jesse shut the door cheerfully. He's the unfortunate one in all this, Koko thought suddenly. So many things had been forced on him as a result of a bed he had nothing to do with.

As Koko lay there thinking, Rick sighed. It was a sigh that had lost all strength to go on.

"Koko."

"Yes?"

"It sucks."

"What does, Rick?"

"I still don't want to lose you."

Koko was silent.

"But it's my fault."

"It's my fault too," Koko said. "I'm not being ironic, but at least now you can go drink all the liquor you want, every day if you want."

"What for? What should I drink for? Because I miss the life we had? What a joke. I don't even have a reason to drink anymore. I'm a middle-aged man who can't even say it's unfair."

"I'm sorry."

"You don't have to apologize." Rick closed his eyes.

"I understand how you feel, Rick."

"Do you?"

"People are attached to each other in different ways. What I can give Randy isn't what I could give you. You show one side of yourself to one person. No other person can bring out that same side."

"That makes me feel better. At least that other guy isn't a replacement for me."

"Rick." Koko lifted his face to look at her. "There isn't any other person like you."

Rick stroked Koko's hair quietly. They'd never before seen things from each other's point of view as much as they did now.

"Can I go?" Koko asked.

Rick nodded. Koko stood up and straightened her rumpled clothes. Her face in the mirror was terribly pale. Only her eyes were strangely gleaming. I'm not happy, she thought. I'm not unhappy, either. I'm not anything right now.

No words were said in parting. Their memories made them unnecessary.

BUCKEY'S LARGE, moist Bambi eyes were on Koko the whole time it took her to tell her story.

"Did I do the right thing, Buckey?" Koko looked at him anxiously.

"I know what you're thinking," Buckey said. "Breaking up with Rick has made you worry about him all over again. But you know there's another person you have to worry about not hurting. You have a man now who laughs and cries according to your every move. Listen, girl. You have to make a decision here and now not to repeat what happened with Rick. Or else you don't have the right to love a new man."

"Yeah, you're right."

How was it this dear, dear friend of hers understood her so well? Koko wondered, laying her head on Buckey's shoulder.

"Tired?"

"No, I slept well just now. You know, Buckey, people who can hate someone with all their might are lucky. I envy them."

"That guy you were in love with was really pathetic, wasn't he?"

"Yeah. I hate it, but I can't help wondering what he's doing now. Jesse's out, and I'm gone. He must really be in a bad way."

"Are you worried?"

"Uh-huh."

"Time'll be kind. You got to wait it out. There are lots of things you can worry yourself over, Koko. But the one thing you can be sure of is that pot of hot soup Spike is making for us. That's one happiness we can count on."

"Things are going well with him?"

"Yeah, real good."

"I'm glad. If you guys weren't getting along, it'd be hard to have me here."

"Oh, come on, Koko. You're treating me like a late-night deli. You *know* you always have a place with me, girl."

"You *are* a late-night deli, Buckey. Just seeing your light on in the dark is a great comfort to me. I love you, Buckey. I mean that."

Buckey thought of what lay before Koko. It made him a little anxious. This girl cannot stand up by herself, he thought. She can't throw her crutches away. Buckey knew that people like her could never be satisfied with the soup in front of them.

WHEN KOKO arrived at Randy's apartment the next evening, she was surprised at the scene that confronted her. An Asian boy opened the door, dressed in nothing more than a towel around his waist. He greeted Koko, who merely stood in the doorway unable to think of a single thing to say. Luckily for her, James came out of his room just then, and the boy in the towel returned to the bathroom, laughing.

"Hey, Koko. How's it going? Randy called from work. He said he was stopping by the supermarket on his way home. Should be back pretty soon."

"Uh, was that guy just now your lover, James?" Koko asked.

James pointed at himself in shock. "Me and Lee? You gotta be kidding. He's a friend from school. Jesus God, Koko. You know I'm not gay, don't you? Lee's not gay, either. Can't you hear what's going on in the bathroom?"

Koko listened. She could hear the shower, and after a few moments she realized that under the cascading water were the more muted sounds of a man and a woman making love. She reddened and turned to James, who shrugged and motioned her to sit.

"You want something to drink?"

"Sure. You have anything alcoholic?"

James got some ice out of the freezer and mixed two large gin and tonics.

"Lime?"

"Don't put it in the glass. Just give me a wedge."

James brought over the two glasses and some lime on a plate. He sat down in front of Koko.

"Is it always like this?" Koko asked.

"Like what?"

"I mean, do your friends always bring girls over here and —you know, do *that*?"

"You kidding? No way." James squeezed lime into his glass. "By the way, Lee's girlfriend is not a girl. Far from it, as a matter of fact."

"She's a boy?"

James nearly choked on his gin and tonic. He guffawed loudly.

"'Not a girl' means someone a little older, like a woman."

Koko squeezed her lime into her own glass, then sipped at her drink.

"I'm older than Randy. Quite a bit older."

"I know, but Mary's older than you and, what's more,

she's married. And what's *more*, she's married to a professor at our school."

"Not good."

"That's right. As far as we're concerned, it's a hopeless situation. But that makes them all the more hot for each other. They're totally gone."

"They use your place here to meet?"

"Not all the time. Lee commutes from Jersey. There're all sorts of inconveniences."

Koko glanced toward the bathroom. The water showed no sign of stopping. She sighed. It's not so great being an adult, she thought. There was no way anyone could stop a person from falling in love.

"By the way, have you broken up with that guy?"

Koko lowered her eyes at James's abrupt question and nodded.

"Have you really?"

Koko was offended. "Why would you say that?" she asked.

"No reason. You just don't look like a woman who's thrown everything away."

"That's rude. I *have* broken up. I just have to go back later to get my things."

"I see." James looked at her for what felt like a long time. Koko felt that those gray eyes could see right through her. They said, If you're gonna lie, don't bother talking to me. I only deal with people who are straight with me. Koko could understand why Randy had chosen him for a roommate.

"It's like this, Koko," James said. "I don't want to see my friend hurt. Randy's been worrying about you all the time. He can't concentrate on anything. He's in love with you."

"Well, James, let me tell you this. I'm in love with Randy. That's the honest truth. But it was another relationship that made me what I am today."

"Uh-huh."

"Because I'm in love with Randy, there's a certain person I'm hurting even more than before. So there's more to this than meets the eye, and that's all I'm going to say to you."

"Well, ex-*cuuuse* me," James said with a faint smile. "It looks like you've been pretty hurt yourself."

Koko smiled and shrugged. "I can't hide anything from a smart boy like you, can I?"

James laughed, as the bathroom door opened and the two lovers came out. They looked distinctly embarrassed.

"You laughing at us?"

"Don't be stupid. Lee, this is Koko, Randy's girlfriend. Koko, Mary."

Koko took a good look at Mary and was more than a little surprised to find her rather plump and, in a very ordinary skirt and blouse, looking like a housewife who spent her days baking pies and embroidering tablecloths. Lee gave Koko a wide grin, but Mary kept her eyes on the ground. Koko felt warm toward her. She didn't look happy, Koko thought, but she still had her dignity. Koko remembered Eileen, such a different breed. Mary looked ambivalent; she was struggling, determined not to buckle under the weight of love. You couldn't call her beautiful, but she struck Koko as somehow gallant. Koko would have liked to give her a hug.

"We'd better be going," Lee said, running a comb through his wet hair. James looked at him, disgusted.

"What, you think our place is a bathhouse? Randy's coming back; wait until he gets here."

"Yeah, well . . ."—Lee looked at Mary—"she has to be getting on home."

Koko held her hand out again to Mary. "I'm glad to have met you. Hope to see you again. And take care."

Mary's face lit up. "Thank you. You take care, too."

The two thanked James and left.

"Where's Lee from?" Koko asked, sitting down again.

"He's Vietnamese. I think he was born in New Jersey, though. But I can't believe it."

"Believe what?"

"I couldn't possibly have sex with a fat ol' dull woman like that." James spat.

"What an awful thing to say! They're in love, aren't they?"

"That makes it even harder to understand. How the hell could he feel that way about a woman like that? A *married* woman, too. I can only get it on with beautiful women."

"I said you were smart a little while ago, James. Well, I take it back."

"Don't get mad! Being smart and liking beautiful women are two different things. Randy's a good-looking, cool dude himself, isn't he? That's one of the reasons why you fell in love with him, isn't it?"

"Well, that's—"

At that moment, the door opened and Randy walked in. He'd run up the steps and stood before them with beads of sweat on his forehead. The two looked at each other, then rushed to embrace. She needed him so much. All she could think of was how she'd missed him. She realized only now how much she had been longing for him, even for the smell of his sweat.

"I wanted to see you. I really wanted to see you," Randy said.

"Me too."

"When I can't see you, you're all I think about. What're you doing to me, Koko?"

Koko touched him: his eyes, his ears, his lips.

"You smell like lime. Were you drinking something?" Randy asked her.

"Uh-huh."

"Your lady's been ordering me around like a bartender."

"Make one for me too, James," Randy said.

James rolled his eyes up and muttered, "Welcome to James's bar." He got more ice out of the freezer. "Lee was here. Left just before you came back," he said, handing Randy a gin and tonic.

"Oh, yeah? My bed or yours?"

"Neither. The bathroom, can you dig it?"

"Geez, they're really into it."

"I introduced them to Koko. She seemed taken with them. In fact, we were having a bit of a fight about it when you walked in."

"I didn't like the way you were talking about them, that's all," Koko said, handing him her empty glass. He took it, grumbling, and went to make her another drink.

"Whaddaya think, big guy?" he asked. "Could you sleep with that woman? I can't imagine it myself. Far better to have a good-looking woman than somebody's fat wife, wouldn't you agree?"

"I'll take Koko over anyone."

"Fuck you! Puttin' up a good front for Koko. Lee's a good guy, and I don't have anything to say about his coming here to have sex. The problem is that woman. My sense of aesthetics can't handle it."

"I don't mind, as long as they change the sheets," Randy joked, feeding Koko a piece of lime. Lee and Mary couldn't hold his attention. Only one thing interested him at the moment, and she was seated right in front of him.

"I think I'll get out of your way here."

"Oh, James, don't mind us," Koko said.

"OK, I'll stay here all night and bug you. That's what I'd like to say, but I have to go to work."

"Huh? You're working tonight? What kind of work?" Koko asked.

"He's working at a friend's club." Randy answered for him.

After James had gone, the two hunkered down in bed with pastrami and Swiss cheese sandwiches. The room was dim, and music played softly. Then, as if to tease themselves by holding back, they put on the TV and watched Arsenio Hall.

Koko had a hard time getting her sandwich down. Eating was the last thing on her mind. But she and Randy rolled with laughter at Arsenio's silly jokes. Each time they brushed up against each other, they shivered with anticipation. They didn't give in to their desires, though, not yet.

As soon as the program ended, Randy shouted, "It's time!" At Koko's puzzled look, he pounced on her. She giggled uncontrollably, and soon her giggles turned into moans of pleasure. She cried out, not caring if anyone heard, and whispered all sorts of endearments.

Randy returned Koko's words of love in kind. Though he told Koko he loved her, he was vaguely aware there was no proof he could offer her. This was the first time he felt love so keenly. He'd never had the anxious feeling he had now that something bad might happen. He made love to her desperately, trying to make the anxiety go away.

Compared to Randy, Koko was a veteran at losing things. The fear of loss that went side by side with loving was something she'd known for a long time. Even as love was growing, it was being eaten away from the other side. It was only a matter of time. Koko was resigned to this illogic. She concentrated all her strength on clearing her mind and giving herself up to him. She knew if she held back, her frustration would turn into jealousy and despair and ruin their time together. She knew that, like her, Randy was incapable of hating others. Suddenly, Buckey's remark about "the soup in front of you" crossed her mind. The thought brought with it such happiness that before she knew what she was saying she murmured, "I'll never hurt you."

That night, Koko had a dream, a still, quiet dream. Rick was lying in bed, alone. His eyes were open a little, and tears kept flowing out of them. After a while, the tears turned into a river and flowed over the too-wide bed. She looked on vacantly. All of a sudden, the bed started to smell, and she grimaced. It was clearly the smell of whiskey. A whiskey river, she thought. In time, the whiskey turned into sweat. Rick groaned and muttered, "All this sweat I'm sweating." She tried to say something when the sweat turned red; it was blood now. She wasn't a bit surprised to see it. "That's what I was telling you," she said calmly, then laughed in a low voice. The laughter disappeared quickly, condensing into what looked like drops of dew, which fell into the blood. Then the blood became a deluge, and the fear that she'd be swept away lanced through her. I've got to get out of here, she thought, and that's when she opened her eyes.

Randy was sleeping peacefully by her side, the rhythm of his breathing slow and deep. Koko lay perfectly still, looking up at the ceiling. The radio was still playing. The sweet low voice of a woman singing the blues.

"Rick."

Koko uttered the name almost soundlessly. Pitiful man, she thought. Randy lay with one leg over her own. Koko sighed and turned over toward the dear man sleeping beside her. His sleeping face looked just like a little boy's. Koko moved so her cheek lay where his breath would fall on it. There's all kinds of unhappiness in the world, Rick had told her. But I've got to think about myself, she thought.

Some people spend the night happily asleep, dreaming sweet dreams, while others spend it awake. All kinds of homes, all kinds of roofs exist, and every manner of happiness and unhappiness under them. Koko thought about how tiny she was, how insignificant her existence. And beside her lay a man to whom her small self meant everything. Loved as she was, she could, more or less, forgive herself her weakness.

FALL

NEW YORK'S short autumn was passing in a blur when Jesse and Daryl showed up unexpectedly at Koko's gallery. It had been ages since she'd seen them. Koko was delighted. Jesse had shot up by more than an inch, and Daryl appeared ever more grown-up.

Daryl kept looking around the gallery, obviously hoping to find Sue. Koko said she'd bring her along later, after work. They decided on where to meet, and Koko shooed the boys out.

No sooner had they gone than Sue appeared. Peeved, Koko prodded her friend.

"You were hiding, weren't you?"

"Of course not."

"You have to tell Daryl not to come here," Koko said. "No matter how grown up he looks, he's still a child. We can't have him wandering around in here."

"Why? He likes paintings, doesn't he?"

"Sue, listen. I've arranged to meet them tonight after work, and you're coming with me."

Sue looked down at the floor, then squared her shoulders

and raised her head as though she'd come to a decision. She looked Koko straight in the eye. "I'm not going."

"Why not? Didn't you see how Daryl looked just now? He needs to see you."

"That's why I don't want to go."

"I want an explanation, Sue, and I want it now."

Sue sat down, shamefaced. "I want to break up with him," she said.

"Why?"

"Because . . ."

"Because why?"

"Because I'm married, that's why."

Astounded to be hearing such a patently obvious rationale at this late date, Koko could only blink at her.

"I really am married, Koko."

"I know that. But you knew full well you were married when you started going out with him. You're so much older than he is. You have to take responsibility. . . . Listen to me—responsibility! What am I saying?"

"Calm down, Koko. I have someone to go home to. Even if I go and do whatever I like, there's someone at home waiting for me. He's a good man and a kind husband. I don't want to lose him."

"Does he know about . . . ?"

Sue chewed her lip. "No, it's like . . . I don't know. He's been so strange lately. I'm scared. Daryl's too serious about me, and my husband's awfully perceptive about some things, and . . . well, I feel like I have to do something before it's too late. I'm panicked, Koko. I get desperate when I think that maybe he's falling in love with another woman. I like Daryl, I do. But my husband's acting so strange."

"You expect me to sympathize? Well, that's just fine and dandy. As long as everything's all right with *you*."

"Come on, Koko." Sue begged Koko to tell Daryl she couldn't see him for a while. She really was panicked.

Thoroughly disgusted, Koko took a deep breath. She leaned forward and spoke between clenched teeth.

"On the surface of it, I'd say you're just like Rick."

KOKO'S CHEST tightened when she spotted Jesse and Daryl sitting on a park bench waiting for her. Their shoulders, though, had become too broad to accept her pity. They couldn't be cuddled anymore, far from it; they were becoming the ones who would open up their arms to enfold others. It seemed best to tell them straight out how Sue felt.

"Sorry to make you guys wait. Here you go: proof of my sincerity."

She handed them each a soda and a sandwich that she'd bought at a deli on her way over. Jesse stood up and took his happily.

"Hi, Koko. So tell us, how've you been? Sit down here." He brushed off the bench.

"Thanks. How have *you* two been? Anything new? Is Rick going to work every day?"

"Pretty much," Jesse said, unfolding his deli bag. He popped open his soda and licked up the foam that came spurting out. Wiping his hand, he urged Daryl to dig into his bag.

"I don't want any," Daryl said. He was hunched forward, elbows on his knees, hands clasped in front of him. Koko looked at Jesse, her eyes asking him what was up. Jesse shook his head slowly a couple of times.

"You're not hungry, Daryl?" Koko asked.

Daryl shook his head. The three sat silently on the bench for a while.

"You called me out here because you had something to

say, didn't you? I'll tell you straight, talking in a park in the early evening is not my idea of fun. This is the time when I need a drink to warm me up."

At that, Daryl kicked the ground with a muttered "Shit." Raising his face, he looked at Koko. "Did she tell you something?" he asked.

"Yeah. Things haven't been going well with you two, I gather. Since when?"

"It's nothing to do with Sue and me. It's Sue's problem. She won't see me at all. I call her at home and her husband answers; I call her at work and she's there, but she never comes to the phone. It's always 'She's on another line' or 'She's not at her desk right now.' If she wants to say something, she should tell me straight. If I did something wrong, she should tell me."

"You don't have any idea what the problem is, do you, Daryl?"

"No, I don't. It's not like we had a fight or anything, but all of a sudden she won't see me and I have no idea why. I can't concentrate on anything, hanging like this. I love her."

"You love her?" Koko looked at Daryl. He was red-faced.

"What's wrong with that? Is it strange for me to love her? I'm not indulging myself in a whim here. When I think of Sue, I feel like I'm about to go crazy. I can't stand it, knowing she's married."

Jesse didn't have any words yet about being in love. He sat, scowling, chewing on his sandwich.

"Daryl." Koko put her arm around his shoulder. "Don't go trying to read too much into this. If you're sad, go ahead and cry. If it hurts, you can curse. It's true Sue was attracted to you for a while. But that was only because her life with her husband is secure. There are women who get involved with men with that as a basis. When all is said and done, the only thing she really cares about is her husband. It's not like she loved you, Daryl."

"So you're saying she was just having fun?"

"You could put it that way. The one thing you can be perfectly clear on is that you loved her, but she didn't feel that way about you. Love on the side for a married woman is a deadly serious game, but a game all the same. She's not going to go so far as to stake everything on it. A serious game always brings regrets with it as well as fun. If she were really in love with you, she'd be going through a divorce about now. At the very least, there'd be some kind of huge uproar. Did you really think that Sue cared about you while you were with her, Daryl? She wasn't suffering at all, was she? The truth is, she wasn't feeling the least bit bad. The only time she starts to feel some real grief is when she's afraid of losing her husband. Face it, you didn't mean that much to her."

"Why not? Because I'm too young?"

"I don't know about that. You're young, but you're a terrific man. It's just that Sue didn't want the sort of affair where she'd end up throwing away everything she had. Daryl, a lot of men have the same kind of affair with women. If you get involved with these people, you have to go with their flow. That's one of the stupid rules of the adult world. The unfortunate thing was that you were too young to know that. But it doesn't matter. The only thing that does matter is that you've lost her. But you know, this will happen again and again. That's the way it is with men and women. You get someone, you lose them, and after a while you get someone else, and so on. You're OK. You'll meet another girl. You should be thinking about the next time."

"I don't want anyone but Sue."

Daryl held his head in his hands. Koko felt pained for him and, at the same time, for herself. It has to be this person and

no one else: how many pairings had this wildly illogical stub-
bornness created for her? There were so many men, she
thought, but when you can't help chasing a certain someone,
the wrong someone, you set yourself up for all kinds of
heartache. If only she could have decided things on the basis
of logic, she could have saved herself so much pain. Koko was
ashamed of herself for preaching to her young friend about
the virtues of logic. I can't even say I'm never again going to
go through what he's going through now, she thought.

"I'm sorry, Daryl. I spoke out of turn. I'm the last person
who should be advising you. I'm as messed up as you are,
and I should know better at my age! But I'm constantly getting blindsided. I do know, though, that Sue's not coming
back to you. And I don't think she ever suffered over you."

"So she was a bitch, plain and simple!" Jesse exclaimed,
furiously balling up his bag and sandwich wrapper.

"But it was Daryl's choice. He can't say that Sue tricked
him into going to bed with her. Unless you take some of the
responsibility yourself, you have no business making love
with a woman. Sue never once tried to hide the fact that she
was married. And I don't think she ever tried to give Daryl
the impression that she might want to leave her husband."

"Even so, if a woman doesn't send out the signals, a man
isn't going to get interested. Sue took advantage of Daryl's
age right from the start. He was easy to twist around her little finger. Sue's a terrible woman, a right bitch, and that's
the truth!"

"Daryl's youth was part of his attraction."

"But she got tired of it after a while, didn't she?"

Daryl merely hung his head sadly as the two argued.
They finally noticed he wasn't saying anything and looked
at each other in distress.

"Come on, Daryl," Jesse said. "Forget about her. Shit—
you and Daddy both. You lose one woman and that's going

to put you in the dumps the rest of your life? I don't believe this shit."

Ignoring him, Daryl looked at Koko.

"I don't care who's responsible, or who took advantage of whom. All I want to know is, does this mean I'm never going to sleep with Sue again? I'll never be able to be with her again like that, ever?"

There was so much pain in Daryl's eyes that Koko was unable to answer him.

"She and I are never going to make love again, Koko?"

"I think, probably, you won't," Koko said.

Daryl's eyes filled with tears. He rubbed at them with clenched fists, then pressed the backs of his thumbs against his closed eyelids.

Jesse tried to comfort him. "Be strong, dude. All the high school girls dig you. The only thing is that you can't sleep with Sue anymore. There're lots of others who'd sleep with you in a minute."

Daryl fought down his sobs. "Sleeping with Sue was very private. Our own private pleasure. It won't be the same with any other woman. You can't understand, Jesse."

Jesse looked away. Koko understood how Daryl felt so well it hurt, and she would have given anything to be able to help him. She took his hand and held it tight.

"Are you all right, Daryl? Are you all right?"

"Uh-huh. But I don't know what to do. I feel like a dog who's lost its master. I was always wagging my tail at the scent of her perfume."

"Everyone's like that. I've felt the same way. Not being able to forget the touch of the person you love—I know exactly how it is. There's nothing you can do about it, you just get through it." Koko took a handkerchief out of her bag and handed it to Daryl. Jesse looked disgruntled at the sight of the two huddled together, consoling each other.

"You can talk, Koko, but you've got yourself a man," he snapped.

"That's right," Koko shot back. "And I constantly worry about what I'll do if I lose him. That's why I know how Daryl feels. Daryl, the one thing you have at your age that I don't is your family around you. Maybe you've lost your love, but when you go home, everything's going on just the same—nothing's happened. It's not like that when you get to be my age. You have to remake your whole life then. It's not easy."

"So I'm lucky?" Daryl raised his face.

"Yes, you are. You've got to believe that."

"But I can't forget her even if I tried. Not for a long time, at least."

"I know how you feel."

"Hey, Koko, what's your guy like? Are you two living together?" Jesse asked.

"He's a wonderful person. He treats me very well. But we're not living together. I'm staying with some friends. It's hard on them, I know, but I have to save up a bit before I can rent my own place."

"Them? You're staying with more than one person? Are they a couple?" Jesse asked.

"Uh-huh. They're both guys."

"You mean—?" Jesse held up a hand and let it hang limply from his wrist. "Fags give me the creeps," he said.

"Me, too," Daryl said.

Koko shrugged and looked at them.

"What do *you* know?" she said tersely. "You've only just begun to get used to girls. Their tastes are a little different, that's all. By the way, Jesse, how's Rick been?"

Jesse crushed his empty soda can and popped it into a nearby garbage receptacle. "That son of a bitch," he muttered.

"Don't use that language about your father."

"He doesn't change, that guy. He sits around every day, looking at nothing. Sometimes he gets really drunk, comes home at dawn, and passes out in the kitchen. Mom came over a while ago and was shocked. Daddy didn't want her to see how much he'd been drinking, so he went around trying to hide the empty liquor bottles, but she found them. I'm so sick of him. He's the pits, man, the absolute pits."

"What was your mom doing there?"

"She says she broke up with that guy. But it's no use. I think Mom's maybe trying to get back together with Daddy, but—"

"Your mother wants to get back together with your dad?"

Koko was shocked to feel her heart lurch. Jesse shot her a look and continued.

"Uh-huh. She says she's tired and she doesn't feel like trying to look for another man, says it'll be hard to find one. But I don't think those two can make it together. Neither of them think about their mistakes. You and I are the only ones who think about what we've done. Sure, I'd like to see them back together. Nothing would be better as far as I'm concerned. But I'm going to be independent in five more years. I'll be grown up. I don't want them both coming after me then, wanting to depend on *me*."

"So you don't think it'll work with them. And? What're they saying to each other?"

"Who wants to know? You saying it bothers you?" Jesse looked at her.

Koko had the grace to be ashamed of herself. She had no idea why the possibility of Rick and his ex-wife making up disturbed her so much, but it did.

"They had a big fight and haven't talked to each other since," Jesse continued. "That's when Daddy told me he was through with lying. He said he wants to make it work with the next woman he's with. But he's hopeless. He can want the next time to be right, but he always goes straight for the bottle. He can't control himself. Sure you don't want to come back, Koko?"

"Yes, I'm sure. But I'm always worrying about him. He's so terribly weak, and I'm not strong enough to help him."

"Why don't you come and visit sometime, then? Your stuff is still there, and all."

Koko didn't answer. She could envision Rick wasting his days. He must be very close to desperation, she thought. Koko was beyond mistaking pity for love, though. She had learned that people can only accept love when it comes from an equal.

"Tell Rick not to drink so much," she said.

"Shit. Tell him yourself. If only you'd come back, things'd be a helluva lot easier on me."

Daryl hunched over again. "You really think I'm never gonna get to be with Sue again? Damn it all, she *liked* sleeping with me. Shit. Can't trust women."

Koko and Jesse exchanged glances. Jesse shrugged and said to Daryl, "I knew that a long time ago. I learned it from my mom. Men are almost as bad—my dad taught me that. Having children don't help none, either."

Jesse looked strangely grown up as he rubbed his nose. Koko suddenly felt very tired. For better or worse, she thought, these children were learning about the world a whole lot faster than she had. She was looking at a couple of kids who were resigning themselves to a lack of love.

KOKO WAS waiting at Fanelli's for Randy. They'd arranged to meet there for dinner. So I get to see him again today, Koko thought, as Randy bent down to kiss her blushing cheek. No matter how often they met, she could never get used to seeing him. She'd freeze with anxiety if he was so much as five minutes late. Sometimes Koko would wonder why the thought of losing Randy terrified her so. What a 'fraidy cat she was, she thought. That was when Koko would tell herself that no matter how many times a person breaks up, she never gets any stronger for it.

"What's with you, Koko, lookin' at me like that, huh?" Randy was looking down at her and laughing. Koko threw her arms around him and held him tight. Breathing in his smell, she felt herself relax.

"Did you miss me that much?" Randy whispered against her ear. He looked incredibly happy. Koko nodded fiercely, glad to be with someone who accepted how she felt about him. The only thing she wanted was to be able to express her love and have that love accepted exactly as it was.

"I'm so happy I could see you again," she said.

"Of course you're seeing me again. Koko, you're gonna see me and see me until you say you're sick of me. But, babe, I'm gonna make sure you never do get sick of me, you hear?"

Koko looked into Randy's clear eyes. Those eyes must never get cloudy on account of her, she thought.

Randy looked up suddenly and frowned. Koko followed his gaze.

"Shit. I can't believe *those* guys are coming in here," he said.

Two young men had walked in. Seeing Randy, they waved and headed over to greet them.

"Friends of yours?" Koko asked.

"Yeah. They're from my school," Randy said.

One boy was black, the other white. They said hi to Koko and poked Randy in the head, one gripping him around the neck in a mock headlock.

"Introduce us to your lady friend, Randy," they teased.

"No way. She's my girl. I introduce you two jokers to her

and you'll horn in for sure. Go sit over there," Randy said. The white boy held out his hand to Koko.

"I'm Victor. Pleased to meet you. This is Art. We're *very* good friends of Randy's."

"Good friends, my ass. Go take a hike. Preferably off a very short pier."

"Ooh, ooh, hurt me, hurt me! Come on, Randy, be nice. That's no way to treat your friends now, is it?"

Laughing, Koko shook their hands. Not waiting for Randy's permission, they plunked themselves down at the table and motioned to a passing waitress.

"Sorry, Koko. These two clowns're always like this. A couple of pests."

"That's OK. I don't mind. I like meeting your friends," Koko said.

Art laughed and said, "See? We're not bothering you."

"Dude, when did you start going with such a fine-looking woman?" Victor asked.

"Shut up," Randy replied.

"From last summer," Koko said. She was having fun. Koko liked boys Randy's age. They were easygoing and frank, yet one sometimes got a glimpse at how desperately they were trying to forge their own style. People around her at work were more relaxed but endeavored only to be conventional, to avoid making waves. Randy's friends were a refreshing change for her.

"So, Randy, you seen Lee around lately?" Art could barely suppress his merriment.

"No, not recently, but it seems James has. He comes to the apartment sometimes."

"With that woman?"

"Guess so."

Koko was thinking of Mary when the three boys burst out laughing.

"The other day"—Victor struggled to speak through his laughter—"Art 'n' I were at this movie, and I was just about to say, 'Hey, isn't that guy from your class?' when, whaddaya know, it was Lee. With *that woman*. Me 'n' Art were wondering what was going on, but we didn't call out to them or nothin'. And then they came and sat down right in front of us."

"And?" Randy opened a bottle of Tabasco and looked at the two in turn.

"So Lee, he puts his arm around her and starts kissing the old bag. I mean, really tonguing her, the whole bit. I tell you, Art 'n' I were shitless, *totally* grossed out, man. Forgot all about watching the movie."

"What's so strange about that?" Koko asked. She felt as if she were being strangled.

"I thought I was gonna barf," Art said.

"Why? All lovers kiss in the movie theater. Randy and I do, too."

"Koko, if you and Randy kiss, nobody's gonna say nothin'. What's gross is seeing Lee get really into it with that fat, homely woman. It's just too gross for words."

"I have no idea what you're talking about," Koko said.

Randy glanced at her. He could tell she was angry. For Randy's sake, she decided to keep her cool in front of Victor and Art.

"Looks like that piggie has something Lee wants."

"Yeah. Did'ja get a load of that belly? I wonder if there's something good hidden under all that flab."

"If so, that makes it all the better."

That's when it happened. Listening to the pair's exchange, Randy let out a guffaw. Koko watched him, aghast.

"What's so funny, Randy?" she asked.

Randy tilted his head as if he didn't understand what she was asking. Victor and Art fired off one bad joke after another about Mary, laughing uproariously the whole time. Koko listened in shock. She learned then that those who've been raised to accept affection with open arms can be incredibly arrogant about love.

Koko felt oppressed all through dinner, but she didn't say a word. She didn't want to spoil Randy's good mood, and besides, there wasn't any malice in their jokes. It wasn't as if they disliked Lee or Mary. They simply said whatever they felt like, confident that no one would mind so long as their insults weren't directed at the people in front of them.

Koko would sometimes see students like these organize symposiums to discuss issues such as racism and problems in the government. They'd debate them earnestly, truly distressed over problems that had little or nothing to do with their own lives. Never once did Koko see them waver in their passionate sincerity. Even while admiring them, Koko knew they couldn't maintain that idealistic posture when they confronted personal dilemmas; she doubted they could keep shouting those lofty-sounding principles then.

"Something wrong, Koko?" Art was looking at her. Koko reddened. They were nice guys, she told herself, not malicious. She didn't know what to reply.

"Guess we're butting in on you two," said Victor.

"No, not at all. I'm sorry, I was daydreaming."

"She's mad because we were saying nasty things about Mary."

Victor was surprised at Randy's comment. "Wow!" he exclaimed. "You're really nice, aren't you?"

"Nice?" Koko said weakly. "I don't know if you would call it nice. It's just that everybody gets old, and some of us are going to get ugly. It could happen to anyone. That's why I don't like to say anything about someone who's having a hard time of it."

"But you don't know," Art said, "that they're having a hard time, do you? If we don't see it, it's not our problem, is it?"

"I've only just met you, Koko," Victor added, "but I think maybe you worry too much. How 'bout if you concentrate on just having fun with Randy? He's a great guy, and besides, he's nuts about you."

Embarrassed, Randy elbowed him.

"I'm nuts about Randy too," she said. Randy's eyes beamed with pleasure, and he covered her hand with his own. Koko had mixed feelings as she put her other hand on top of his so as not to let that warmth escape.

"Did those guys bother you?" Randy asked on their way home.

"No, not at all. They're nice. And they like you. Everyone likes you, Randy."

"Is that so."

"Yes, that's so. You can't even imagine people not liking you."

"Are you being sarcastic?"

"No. I'm just saying what I think."

"As long as you like me, sweetie, that's enough for me."

"I don't think so. Your love for me is based on the satisfaction that comes from others liking you."

"Is there something wrong with that?"

"No, it's a good thing. I like seeing you happy. But I'd like you even if you weren't happy," Koko said.

"Don't say that. It sounds sad somehow."

"Just be selfish and playful. And love me."

"Like now, you mean?"

"Yes."

Koko believed the one difference between her and Randy was that she worried over losing him while he didn't worry over losing her at all. It seemed to her Randy simply could not envision a time when their love would be over. Koko knew that one could never tell when the happiness created between people might end. She also knew that love's destroyer didn't always come from the outside, but rather from within a person's own heart. There was no such thing, she thought, as a love between a man and a woman that lasted forever.

"I don't want to lose you," she said.

Surprised, Randy drew himself away from her.

"Why would you say that? There's no way I'd ever leave you, Koko." He looked at her earnestly.

"You're a sweet boy," she said. "But the world never goes just the way you want it."

Randy sulked, while Koko twined her arms in his and held him close.

"I'm lonely when you're not with me," she said. "I need to have you in the corner of my eye. And it's awful to go to sleep at night in a place that doesn't have your smell."

"Koko, let's live together."

"Maybe someday. I want to be alone for a while. More important, do you know what it's like to live with someone and still feel lonely? To want each other, and yet not be satisfied with each other? I had that kind of life. I don't ever want it to be that way with us. That's why I'm a little afraid, to be honest."

"Is that my fault?" Randy asked. "You think I can't handle it because I'm young?"

"No, it's not that. Failure doesn't always make a person strong. It's my fault. Maybe I'm a coward. I've started thinking stupid things—like what if I lose you?"

Randy's eyes widened.

"When you're always thinking about the loss of someone that's irreplaceable to you, it's a sign of how much you love that person. I haven't told you yet, have I? Randy, I love you."

Randy held Koko tight. Maybe I'm the coward, he thought. For the first time, he could taste the anxiety that comes with the ever-present possibility of losing love. A vague loneliness stole over his heart. Koko, he thought, always exposed tiny fragile seeds within herself that became the little sprouts of more love for him, and also of her resignation. Randy wondered if he'd ever be able to love her as much as she loved him.

"Randy, let's have a drink and then go home."

"OK," he said.

A homeless person passed by and shook his paper cup at them. Koko dropped a few dimes in, murmuring, "Takes guts to get like this." Randy didn't understand what she meant.

It was noisy inside the bar. As he went in, Randy looked back. The homeless person was giving them the finger. Randy shrugged and shook his head. Jerk. He got his money. She's really too nice to people, he thought, his eyes on Koko's back.

WINTER

WINTER HAD crept up on them before they knew it. Everyone around Koko was caught up in pre-Christmas excitement, asking each other about this and that party. Buckey decided to host one. Spike, an excellent cook, announced he'd take care of the food. Buckey ran around getting the apartment in order and setting up a bar in the corner. He assigned Koko the role of bartender.

Koko sat on the living room couch and began to write a list of drinks they'd need. She called out to Buckey, busily at work in the kitchen, "What should I get for champagne? I can't afford anything very expensive."

"Pink'd be good," Buckey said, sticking a wire bottle brush down the kitchen drain—it had a tendency to clog.

"Pink! What kind of pink? There're a zillion kinds of pink. Men are so vague."

"Men? You mean me?"

"That's right. More or less. What does Spike drink?"

"Oh, he won't touch anything but vodka martinis. He likes Absolut for the vodka."

"Is that the one with the silver label?"

"I thought it was white."

"It is?"

"Hey, Koko, you *are* inviting your boyfriend, aren't you? We're finally going to meet this Randy boy, aren't we?"

"Yeah, but don't go stealing him away from me."

"You kidding? Me? I'd never do such a *woman*like thing."

"Well, ex-*cuuuse me*."

Buckey's telephone rang and he handed it to Koko.

"It's your kiddy," he said.

Koko took the receiver from him. Jesse was on the line.

"How you doin', Koko? What're you up to for Christmas? You wanna come here?"

"I can't make it for Christmas Eve or Christmas Day. Why?"

"Well—uh, I was wondering if maybe I was—uh, getting a present from you this year."

Koko snorted. Children always try to widen their circle of adult acquaintances around Christmas time.

"What do you want?"

"A suit."

"A suit? What for?"

"I'm going to Tanya's house for New Year's Eve."

"Tanya? Who's that?"

"My girlfriend."

"What happened to Tracy?"

"We broke up."

Koko was silent. Putting a palm over the receiver, she turned to Buckey, who was looking on with great interest. She rolled her eyes and shrugged, silently saying, Can you believe this kid?

"Koko, you still there?" Jesse said.

"Of course I am. I'll make some time around the twenty-third. I'm not going to see Rick, though, so let's meet somewhere outside. How about Blimpie's on the corner?"

"OK. Daddy won't try to get you to do anything, Koko. Eileen's been coming around a lot."

"Are they going together again?"

"Dunno. That woman's a real pain in the butt. Sticks me with that crybaby brat of hers and makes me watch him. She's always getting smashed with Daddy and passing out on the couch."

"I don't believe it."

"So it's OK. Daddy gets drunk, but it's different from before. He's like soda with the fizz gone out."

"You'd better not say that to your father's face, young man."

"Well, it's the truth. I know him better than anyone else. I am his son, after all. Unfortunately."

Koko sighed. Jesse reminded her about the suit and hung up.

"You're going to buy him a suit, Koko? That's just like a mom," Buckey said, handing her a glass of wine.

"I can't believe it."

"Why not? He's growing up."

"Not Jesse, *Rick*. Remember I told you about that woman, Eileen? She's been visiting Rick a lot lately."

"Why do you find that hard to believe?" Buckey was amused.

Put out by his attitude, Koko buttoned up.

"You're not going to get jealous now, are you?" Buckey asked.

"Are you kidding?" Koko shouted. Buckey peered into her face.

"Calm down, now," he said. "Honey, you're not Rick's woman anymore, and he's not a part of you either. You're in love with Randy, right? Well, Rick's life is going on, too. If your relationship made it impossible for you to be friends once it was over, you don't have a right to go saying this and that about how he's living his life."

"Yeah, I know. You're right. But I can't help wondering what's going on with those two. Rick's really messed up."

"Why don't you go find out?"

Koko looked up at him.

"I'm serious. Why don't you go and see for yourself if he's all messed up?" Buckey said. "You'll find out he's getting along without you. People will surprise you; they're amazingly resilient. You think too much, Koko. Relationships are gravy, they're a gift from God. You should ease up a little."

"Maybe I'm arrogant, Buckey. Do you think so? I can't imagine that I wouldn't leave an impression on people. Damn it all. Maybe I'm too pushy. I wonder if that's partly why it didn't go well with Rick."

"You're always quick to analyze yourself. It's your strong point and your weak point, both."

"I didn't used to be like this. I became so analytical living with Rick. It's like I need to find a reason for everything that goes bad or I can't go on."

"Why don't you try living more by the seat of your pants? Do whatever it is you feel like doing, like the time you jumped into Randy's arms without thinking."

A light snow had begun to fall. Buckey went to stand by the window. He called Koko to come and see.

"The first snow of the year, isn't it?" she said.

"Uh-huh. Might get cold tonight. But it's warm inside. We're pretty fortunate. We have a nice life. Don't you think so, Koko?"

"Yeah. I'm glad I have a friend like you, Buckey. Happiness is something you don't really notice unless you have someone around to point it out."

Buckey and Koko stood at the window silently for a while. This screwed-up world, she thought. Finally she felt able to accept that she couldn't control most of it and that this was no sin on her part. If there were such a thing as the sound of chewing on happiness, it would have been echoing in that still room. Koko and Buckey bit down on it, and savored it, and forgot for a while to speak.

KOKO HAD asked Randy to come with her to some stores on Broadway to help look for a new suit for Jesse. Randy searched through the shirts and ties earnestly for items that might match the suit he selected, but he seemed moody. He was afraid Koko might see Rick again. He tried to imagine how she might feel seeing her old boyfriend, but nothing came to mind.

Koko couldn't help smiling at him: he'd pout, then get engrossed in scrutinizing the tags on a suit. He was adorable, Koko thought, and a really kind man.

"Does it bother you, Randy?"

"Well, actually, it does. You loved him, didn't you? I don't want you going back to the place where it all happened. You'll remember all kinds of things. And then you'll forget about me."

"That's stupid. What do you think memories are? Once you're totally involved with a new love, memories of an old boyfriend are like so much trash. Once it's over, it's over. At least that's the way it is for women."

"By new love, you mean me?"

"That's right."

Feeling better, Randy grinned. "You sure are good at saying nice things. But I know you don't think of your time with him as trash. And what's more, if it hadn't been for him, you and I might never've gotten together. If a past love is trash, then maybe it's fabulous trash that you can never ever throw away."

"Wow, that's some metaphor, coming from you."

"Come on, Koko, now you're making fun of me. But really, you know a lot more than I do, and part of what you know came from Rick, so what can I say? I'll try not to mind. But promise me one thing."

Koko fell back a step at the serious look in his eyes.

"What?" she asked.

"That you won't ever hurt me."

"Randy." Koko took his face in both of her hands and kissed him. "If there's one thing I've learned from Rick, it's that," she said.

Randy returned Koko's kiss and didn't speak of the subject again.

JESSE WAS delighted with the suit Randy chose. Koko had known he'd like it, but it was more of a hit than she'd even expected. They went from Blimpie's to Rick's apartment, as Jesse promised her his father wouldn't be there.

Brushing off her admonishment to wait until Christmas, Jesse said, "I just want to take a look," and started to dismantle the carefully wrapped box. "I'll put it back together. Then on Christmas morning I'll open it up again. That's OK, isn't it? Wow, this is great, Koko! I was right to ask you. I didn't know you had such great taste!"

"I didn't pick it out. My boyfriend did."

"Oh, yeah? How're things going with you guys?"

"OK."

Koko looked around at the room. It wasn't as messy as she'd expected. The surfaces looked like they'd been cleaned recently. She sighed, slightly disgruntled.

"You two're keeping things pretty neat around here, aren't you?" she said.

"Of course. If we let the apartment get messy on top of everything else, it'd really be the pits. Daddy gives me spending money to clean."

"Where is that daddy of yours?"

"He's out buying a new pipe for the clothes rack. The old one broke—you know, the part you hang the clothes on. You wanna see him after all? I didn't tell him you were coming today."

"No. I wouldn't know what to say. I'll just take some sweaters and a coat and go."

"I guess they're wherever you left them. In the bedroom, maybe?"

Koko stood up and hesitantly opened the door to the bedroom. It was like looking into a stranger's room. It pained her to see not a trace of herself there. The bed hadn't been made; it was no longer the bed that caused her so much anguish; it was merely a bed, sweat-stained and sagging, nothing to do with her.

Koko lowered herself onto the edge. A number of cigarette butts that weren't Rick's brand lay in the ashtray on the bedside table. Koko began to feel strangely comforted. She sat vacantly in the dim light and realized suddenly that she was smiling. She was able, finally, to forgive Rick and to forgive herself. She could feel affection for him once more. For the first time, she knew that they hadn't been a mistake. Their relationship hadn't been so much trash. It was simply something that had happened, she thought. A firmly planted milestone in her life.

"What're you thinking, Koko?"

Jesse was standing beside her. He looked about to cry.

"Sit down, Jesse." Koko patted the bed.

Jesse did as he was told, and Koko put her arm around him. Every time she saw him, his frame and posture appeared more adult.

"What did living with me mean to you?" she asked.

Jesse thought for a while.

"It was convenient. In all kinds of ways. I got sick of you

sometimes, but you were very convenient to have around. I was still a kid and I couldn't get along by myself. Daddy's like that, too. . . . Well, I don't know if 'convenient' is the right word. I don't mean anything bad by it. I'm grateful to you. I really mean that."

"I know. And I know what you're trying to say. You were convenient for me, too. I wasn't enough of an adult to share Rick's loneliness. I'm grateful to you, too. And I'll continue to be."

"What's going to happen with me and you after this? Once you get all your stuff, it'll be over, won't it?" Jesse sniffled.

Koko squeezed him tight. "It won't be over," she said.

"But you and Daddy are over, aren't you?"

"As far as being together as boyfriend and girlfriend, we are, yes."

"It's the same with Mom and Daddy. I hate it. I've seen too much of what happens with men and women."

"Maybe that's a good thing. Now it's your turn. Is this Tanya a good girl?"

Jesse chewed on his lip, embarrassed.

"Uh-huh. I made Tracy cry. Got my ass kicked by Roxanne for it, too. It was awful. I feel bad when I remember it, but I forget when I'm with Tanya."

Koko laughed. What a story, she thought. She herself had done the same thing over and over. People were so stupid. And lovable, somehow.

"Don't laugh, Koko."

"I'm sorry. So, have you slept with her yet?"

"Uh-uh. She's stingy, so she's not letting me."

Koko laughed aloud again. At that moment, the bedroom door opened. It was Rick. He was so surprised to see Koko he merely stood there, unable to speak.

Jesse raised a hand and said, "Hi, Dad."

Koko spoke too. "Hi, Rick. What's up?"

Jesse looked at Rick and Koko in turn, then stood up.

"Where're you going, Jesse?" Koko asked. Flustered, she half stood up herself. She had no idea what to say to Rick if left alone with him.

"Where? I thought maybe I'd go to Daryl's or something. You two don't want me around, do you?"

"That's not so," Koko said.

Rick's grin was pained.

"Come on out to the living room, Koko," he said. "It's been a long time. I'll fix tea. Jesse, clean up your room by tomorrow. Your mom's coming over with your presents, isn't she?"

Jesse dragged himself back to his room, looking distinctly put out. Koko was uncomfortable as she followed Rick to the kitchen and sat down. It takes quite a bit of energy to get a conversation going when you're not friends or lovers, she thought.

Rick waited quietly for the water to boil. Koko watched him closely as he lit a cigarette. He didn't seem interested in forcing a conversation. He looked like a person who'd long ago ceased to struggle. He had the quiet of the resigned about him.

The water began to boil with its soft bubbling sound and the kitchen window fogged up. Moving almost languidly, Rick got out a couple of tea bags, one for each cup. Koko watched him, cheek in hand. She gazed at his large hands with nostalgia. His fingers were very long and his knuckles prominent. Koko knew now that her dream could never have come true: those hands belonged to Rick and, as such, weren't anything Koko could own. A man's body, she realized, was not like a child's plaything, something you could get if you threw a hard enough tantrum. Koko gazed at Rick's hands intently, without longing.

"You want sugar?" Rick asked.

"Please."

Rick set a cup down in front of Koko, then settled himself into a chair.

"You know, I don't think we've ever had a cup of tea together before," Koko said. "What do you think?"

Rick looked at Koko and took a sip from his own cup. "You're right. I didn't even know whether you took sugar or not."

"It seems like we really didn't know much about each other's habits."

"Well. That was because just being together was a habit."

They smiled quietly.

"So what have you been doing all this time?" Koko asked.

"What've I been doing? Same as always. Go to work, go to bars, get drunk, spend some time sometimes with girls. Jesse lectures me 'bout this and that and I get pretty sick of myself, having to be lectured to by my own son. But I end up thinking, Well, that's the way it goes. It's a life a lot like my father's."

"Are you mad that I left?"

"Can't be helped. Ain't the first time a woman's gone and left me."

Rick laughed in self-derision. He didn't seem desperate, or tired. He seemed, in fact, rather nonchalant about it all. Koko was relieved, but at the same time she felt strangely saddened.

"How've you been?" Rick asked.

"Not bad."

"That guy's being nice to you, as always?"

"Uh-huh."

"That's good. I'm not saying that to be ironic or anything. You can come here because things're going well. You couldn't go anywhere when we were together. You couldn't even if you wanted to because you always had to wait here for me. I used to get pissed at you for that, but now I can see it was really me who was keeping you here. I had you tied down with invisible ropes."

"No, Rick, it was just the opposite. I was trying so hard to tie you to me that it didn't work. The way I see it now, I didn't know how to do anything. It's hard to love a person."

"Did you love me?" Rick asked.

"Uh-huh. And you? Did you love me?"

"Sure I did. But to tell you the truth, you were a royal pain in the butt." Rick's laugh was deep.

"I hear you've been seeing Eileen."

"Jesse told you that? What a brat, that guy. Always sticking his nose into his parents' business."

"He has a right."

"Bet it gives you the creeps, remembering her."

"Well, I can't say it doesn't. But it's not my place to say anything."

"She's all messed up. Same as me. But she's a good friend to me. I can relax around her. She doesn't want anything from me. We're a lot like each other, Eileen and I. I don't want anything from her either. She doesn't love me, and I don't love her. That's why we can make each other feel better. Sure, I think it's pretty dumb, and I don't like it, but that's why we're together. She 'n' me, we've both given up any hope that anybody might do anything for us."

"Don't you have to do something for someone before they do something for you?" Koko asked.

"Only the fortunates like you can think that. There're others where that doesn't apply. You just don't know about them. Jesse's mom is probably one prime example. She was always worrying too much 'bout what she was gonna be getting back."

"If you don't expect anything back, you can give love like a gift. I finally learned that after I left you."

"He must be a good guy."

Koko looked at Rick's profile, not knowing how to reply. She could see he was no longer the person full of hatred and weariness that he'd been when they were together. He certainly didn't look happy, though. He pushed unhappiness far away from himself. He was insulated. At last, Koko thought, he's learned how to let himself rest, to make things easy on himself, however cheerless that might be.

"Hey, you mind if I set up the pipe I bought?" Rick asked.

"Sure. The clothes rack broke, right?"

"Yeah. Jesse's really into clothes recently. Been buying all sorts of junk. I guess he's growing up."

"I'll help you," Koko said.

Rick and Koko began to clumsily work the screwdriver, looking at the directions for setting up the rack as they went along. The pipe was exceptionally long. They soon broke a sweat as they wrestled with it.

"Maybe you bought the wrong pipe. It just won't go in."

"No, that can't be. Can you take out that screw next to you? The one right there. Oh, I see now. Nut was facing the wrong way."

Muttering, Rick got the screws in order. Watching him from the side, Koko couldn't help laughing.

"I don't believe it," she said. "Men are usually pretty good at this stuff, aren't they?"

"Jesse's good at it. He even fixed the VCR by himself. Can you hold this screw right here, Koko?"

Tightening down the screw, Rick chuckled to himself. Koko looked at him dubiously.

"What's with you?" she asked.

"Hey, Koko, maybe we should change our jobs."

"What's that supposed to mean?"

"It'd be nice to make a living doing stuff like this with you all the time. It's dumb but kind of fun, you know?" Rick sighed. "I'd like to live out the rest of my days like this."

Koko let go of the pipe, her jaw set. She was ready to cry.

"It'd be great, don't you think?" Rick continued. "Working with our hands, you and me, not thinking about anything, doing simple stuff. Like two little kids."

"Don't say that."

"I mean it. Hey, Koko, can you do me a favor?"

"What?"

"Go on a date with me."

"Are you serious?"

"Sure. Let's go listen to some jazz or something."

"I didn't know you like jazz."

"Don't be so cold. Is it a yes or a no?"

"I don't know what to say."

"There, all done. What a hassle that was. Hey, Jesse," he called. "You can get your clothes off the sofa now."

Jesse came out of his room carrying a load of coats and jackets.

"What're you doing? Put the rack in your room first and then hang your jackets up."

"I don't have any more room in there anymore. Can't we put it in your room?"

"It's your fault for buying one thing after another that you don't need. Don't you know how to save money?"

"No, same as you, Daddy," Jesse said. "That reminds me, Koko bought me a suit for Christmas. I'm going to wear it when I go to Tanya's place for New Year's Eve. It's really terrific."

"How 'bout tomorrow? You're having dinner out with Mom, aren't you?"

Koko glanced at Rick and realized he would spend Christmas Eve all by himself.

"Rick, can I take you up on what you said a minute ago?"

"Huh?"

"About going on a date with me."

"Sure. But why?"

"You really want to go on a date with me?"

Rick shrugged and grinned. "Yes, I do," he said.

"Then let's do it."

"OK. But that's when I really will lose you. That's the day you'll put me out of your heart. And the day I'll leave, myself."

"I don't understand what you mean."

Koko looked at the ground. Rick put his fingers under her chin and gently raised her face.

"Koko, I still love you," he said. "So I get mad sometimes and I still get pretty jealous. It sucks, doesn't it? I'm the one who always goes with the flow, who can never make a decision and stick with it. I sit and wait for things to happen. I don't like it, but that's the way it is."

"Are you saying you want me to make something happen?"

"Well, you'll be sad on down the line if we leave things like this."

"You're feeling sorry for me?"

"No, I just wanted to do something fun with you at the last, that's all. I want to be able to nod my head and think, Yup, we had some good times, too. That's all. I like seeing the girl I'm with happy. I want to see you laugh one more time. I think maybe now I can make you laugh."

Koko sighed. "Can I have a drink, Rick? You can have one, too. Not that my permission means anything anymore."

Rick stood up and got ice out of the freezer. It made a clear clanging sound as he dropped it into a couple of glasses. Koko thought, as she watched him pour out the Bacardi,

What he needs is a woman who'd make him into her own personal bartender. A woman whose eyes would narrow with his at the smell of liquor. A woman like him.

"Any relationship has its problems," Koko said. "It wasn't like things were especially bad with you. It couldn't be helped that it ended the way it did. I don't know what's going to happen with Randy and me. No one can say anything about the future. I don't think it has anything to do with one person being wrong. After all, I'm the one who chose you. There's no reason for you to feel sorry for me."

Koko spoke all in one breath. Then she took a long sip of her rum Coke. Rick looked at her without touching his own drink. Her eyes, he thought, looked different from his own or Eileen's. Unlike Koko, Rick didn't believe that relationships brought problems with them. Trouble chose its victims, he believed, and one was chosen according to what lay in his or her own heart; unfortunately you fashion the magnet for trouble without knowing it.

"I really do want to make you laugh," he said.

"And what if I said it was too late?"

"I'm not talking about happiness. That's for your guy to give you. It's not too late for laughter."

"Thanks. But you and I are different, Rick. I know that only too well. I can't laugh if I know it's the last time. It's too sad to think of things ending."

"Breaking up with me wasn't a sad thing, was it?" Rick asked.

"Rick. You can say it's none of my business, but it hurts me to think you're going to be all alone on Christmas. But if we go out on a date, it's not going to be to get back into things."

"You feeling sorry for me?"

"I think we're going around in circles here. I am not feeling sorry for you. I'm just a little sad to think of you alone."

At that, Rick felt a great weight lifting from him. He was already something in the past for her. He could finally breathe easy. He lifted his glass to his lips. It burned going down, as always, but this time the taste brought relief as well as a sense of futility. Rick needed to avoid anything that might have any great meaning to him. Maybe what he really wanted was nothingness. One great absence. All at once, his body temperature seemed to drop. Geez, it's cold, he thought, shivering. He wanted something warm. There wasn't anything anywhere that could warm him up. He finally understood what it was he had lost.

"Are you all right, Rick?"

Koko's question seemed to revive him. He looked up with bloodshot eyes.

She put her arm around his shoulder and said gently, "What's wrong, Rick? Are you sad?"

"Yeah."

"Did I make you sad?"

"No. I made myself sad."

"Why?"

"Koko, don't you think you ask too many questions?"

Koko closed her mouth. Rick took her hand from his shoulder and pressed it to his lips. He held it there for a while, his eyes closed. Koko sat quietly, letting him kiss her. He looks like a child, she thought.

"This is what I should've done," said Rick.

"Huh?"

"This is what I should've done from the start. It would've been so easy. Pure and simple. Like a lonely child reaching out for someone. This is how people should be when they love each other," he said.

Koko smiled. "Silly Rick," she said.

Jesse, hardly breathing, opened his door a crack and

peeked out at the two. They looked to him like two people who were getting along very well indeed. It puzzled him. He couldn't understand why they would start to get along well just when they were breaking up. Adults are weird, he thought. He could sense there was a big difference between his father and Koko's relationship and his own experience with girls. He knew these two, who looked like they liked each other so much, would probably not be seeing each other again. The premonition disturbed him. They were sitting there so quietly. He could see the decision had been made. But maybe if he could get them to promise to get together once a month, the three of them . . . ? The thought shocked him. Not even when his parents had split up had he been so panicked. What was this all about? What was Koko to him, anyway? He remembered there'd been times when she'd leaned on him, when she'd looked to him, Jesse, for help. She was the first woman who'd taught him the happiness of being depended upon. He felt he had to say something. He was just about to burst into the room when he saw them embrace. Shit, he thought, can't go and butt in on them now.

Koko was on the verge of tears. Oddly enough, she'd forgotten all about Randy. Drunk with happiness, she buried her face in Rick's chest. It was the first time she'd ever felt such contentment with him. The bad memories faded away as she breathed in his smell. It had been so long since she had been in his arms. They held each other tight.

"It feels so good here in your arms. It's the one thing I'm going to miss."

"You think so?"

"Yeah. Thank you, Rick. I'm not mad or sad or anything."

Rick didn't reply. He knew that this time, for real, he'd be brought to his knees by despair when he lost what he held in his arms. It was too damn early for despair. The thought of all that living he still had to get through made his vision darken for an instant.

His arms tightened around Koko. God, he didn't want to let her go, he thought. Even so, he found himself saying, "You'd better hurry up and get yourself back to Randy's place."

Koko looked up. Rick's face was twisted with regret at what he'd just said. He'd meant to tell her how much he needed her.

Koko stroked his cheek, then nodded as though she understood what he was thinking.

"It's OK to go?" she asked in a tiny voice.

"Uh-huh."

"This is the end."

"I know."

"What a pity. It was just starting to be so nice," Koko said.

"That's because you're happy with someone else. You can be considerate of me. You knew I wanted to see you relax with me, so you did."

"I really did relax, you know."

"I know. That's your last gift to me. I appreciate it."

"Oh, Rick . . ."

Koko got up to go. Rick held the door open for her. She walked out, then turned.

"When you fall in love next time, make sure you hold her like that," she said.

Rick wanted very much to stop her, but he fought to hold himself back and didn't say a word. After she'd left and he'd pulled the door shut, he stood there, stunned. It was as if everything within him shut down all at once and his mouth sagged open with the pain of it. He felt he had to shout something, but his tongue seemed to weigh a ton.

Outside, Koko cried for a while. The freezing wind cut

cruelly at her cheeks. She was thankful that she was the one, not him, who had to be walking out in this cold. She knew, of course, that Rick must be feeling infinitely colder up there in the apartment. She walked more and more quickly, hurrying to a warm place.

THE CHRISTMAS PARTY was a huge success. Spike's food was exquisite and Buckey was in his element as host. Koko's friends greeted Randy warmly and made him feel welcome. Koko kept busy making drinks for everyone and firing off jokes.

Buckey came over and whispered into her ear, "Koko, you don't have to push yourself so hard."

"I'm not doing anything of the sort." Koko looked at him, a little offended.

"I wonder. You can be honest, girl. I think you must be feeling a bit down. You just broke up with the man you lived with for so long."

"Don't be ridiculous. Randy's here."

"Did you tell him about it?"

"Uh-huh."

"What'd he say?"

"He was a little jealous."

Buckey snorted. "He's so cute," he said.

"I know that without you telling me. Don't you go sticking your finger in the pot."

While the two were razzing each other in the corner, Koko heard Spike shout her name from the other side of the room. There was something in his voice she'd never heard before, and it sent a chill of dread through her. She hurried to the kitchen, with Buckey trailing behind. When Buckey caught up with her, Koko was sitting on the floor, her face white.

"What's wrong?" Buckey asked, shocked.

"Rick's been in an accident," Spike replied. "I don't know the details. That was his son on the phone. The boy was crying and carrying on. I couldn't get a thing out of him."

A WORRIED Buckey and Spike ushered Koko into the apartment when she returned, exhausted, from the hospital. Buckey brushed the snow from her hair and Spike rushed to the kitchen, saying he'd make her something hot to drink. Koko let Buckey take her coat, then sank onto the couch. Her body felt very heavy.

"I'm so tired," she said.

Spike came out with a cup of Ovaltine.

"So how is he? Was he badly hurt?" he asked.

"It doesn't look good. They don't know yet if he'll pull through. He hasn't regained consciousness."

Buckey sighed. "Honestly. Why did this have to happen? What are the police saying?"

"I don't know."

"You don't know? Koko, didn't they tell you anything?"

Koko looked at Buckey. "It doesn't seem to have much to do with me."

"What's that supposed to mean? There's lots of stuff you have to take care of, isn't there? With Jesse and all?"

"No, there isn't. When I got to the hospital, Rick's wife was there. I had no idea, but apparently they never got divorced. Not that it matters. And it wasn't only Rick. Eileen was in the car, too, when the accident happened. So you had the wife, the girlfriend, and the . . . what? Me. I wasn't anything there. Nobody had time to pay any attention to me. Eileen's husband came, Jesse was crying, and Rick's wife was there. I was a concerned friend who came rushing over, no more," Koko said, between sips of her drink.

Buckey put his arm around her shoulders. He stole a look

at her profile, trying to determine how she felt. All he saw there was exhaustion.

"How's Eileen?" he asked.

"She's been injured badly, but her life's not in danger."

Koko looked around the room as though she had just remembered something.

"I'm sorry, Buckey. I didn't even help you clean up. How did the party go?"

"That's nothing for you to worry about. I only told a few people about Rick's accident, so the party went on until after dawn. But you should give Randy a call. After you and Sue left for the hospital, he looked so worried. I felt terrible for him. He tried to joke around with everyone as if to get his mind off you and Rick, but he ended up looking out the window a lot. I'll bring the phone, OK?"

"No."

"No? Koko, you've got to call him."

"If I talk to Randy, I know I'll start to cry. It's strange, but when I'm with you guys I can pretty much keep myself together. The reason why I'm not crying now, Buckey, is because I know I can cry here anytime and it's all right. But it's not like that with Randy. I don't want him to see me crying over another man. I'd rather die than hurt him."

"What Randy wants, Koko, is for you to depend on him. He needs that. It's the only thing that's going to reassure him."

"I know. That's why I don't want to talk to him. Please, Buckey, you call. Tell him I'm here and I'm a little upset but basically all right."

"I can't do that. You do it yourself."

"If I talk to him, I'll end up telling him everything. If he sees me crying, he'll really be hurt."

Scowling, Buckey went off to make the call. Koko sat on

the couch, all but catatonic. The noise and laughter from the Christmas party the night before seemed like something from a million years ago.

"I BELIEVE we've met twice before," Jesse's mother had said, looking at Koko. A tight smile cut into her cheeks. "I never imagined we'd be meeting again over something like this."

Koko acknowledged her with a slight nod. "Where's Jesse?" she asked.

"He's in the waiting room around the corner, crying his eyes out. Just goes to show, even a man like that's a father." Jesse's mother spat the last words. Koko felt her blood begin to boil and took a deep breath to keep herself calm.

"You're not sad?" she asked.

"Sad?" The woman looked at Koko incredulously. "Anyone who can be sad at a situation like this is either an idiot or a sucker. Or both. Koko—do you mind if I call you Koko? You can call me June. Koko, do you have any idea what I'm feeling right now? 'Jesus, he's gone and done it to me again'—that's how I feel. When we were together, it was the same thing over and over. And in the end, the tab for the whole thing always came to me. I'd have to sign for the entire load of shit."

"I don't understand what you mean by tab."

"You wouldn't, would you? Not a nice young lady like you. It was a miracle that a person like you actually lived with him for a few years. But that miracle was a reality for me."

"I don't understand a word you're saying."

"Don't get mad. Go and see Jesse. He seems to like you. I envy people who can dispose of things just by liking them or not liking them."

"Are you saying I do that?" Koko asked.

"Don't you?" June returned.

"You don't know a thing about Rick and me."

"Then let me ask you. Who stands to lose the most if he dies? Me. I lost the most when we were married and when we lived apart, and I'll be the one to lose the most if he dies. I'm the one who'll have to take on the whole burden."

"I don't think this talk is getting either of us anywhere. I'm going to go and look in on Jesse."

Koko walked past her, her lips set. June's voice followed her.

"Koko, Rick wasn't alone in that car," she rasped. "That woman Eileen was with him."

Koko couldn't help but look back at her. June's face was pale.

"There's no reason for you to be looking so anxious. Nobody's going to take you seriously. As long as he doesn't die, that is."

There was a trace of real pain in June's voice. Koko felt a little sorry for her. Something in that voice that was very similar to Rick's. It was something that invited unhappiness.

Jesse was sitting bowed over, his face in his hands. He didn't seem to be crying anymore. Koko sat down beside him and put a hand on his knee.

"Is that you, Koko?" Jesse asked in a small voice, not raising his head.

"How did you know it was me?" Koko asked gently.

"I remember how your hand feels. You're the only woman whose hand I remember."

Koko pulled the boy's head to her shoulder. "I'm sorry, Jesse. I don't know what to say. I'm in shock, too."

"I know. Whenever I'm in shock, you're in shock, too."

Koko smiled weakly.

"Did you see Jeff's dad?" Jesse asked.

"No."

"You know, don't you? That Eileen was with him."

"Your mom told me."

"Jeff's dad kicked in a hospital door and got yelled at by a nurse."

"It's no wonder he lost his temper."

"He said something about 'That nigger's really gone and done it now.' Then Mom said, 'Your bitch is just as much to blame.' I was crying and all, but it sure was funny."

"What a mess," Koko said.

"You know, Koko, Daddy and Eileen were getting along pretty well together. There's no cause to go calling them bitch or nigger. They're even as far as I can see."

"You're absolutely right. But I can understand what made them say it."

Jesse raised his head and stretched out his legs. "People like you and me don't say stupid things like that about others. But what I don't understand is why grown-ups are always messing things up for us. How come people can't keep their shit wired tighter?"

Koko squeezed Jesse. That was exactly what she herself often wondered.

"What an awful Christmas. All Daddy's fault. But it's worse for him."

Koko thought so too. She wondered if what Jesse said was true. She remembered the look in Rick's eyes as she left the apartment for the last time. There had been silent despair there. She'd seen it, and she'd shut the door on it. But she wasn't so presumptuous anymore as to think she could've saved him.

"Did you hear me, Koko?"

Koko looked at Jesse blankly.

"I said, I wonder if Daddy's going to die."

"I don't know."

"He can't die now. It's no fair! Him dying now is no fair;

his whole life hasn't been fair! I have a right to protest. I'm the only one who does. He's my father, after all. But who can I complain to?"

Jesse began to cry again. Koko felt like crying too, but she fought back the urge. All she could do for him was hold him and keep from crying herself. The best thing for a person in pain was to be with someone stronger who was feeling the same pain.

Koko told Jesse she was going to the bathroom and instead went back to see his mother. June shrugged when she saw her.

"It doesn't look good. He might not make it," she said, running her hand through her hair. There was a fine sheen of oil on her forehead.

"And Eileen?" Koko asked.

"Her back is broken, but I don't think she's going to die from it. Shit! That man is always like that. If only he'd done something good for me."

"I'll be going now."

June nodded and said "Thank you" in a tiny voice. Koko wrote down her work number and Buckey's number on a piece of paper. Handing it to June, she asked her to call her if there was any change.

"Koko."

Koko looked down at her questioningly.

"Take care. It's snowing out."

"Thank you. Tell Jesse I said good-bye. He, uh . . . He loves his father very much. More than me and probably more than you."

"I know." June looked away. Koko squared her shoulders and headed for the elevator, but the pounding of her head wouldn't slow down. Maybe she was the one who needed someone's help, she thought, suddenly frightened. This was the most afraid she'd been in all the time since she'd met

Rick. She was gripped by an inordinate, almost physical pain. Now she could see how necessary it was for her that Rick live. Even if they were to walk different paths, so many things she'd be building would be based on the premise that Rick was alive.

"ALL RIGHT. I told Randy what you told me to."

Koko looked up. Buckey had the look of a person who's just completed a task he found distasteful.

"Sorry, Buckey."

"That's OK. But he seemed about ready to jump out the door and come over. Poor boy. He's very worried about you, love. And jealous. What a load of trouble that Rick is."

Koko looked down and covered her face. Buckey sat next to her and rubbed her back gently. This is exactly like what I did with Jesse, Koko thought. Everyone needs someone like this. Someone who isn't related by blood, a good friend you can be completely yourself with.

"I'm so glad I have you to be with me, Buckey," she said.

"Koko, tomorrow you have to go and see Randy. Do it as a favor to me, won't you? You have to take care of a man like that." Buckey looked at her earnestly.

"He's your type?"

"Idiot. This isn't the time for jokes."

"Yeah. Now that you mentioned it, you're right."

Their laughter was low. Nothing was funny, but they laughed out of consideration for each other, to push back the dark feeling that assailed them both.

KOKO VISITED Randy's apartment the next evening. She halted any number of times as she climbed the stairs, but as she approached Randy's floor, she suddenly found herself unable to bear another moment without him and rushed up the remaining flight.

Randy was beside himself when he heard Koko's voice over the intercom. Unable to wait, he opened the door to the apartment and stationed himself there. They threw themselves into each other's arms before saying a word. As was Randy's habit when he saw Koko, he thanked God over and over. Ever since Rick's accident, he'd been in a state of unbearable anxiety. A vague fear that Koko was destined to be somehow taken away from him was eating away at him. Randy knew that such thoughts were absurd, but it was useless. He was afraid of what would happen if Rick died. Rick meant nothing to him alive, but from the moment he heard there was a possibility he might die, Randy thought for the first time that Rick might actually get Koko back. Not Rick the person, in the flesh, but the memories of him that Koko had created within herself.

"You must've been freezing out there," he said.

"Uh-huh. But I'm OK. You're always so warm."

"That's 'cause I'm hot, baby."

Randy tried to shrug away his dread with a joke, but it was no use. *I'll always warm you* is what he really wanted to say. For some reason or another, he himself felt like crying. How weak he was. Unable to trust himself to speak, he merely motioned her inside.

"I could use a drink," Koko said.

Randy nodded and broke open the seal on a bottle of Ronrico. While he was fixing her a drink, Koko briefly filled him in on Rick's condition, what Jesse's mother had said, and so on. She sounded as though she were relating facts from a newspaper, she was trying to keep herself under so much control, not wanting to let a hint of anxiety or worry loose. Her effort had the opposite effect of what she intended; it threw into relief just how bad things were for her.

Randy had certain ideas about how love should be, and one of them was that he should be able to save his loved one before she felt the need to show consideration toward him. He felt ashamed at his own helplessness.

Koko continued to talk. Randy gave her the glass, then settled down at her feet and looked up at her.

"Koko, it makes me sad that I haven't been able to catch up to you yet. But you don't have to be so careful of me. You're intelligent and your love is deep, so you sacrifice yourself trying not to hurt me. Please don't do that. Don't think you have to make everything go well by yourself. You've lived a little longer than I have, so you've had lots of lessons in how not to hurt people, but you don't have to use them all on me. If you really want to make me happy, let me help you with your hurt. As long as I haven't been the one to cause the pain, I think I can help you with it."

Koko looked surprised. "I must really be worrying you, huh," she said.

"No, you aren't. You look like you're in pain. Drink your drink and try to relax. No matter what happens, you're still you."

Koko sighed and took a swallow. The instant the strong liquor slid past her throat, she felt the room become warmer.

"This is really strong," she gasped.

"Should I put some more Coke in it?"

"No, that's OK. Maybe it's just right as it is. But what do I do? I feel like bawling."

"What's wrong with that? You used to cry a lot in front of me."

"Yeah. But Randy, it's one thing to cry out of emptiness, it's another to cry over something you don't want to lose."

"Is Rick the something you don't want to lose?"

"I don't know. Not Rick himself. Something that should be resting quietly within me."

"What can I do?"

Koko thought for a while.

"You know, Randy, I'm hurting. I'm really, really hurting. I feel like, why did he have to go and do this to me? I almost hate him. They say he was awfully drunk. He tested positive for drugs, too. He didn't give a damn about what would happen, I'm certain of it. But why couldn't he understand that it's different for the people around him? He was always like that. He said a long time ago that the only person who'd be sad if he died was Jesse. How could he have thought he had so little value? Why didn't he try to understand that the people around him were weak as well? It's too much."

"Koko," Randy said, as he took her by the shoulders and shook her gently to calm her, "look at me."

Koko did as she was told. His eyes were moist and she could see herself reflected in them. She burrowed her face in his chest.

"Koko." Randy stroked her hair. "There's my girl. Everything's gonna be all right."

Koko's breathing slowly became regular and she rested against Randy's chest for a long time. He was finally able to comfort her in her loss; she was finally able to entrust herself to him.

"Let's go to bed, Koko. I'll warm you up. I'll hold you so there won't be any cracks for bad things to come through. I'll cover you up, and whenever you open your eyes, you'll be seeing me." Randy held her glass to her lips. She parted them weakly and drank the liquor that flowed in.

"Hey, Koko?" Randy asked after sipping at the drink himself. "How many flavors does Baskin Robbins have?"

Koko looked up, puzzled. "Thirty-one. Why?"

"Even ice cream has that many flavors. So how many ways of loving and being loved do you think there must be? No matter how much of an adult you are, Koko, you still don't know everything. It's not like Rick was the be-all and end-all of everything. Let's go taste all those other things there are to taste together from now on, OK?"

Koko nodded over and over at Randy's words. Her heart was gradually growing lighter. She felt the lightness she'd sought for so long in her relationship with Rick.

"I want to go to sleep with you, Randy."

"I can't think of anything more wonderful. Come. I put the heat on in the bedroom. Should be just right by now."

Koko woke up many times that night. She'd check to make sure that Randy's arm was still under her head; then, feeling better, she'd close her eyes. Koko would think of Rick in the hospital, and her eyes would well up at her own good fortune. It didn't occur to her that what she had wasn't a matter of chance; rather, it was something she'd struggled and suffered for.

KOKO AND her friends were stationed at their favorite club to ring in the New Year together. All were giddily drunk; a few who couldn't wait had already passed out on the floor. Koko and Randy sat in the midst of the general exuberance, one minute gazing into each other's eyes, the next minute fending off everyone's teasing.

At the stroke of midnight, dozens of champagne corks popped amid a storm of kissing and hugging. Buckey was soaked, having poured a bottle of champagne over his head. Spike did the same.

Koko was watching them, laughing, when someone tapped her on the shoulder. Turning around, she saw Daryl grinning at her.

"Happy New Year, Koko!"

"Daryl! What are you doing here? You're not old enough to get into a place like this, are you?"

Daryl gave Koko a kiss. "No one ever cards me. I don't

look any more than twenty-three or -four, wouldn't you say?"

Koko looked him up and down, then realized he was holding the hand of the woman next to him.

"Is this your girlfriend?" Koko asked.

Daryl nodded, embarrassed, and introduced her to his date. The woman smiled and greeted Koko cheerfully, then said she was going to the bar to buy drinks.

"Isn't she a lot older than you?"

"Uh-huh. You know I don't go for children. I prefer fully mature women, especially you, Koko."

"Why, thank you, Daryl, but I don't go for children either."

"Hey, that guy you were with is your boyfriend, right? He's not much older than me, is he? A student, I'll bet, huh?"

"As a matter of fact he is. What of it? He's certainly not in high school. Oh—Sue's here. You didn't see her?"

Daryl grinned and gave her a thumbs-up.

"I've already given her a New Year's kiss. And I introduced her to my girl."

"I give up."

"'Course you do." Daryl suddenly became serious. "It's awful about Rick. Jesse's been either at the hospital or his mom's place since it happened."

"I know."

Koko had heard from Jesse's mother several times. June said she wanted to meet with Koko to talk.

"What did you do to Jesse?" she'd asked Koko once over the phone.

Koko had been silent.

"I can't handle the kid. How in the world did you raise him? It's like he hates me. He doesn't pay any attention to anything I say. I'd like to see you, Koko, and talk. Could you please make some time for me?"

Daryl's girlfriend came back and handed him a drink. She kept pulling at Daryl's sleeve. It seemed she wanted to dance. Daryl leaned over and said hastily into Koko's ear, "Jesse's thinking he wants to live with you."

Koko looked at Daryl, shocked.

"It's true. He told me so," Daryl said.

"I can't take Jesse. There's no way."

"Why not?"

Daryl's girlfriend was pulling him away by the hand now. He turned back to Koko with a puzzled look.

"Jesse and I aren't anything to each other. We're not mother and son, not lovers; we can't even say we're friends."

"There're lots of cases where parents and kids, lovers, and friends don't live together. So what's wrong with the opposite? Jesse likes you, Koko. Isn't that enough of a reason?"

Daryl smiled as he spoke, then stepped out onto the dance floor. Koko merely stood there, slowly shaking her head.

The wild partying finally wound down a little after seven in the morning. Koko and Randy walked to the East Village as they sobered up. They were exhausted but clear-headed. It was so cold that their cheeks were frozen and threatened to crack every time they spoke.

Koko told Randy what Daryl had said. She found herself getting madder and madder. Of course she liked Jesse and was worried about him. But when she felt fate throwing them together, forcing him on her, she realized she absolutely could not take him in. She wasn't the same person she'd been when she lived with Rick. She didn't have room in her heart anymore to be dealing with Jesse every day. This realization, in turn, made her annoyed with herself.

Randy, for his part, was looking around for a café that was

still open. He had to get some coffee into this girl and calm her down, he thought. She was always agitating herself over other people's problems. Ever since Rick's accident, Randy had been expending all his strength on calming Koko down. It was making him grow up very quickly. His arms were becoming very adept at surmising Koko's anxiety level. He wasn't a young kid running after her heart anymore. He'd become a man capable of patiently reading his lover's emotions, then dealing with them.

They finally found a tiny diner. They hurried inside and ordered coffee, exchanging New Year's greetings with the manager before sitting down at a corner table. The place was a mess. Shreds of paper from firecrackers and streamers from party poppers lay everywhere.

"Koko, you still don't know what's going to happen. It's much too early to worry about it."

"I know. But I wonder if maybe I'm really a very cold person, and then I feel awful. Then again, there's absolutely no way I'm going to live with Jesse."

Randy took Koko's hand and held it gently. "What is Jesse to you? I want to know. Sometimes you talk about him like he's someone very dear, and then sometimes you complain about him as if you really hate him. It's not like he's a friend. But he's always on your mind."

Koko took a cigarette out of her coat pocket and put it between her lips. The manager called out from behind the counter that if she smoked now she'd be smoking all year. Randy grinned at him and lit a match for her.

"You're right, Randy. It's exactly like you say. I always think, this is *it*, this is absolutely *the end*, but when all is said and done, I can't leave him and he can't leave me. Inside of myself, I'm always holding his hand."

"Like a younger brother?"

"Maybe. It's weird. I could leave Rick, but I can't leave

Jesse. It's not like I love him, though. I have never once thought that I can't get along without him."

"If Jesse really starts saying he wants to live with you, Koko, what're you going to do?"

Koko shrugged. "It's impossible. You know that adults don't live with their families. I don't, and neither do you. I don't want to be saddled with Jesse until he grows up. I can only open up to my lover. And to a very few of my friends."

"I'm sure glad you're not my sister."

"Don't be silly."

They left the café when both their insides and outsides were warm. The manager was smoking and muttering something to himself. Randy made Koko laugh by whispering to her that there's nothing like New Year's resolutions to make people feel like chucking it all.

KOKO GOT word of Rick's death about a week after that. She stood for a long time by the window after the call from June. It was snowing out. She leaned her forehead against the glass, wet with condensation. It looked foggy outside, but that might have been an illusion from the heat in the room or from the tears filming her eyes.

Buckey and Spike were out visiting an artist friend's exhibition. Koko felt sadness, but relief too. Rick's death had released her from all the unhappiness she'd had with him in life. There was a time when his not being there would have been a tragedy, but now Rick didn't have much influence on her. Rick was dead. Koko tried to absorb that fact.

I can't go judging Rick, she thought, according to my values. He was a man, a black man, born in this country. He was raised by different parents from mine, he had a different religion, a different way of thinking. He was a totally different person. When love sweeps you away, you want to think your lover is the same as yourself in body and soul; but no, everyone is born apart, she realized, and everyone dies alone.

Koko breathed deeply to calm herself. The phone rang a couple of times, but stopped ringing before she could answer. I don't care how petty or worthless my life is, Koko thought, I can't get through this alone.

THE NEXT THING she knew, she was lying on the couch and Buckey and Spike were peering into her face. Koko slowly pulled herself up and wiped the sweat from her forehead.

"I'm so hot," she said.

"Of course you are. You collapsed right in front of the radiator. Are you all right?"

Koko took the hand towel Spike held out and patted away her sweat.

"I didn't collapse. I fell asleep all of a sudden."

"Yeah, right. It's too bad about Rick. His sister called just now."

"Grace?"

"She said, 'In the end Koko couldn't do it either.'"

Koko covered her face with the towel. "What the hell does that woman think I am?" she said. "What does she think I could've done for him? She's gotta be kidding. She thinks a woman can handle a man's life, is that it? She thinks a relationship is anything so monumental? I was living with Rick like any ordinary woman, and I'm living with his death like any ordinary woman. The only thing I have is the reality of that death. I loved Rick. That's all. I had happiness with him, but I also had so much unhappiness it erased anything good. So what does she think I could've done?"

"Koko, it's all right."

Buckey and Spike sat down on either side of her. They patted her hair and kissed her cheeks, trying to comfort her.

"I don't want to go to the funeral," Koko said flatly.

"You should go. You'll feel better."

"I wouldn't know how to act."

"Spike has to go uptown anyway, so he'll take you as far as Lenox Street."

"Really?" Koko looked up at Spike.

"Sure. And on the way, we can buy a nice hat for the funeral," said Spike.

"Good idea," Buckey put in. "How about Renny's Studio in SoHo?"

"If you wear one of those eccentric things to a funeral, the corpse will sit up from shock!" said Spike.

"I wonder. I like them. The other day when we were at that new club that they made over from the Power House—what's the name of that place?—anyway, someone there was wearing one, remember? Didn't you think it was absolutely dreamy?"

Koko looked at both of them in turn. "I don't believe you guys. Do you have any idea how I'm feeling?"

Buckey rubbed his face, embarrassed. "I'm sorry, Koko. But in the first place, we never even met Rick. You can't cry over someone you don't know. Not that we're not worried about *you*, darling; we most certainly *are*."

Spike had to choke back his laughter at Buckey's consternation. He clammed up quickly enough, though, when Koko glared at him.

"Thanks, you two. I feel a little better. Actually, it's a relief to have people around me who aren't crying about Rick. That's why I don't want to go to the funeral. I'm scared I won't be able to breathe. But I'll be OK."

JESSE'S MOTHER called Koko again, this time at work, a couple of months later.

"I'd like to talk to you. Can you make some time tonight?" June asked.

"Is Jesse all right?"

"More or less. I'd like to discuss him with you as well. Can you come to my place? It's in Parkchester."

"In the Bronx?"

"You don't have to sound so put upon. I just want to talk to someone who had the same man in common. Jesse would like to see you too. I couldn't talk much the last time we met, so please, will you come?"

Koko was silent. June plowed on, giving her directions from the subway station, then hung up. Koko was annoyed as she put the receiver down. She stalked around the gallery for a while, fuming at June's oddly intimate way of speaking to her, as well as her high-handed presumption. Ordering me around like I'm a delivery girl or something, she thought. The nerve!

Sue looked up, puzzled.

"I assume that wasn't your honey asking you for a date," she observed.

"Far from it. That was Jesse's mother. What in the world could she be thinking? She wants to see me at her apartment tonight to talk."

"Maybe she likes your company."

"This is serious, Sue! I can't stand that woman. She's up to something, I know it. She thinks I'm a stupid little girl she can push around. She's taking me for a ride, don't you think?"

"She's taking you for a ride," Sue said with a straight face, then burst out laughing. "Maybe she wants to talk about old memories of Rick," Sue went on, getting hold of herself. "How was she at the funeral?"

"The perfect wife and the perfect mother. Everyone was

taken in except for Grace. Everyone gathered around her, offering their condolences—made me feel really out of place. I was miserable before, during, and after, but I discovered I'm not the type who cries at funerals. Maybe I shouldn't have gone wearing that René hat."

"René? Not the designer René Miller?"

"Uh-huh."

Sue laughed aloud. "I don't believe it. You didn't wear one of those upside-down garbage cans on your head, did you? Or one of those mushroom-with-a-brim things?"

"No, of course not. I picked one that was pretty conservative. But getting back to June: she was a real piece of work. I don't think anyone guessed she and Rick had been living separately. She played the part of the bereaved widow to the hilt. I was speechless, I was so impressed. Grace kept muttering, 'Bunch of bullshit.'"

"And Jesse?"

"He was silent, from beginning to end. The only thing he said to me was 'Hi, Koko,' in a little voice as we were filing out to go to the cemetery. I've never seen him look like such a gentleman." Koko's voice trailed off with the memory. Then she continued. "While the minister talked, I remembered all sorts of things from when Rick and I were living together. He was dead, so I wanted to think really good things about him. But it was impossible. He wasn't a good man. I felt confused, and everyone crying and carrying on made the whole thing seem so vulgar. After a while I began to think it *was* vulgar. Everything about human society is vulgar! Death doesn't all of a sudden make life noble. Any tears I might've had dried right up."

"Hmmm." Sue had a pen hanging from her mouth as if it were a cigarette. She didn't even try to feign interest in Koko's philosophizing. "Do you miss him sometimes?"

"Yeah."

"Even though you've got Randy."

"I think of Rick with one part of me, and Randy with a totally different part. One doesn't interfere with the other."

"That's convenient."

"People are disgusting. I told you, didn't I?"

Sue eyed Koko's profile, baffled. She couldn't see the desolation that lay behind those words.

KOKO RAN into Jesse at the Parkchester station. He said with a sheepish grin that he was coming back from Tanya's place.

"How are things going with you two?" Koko asked.

"OK. But, Koko, I never thought I'd run into you here. When Mom told me to come home early today, I thought maybe Derek would be coming over for dinner or something."

"Who's Derek?"

"Mom's boyfriend. He's a cop. Kind of fat, but a good guy."

"You don't say."

June was surprised to see Koko and Jesse come in together, but she took Koko's coat graciously.

"You must be hungry. Would you like something to drink first?"

"I'd rather not eat. I'll just have something to drink," Koko said. "You said you wanted to talk to me?"

"Don't be in such a hurry. Have a seat." June motioned her to the dining room table. "Jesse, go and serve yourself. It's all ready."

"OK."

Jesse fixed himself a plate and then disappeared into a back room. He didn't want to be anywhere near Koko and his mother when they were in the same room. He had no idea how he should act.

"So how've you been, Koko? Have things settled down for you?"

"There was nothing to settle down. Rick and I stopped living together quite a while ago. And I have a boyfriend."

"I do, too. But I don't feel like getting married. I know he'd make me happy. And he says Jesse can live with us. Jesse didn't say anything about him to you?"

"Not really."

"Oh. Well, I guess doubts are inevitable when it comes to marriage, no matter who you're with. I just can't seem to fall head over heels."

"You're with someone even though you don't love him?"

"Love? Don't be silly. All I ask of a man is that he be kind to me. I've had enough of men like Rick. That man was bad news. Things went well for only about two or three months into our marriage. The rest was hell. Things seemed to go pretty well with you and him, though. I was impressed. I wondered how you could put up with that man for so long."

"Then why didn't you finish going through with the divorce?"

"Well, you see, I wanted to make sure *he* wouldn't go and get married to some other woman and live happily ever after. I would have divorced him in an instant, though, if I'd found someone I wanted to marry. I wasn't about to give him up completely until then."

"That's a lie!"

June flinched and blinked several times.

"You wanted to go back to Rick. You were waiting for him to get old and weak so you could move in with him. It wasn't me or Eileen who was the most tenacious with him; it was *you*. I know you hated him. Probably a lot of women hated him. I was one of them, of course. But I don't think anyone could have hated him enough to forget him. That's the way he was. He made women want to be with him at the same time that they hated him."

June stood up and went to fix the drinks. She was silent the whole time she was mixing them, but her hands trembled ever so slightly as she came back with the glasses. June downed her gin and tonic in one long pull, then finally spoke.

"You're pretty smart for your age," she said. Watching the woman closely, Koko felt her own anger start to dissipate.

"Thanks to that man's bad influence," June said, "I can hold my liquor extraordinarily well. Is gin and tonic OK for you?"

Koko nodded. June set the other glass down in front of her.

"Hate and tenacity side by side is a hard thing to handle. You can't call it love," June said.

"I think it's a kind of love. I managed to get myself out of it. I think you're the only one who didn't. Am I right? You *were* going to go back to Rick someday, weren't you?"

June shrugged. Her laugh was low. "You're right. I figured I'd wait until he was ground down by life and liquor; then I'd take care of him. Laughing all the while."

"Why would you want to do that?"

"Why? Because if I didn't, I'd never be able to get myself back. Do you have any idea how much I suffered on account of that man? I used to be a lot like you, Koko. A young woman who dreamed of love and romance, who thought marriage was some kind of honeyed candy. He destroyed my hopes one by one. I tried to be optimistic at first. I'd think, He doesn't like how I do things, or things at work must be bugging him. I finally understood I was fooling myself. Rick could only remember how life was when he was growing up, and then he'd drag that old life into our lives. That dirt town had its hooks in him too deep. You know where he grew up?"

Koko shook her head.

"The armpit of the universe. He lived in North Carolina until his parents split up. Rick took me there once, and that's when I understood. New York's terrible, but in a completely different way. Where Rick grew up, your race decides your whole life. There aren't any interesting, open-minded people like you find around here."

"So why didn't you divorce him then? You can't use Jesse as an excuse; you didn't raise him afterward."

June finished off her second gin and tonic. "I was the opposite of Rick," she said. "I couldn't believe I was unhappy. I believed so strongly in happiness that I couldn't see myself as unhappy. I didn't understand anything. I was so stupid. I just couldn't accept the fact that it was hopeless."

Any lingering animosity Koko had toward June had disappeared. This lonely woman had fought a long, hard battle and her wounds ran deep. Koko's heart ached to see how defenseless she looked.

"Was Rick good to you?" June asked after a short silence.

Koko hesitated, groping for words.

"I'm sure he was good to you," June said. "At least better than he was to me. You're a lot younger than he was, and you're not as strong-willed as me. You two probably didn't have too many run-ins."

"No, we did. If things had been good, I wouldn't have left. But I don't hate Rick. I gave up on him ever being able to love me, but I don't hate him."

"You're just saying that because he's dead. Koko, you don't always have to say good things about the dead. Face it, Rick was a real worm when it came to relationships. I think I could've forgiven him if he'd told me honestly how he felt. He never did, though. He didn't have the words to do it. He knew I would've taken his part and comforted him if he'd owned up to even a few of his faults. But it was no use. I'd get all worked up trying to force him to acknowledge his failings, and he'd run away every time. We kept going around in circles, and after a while I didn't know if I was chasing him out of love or hatred. It's the same now even though he's dead. I just want to kill him. Idiotic, isn't it? I think I'll always feel this way."

Koko could understand how June felt, but the idea of harboring such strong hatred, so strong you could call it a passion, toward someone who was already dead made her uncomfortable. To Koko, death had an absolute power that wiped away any ill feelings she might have had.

"Hey, Koko, remember the first time I went to see you and Rick?"

Koko nodded. She remembered the day June had come to Rick's apartment, ostensibly to see Jesse.

"Yeah, you didn't make a great impression on me," Koko said. "You had a very unpleasant, nervous way about you. I even felt sorry for Rick. I thought it was a good thing he'd split up with you. I don't feel that way anymore, though."

"Oh, God." June laughed in self-derision.

"Please don't take it the wrong way. Rick and I were happy then. That's because I wasn't heavy to him. I was a sunny young girl. Everything began to change when I started getting serious. I could imagine then how it must've been when you two were together."

"I wonder. Things were a lot better with you than with me."

Koko could feel her anger return. What the hell is this woman trying to say? she wondered. It would be pathetic if she was still jealous.

"I don't think Rick changed much between the time he was with you and when he was with me. The difference had to do with you and me. You and I were different toward him. I wanted to be happy and I made an effort to make it happen."

June looked up at Koko's words. "Effort? What's that? Don't make me laugh. You left—you ran away from your life with Rick without taking any responsibility."

"Responsibility? What do you mean, responsibility?" Koko shot back. "I don't go around saying anything about *your* failed marriage with Rick. I'd like you to give me the same courtesy. Everyone's relationship is different. I don't see what responsibility has to do with it."

June bit her lip and looked away. "I'm the one who's the loser, the only one. There's no way you can understand. The only memories I have left of Rick are of how he hurt me. I'm not young anymore, either. I can't get myself any man I want. On top of everything, there's Jesse. I have to raise him. What did Rick ever do for me, huh? I'm a wreck, thanks to that man."

Koko sighed. She wanted to think June's spiel came from hysteria over Rick's death. Otherwise, there'd be no good reason Koko could imagine for her having to listen to it. The two sat silently for a while, pulling on their cigarettes.

"You think I'm pathetic, don't you, Koko? You're wondering why I'm saying all this. He's dead, after all, right? But you can't understand how panicked I am. I've lost everything now. Can you imagine what that's like? I used up all my kind and tender feelings, all my hopes, on Rick. The only way I could ever have them again would be for him to return them."

"What about Jesse? Don't you have any hopes for him?"

"It's no use."

"But he's your child. Your son."

"That's right. But when it's no use, it's no use. I feel sorry for him, but living with him again has made me see. He hates me."

"No child hates his own mother."

"Some children don't need their mothers."

Koko sprang to her feet and slapped June across the face. It took a moment for Koko to realize what she'd done. She stood there, her hand smarting. June wiped the corner of her mouth again and again. The blow had cut the inside of her mouth on a tooth.

"You don't understand anything!" Koko shouted. She dropped back onto the chair and buried her face in her arms on top of the table. "You don't know how I struggled with Jesse. That boy always, *always*, longed for his mother. For you! He couldn't accept me. I wasn't his mother; we didn't share the same blood. I knew that, and so did Jesse. No matter how close we got, how much we confided in each other, that last little bit always got in the way. We never actually saw each other naked. And we probably never will. That's important! It should be no big deal to see each other without any clothes on. Most families, blood-related or not, have been together since before any of that matters. But by the time Jesse and I started living together, if one of us opened the door while the other was in the shower, we had to say 'Excuse me.' We couldn't become mother and son. We really struggled to make something out of our relationship. You know, I'd like to think you have no right to be Jesse's mother, but you *are* his mother. Nothing can change that."

Koko scrubbed furiously at her tears.

"Mothers are so incredibly self-centered," she said. "You and Eileen both, you don't think about the things you can do so much more easily than I can. You walk around like only you have problems. You can think all you want that people like me have it easy, but we can't use our children as a reason for failing to do something. Jesse and Rick are two entirely separate matters to me. I can't believe you count Jesse as one of the reasons why you're not happy."

"Calm down, Koko. I didn't ask you over to make you mad. I apologize if I said something to upset you."

The ice in Koko's drink had melted. June picked up the glass and went to make her a fresh drink. Koko wiped her tears away with the back of her hand and tried to relax.

"The only thing I can do is hate Rick," June said flatly. "That's the kind of woman I am. It's awful, I know. All Jesse and I do is fight. The other day I hit him with a shoe. He told me then, 'Daddy's not the only one; *I* don't want to have anything to do with a woman like you, either.' I hit him over and over, crying the whole time."

But he didn't hit you back, Koko thought. Jesse was big enough now to throw her off. But he didn't, and he didn't run away. He let his mother hit him. It didn't occur to June that he was letting her hit him; June didn't even understand, thought Koko, why a child needs a mother in the first place.

"I don't know how to raise that boy," June said. "Long ago, when Rick and I would fight late at night, he'd come to our room and say, 'Daddy, Mom, how come you won't let me sleep?' He was five years old. We couldn't stop fighting even then, we were so taken up with ourselves. We'd scream, hit each other, then make love. The same thing, every day. Then one day I realized that Jesse wasn't saying anything to me other than what was absolutely necessary. He'd given up on me."

That's not so! Koko wanted to scream. "When I first started living with Jesse, he used to talk about you all the time," she said. "He'd start off with 'My mom, she . . .' and off he'd go, so proud, like he was telling me about the best thing in the world."

June shrugged. "If he had anything to be proud of me about, it must've happened while he was still in my womb."

Koko knew June was making herself unhappy. She'd stopped examining herself and trying to make sense of her life.

"Jesse wants to live with you," June said suddenly. "He's always saying it was fun living with you."

"It wasn't fun. We worked desperately to try to keep Rick together and with us. We were solid on that. But Rick isn't here anymore. There's no way Jesse and I can live together again. I like Jesse. But there's no reason to live together anymore. Why would you bring that up?"

"Well, the reason I asked you over tonight, Koko, was to ask you if you would take him."

June blushed. Relief that she'd finally said what she wanted vied with her shame at the unreasonableness of her request.

"Don't you love Jesse?" Koko asked.

"I love him. But that's a different thing from living with him. I know I'm not fit to be a mother."

There was sympathy in Koko's eyes. "I used to despise you when I first started living with Jesse," she said. "I was taking care of him, and where were you? I'd think that even an animal can bear young, but it takes a human being to raise a child. Now I understand that animals raise their young too, but a human parent's job is to raise a true adult. I'd be happy to help with that. But the child part of Jesse was taken away from him when he was small. You did that, June. And now you're doing the same thing to your son that Rick did to you when he stole your happiness and then died. You'd better think about it. Think about what it is that Jesse needs."

A shadow seemed to move behind them. Koko and June

turned at the same time to see Jesse standing there. Koko was about to say something when he spoke.

"I'll live by myself."

June laughed shrilly. "What are you saying?" Her voice was harsh. "You're still a kid and that's that. You shouldn't be saying stupid things. Are you done with your homework?"

"I want to live by myself," Jesse repeated, not paying any attention to her. "Nobody wants to take care of me. It's for the best."

"Jesse, go to your room. Listen to what your mother tells you," June said.

Jesse's lips twisted. "Mom, you've got something wrong here. I'm not a five- or six-year-old kid. You think I haven't grown any older since the time we stopped living together all those years ago. Well, I'm totally different from back then. You are too. Maybe you think you haven't changed, but you have. Daddy changed, too. He didn't love you anymore. That's why he didn't even hate you. It was Koko who was in his heart. She was the last woman in his heart when he died. Not you."

Koko looked nervously at Jesse and June in turn. However, they didn't look particularly upset. It seemed they had been arguing like this since Rick died.

"I hated your father. Meeting him ruined my life. Won't you please stop talking about him?"

"You ruined his life, too. You like to yammer on about how he was raised and his character, but it wasn't only that. Meeting you was the worst thing that ever happened to him."

"Jesse! Go to your room!"

"No."

"Go, I said!"

Jesse looked at Koko and shrugged, his hands spread

wide. Koko thought he was purposely trying to provoke his mother.

June heaved a great sigh when Jesse disappeared reluctantly into his room.

"You see how it is?" she said. "It's always like this. We're a miserable pair, don't you think?"

"I'm sad for you, June," Koko said.

"Does that mean you feel sorry for me?"

"Not sorry. It seems you always take the bad side of everything. Are you so loath to become happy? Blaming some man for all your problems is no answer. And is it so difficult to understand how Jesse really feels when he talks to you like that? It wasn't you who lost the most when Rick died. Needless to say, it wasn't me either. It was Jesse. His very youth is his biggest handicap. If we don't do something for him, who's he going to go to? I have someone to love. You're OK; you have memories of Rick to curse at. But what does Jesse have? He hasn't had much experience in dealing with grief. How's he going to get through this? Ordinarily his mother would help him, but you're incapable of that. You're a selfish, miserable woman."

"You despise me, don't you?"

"I told you, I'm sad for you, that's all. I'm amazed, frankly. There aren't any people like you around me. Rick is dead; you can't lay everything on him anymore. It's up to you from now on: you're responsible for your own happiness and unhappiness." Koko stood up.

June looked at her timidly as she put her coat on. "Do you want me to call you a cab?"

"No, thanks. It's still early; I can take the subway."

Jesse appeared, wearing his jacket. "I'll walk Koko to the station, Mom," he said.

June nodded and followed them as far as the door. Koko looked back at her as she turned the collar up on her coat.

"I guess we didn't get anywhere," she said.

"Thanks for coming, anyway," June replied. "Do you mind if I ask you one last question, Koko?"

Koko waited.

"I don't understand why someone like you lived with Rick. There must've been lots of other men, men who'd take you out, who'd make time for you on the weekends."

Koko shrugged. "Well," she said. She tilted her head in thought. "I suppose I thought that having someone around to escort me on the weekends was cheap compared to love."

"You loved him?"

"Yes I did, same as you. The difference was that I also loved myself."

Koko closed the door on June's startled face. Jesse was waiting for her in front of the elevator.

"Thanks for walking me, Jesse."

"No problem. It looked like Mom and I were headed for a fight anyway. It was best to get out."

In the street, the cold wind beat at them as they walked along. Jesse pulled his hat down past his ears. It was knitted from brightly colored wool.

"You look like a kid in that hat," Koko said.

"I am a kid."

"Oh, yeah? A kid who already knows about girls."

"Maybe. You look like a teenager yourself, Koko, in that ratty old coat."

"Thank you. I know too much about men, though."

"That's good." Jesse sniffled.

"You caught a cold?"

"Uh-huh. Hey, Koko, my mom's pretty messed up, isn't she?"

"Yeah."

"She doesn't know enough about men. All men aren't like Daddy was. She dates lots of men, but she ruins it almost from the start. Men get scared off because they can see she picks them for what kind of life they can provide."

June's face appeared in Koko's mind's eye, along with a sense of oppression.

"What are you going to do, Jesse?" she asked.

Jesse hung his head, his hands jammed deep into his pockets.

"What'm I going to do?" he asked. "There's nothing I *can* do."

"I can help you, but I can't live with you. I'm in love with someone, and there just isn't any room for you between us."

"I understand."

"I think you really should try living with your mother for a while. In another five years, you'll be able to look after yourself. It won't be too late to think about it then. Maybe we can be roommates."

"Yeah." Jesse scrubbed at his eyes with his arm. "I wish I were grown up already," he said. "Why did Daddy have to go and die now? Why couldn't he have waited a little while longer? I didn't care how much he drank. I always forgave him. He was a basket case, but I didn't care. He was my father . . . my own flesh and blood. It's not fair."

Koko put her arm around Jesse as they walked. All she could do was hope her arm around his shoulder would reassure him of his own existence.

They arrived at the station and Koko fished around in her purse for money to buy a token.

"Will you come again?" Jesse asked.

"I don't think so," Koko said.

"Oh. I guess you're right. Well, can I call you sometime?"

"Sure. And come see me anytime. Bring Daryl along. I'll treat you guys to a meal."

"That's great!"

Jesse looked down with a laugh. His relief was evident.

"'Cause, Koko, out of all the women I know, you're the one I'm closest to. Of the ones I'm not related to, I mean. I listened in a little on your talk with Mom, and it got me thinking that it's best *not* to be related sometimes, you know? It can make things easier."

Koko grinned and mussed Jesse's hair. I'll be there whenever you need me, she said to herself. Not relatives, not lovers, not friends. An odd relationship. But she knew now that both she and Jesse would always be praying that the other was OK.

DROPPING BY Randy's place on the way back, Koko told him about what had happened. At first he was furious at Jesse's mother, but by the time Koko finished her story he felt sorry for her. It was futile to blame anyone who loved someone so much, he thought. She couldn't help it, he almost said aloud.

"What if I become like her?" he mumbled.

"What do you mean? I'm not an alcoholic like Rick; I don't go stumbling out at night to hit the bars. You don't have anything to worry about."

"Sometimes I get afraid about what'll happen if I love you too much. If I'm ever sent to prison, I already know the reason why. It'll be if anyone ever hurts you or tries to hurt you. Do you understand?"

Koko had to hold him tight to make him feel better. Stroking his back, she thought, Whoever decided that men were strong? Everyone lives with the fear they'll lose the person they love most. There's no difference between men and women about that; there's a fundamental equality about the strengths and weaknesses of people's hearts.

Koko tightened her arms around Randy. Although his presence reassured her, she was gripped by a new fear of hurting him.

SPRING

SPRING DESCENDED upon New York all at once, filling the air. As the days passed, those who grieved Rick's death were getting used to it in their own way.

June sent Koko a box jammed full of clothing and other small articles left behind at Rick's place. An earring and a carton of cigarettes that weren't hers brought a wry smile to her lips.

"Hey, Buckey, would you look at this?" she said. "You think I could ever wear an earring this ugly? Really irks me."

Buckey was on the couch, going through the *Village Voice*. He laid the paper on the coffee table and peered into the box with great interest.

"Maybe it was Rick's," was his only comment.

Koko glared at him.

"That wasn't funny? I'm sorry," he said.

"Your jokes recently are way *way* off, Buckey. Aaagh, what could that woman be thinking? What's this? A romance novel? Janet Dailey. What the hell would I be reading her for, huh? And these cigarettes. Spike smokes, doesn't he?"

"Uh-huh."

"What brand?"

"Benson and Hedges."

"Well, then, you take these for him. They were probably Eileen's."

Koko handed Buckey the carton. He gave her an odd look.

"You don't think he'll want them?"

"Uh, Koko, there's something I should tell you."

Koko looked at him, puzzled. "Is something wrong?"

Buckey looked uncomfortable for a few moments. He finally said in a tiny voice, "I think we're going to break up."

"What?"

"Spike's fallen in love with someone else." Buckey hung his head. He looked as if he was the one who had done something wrong.

"Oh, Buckey, baby. I'm so sorry. I didn't see what was going on at all. I'm terrible. You're always helping me, and when you're in trouble I don't even notice."

"It's not your fault, Koko. You've had your hands full. And I didn't know myself until a week ago. I kept thinking I should tell you, but the right time never came up."

Buckey put his head on Koko's shoulder and sighed. Koko put her arms around him and patted his back.

"You two looked like you were getting along so well. What happened?"

"He met someone at a club. You know where Christopher Street crosses Washington? There's a place called the Blue Ribbon."

Koko consoled him, but she couldn't help thinking that the way he loved men was very different from the way she did. It was as if he didn't know about the hatred that was the other side of love, she thought, or he avoided the sort of love that would bring him too close to it. He managed to scoop up pure bits of love and goodwill, leaving anger and confrontation aside. The tears that filled his eyes and threatened to spill over were clean and clear.

"You don't hate Spike, do you?"

Buckey looked up, and she saw tears run down his face.

"Of course not," he said. "He said he was grateful to me. I was happy to hear that from him. We had so much fun together. But I guess he likes what's new and different. He said I was too good to him, that I was too understanding and it suffocated him. When he started thinking that he could never cheat on me, he lost it and started going to the Blue Ribbon again. It seems you can't make love last unless you leave a little space open for the other person to feel like he can betray you if he wants."

"It's gonna be hard for a while," Koko said.

"Yeah. But I'm better off than you."

Koko opened her mouth to say something, but nothing came out. She knew what he meant so well it hurt. He was referring to the difference in their styles of loving. Although he lived with Spike, one couldn't say they had a life together. Sharing the same space didn't change the fact that everything they did together culminated in bed and the passion they had for each other there. Theirs was a romance, no more, no less. Neither of them seized the inner essence of the other. It was never that way for Koko. The life she shared with the one she loved was the same as life itself to her. If her love died, a cog in the works would slip out of place, and she'd have difficulty figuring out which shoe went on which foot.

"When is Spike going to move out?" she asked.

"Pretty soon, I guess. Koko, do you think maybe you can start paying me rent?"

"Idiot. What a thing to think about now." Koko smiled and took Buckey's face in both her hands. "Don't cry, sweetheart."

Buckey did cry, though. Everyone needs someone to help them cry, Koko thought, and she was glad to be there for Buckey. Her thoughts wandered to Jesse. He was grieving over the loss of his father, and the loss of her on top of that. She'd deserted him, too. Was there anyone with him now who could help him cry? He was too young to cry at a girl-friend's breast. That comfort was something reserved only for fully grown men who could throw away their pride. Koko couldn't imagine Jesse being able to cry in front of his mother.

"Buckey," Koko said, her voice breaking, "did I abandon Jesse?"

Buckey wiped away his tears and looked at her. "Why would you think that?"

"Because he doesn't have anyone to cry with now."

"So what?"

"So what? So . . . it's sad, that's what."

"Ha!" Buckey exclaimed.

"What do you mean 'ha'? Did I say something funny?"

"Damn right it's funny."

"Why?"

Buckey roused himself and sat up straight on the couch. "I didn't have anyone to cry with when I was a kid, either. You're too nice, Koko. A person has to make a place to cry by himself, with his own two hands. He can't have someone hand it to him. If Jesse doesn't know how to make one, he won't cry, that's all. And that's OK; he won't die from it. He'll gradually learn how to build one as he gets older. That's 'cause he'll learn how to help people cry on his own shoulder. It's part of getting to know how to take care of people, how to be good to them. If you don't know how to do that, you can't go borrowing anyone's shoulder to cry on, can you? You wouldn't have the right."

"You think so?"

"Yes, I do."

Koko gazed at her friend. He was blessed with such physical beauty, she thought, and someone who didn't know him might mistake him for one of the many flighty gay men who gathered at the clubs downtown into the late hours: one of those shooting stars bedazzled by his own brilliance, indulging himself in food, love, and music while knowing nothing of struggle or pain, and who turned his back on a society that had turned its back on him. He'd learned not through money or education but from life itself, and then made himself into the compasssionate, strong man he was.

"You're smart, Buckey. You don't hate anyone, do you? I wish I could live that way."

Buckey chuckled. "Is that how I look to you? If so, I'm glad. Guess I used up a lifetime's worth of hate when I was a little kid. It got so I knew if I hated anymore it'd be the end of me. So I stopped. Things got easier after that. If I'd kept on going the way I'd been, I would've died long ago from an overdose or a bullet. That reminds me, Koko, I wanted to tell you—that's one thing you have to be careful of with Jesse. You don't want him getting into that shit."

"You're kidding."

"No, I'm not. It's OK as long as he's still upset about things, but the moment he loses the strength to feel upset, he's done for. He won't give a damn about anything. I think you really should give him some concrete help. You can't do anything about how he feels or whose shoulder he's gonna cry on. He's not a pet dog. But you could take him to a movie now and then, just be a friend, and talk to him about drugs."

"Thanks for the advice. You're incredible, Buckey. You've just been dumped, and you're still thinking about me and my problems."

"Don't say that. Aaagh—now you've done it. Spike's probably in bed with that guy right now. Oh, geez, it hurts.

Nothing I can do about it, though; it's not me he wants anymore."

Koko vowed then to always do anything she could for this good-hearted friend of hers. She admired his integrity and his dignity. She even felt like telling him she loved him.

"Shall we throw a going-away party for Spike?" she said.

"You mean it?"

"Sure, I mean it. He's being a jerk right now, but basically he's a wonderful person."

Buckey thought it over.

"So, Buckey, you want me to go get the champagne?"

"Great idea!"

Koko got up to get a garbage bag for Buckey's used tissues and came face to face with Spike. He stood behind them, a pained look on his face. He had apparently been standing there, struggling for something to say, for quite some time. Koko motioned him with her eyes. He came around the couch and knelt before Buckey. Taking both of his hands in his own, he kissed them. Koko all but fled to the kitchen. She absolutely could not stand this sort of scene. Cowering there, she could hear their quiet voices from the living room. I shouldn't be here, she thought, peering into the refrigerator. She opened up a bottle of beer for herself. She couldn't help laughing, though, when she saw the label: Blue Ribbon. Poor Buckey. Well, best drink it up now before he sees it, she told herself.

SPRING ALWAYS awakens the five senses, but what brought home the change of seasons more than anything to Koko was seeing Randy's bare skin peeking out of the space between his loafers and the bottom of his pants. Koko loved those ankles of his. They looked so innocent and vulnerable, like a little kid's. She'd grown especially fond of his habit of not wearing socks.

"Has Buckey gotten over that guy yet?" Randy asked, leaning toward her, one elbow on the bistro table. Koko was flipping through a magazine across from him. She looked up. The green of the trees behind him was dazzling.

"Uh-huh. Sometimes he gets really quiet, but he's OK," she said.

"What're your plans now?"

"My plans?"

"Yeah. Are you going to keep staying with Buckey?" Randy asked.

"I guess so. How come?"

Randy was silent. Finally he said, "I don't like it. You living with another man and all."

Koko was stunned for a moment; then she burst out laughing. Randy looked away and chewed on his lip.

"Yes, he's a man, but this is Buckey we're talking about here. You know he's gay. Come on, Randy, you're not going to get jealous over *Buckey*, are you? That's ridiculous," Koko said.

"A man's a man."

"Yeah, but—"

"You don't get it, do you? I'm always thinking and worrying about you. I know I shouldn't, but I can't help it. You've had a lot more experience than me; you know a lot more. I can't compete with that. I'm still a student; I can't even take you out properly. I keep thinking some older, more experienced guy is gonna appear and take you away."

Koko's eyes danced with amusement. Randy hung his head, more hurt than ever.

"Randy, look at me."

Randy refused, his face set. Koko took his chin in her hand and forced him to raise his head.

"Look at me, I said. What are you so scared for, huh? Have confidence. I'm going to be staying with Buckey for a while. He can't pay the rent all by himself. But there's nothing, absolutely nothing, for you to be worried about. He's a dear friend. I'll move out when he gets a new boyfriend."

"I want to live with you, Koko."

"Randy." Koko tilted her head and looked at him. "I can't live with you while you're so full of me. You're not ready. My being with you all the time would only make it worse. Sometimes it's far more lonely to be with someone than to be alone. I've been through one disaster like that; I couldn't bear another. It won't work so long as you don't trust me. The next time I live with a lover, I don't want to have any regrets. I want to be really, really happy. I don't want to mess things up with stupid jealousies and misunderstandings. Can you understand what I'm saying?"

Randy nodded. He still didn't look satisfied, but he seemed, in his own way, to accept her point of view.

"I guess I'm still a kid, aren't I? I've been a wreck ever since I fell in love with you. I wonder if I'll ever get used to this."

Koko grinned. "You don't have to get used to it. I'm always terribly lonely on the days I don't see you. I'm only saying we can't live together now because I don't want to make things any harder on you than they have to be."

Just then a young woman passing by their table thumped Randy on the shoulder. He turned around, his eyes widening in surprise.

"Hey, haven't seen you in ages," he said. "How's it going? April, this is my girlfriend, Koko."

Koko smiled and said hello. The woman Randy called April studied her with open interest. Then, with a flip of her chestnut-colored hair, she said, "I slept with Randy three times."

Randy's discomfort was evident. He looked first at April,

then at Koko. Koko was merely stunned. She fixed her eyes on April.

"Randy's very popular with the girls. You don't mind?"

"I think that's a good thing," Koko said.

April looked a bit deflated at that. "Art said you were a real lady. 'An adult in the best sense of the word'; that's what he said. You know, Koko, if things start going bad with you and Randy, I'm going to be right there. You don't mind?"

"That's Randy's decision."

April shrugged. "I was joking. Jesus, if you aren't watching for two minutes all the good men get snapped up. I can't waste time with you guys. See you later, Randy!"

She hurried off and Randy looked at Koko sheepishly.

"It was a long time ago."

"I'm not asking any questions."

"You're not jealous at all, are you?"

"I'll be jealous enough when I have cause to be."

"Oh, yeah? Like when?"

"You should figure that out for yourself, then make sure I never have to get jealous. You'll do that for me, won't you? I'm sick of being jealous."

Randy nodded, satisfied. "I love it when you tell me what you like and don't like," he said. "That way I can learn all sorts of things about you, one by one; then after a while I'll really be your man."

"You already are my man, Randy. You have no idea how good you make me feel. You should tell me how you want to be loved, too. I need to hear it."

Randy chuckled and whispered something into her ear that made her blush.

DARYL CALLED a few days after that. It was a warm, almost summery night. Koko had asked Randy over to play cards with her and Buckey. They were immersed in the game when the phone rang.

"Who is it?"

"Daryl," Buckey said.

"Daryl? What does he want?"

"I don't know."

Buckey and Randy glued their eyes to their cards as Koko took the phone.

"Hi, Koko. Is this a bad time?"

"Uh-uh. What's up?"

"It's not an emergency or anything, but I guess you know things aren't going well at all with Jesse and his mom."

"Uh-huh."

"He's skipping a lot of school, too."

"He's not into anything he shouldn't be, is he?"

"I don't know. A friend of mine said he saw him going into a shooting gallery."

"He's not doing drugs, is he?"

"I can't say for sure. Hey, Koko, do you think maybe you could see him and talk to him? He's been avoiding me, won't talk to me at all."

"Sure, but I wonder what's got into him. If he's not talking to you, I can't imagine he'll talk to me."

"That's not true. He really likes you, Koko. And he respects you. He'll listen to you; I'm sure he will."

Koko hung up with a sigh. Buckey and Randy looked up.

"What'd Daryl want?" Buckey asked.

Koko shook her head silently.

"It's Jesse," she said, sitting down and taking up her cards again.

"Girl trouble again?" Randy asked.

Koko shook her head and told them what Daryl had said.

"I told you this might happen," Buckey said. "He's just

doing what everybody else is. Almost every kid with a bad home situation ends up doing drugs."

Koko was furious at Buckey's complacency. Randy looked at her anxiously.

"Do you think he's really doing drugs, Koko?" he asked.

"I don't know. But it looks like he's going in that direction. Oh, why is this happening?"

"Shit happens, Koko. He's rebelling. It's a stage."

"Buckey!" Koko grabbed his cards and slapped them face down on the floor.

"Is it something I said?" he asked.

"How can you be so blasé about this? A stage, my foot! If it's a stage, that's fine, but what if it turns out to be more serious, huh? You could a least look a *little* worried, couldn't you?"

"First it's girls, then it's drugs, then liquor. You have to do something about it, of course, but it's such a common pattern. I'm surprised he's not more original. Anyway, I don't know this Jesse boy."

"You're cold, Buckey, that's your problem. You only care about what's directly in front of your face."

"What's wrong with that?"

"I wonder if it really is inevitable," Randy muttered. Buckey and Koko looked at him, surprised. He looked back at them, a little embarrassed.

"Well, I wonder if it really is inevitable to get involved with drugs and liquor because you come from a bad home or because you have a hard life. I mean, it's not carved in granite or anything, is it? I don't like that way of thinking. It's old-fashioned. There're lots of people with problems, but they can't all check out like that. It's stupid. You should tell Jesse's mother she has to get a grip on her son—that's what mothers are for. My mom yelled at me a lot. Not that I ever went anywhere near drugs; I hated the whole idea. But why does Koko have to deal with all the shit, huh? It's not fair. It's not her responsibility."

"It seems you haven't any empathy for people who can't help leaning on old-fashioned ways, have you, Randy?" Buckey observed coldly. Randy was startled by his unexpected hostility.

"But you're clean yourself, Buckey," he said. "You're not taking Jesse and his mother's side, are you? That's crazy."

"You don't understand anything, student boy. There's a *big* difference between a clean body that has never known a thing and one that has experienced filth, picked itself up, and cleaned itself off. You probably don't know which is the more virtuous, do you? I think it's the latter. You know why? Because that's the one that requires *effort*. A pampered suburban prince like yourself couldn't understand, not in a million years."

"Is there something wrong with coming from a good home? It's true my dad has a good position in his company and my mother's a terrific woman with her own career. But I don't feel superior. I'm honestly grateful. I want to help poor people, but at the same time I can't stand it when people use a bad home environment or the fact that they're a minority as an excuse to be lazy and give up on everything. I'm proud that I'm black—"

"*Really?*" Buckey's lips curled into a sneer. "And just what do you think it means to be proud to be black?"

Randy was at a loss for an answer.

"You can't answer that, can you? People who have never had their pride injured have no idea what pride is."

Buckey began to gather together the cards. Nobody said anything. It was obvious the game was over.

"In other words, my dear boy, you are spoiled. You live in your own pretty little dream world, and you can't think anything but happy thoughts. You're gonna end up a burden on Koko for sure, no different from Jesse."

"Are you saying there's something wrong with me?"

"Not *wrong*, per se. It's simply that if you think the world turns according to clear-cut, mutually agreed upon rules, you're an idiot and a snob. You're from Queens, right? Try going to Jamaica Avenue and shout what you just said as loud as you can. I guarantee everyone will shrug and turn away."

Randy lunged at Buckey. Koko screamed and threw herself between them. The three fell to the floor and rolled around like wrestlers on a mat.

"What's wrong with you two?"

"Randy's such a baby, I felt like teasing him, that's all."

"Yeah? Well hearing that from a faggot like you is enough to make me puke!"

"I might be a faggot, but at least I'm not an asshole."

"Stop it! Both of you, get up," Koko said, sitting up herself and raking her hands through her hair. The two men lay on the floor drained of strength, but after a while Buckey sat up.

"You can hit me, just don't hurt the face," he said.

Randy remained sprawled on his stomach, his face buried in an arm. He slammed the floor with a fist. Koko, her brows knit, laid a hand on his back.

"I can't stand ugliness and ugly people," Randy said, his voice muffled. "Poor people, slums, I hate 'em all. People like that are always jealous of people that have it better 'n' them. They've never thought it's not my fault they live like that. I hate Jesse's father, even if he is dead. He leaned on Koko when he was alive; he's leaning on her now, from the grave! I'm not the spoiled one. *He* is. I'm trying my best to love Koko, but *he's* always getting in the way."

Randy's voice was barely audible. Koko glanced at Buckey in consternation. He ignored her, his eyes on Randy.

"It's one thing, Randy, for you to be thrilled about Koko being in love with you. That's fine. Just don't get a swelled head over it," he said.

"A swelled head? Are you kidding? I'm always half out of my mind with worry!"

"You are arrogant toward everyone except Koko," Buckey said flatly.

Randy raised his head and looked at Koko. "Is that what you think, too?" he asked.

"Sometimes," she said. "But that comes with being young."

"You guys're ganging up on me and treating me like a kid. I'm not that much younger than you."

"It's not a question of age," Buckey said. Hurt, Randy buried his face again in his arm.

"Randy." Koko leaned forward and kissed the back of his neck. "You say it's not my responsibility to help Jesse with his problems, but I don't, really. People can't go around fixing things for each other; it's just not possible. It wouldn't work even if we tried. I loved Rick. I don't have any regrets about that. The truth is, even though I love you, I still think of him sometimes. I remember good and bad times. Why should I feel guilty toward you about that? After all, what happened between him and me is a fact. It can't—it shouldn't be erased, and not you or anyone else should make me try to do it. If you love me, you have to accept that part of me as well. Everyone has a past; it's what makes us what we are. Maybe some of those memories are painful, but that doesn't mean they should go into the trash."

Randy slowly pulled himself up and wrapped his arms around his knees. Tears filled his eyes. He looked like an abandoned child.

"You really think about Rick sometimes, even now?"

"Yes, I do. But that has nothing to do with my love for you."

"Shit."

"I don't do it to hurt you, Randy."

"That son of a bitch. He was an alcoholic, good-for-nothing fuck, and you know it. All he did was cause you grief."

Buckey had opened a new bottle of wine. He pulled the cork out and poured some into Randy's glass.

"Well, darling, that's the way it is between adults sometimes," he said.

"Would you quit talking like that?" Randy glared at him. "I can't stand fag talk."

"I like to talk this way. It's my style, it doesn't hurt anybody, and it's friendly. You're nice to Koko, but as far as anyone else is concerned, forget it. You know why? Because you only love people for your own sake. It must be nice to come from a privileged black home. But you know, there are all kinds of families in this world, all kinds of kids growing up. Everything isn't like on the *Bill Cosby Show*. I didn't get to meet Rick in the end, but I think I can understand him. He wasn't good at living, but I don't think he was totally fucked up. Somewhere along the way he lost his will to live. We all get like that at some point or other. They don't teach you in school about what to do when that happens. And you can't expect to luck out and get good parents who will help. I'll bet you think you can do anything, Randy. You probably think you can do right by Koko, too. But your belief is a fragile and brittle thing. You're the only one who can build your own core essence.

"Home? Environment? All that can eat shit. Jesse will either learn or not. If he doesn't, he'll do some stupid things. If that happens, a little warmth, a little comfort, will go a long, long way. If Koko wants to provide that, who are we to stand on the side and criticize? It was a wonderful man who was there for me when I needed it. He didn't despise me when I felt despicable; he didn't solve all my problems for me. He was broad-minded enough and grown up enough to understand what people go through sometimes.

"I don't think you know, Randy, that losers are also winners when it comes to relationships. People who don't understand that are foolish. Koko was a loser. But she knows she was also a winner. That's why she can recognize when others are in pain. The way you are now, you're only going to be a loser. That's why I say you're arrogant and you say you feel insecure. So where does that leave Koko? If she feels insecure, she can't show it because she'll be afraid it'll scare you. She can never let herself rest."

"She rests with me. You don't know what you're talking about, Buckey."

"Excuse me, but I do know. We live together, Koko and I; we're like brother and sister. I see how careful she is with you, and that's how I know she's not completely relaxed around you. This woman here is too attuned to other people's feelings; she forgets about herself. Unfortunately for her, she hasn't yet met a man who can make her feel easy as well as love her. You give her about as much comfort as a Band-Aid. You think a few hugs and kisses are going to do the trick? Those are emergency measures, nothing more."

"You're saying I'm not good enough?"

"No, but if *you* don't think you are, you should maybe try to improve yourself. I'm not saying you should do anything radical, but you really ought to love her through the tough times."

Randy looked at Koko. "Is that what you think?" he asked.

Koko hesitated. She thought Buckey was right, but she was used to how he put things. She could see that Randy, talking to Buckey for the first time about personal things, wasn't taking it so well. Randy was the guy who had, after all, used different flavors of ice cream to explain love. There was an earnest sincerity in his clumsiness that Koko found endearing, and she didn't want to destroy it. She struggled to find the right words to let him know how she felt.

All at once, Randy got to his feet. Surprised, Koko looked up at him.

"Where are you going?" she asked.

"I'm leaving. This place isn't for me. Gives me the creeps."

Koko stood up. She felt she had to stop him.

"I'll see myself out. You can stay here with this faggot."

Koko slapped Randy's face. His eyes widened with disbelief, but then he smiled wryly.

"That's the first time I've ever been hit," he said.

"I can't hit you? You think love is just being sweet and nice? Apologize to my friend!"

Randy, his jaw set, threw a glance at Buckey but didn't say a word. He left, slamming the door behind him.

Koko stood there, stunned, for a few long moments, then sank down next to Buckey on the couch.

"Sorry about that, Buckey," she said, chagrined.

"That's OK."

"I hit him."

"I saw." Buckey chuckled. "He's good at grabbing onto happiness."

"Huh?"

"He's got talent."

"I wonder."

"I guarantee he won't turn out like Rick. He don't know nothing 'bout nothing yet, though."

"I love him. I can't help it. With all his faults, I really, truly love him."

"You think I don't know that?"

"Yeah, I guess you do."

Buckey and Koko looked at each other and shrugged.

TEN DAYS PASSED, and not a word from Randy. Now and then anxiety would overwhelm Koko, and she made any number of mistakes. Her friends were exhausted by her, but no one was more disgusted with her than herself.

"Why can't you stop by on your way home from work? He lives in the East Village, doesn't he?"

Sue couldn't understand what held her back, but Koko merely nodded absently. All she could think of was how hard it was to suddenly not hear the voice she'd been hearing every day. It was times like this when not living together was a true pain in the ass, she thought. Every now and then she'd reach for the phone, but she always stopped herself before pushing that last button. Randy, she felt, would have to be the one to call.

Koko stomped around the apartment, going crazy, but Buckey paid no attention. She would've liked some sympathy from him or maybe some jokes. She tried different ways to draw him out, and even went so far as to sing a stupid song at the top of her lungs. Buckey merely rolled up his *Village Voice* and threw it at her.

"Hey! What was that for?"

"You were yowling."

"You don't understand what I'm going through, do you?"

"I'm not interested in the state of anyone's love life."

"I'll have you know this mess is partly your fault."

"You were the one who hit him."

"I wonder if he's ever going to call. Do you think maybe he got a summer job? He can't be so busy he can't pick up the phone, can he?"

"Love is a fragile, ephemeral thing."

That was the last thing Koko wanted to hear. She flung herself onto the bed and buried her face in the pillow. I'm lonely, she thought. But I'm alive, that's one thing for sure. She remembered how she'd longed for a bed that would enfold her, pull her down into a deep, dark, dreamless sleep. How exhausted she'd been from her life with Rick. That bed wasn't what she wanted now.

Although she'd experienced yearning in her relationship with Rick, she realized now that she always felt a certain satiety with him. It was different with Randy. But even half mad with loneliness and anxiety, Koko had a feeling that Randy wasn't going to leave her.

Koko stood up and went to the kitchen where Buckey was reading the directions on the back of a Rice-A-Roni box. He had a pot of water heating up on the stove in front of him.

"You're gonna cook, Buckey?"

"What does it look like I'm doing? Shit, I'm no good at this. Why'd Spike have to go and leave, huh? My next boyfriend is gonna know how to cook for sure."

"Rice-A-Roni and frozen peas? What's the main dish?"

"There is none."

"You mean this is it?"

"Yep."

"Since when did you become a vegetarian?"

"Shut up."

Koko snorted and opened the refrigerator. The champagne was still there. Spike had begged out of his own going-away party. Koko remembered how good a cook Spike really was, and all at once she felt mournful.

"Buckey." She turned to look at him. "I think I'll go over to Randy's place this weekend."

Buckey glanced up. "Good idea," he said. "But I don't think you'll have to."

"What do you mean?"

"He's on his way here now. He called a little while ago."

"Really? And?"

"I asked him to pick up a bucket of fried chicken on his way over."

"No, idiot, what did he say?"

"He said he's bringing someone."

Snapping her fingers, Koko slammed the refrigerator shut. "Hey, Buckey, let's drink that champagne. Oh, I'm so happy! What should I do, what should I do? I have to take a shower!"

"They'll be here for dinner." There was a touch of exasperation in Buckey's eyes as he glanced up at his happy friend. It was nice to see her like this again, though.

"I'll pick up the apartment!" Koko exclaimed.

WHEN THE DOORBELL RANG, Koko bounded to the door and whipped open the locks. Randy stood there, smiling shyly, a paper bag from the liquor store in one hand and a bouquet of flowers in the other. Koko stripped him of his parcels, setting them on the floor, and embraced him. When they'd finally caught their breaths after exchanging feverish kisses and looking into each other's eyes, Koko noticed, with astonishment, who it was Randy had brought. Jesse was standing there holding a big bucket and looking distinctly ill at ease.

Koko's eyes widened as she looked at the two in turn. Randy shrugged and explained that he'd asked Sue for Daryl's phone number and gotten in touch with Jesse through him.

Not knowing what to think, Koko ushered the two in.

"We brought some fried chicken and red wine," Randy said, and raised a hand at Buckey in the kitchen. Buckey winked back.

"Did you know who Randy was bringing, Buckey?" Koko demanded.

"Well—"

"You guys're awful, leaving me in the dark. I'll bet you've been in touch for ages."

"No. I just called him to apologize," Randy said, putting an arm around Koko's shoulder. Koko tried her best to pout, but her laughter broke through soon enough. She couldn't hide her elation. Her eyes drank Randy in, and she told him softly how much she'd missed him.

They started their dinner of fried chicken and Rice-A-Roni. Randy uncorked the red wine.

Jesse wasn't very comfortable as he drank his soda. Never before included in a group of adults like this, he felt very much out of place.

"Have another piece of chicken, Jesse," Koko said.

"I'm full already."

"Now, Jesse, you're so skinny! You've got to get some meat on those bones. You're getting taller and thinner all the time. You didn't have that much to start with, either."

Jesse reluctantly put another piece of chicken on his plate and shook some Tabasco onto it.

"So whatever did you and Randy talk about, hm? Come on, out with it," Koko said. "I want to know."

Chewing on his chicken wing, Jesse shot Randy an embarrassed glance. "He said he could sympathize about my home environment, but what I was thinking of doing wasn't happening at all."

"That's an improvement," Buckey observed teasingly.

Koko silenced him with a look and turned back to Jesse. "And then what did you say?"

"I told him he didn't have any idea about what was going on with me. But I wasn't doing drugs or anything. I was interested, that's all. The guys doin' it were kinda cool."

"Drugs're no good for your health, Jesse."

"Neither are cigarettes, Koko."

Koko reddened through the smoke of the cigarette she had just lit.

"I was mad," Jesse said. "Everyone'd started taking Dad's death for granted. Maybe he wasn't good for anything, but he was my father. If it weren't for him, I wouldn't be here. But what was worse is that I started to accept everyone forgetting about him so quick. I was mad at myself, mad at everybody. I kept thinking, Why did it have to be like that? Goin' over and over it in my head, you know. Then finally I realized that I knew him better 'n anybody. I knew exactly what kind of man he was. I hate to say it, but maybe the way he died suited him."

"Suitable or not, that's not for you to decide," Buckey said. Jesse frowned, ashamed.

"I thought I had the rottenest luck," he continued. "My mom doesn't love me. It's a lie that moms always love their kids. She's been saying a lot of awful things lately about me being half black. Mom's known all kinds of people, and she's had lots of chances to get together with other guys, but Daddy turned her off of all black men. She doesn't even look at any. I thought, How'm I supposed to be a good kid living in a place like that? I didn't know which way was up; I didn't have a thing to be proud of. It's the pits, I tell you, livin' with a woman who talks shit about the black man who was the closest to you. On top of that, everything she says is true. Even so, I loved him. Then this guy shows up." Jesse motioned to Randy with his chin. "He said I was lucky; that people who have their pride kicked around from the beginning know what pride is and start off from a much higher level than those who don't. They have a chance to be better people."

Buckey burst out laughing and Randy hung his head. Koko sent Buckey a swift kick under the table. All Jesse could do was look at the three adults in turn, completely bewildered.

"I thought maybe he was right," he went on. "But I told him he was trying to give me a snow job. Then he gets mad and says he didn't go out of his way to talk to someone who was connected with Koko's old boyfriend for that. He came to talk to me because he wanted to understand everything there was to know about Koko. He didn't know if I was on my way to becoming a juvenile delinquent or not, but he thought that wouldn't happen as long as Koko still cared about Daddy and me. Also, he said he came because he was curious about me and wanted to know more. I felt a lot better after I heard that. I hate sermons and people feeling sorry for me: 'That kid's gettin' into drugs; oh, God, how awful, we have to save him.' I can see through that shit. This guy—I'm sorry, I mean Randy—wasn't like that, so I started thinking he was kind of OK. But then he started goin' on and on about how cute Koko was, how sexy—I started gettin' tired of him again."

Koko reddened and looked at Randy. He tried to look disgruntled as he raised his wineglass to his lips, but she could see he was on the verge of laughter.

"Koko, do you still like Daddy even now?" Jesse asked.

"I like him."

"But Daddy's dead. You still like him even so? How come you still worry about me? Is it 'cause you're supposed to?"

"No, not at all. I think of you and your daddy as separate."

"Well then." Jesse scrunched up his face and stared fixedly into space. "Does that mean you love me?"

Randy and Buckey turned to her simultaneously. Keenly aware of those two pairs of eyes, Koko still managed to answer firmly.

"Yes, I do. I love you, Jesse."

Jesse didn't look surprised. "Hm," he said, and nodded once. "I don't really get what love is, but I guess it's when that person is always stuck to your heart," he said.

"Very much something like that, I'd say," Buckey put in with a smile.

"Well, if that's so, then I guess I love you too, Koko. Whaddaya think?"

Jesse's unexpected question sent Koko into confusion.

"How should I know? Whaddaya think yourself?" she said.

"Ha, ha! Koko's embarrassed."

"That's about enough out of you, Buckey!" Koko said.

"Can I have another soda?" Jesse asked.

Buckey nodded and went to the kitchen.

"Tanya, wasn't it?" Koko asked. "How're things going with you two?"

"OK. Sometimes we fight, though."

"You're being careful with birth control?"

"You're always asking that, Koko. Are you?"

Randy looked as guilty as if the question had been directed at him. He was surprised that Koko and Jesse talked to each other as two equal adults.

"Yes, I am. You've nothing to worry about on that account."

Koko grinned at Jesse. It hadn't been that much time since she'd seen him last, but he looked more grown up now. Pretty soon he won't need me anymore, she thought. The realization made her miss the skinny little brat he'd been when they first met. We didn't know anything back then, not one thing, she thought. Not that either of us is so wise now, but as the years pass, what we know is growing little by little; maybe, she thought, we're each growing more tolerant. People who are able to forgive can look at things with a broad and fair eye.

"Do you love Randy?" Jesse suddenly asked her.

"Yes, I do."

"But you won't forget Daddy, will you?"

"No, Jesse. It's because of your daddy that I can love Randy. Your daddy made me a little wiser."

"Hm. Well, then, maybe he was good for something after all."

"That happened because Koko is who she is," Buckey said, returning from the kitchen. "If it weren't for Koko, you might not be here listening to what we have to say to you. People aren't much, but sometimes they can have a huge impact on others. You have to keep the good bits of that impact. Won't be long now before you start having an effect on a girl of your own."

"The way you did on Randy?" Jesse asked him. "He told me about the fight you had. He said he'd never thought that there might be people who are born into unhappiness, who can't help choosing it. He said it'd never occurred to him that there might be something else besides discrimination from the outside that ground people down. What you said made him realize things were more complicated than he'd thought."

Randy cleared his throat awkwardly.

Buckey was looking at Jesse with great interest. "It's very difficult to say what's good and what's bad in this country," he said. "You might think you're fine and then find you're completely excluded because you're some kind of minority. Happens all the time. On the other hand, you'll never get anywhere stewing about it. You have to think calmly and clearly, then make your moves. There're lots of people who try to do that, but you're the loser if those are the only people you think are worth anything. Whether helplessness makes a person bigger or smaller, we're all the same underneath. So, Jesse, you need to decide for yourself what your daddy was to you and hold on to that, no matter what anyone says. You understand what I'm saying?"

"Hmmm. Yeah, I think so."

Pleasantly drunk now, Koko propped her elbows on the table and gazed fondly at Jesse. It seemed to her that she'd never before felt this way about him. Must be because he's on the verge of becoming an adult, she thought. How many times in a person's life do you meet up with someone who loves you? She wanted to be one of those people for Jesse; then, if he were to run into hard times, he could remember that. She wanted to always be free enough to lend a hand to a loved one who needed it. Koko thought maybe Jesse would be able to understand that now.

"Even so, I'm lonely. I've been feeling so alone lately," Jesse said.

"Everybody's alone, when you come down to it."

"You feel lonely too, Buckey?"

"You bet. That's why I try to take such good care of the people around me."

"Shit. Maybe everyone's like this. You too, Randy?"

Randy's look at Koko was distressed. He had no means of answering such a question, but when he tried to think of himself without Koko, he grew suddenly disconsolate.

"Daddy made me feel like I wasn't alone. Degenerate as he was, I guess he took care of me."

"You'll get that next time from a girl; you'll see," Randy said.

Jesse looked first at Randy, then at Koko. He opened his mouth as if to say something, but then closed it and shook his head instead.

"I'd better get going," he said.

Buckey said he'd walk him to the subway.

As Jesse was getting ready to go, he looked around the apartment. Everything seemed unusual to him—and so different from the place he'd shared with Koko. His intuition told him that even the air was different, depending on who got together with whom. *Koko has a different life from me.* The thought made him feel strange.

"Wow! You're so much taller than me already!" Koko exclaimed when they hugged good-bye. Jesse shrugged, laughing.

"Well, I'm still shorter than *him*."

Randy pointed at himself. "*Him*? I do have a name, you know."

"Sorry, Randy. Thanks, guys, for everything."

"When did you get so polite, huh? I know all about you, Jesse."

"Yeah, I guess you do," Jesse said. He looked down at the ground for few moments, then raised his head. "I finally understand, Koko. You have your own life. You don't have room for me."

Koko lightly slapped him on his cheeks twice, three times.

"You can come in any time, but you have to come on your own. Nobody's going to go and get you no matter how long you wait."

"OK, I will."

Jesse kissed Koko and Randy on their cheeks in turn. Buckey came out wearing a gaudy shirt and matching hat. It seemed he was planning to hit some clubs after dropping Jesse off.

"You two lovebirds take your time. I think I'll be a little late," he said.

"Koko, make sure you use your birth control," Jesse said in parting.

Randy burst out laughing and got himself pinched by his girlfriend.

After Buckey and Jesse left, Koko and Randy sat on the couch and started on the rest of the wine. Koko was quiet, out of sorts. She felt let down, somehow. Randy was solicitous, stroking her hair with an understanding hand.

"I can't believe you pulled it off," Koko said.

"You mean Jesse?"

"How did you get him to come?"

"I told him how I felt. At first he was mad at me, saying it was all my fault for stealing you from his father. I got mad, too, and shouted back that it went two ways. He didn't really believe it was my fault, of course. I guess he just needed someone to take it out on. Later on he said he was mad because nobody was doing the stuff for him that you used to do. I said that if he felt that way, he should tell you so himself and that when you ask someone to do something, you have to ask nicely, or they won't feel like helping you."

"That's OK. I don't mind."

"Then, as I was talking to him, I started to feel ashamed of myself. I never asked you nicely for anything. I wanted you to love me, but I refused to accept anything I didn't like or look at things I found uncomfortable, things that're real. I was a spoiled brat, just like Buckey said. I guess I'll be seeing more stuff like that in me and hating myself for it."

"Silly. You should ask me, like you just said. Ask me to help you."

"You'll help me?"

"Of course. And you'll help me."

All at once it began to rain outside. Koko went to the window and looked out. Randy picked up their two wineglasses and went to stand behind her.

"I wonder if they're all right?" she said.

"They're fine. It's only rain."

"I feel bad. Only we two get to be nice and dry like this."

The raindrops pattered against the window as if battling the night. They hit the glass, then ran down. Their sparkle and movement made Koko and Randy feel they were looking at stars on this starless night.

Koko gazed at the reflection of her lover beside her. The small diamond in his ear sparkled more brilliantly than ever in the raindrops on the window. The diamond moved down, and she felt Randy's warm lips brush her neck. It looks just like a falling star, she thought. There was one thing she had to ask him, and only one. She turned around to do so, but then her lips were sealed by his and she forgot all about it. The darkness enfolded them in sweet silence; only the hushed whisper of the rain could be heard. Listening to it, Koko thought of many things. She met him in the summer, fell in love in the fall, and they warmed each other over the winter. Now spring was almost over and soon it would be summer again.

Some say that time is kind. But you can't use it like dirt to bury things. So then what is time? Koko remembered the person who lived quietly within her heart. The painful memories hurt a little. Koko thought about what it was she wanted.

What she wanted was a soft blanket. A blanket of time to cover the memories of nothing special that lay about in her heart. She wanted to tuck in that flock of memories so they could sleep, safe and sound. Koko looked up to find Randy's laughing eyes upon her. He'd hit on an excellent idea for passing the time.

"Hey, how about if you and I open up that bottle of champagne?"